In Her Sights

John Kimbrey

Clink
Street

London | New York

Published by Clink Street Publishing 2019

Copyright © 2019

First edition.

ISBN:
978-1-913136-92-5 - paperback
978-1-913136-93-2 - ebook

*To friends, who have provided me with much
inspiration for my many characters, and to my
selective group of readers. Thank you...*

This for Haze...

Tony

Best wishes

Kimberley

Chapter 1

Ed looked ahead through the light morning mist, across the wilderness of No Man's Land, towards the enemy lines. The sound of spoons scraping on metal echoed across to their position, as their opponents in this war of all wars ate their morning meal. Muttering German voices and some laughter drifted across to them, the soldiers oblivious that they were being watched by a highly trained British sniper team. If only they had been taught basic German, they could have gathered useful information and reported back to Divisional HQ. Sadly, all they could do was wait until an unsuspecting soldier raised his head just enough for them to end his war prematurely.

Their overnight insertion had gone well, their position secure, and the morning was now quiet. Ed had been on watch for two hours. She glanced down to where Frank slept beside her, his head tucked neatly into his arm to muffle his breathing. This was the boring part of being a sniper, but discipline was the single most important factor in staying alive. Frank could stay put for another hour.

Their position was a good one, just one hundred and fifty yards south of the enemy lines, and well protected from both flanks, with a good escape route. To the left, an old vehicle, blown up long ago lay rusting in the dirt, surrounded by shell holes and detritus from dead trees. Low wire entanglements as far as the eye could see, littered the area, on this quiet sunny morning. They were vulnerable only from the air, and whenever a German aircraft flew over, they simply followed standard operational procedures and stayed perfectly still, their bodies well hidden amongst the mud and debris of the barren landscape, until the aircraft had gone.

The hour passed by slowly, with nothing happening, and Ed took the opportunity to relax her bladder, feeling the warmth quickly spreading around her thighs, the layers of dirty clothing soaking up some of her urine before it filtered away into the soil beneath her. This brief sensation of relative comfort disappeared sharply as she once again focussed her mind on the target, her training ensuring it hadn't affected her concentration. Then, out of nowhere, a sudden commotion rose up from the German lines, with loud laughter erupting, at a twenty-degree arc from her position. She scanned across carefully for several minutes, not daring to move, and then, without warning, a German officer appeared, his torso clearly visible above the parapet, yelling loudly. 'Englander, Englander, wherefore art thou, Englander?' before disappearing back down out of sight, his gratification obvious as the laughter from the soldiers below him in the trench increased. She was about to nudge Frank when he slowly lifted his head up, raising the veil of his camouflage netting. He moved in tight beside her, lining himself up as he had done a hundred times before, before easing off the safety catch of his rifle. She leaned over slightly, to brief him, without taking her eyes from the top of the ladder.

'We are in luck, dear friend; our man is active,' she whispered. They both lay wide-eyed, motionless, waiting for another chance. The slightest movement could now be fatal, as any German sniper in range, with his advanced rifle sights, would soon try to ruin their day. Ed knew they were vulnerable to attack in this advanced position, and although they did have reasonable cover, they simply could not take any chances. Then suddenly it happened again!

Quite extraordinary actions by the German officer. The impetuous fool, Ed thought, and smiled down the barrel of her rifle as he stepped into her sight line. He stood high in the air, being cheered on by his audience below, waving his cap, singing.

'God save our gracious King,' he sang and then dropped down once again, having only stayed in view for a few seconds. Laughter from his men reached their ears. Frank smiled to himself, not uttering a word. The German was playing with fire and thought he was impregnable, but death was now only moments away. Ed was ready, and tightened her grip, awaiting her chance.

In less than a minute, he rose once again, this time wearing an ornate officers' helmet, the gold spike pointing upwards, the eagle on the front catching the sun. He stopped for a valuable couple of seconds, peering upwards into the bright sky, a cigarette hanging from his mouth, uttering something quite indistinguishable to someone below him in the trench. He had no idea what was about to happen...

Index finger now poised, tightening gently on the trigger, Ed breathed passively, her shot just seconds away. A pause as the target was hidden slightly behind a cloud of cigarette smoke that hung in the still air. These were his last seconds of life. He was not known to his assailants, and sorrow was never considered as

Ed calmly drew in the final killer breath. She held it for a single moment before tightening her body. Frank looked on through his camouflage veil, he too on aim, waiting for his partner to complete the shot. Crack! The bullet was gone.

The German officer's face suddenly twisted to the right, blood erupting from his eye socket in a bright red arc. His helmet flew sideways, his body arched dramatically as the .303-bullet smashed his brains skywards, his limp body falling downwards out of sight. Stillness then met the day.

Frank gently nudged Ed's ankle with his foot, acknowledging her shot. Periscopes then appeared along the line, first one or two, then a dozen or more, as German eyes sought any sign of the person who'd made the deadly shot! Ed relaxed and exhaled slowly into the crook of her arm, aware her breath in the cold air could so easily give their position away. With their lives now in their own hands, they settled down for a long wait. The German soldiers were searching for any sign of their enemy, and suddenly a machine gun on their flank fired several bursts, firstly at the old vehicle, then sweeping blindly across the plain, keen to slay the bandit that had killed one of their own. They wanted revenge.

Ed and Frank were now in a dangerous situation. They had several hours to wait until darkness fell, when they could withdraw, and they lay with their heads low, fingers poised, safety catches off, waiting. All gunfire had stopped, but several periscopes remained, turning slowly, seeking the hidden enemy. The German soldiers knew the British snipers would have to move at some point and were determined to catch their foe. Finally, the sun started to dip towards the horizon and within a short while it was too dark to see.

They were cold and stiff from their prolonged wait and hadn't drunk anything for several hours. Thirst was always preferred to death! They both knew this was not the time to move and stayed properly alert, scanning to their front, waiting for the sky rockets that were sure to follow. They knew their enemy well, and after just ten minutes, several rockets were fired aloft, providing enough light to see the slightest movement, as they slowly descended on their tiny parachutes. The Germans were clearly not giving up on finding the sniper hidden in the darkness. Frank and Ed prayed for a let-up soon.

Eventually the lights ceased and the peace of earlier returned. As Ed shivered in the mud, seven hours after slaying the German officer, it was time to move. She nudged Frank twice on his foot, a well-rehearsed sign for him to move, and he quietly slipped back to the rear before dropping down into the shell hole behind their position. It was a full ten minutes before she joined him and lay next to him in the darkness, staring into the night sky. They were terribly stiff and slowly stretched themselves, before reaching for their water, emptying a whole flask to quench an urgent thirst, then quickly eating some army biscuits, before readying themselves for the long crawl back to their own lines.

No words were spoken, and as they had done many times, they followed their wits. Staying low they headed south, taking advantage of any cover available to them, to run in a crouch. They made good speed, but after only fifteen minutes they reached a line of wire right across their line of withdrawal. They dropped to the ground as Frank sought a way forward, Ed turning to cover their rear. Just a minute later, he tapped Ed on the shoulder then headed to his right and scrambled over a small rise, before disappearing into a shell hole beyond. Ed waited until the noise of his movement had ceased before she made her move. In seconds, she was at the top of the rise and was just dropping down when a sudden burst of machine gun fire opened up behind them. Frank heard the bullets fly overhead and ducked instinctively. Then he heard Ed groan. He swung round but could see nothing, so quickly reversed back to where she was, knowing she was in trouble.

Ed lay quite still, face down in the dirt, breathing rapidly. She turned her head to spit gravel from her lips and brought her hand up to feel inside her ghillie suit. It was wet, and she felt quite sick. She began to sweat and then the pain hit her!

Her breathing became shallow and quite harsh as her body went into shock. She heard a noise in front of her but stayed still in the darkness. Her best friend, she knew, would come for her. Then Frank's hand reached for her, pulling her by the collar as he dragged her along the ground, staying low until they slid down into a shell hole. He sat up and ripped his hood from his head, speaking softly to her, but with urgency, his heart racing as he sought answers.

'Where have you been hit?' he whispered. She didn't answer and so he repeated her name over and over, but she still made no sound. God, he thought, is she dead? Then he heard a murmur and sighed with relief, asking her again where she was hit. Unable to see her too well, he put his ear to her mouth.

'On my back, at the top of my back,' she said hoarsely. 'But I think it's gone right through as my chest is agony.'

Frank rolled her gently on her back, knowing the exit point would be the worst injury. He opened the buttons of her ghillie suit and pulled it down, reaching inside her tunic until he felt a large hole in her chest. It was pouring blood! He quickly reached inside his own tunic for a field dressing before opening her tunic fully. He unravelled the dressing, placing it firmly over the exit wound and pressing down to stop the bleeding, making her whimper softly. He struggled to wrap the bandages attached to the dressing around her body, but finally tied them off at the side. She arched her back in acute pain, but never uttered a sound. She bit her lip until the pain was under control. He then spoke to her softly.

'I am going to have to turn you.'

'Just get on with it,' she said, groaning.

He turned her over, freeing her arm so he could access her shoulder. He yanked the back of her tunic down, reaching inside her shirt and following the sticky blood trail until he located a tiny indent, a hole. Keeping one finger over it, he reached for her own field dressing with his other hand and ripped it open with his teeth, quickly covering the small indentation that was still bleeding, and tying the dressing off as before. He pulled her tunic back up and pushed her arm into the sleeve, buttoning up her ghillie suit, and laid her flat. He knew he had to move rapidly now, or see his friend die in front of him!

He looked ahead into the darkness, hoping they were not too far from their own trenches, and quickly slung both rifles over his shoulder. He then grabbed a handful of Ed's ghillie suit behind her head and began to drag her up out of the shell hole and along the ground. It was clear to him within a few seconds that even though she was relatively light, this could easily kill her. He decided there was no point in taking her back carefully if she died on the way! He knew what he had to do was risky, but he clearly had no choice.

'Ed, I am going to have to carry you, it's going to hurt,' he whispered. He bent down, gathering her up across his body so her head lay on his shoulder, clasped his hands and taking a deep breath started to lift her up. He hoped that as he couldn't see anything, the Germans certainly wouldn't be able to either. He looked down at the friend he treasured most in his life, and as he set off in the darkness, he heard a volley of shells suddenly whistle overhead, landing seconds later deep into the British lines. The morning barrage had begun!

He wasted no time and set off at a fast walking pace over the undulating ground before him. Progress was swift, and he made a hundred yards before stumbling into more wire, where he dropped to a crouch, pausing for a few seconds to rest. As he rose up, a barb snagged Ed's ghillie suit and even though he pulled on it several times, he was forced to lay her down to free her, wasting valuable time. Sweat from his exertion ran into his eyes as his fingers fumbled, but quickly he bundled her up once again and set off through the gap, all the while the shells exploding ahead. He was the most frightened he had ever been, and as his arms started to ache once more, he found himself shouting to himself to finish the job! He yelled to Ed over the increasing noise of the shells, her head just inches away from his, but she remained silent, her eyes closed. He kept telling himself they would make it and shouted to her over and over; 'It will be OK Ed, it will be OK,' as he maintained his pace forward towards safety, flinching each time a shell landed. He was convinced that they could not be far away now and worked his way through the wire, the bombs shattering the ground all around him. He was sweating heavily, his eyes stinging as it washed into them, his breathing rapid, and then suddenly, the ground disappeared beneath him! It was a second later and he landed in a heap in the mud, Ed now lying across him, groaning.

***

Ed had been in and out of consciousness since she first felt the burning in her back, the pain forever present, the noise now incessant. She could feel Frank's great strength as he carried her, his hands holding her tightly to his body as he panted, head down, moving swiftly on. She tried to breathe in the rhythm of Frank's steps, but then he stumbled, and pain ripped through her body. Tears pricked her eyes, and she buried her head into his shoulder until finally the pain had eased.

Suddenly, her memory started to return. She remembered taking the shot, but wasn't sure when it happened, although she could visualise the German officer's head exploding as the .303 round hit home. She could picture them crawling back homewards, before the sudden burning in her back and lying in the dirt. Frank was fussing over her and talking as he applied the dressings, before lifting her up and carrying her away in the darkness, as the early morning bombardment began.

She felt secure in Frank's arms, and her mind started to wander, remembering all they had done together. Her army training in Bristol flashed through her mind, then the rifle ranges where she had thrived amongst her peers and so eagerly learnt her new skill. She thought of her journey to the war, and then suddenly she was back on the farm with her brother, Edward. She could recall how hard the past years had been, and how capable she had become, remembering when it all started, that wet spring day in 1914, a brutal day for one as young as she.

Chapter 2

It had rained all morning and a cold breeze from the north meant for an uncomfortable day ahead. With over half the field yet to complete, the plough finally became stuck, caked in deep mud, the seasonal rains making the field almost unworkable. Edwina pulled the horse to a standstill and noticed the underside of the furrow was now almost completely hidden, rendering the chisel essentially useless. The horse was sweating heavily from pulling up the slope, and steam rose gently from her withers into the morning air. Ed jammed a steel peg deep into the soil to stop any forward movement and knelt down to try and clear the blockage. The horse, seeming almost human, peered round and stamped her hoof impatiently at standing idle. Ed's knees had sunk deep into the sodden earth, and the water had quickly penetrated her corduroy trousers as she bent double to clear the blades with an iron grip! As she scraped away feverishly with her knife, she breathed deeply, the effort causing the muscles in her arms and shoulders to ache, her hands slowly becoming numb.

Working the land during this time of year was a difficult task for any farmhand, especially one as young as she. But ever since she was a child, hardships had been part of her daily life, teaching her disciplines way in advance of her tender years. Edwina had demonstrated to her father time and time again that she was more able than her twin brother, who shirked his duties on a daily basis. She had, over time, become as capable as any man, now more than ever, following their parents' watery demise just two years ago…

She remembered the day clearly when their vicar charged into the kitchen without invitation, slamming the scullery door behind him. He walked straight towards her, looking deeply troubled, staring briefly before turning towards the hearth. He reached for his bright red handkerchief and blew his nose, loudly, before wiping his eyes, as he rested one hand on the mantelpiece, staring into the flames. She was perplexed as she realised something was terribly amiss.

'Where's Edward?' Bryan asked, without looking up.

Edwina was about to answer when the latch on the door from the hall suddenly clicked, the rusty hinges protesting loudly as the door opened. Edward appeared from the gloom with an armful of clothes, heading towards the sink. He offered a brief hello to Bryan as he walked over, dropping his washing to the floor next to the old Belfast sink. He then turned to greet their friend properly, but it soon became evident that Bryan was not visiting to exchange pleasantries.

She snapped back to reality as the rain ran down her neck and into her open mouth and eyes. She blew the water away from her lips and felt a shiver run up her back. Her knife finally cleared the mud, but it slipped from the iron plough blade, tearing the skin on the back of her hand in the process. She flinched, swearing to herself, and stood to wrap her now bloodied hand with her dirty handkerchief before forcing it into her old leather glove. She removed the peg and gathered up the reins once more and with a yell of encouragement set off again, the horse pulling away strongly, the soil now rolling evenly once again like a small wave on the seashore. She realised, with a certain pride, how good her ploughing had become since starting just two seasons ago, her personal strength playing an integral part in mastering this ancient art. She had accomplished many personal goals over the past year and was proud of her achievements. She was especially pleased how she could now lift a fully laden pitchfork up onto her shoulders and carry it right up through the two lower fields to the top paddock, in one mammoth effort! Although the pole dug deeply into her flesh, she never flinched, and she smiled inwardly thinking of her father, who had struggled, himself, to complete that very task.

It was after eight o'clock when Edwina finally came in from the fields. Dinner was ready, but much to her annoyance, Edward had already eaten, so the table was only laid for one. He was sitting in front of the warm fire, reading, chores still to be done. She had almost given up moaning at him anymore as he paid little attention and would often just shrug his shoulders saying, he would get to it tomorrow! Standing sombrely at the old Belfast sink in the scullery, she scrubbed her hands with a bar of cheap soap smelling of disinfectant under the cold water that flowed forcefully from the large brass tap. She looked across at Edward as she twisted the soap in her hands, washing her wound carefully before reaching for the grubby towel hanging from the hook on the back of the door. She stepped into the warm kitchen and took a seat at the table. Ed looked across at her but said nothing, just placed his book down and reached for the cloth, taking a large dish of stew from the top shelf of the oven, and setting it on the table. Ed already had the serving spoon in her hand, and quickly spooned a big helping into her dish. The first mouthful was bliss as she savoured the rich meaty gravy.

'It's chicken again, same as yesterday,' Edward said, and sat back down staring into the flames. 'Did you see the paper?' he asked. 'Do you think there will be a war?'

Edwina looked up with a full mouth and a confused expression. As she finished swallowing, she remembered the newspaper from the previous evening. Looking across the room, she saw the paper was still on the floor where she had left it.

'Oh yes, of course,' she said, and went over to retrieve it, folding it neatly as she sat back down. Scanning the text again she reached for a piece of bread and spread butter thickly before taking a large bite. She started reading again as Edward shuffled off to get more water from the sink. When he returned, he dropped into his seat next to her, seeming a little agitated, as Ed read in silence.

'Britain surely won't get involved in a European argument, what have we got to gain?' said Edwina indignantly, wiping butter from the side of her mouth. 'What are you worrying about anyway? It's really not our war, is it?' she said, reaching for the dish.

'That's not what the papers are saying! Britain has a vested interest; the German Kaiser and the Russian Tsar are cousins, you know, and are related to our King. If this is to become a European war, it is bound to include us!'

'I doubt that,' Edwina said tartly. 'We are surrounded by water, and in any case, we are miles away, no-one will invade us.' Edwina turned back to the newspaper, leaning gently backwards on her chair, making the old wooden legs creak.

'We are, yes,' said Edward. 'But that hasn't stopped us getting involved in wars over the centuries, crikey, we have been in most of them.'

Pausing on that thought, Edwina took another slice of bread and butter as Edward gazing into space, was clearly miles away. As she looked at him, the fire suddenly belched a great plume of smoke from the chimney, which slowly crept upwards in a ghostly cloak before it joined a long, grey cloud of smoke hugging the ceiling! Without another word, Edward went over to retrieve his book and left the room. She sighed as she looked around the empty kitchen, utterly fed up with life as it was. She sat in silence, wishing for change, hoping her life would not be stuck forever in this daily circle of routine, with nothing to look forward to. With just the noise of her spoon on the dish as she served herself another helping, the silence in the room was painful to the ears. Her belly swelling to bursting point, she drank the remains of her tea. She looked up to the photo of her father on the far wall, her mind drifting back to happier times and his end of day ritual.

She remembered him standing next to the mantelpiece and reaching for a small cigar from the packet tucked behind the clock, which he would light with a fire stick from the pot in the hearth. With the short brown cigar wedged in the side of his mouth, he would puff away before pulling off his boots, using the large iron boot hook that resembled a giant beetle. As he eased his feet clear, his socks would hang half off his feet, steaming with perspiration, having not seen the light of day since the early hours. She smiled to herself as she pictured him puffing away contentedly and remembered how he would often look across at her, acknowledging her efforts with an approving double nod. No words were ever spoken, but the image was now engraved in her memory, making her still glow with pride. She missed him greatly. As she walked over to her seat by the fire, she dragged the memory of earlier times back to the present, remembering how Bryan had filled the void their parents left, and the day he had revealed their worst nightmare.

'Whatever is wrong, Bryan?' Edwina had asked, the concern evident in her voice. Edward stood and stared expectantly, firstly at his sister and then across the room towards Bryan.

Bryan blew his nose for the second time, before pulling out a newspaper from his inside coat pocket. He looked at them both, holding it to his chest, walking slowly towards them. Tears suddenly started flooding his eyes and he closed them for just a second, a tear dropping onto his cheek. He steadied himself, breathing out deeply, then placed a copy of the London Herald *on the kitchen table. The huge headline shouted out at them!*

'TITANIC SINKS'

A picture of the ship docked in Southampton was positioned under the headline. The twins leant forward together, straining to see the picture and then, as one, they froze with open mouths, staring down.

Edwina turned, gasping as she faced Edward, her hand covering her mouth. Edward was still immersed in the front page, glaring at the paper, then suddenly stepped back without warning, utterly lost in the moment!

Below the image of the ship, a second headline struck them.
*'**Great Loss of Life**' began the report. '**Titanic, the Tragic Story…**'*
Bryan pulled out the heavy wooden chair and gently lowered himself onto it and spread the paper on the kitchen table. He adjusted his glasses and ushered the twins to sit. They paused for a brief moment, before Edwina moved and tugged at her brother's hand. He was staring at Bryan, motionless. She pulled his hand again until he slowly sat down next to her. The priest read for several minutes to his tiny audience, who hung on his every word. As he finished, he looked up and removed his spectacles.
'What about survivors, Bryan?' Edwina said softly.
'We will have to wait, but I am sure they had as good a chance as anyone,' he said, attempting to console them. Edwina tightened her grip on Edward's hand and pulled him close to her. Bryan began to read again, slowly and deliberately. They sat quite numb, listening attentively to every single word. Bryan then dropped the paper and held his hands out to them to deliver a prayer. They clenched hands and bowed their heads.

Ed remembered that day so clearly. What had started out as a perfectly normal morning had finished with their lives torn apart. It took many weeks for a preliminary list of survivors to appear in the press, but their parents' names were never listed. They had read many news reports since the tragedy, the press raising much conjecture and suspicion. Conversely, there were stories of heroism by the crew and, as is the nature of the human race, cowardice too, as reports filtered out of affluent male passengers being able to pay for a seat on lifeboats, while women and children perished!

Peering through the gloomy pantry, she saw the wedding photograph of her parents collecting dust above the oak sideboard, which forced tears to rise in Edwina eyes. She hadn't cried since that fateful day, but suddenly and quite uncontrollably tears flowed down her cheeks. She stood quickly, to shake off her emotions, and wiped her nose on her sleeve, muttering to herself. She smiled at her dad looking across at her from the old photograph, hoping he would have been proud of what she had achieved. She had never been a submissive person but had struggled with the huge responsibility of running a farm on her own, and at such a young age. Losing all that her father had worked for now would be unforgivable. Although she'd known the fundamentals of practical farming, she had little understanding of general farm management and the many financial dealings had tested her. Although she had struggled at the beginning, there had been just enough money from the previous season to sustain the farm, and she had sought guidance from anyone kind enough to offer it. Following two relatively lean years, progress had been made and she hoped next season would be better than ever. Edward might even start pulling his weight, without her constantly having to push him.

She blew her nose and sat back down, feeling the warmth from the fire on her face. Suddenly, without warning, her pet chicken Dolly appeared beside her and jumped up onto her lap, offering a welcome distraction from her painful memories. Edwina smiled down at the small bundle of feathers, watching as the chicken jerked its head from side to side pecking the buttons on her trouser pocket in search of food, before settling down quietly. Her father had frowned on animals in the house, even Meg the sheep dog, but Edwina had encouraged Dolly to come in with treats and now the chicken came and went as she pleased, often finding scraps from around the kitchen table. It was a peaceful moment and Dolly sat contentedly grooming herself, like a cat. She was now very much part of the family but was an old bird and hardly productive anymore. Despite that, Ed simply couldn't dispose of her, and as they sat together, her eyes felt heavy and she knew sleep was not far away. Suddenly, a loud crack came from the fire, a glowing ember catapulting across the kitchen onto the cold stone floor near her feet, causing the said chicken to squawk and jump up simultaneously and scurry out of the pantry door to safety! With a tired body, Ed stared into the flames and within minutes had slipped into a deep sleep.

It was the chill of the early morning some hours later that woke her. The candles were all finished, the last embers of the fire providing only the faintest glow in the hearth. Edwina sat up and shivered. She reached for a match to light a candle and saw it was a little after 2 a.m. She quickly threw some logs on the fire and closed the pantry door. Climbing the stairs was a real effort but she was drawn towards her soft feather mattress. She flopped down fully clothed onto her bed, pulling the eiderdown over her as the candle flickered beside her. Within seconds she was asleep.

The weeks that followed seemed to all join together and before long the summer planting had been completed. Their moderate breeding plan was producing good quality animals and Edward surprised her with plans of his own for the following season, even reminding her that Duchess, their old mare, was getting old and would need to be replaced. This would not be easy, but although they were not cash rich and had little in the way of reserves, they hoped to exchange goods or labour to purchase a new mare, as was common practice in the farming community. Edwina knew they would have to make plans for the 1915 season soon, but as the weeks passed both she and Edward found themselves absorbed in everyday matters, although they always found time to read the news reports from Europe. It was now mid-summer 1914 and on 4th August, after much pressure from all sides, war was declared on Germany!!!

The world changed that day. The British Expeditionary Force was formed from volunteers from all over Britain and the Commonwealth. With over 400,000 men signing up to serve their country's call, they were deployed to garrisons around the British Empire and many towns saw their men march off to war. Despite the lofty number of local young men leaving to join the many thousands already serving, Edward was in no mood to even think about volunteering and worried intensely about the prospects of being called up. Edwina did her utmost to calm her brother's fears during their short evenings together, where they would sit at the table and read the paper.

'They say it will all be over by Christmas,' said Ed, peering round at her brother. But in the months that followed the war showed no sign of abatement. Bryan continued to visit twice a week, bringing copies of newspapers, and they were often unpleasant reading. The pictures were a portrayal of reality in the trenches and although it looked horrific, Edwina took a great interest, reading late into the night.

They didn't expect their lives to change much and the village had remained largely the same, with only a few hardy souls volunteering to join up. Christmas that year came in cold and frosty and 1915 arrived all too quickly, with no peace imminent. As the New Year passed by, it was clear that the end of the war was a long way off! In the spring, the second call came and 'Kitchener's Army' was formed destined to fight at the battle of the Somme, where tens of thousands would lose their lives.

Summer was a hot affair, the sun scorching the land, and by autumn the harvest was a little shy of their average; however, it was stored in the barn, and the excess sold off to the local military land agent, who paid a good price. They couldn't sit on their laurels now, so ploughed the acres and replanted a winter crop to see them through to the following year. Christmas was soon upon them once again and in an attempt to maintain tradition, the twins worked together, making a special effort, inviting Bryan their closest friend. Even though it was his most important day of the year, the image of a feast in the warmth of their cottage sped him to their table… The churchgoers on Christmas morning experienced shortened hymns, and a quickly delivered sermon, finishing in under forty-five minutes. After a quick change, the vicar was soon climbing the hill to present himself at the cottage door, carrying with him a bottle of port in one hand and sherry in the other.

'Merry Christmas,' he shouted as the door opened, entering the warm kitchen and savouring the fine smells of a Christmas lunch. Edward had cut a small pine tree from the copse and covered it with paper decorations and a small pottery angel on the top. Ed had killed a large white goose the previous week specially for the occasion, which had she hung in the barn to improve the flavour. She had also steamed a Christmas pudding the previous month, a recipe taken from her grandmother's old cookery book, and now placed it in the oven to warm through. The kitchen table had a clean white cloth and with all the trimmings, looked splendid. Ed placed the food on the table, charged each glass and waited for grace. With heads bowed, Bryan did what he was best at, with the greatest of sincerity. After the amen, there was a moment of silence before they joined hands together, as they had done each year.

'Mum and Dad,' said Edward. 'Amen,' said Bryan again.

They feasted well that day and even with Bryan's appetite, they couldn't quite finish all of grandma's Christmas pudding. Edward's home brew kept them watered, and after several glasses, and some port to finish, it wasn't surprising, that Bryan wandered over to an armchair by the fire and within minutes his head had dropped back, and he was snoring, loudly.

As the twins cleared the dishes, they giggled like school children, at the sounds coming from his mouth, before finally joining him by the fire. At a quarter to five the clock chimed, and Bryan's extended stomach lurched, as he woke with a start, peering at them with squinting eyes. He looked up at the clock before stretching his arms upwards for several moments, a strange groaning sound emerging from his mouth.

'What a lovely day we have had, is there any tea in the pot Edwina,' he asked, smiling. 'I can do better than that, we have cake, would you like a slice,' she said. 'Well how thoughtful, I think I have a little room.'

And so, for the next hour they chatted about the war, about their parents and thanked God for the life they had. As the clock struck six, Bryan lifted his heavy frame from the chair. 'It is time I departed I'm afraid.' And made his way towards the door.

'Merry Christmas to you both,' he said. 'Mind how you go.' Seconds later, he was lost in the darkness. Ed shivered, quickly closed the door and wandered back into the kitchen.

'Just stack the dishes, Edward,' she said. 'They can wait until morning.'

Edward looked round and saw some port remained in the bottle.

'Final glass, Ed?' he suggested. Edwina smiled and brought two fresh glasses. They sat by the fire, enjoying the warmth of the kitchen after a memorable Christmas day. The scullery door suddenly started rattling, buffeted by the wind.

'That storms finally arrived,' Ed said, peering at the window, and went to fasten the bolt.

Little could they imagine the immense challenges that 1916 would bring for Britain, and for Edward in particular as the British Government announced it was finally to start conscription.

Chapter 3

Throughout the night the wind steadily increased to hurricane force, and the siblings rose early to check and feed the animals, before securing them in the barn for safety. Whilst Edwina headed back to the cottage, Edward closed all the doors and secured the badly fitting window in the parlour as best he could before joining her. When he arrived a few minutes later, a huge fire was now bursting from the hearth, the heat quickly filling the cold kitchen. It didn't take long for the kettle to boil for their first brew of the day. As she waited for the tea to mash, she started clearing up from the previous night's celebration, and noticed a small pile of unopened mail tucked under the newspaper on the top of the dresser. She picked out two Christmas cards first and placed them on the mantelpiece next to several others, just as Edward came through the door. She quite forgot the remaining envelopes, instead reaching to pour the tea. Her brother went straight over to the fire and flopped into the chair, stretching his hands to the warming flames.

'Have an awful headache,' he mumbled. But Edwina took no notice and simply handed him a large mug of tea settling down beside him. As she pursed her lips for her first sip, a sudden punch wind hit the side of the house like a battering ram, making the building shudder. Their eyes met for an instant as fine dust particles dropped from the ceiling.

'That sounds a powerful one, Edward, is everything tethered down outside?' she asked.

He took a few sips before answering. 'Well, I'm not sure about everything, but I have checked around the rear of the barn and haven't opened the hen house, they can stay in today. Don't want to lose any birds, do we?' he said. The farm was a perilous place to be and with so much of their equipment not tied down, they were aware some items might get blown away.

The storm raged for two days, followed by a lull, before more high winds returning on New Year's Eve, along with the first of the winter snow. At around three o'clock in the afternoon, Ed heard an almighty crash from across the yard and turned quickly to see a whole section of slates slide from the roof above the door of the barn. Once the momentum had begun, she had to watch helplessly as they smashed to the ground.

'Edward, Edward,' she yelled, but she got no answer. 'Edward, for God's sake come down,' she shouted, and finally she heard hurried footsteps on the stairs. He arrived to see his sister donning her boots and reaching for her heavy coat.

'What's up?' he asked in earnest.

'Quickly,' she said. 'The barn!'

Edward, now realising there was a problem, headed to the porch as Ed was rushing out of the door. She was shouting as she went, but her words were lost in the wind. He peered out through the open door before grabbing his outdoor clothing to join her.

For several hours, they battled the snow and cold wind to fix a large hole of several feet, entrusting a pile of logs and a broken step ladder to reach the top line of slates. Edwina was working feverishly, clearing the broken tiles before nailing new timbers into place, while Edward supported the beams from underneath with self-made props. He was impressed by the speed of work and her ability to adapt to any situation, feeling slightly in awe of her.

She looked round at him standing idle and snapped at him, 'Well, come on, Edward, I can't do it alone.'

He quickly stepped up and started replacing the tiles one by one, the hole slowly disappearing until finally the roof was watertight again. They returned the tools, did a final check on the animals before heading back to the warmth of their humble cottage.

The glow from the fire greeted them as they took off their wet coats, Edwina hanging hers on the hook behind the scullery door, Edward just dropping his by his feet. They stood together, inches from the fire, warming themselves, their fingers tingling painfully as circulation was restored. Edward poked the fire, leaning with one hand on the mantelpiece, before placing the kettle on the range for some tea. It was too late to cook, so they ate cheese and crackers and some left-over meat from the previous day. Once their stomachs were full, they sat contentedly, chatting to each other, a pleasure Edwina had quite forgotten. It was, however, short-lived, as Edward yawned lazily for several seconds before heading off to bed. Edwina walked over to lock the outer door, pinched the life from the remaining candles and banked up the fire to last until morning. As she reached over to the last candle on the dresser, she noticed the letters. She quickly looked through them and saw a plain brown envelope addressed to Mr Edward Mitchell, and marked Ministry of National Service. She knew at once what it might be and instinctively looked up towards the hallway door. Her heart raced as she placed the remaining envelopes back down and taking a deep breath eased her finger under the flap and pulled out a single printed sheet of paper.

'You are hereby notified that you will be required to...'

She paused, just for a second, and bit softly on her bottom lip. She cast her eyes down the page, to see a date: *26 March 1916...*

Oh my God, she thought, how was she going to tell Edward his worst nightmare had finally happened? She drew the letter to her chest, feeling nervous, her body tense and she slumped back into her chair, staring at the dancing flames before her. The single most alarming and frightening thing in Edward's world, which he was dreading beyond all else, had been sitting on the dresser for over a week! She stood slowly, staring at the paper again before reaching for the candle and heading to the hallway. He had to be told, she thought. And now!

She climbed the stairs quickly, knowing she was about to ruin what had turned out to be a good day, but this simply couldn't wait until morning. With her heart pounding, she stopped outside his door, took a breath, placed her right ear against the timber and listened. She could hear him shuffling about, so tapped gently on the door, pushing it open simultaneously.

'Edward, are you awake?' But what met her gaze shocked her.

'Stop, no,' he shouted, but it was too late. Ed was already standing in the doorway, her mouth open. The candle by Edward's bed offered sufficient light for her to see her brother dressed in one of their mother's old frocks!

'No, no, no,' he shouted, bolting towards her, but she was inside the room now and stood her ground as he approached. In his haste to push her out of his room his foot caught on the hem of the dress and he tripped forward, falling at her feet. She was stunned for a moment before leaning down to help him up. He shrugged off her advances, getting to his feet by himself, and dashed back across the room, throwing himself onto his bed, burying his face in the pillow. She went over and sat on the bed, her arm gently lying across his legs. His body shuddered as he let out his emotions, sniffling in the throes of shame.

'It's OK, Edward, I am not angry, and I am certainly not judging you,' she said warmly. He rolled over and stared up at her, wiping his tears from his red eyes with the back of his hand.

'I, I just miss Mother so very much and somehow feel close to her this way.'

Edwina looked at him forlornly. She was more than a little surprised to see him this way but tried hard to find the right words. 'Look, I miss Mum very much too. There isn't a day goes by that I don't think of her,' she said compassionately as Edward sniffed. Edwina cast her eyes across the room to see a large trunk in the corner, that she thought had been disposed of years before. It was clear that Edward had kept it in his room all this time but had said nothing. She cradled her brother in her arms, and when he had finally calmed, she pulled her arms away and reached into her pocket.

'I have something I need to talk to you about, Edward, something rather important,' she said softly.

He looked at her calmly, assuming nothing could be worse than what had just happened.

'What?' he said. 'What is it Ed?'

She said nothing, simply offered him the envelope, her nerve almost leaving her. 'Your call-up papers have arrived, and you have to join the army on the twenty-sixth of March.'

His mouth fell open and he looked at her in a state of shock. He suddenly started panting heavily, before snatching the paper from her hand. He stood up and leant towards the single candle on his bedside table, reading the sheet before lifting his head to look at her, taking a deep breath.

'Oh my God, I knew this would happen, what am I to do now?' he said, shaking. His left hand then covered his mouth and tears rolled down his cheeks. She reached for him, but he pushed her hand away, screwing up the document in his hand, sobbing. They both knew he was not cut out for life in khaki as he was a gentle boy and certainly not a man ready for war! He cried like a baby; a picture so familiar to her over the years. He flopped back onto the bed and reached for her, hugging her tightly. He had never shown her any sign of sibling affection before and so she hung on for several minutes, in silence, feeling his heavy sobbing slowly ease against her shoulder. He finally released his grip and pulled away, unfolded the letter and sitting up before reading it once more. She looked at his sad face, knowing full well she could do little to help him this time.

He suddenly stood, cast the frock aside and stormed out of his room. He was already charging down the stairs back to the kitchen before she had even risen from his bed, and by the time she had caught him up he was sitting in his armchair, poking the logs with anger, his lips pursed tightly together. Edwina watched him before placing the kettle on the range as tea was in order.

'So, what do I do, Ed?' he said. 'I just cannot do this; I have to find a way out.'

She frowned, but his words didn't shock her. He spat into the flames, staining the log briefly until the spit bubbled and evaporated in the heat, then sat back with his eyes closed.

'Perhaps I could avoid the conscription somehow,' he said. 'You know, feign injury or break my leg even, so I fail the medical in some way. Gosh, why didn't I think of that before?' He was now actually alert to his problem and stood up and began pacing around the kitchen.

'How about exemption? Can farmers avoid the draft?' he said bluntly.

Edwina didn't speak as she simply didn't have the knowledge but thought it was probably unlikely, knowing the country had been at war for over fifteen months and tens of thousands of men had already left communities such as theirs. The country needed every man available and he would be no exception. Edward returned to his chair and suddenly started sobbing once again, spilling his tea onto his grey vest, jumping up before his skin burnt.

'Why is it always the men that go to war?' he said between sniffs. 'Why me and why now?'

Ed continued to watch him torture himself, so wanting to help, but she simply had no answer.

'I will need to run away, Ed, yes, that's it, I will go to Scotland or go overseas,' he said, his expression becoming determined. 'I just cannot be a soldier; I hate the idea and...' Suddenly Edwina intervened.

'Now stop,' she said forcefully, putting her mug down and standing up. 'Maybe as a farmer they will indeed want you to remain on the land, with the war effort and all, as there are great demands on producing food for the front. Perhaps that is your way out, but who would you speak to, Edward? Who would make that decision? We should speak to Bryan, he would know, but...' and she stopped, not finishing her sentence.

'What?' said Edward, looking up from the fire. 'What are you thinking?'

She remained silent, pondering what had just crossed her mind. 'Men going to war' she thought, feeling suddenly rather excited. Knowing what was in her mind was a crazy notion even for her, but it just might work! She walked across to the kitchen window, beginning to process the thoughts quickly in her mind, staring out into the darkness. She could hear Edward's faint voice but was not really taking in what he was saying. Her mind wandered in several directions at once and she turned to stare at him from across the room, Edward watching in puzzlement.

'Ed,' he said again. 'What is it, what is going on?'

She could see the pain on his face and knew she needed to answer him, but her mind seemed to be in a trance like state, as her thoughts overtook logic and careered out of control. Suddenly it became real.

'Edward, you need to worry no more.' She said with excitement. He looked at her confused. What had she come up with this time he wondered? Quickly, she moved back across the kitchen to where he sat. She stared at him with wide eyes, just inches from his face. He sat back suspiciously, alarmed, and when he saw her grinning, he mistook it for mockery and stood up abruptly. With his mouth open, about to burst forth with a profanity, she held up her hand to stop him shaking her head and smiled with a cheeky grin. Reaching for his hands, she spoke with a confidence he was unsure of.

'This is going to sound crazy, Edward, but…' She paused, trying to calm herself, her heart pounded in her chest and she bit into her bottom lip before speaking. Sitting now only feet apart and not taking her eyes from his for a moment, she spoke softly.

'I will go in your place!' she said quietly. 'The more I think about it the more it makes perfect sense,' and sat back, waiting for his reaction.

He didn't move a muscle for several seconds, just sank back in the chair once again and sighed, his shoulders slumping forward in despair. He pulled his arms back and placed them out sideways, shaking his head, bewildered.

'Is that the best you can do, Ed, is that really all you can come up with?' And he stood up to walk away.

Edwina remained seated, letting her words do the work, waiting for his mind to work through what she had said. Halfway across the kitchen Edward stopped. She could tell the idea was taking root and he slowly turned to face her. She smiled at him and he realised she was very serious and returned to his chair, next to her.

'How on earth do you think you would you get away with it?' he said. 'You would be rumbled as soon as you got anywhere near the army.'

She suddenly grabbed both his wrists tightly and looked deeply into his blue eyes. 'Listen,' she said, 'you have just asked me the obvious question: why always men? Well, you are right. I am better at being a man than you will ever be. I am stronger than you, more capable and I am a better shot too. You feel a closeness to all things feminine, I know that, so we simply swap lives, completely. What's the worst that can happen? I go away and get found out and then sent home. But that won't happen Edward, not if we plan this properly. I have always hated wearing dresses and feel much happier in trousers and working the land. I can do this, Edward.'

Edward rose to his feet again and walked back across the kitchen, pondering her words. He opened the door to suck in some cool night air. Edwina walked over to join him and hooked her arm into the crook of his elbow.

She spoke to him with a fondness that only exists between sibling, of the days when they were young. 'Do you remember who was first to climb the old oak tree at the top of the paddock? Who fought and won your battles at school when you were bullied by those boys? And, who thrived on farming life without difficulty?'

Edward turned to look at her, nodding.

'And ask yourself who always preferred to be indoors with Mother with a fondness I never had working the household chores? I was always stronger and more capable than you in every way Edward, and father knew that too. This is my destiny, I just need to learn how to be a man in every way and you dear brother, must teach me all you know. Only then, can we ever have the chance to pull this off.'

'Yes, I know your right, but you could be injured or worse still, killed or blown to pieces. How would I live with than on my shoulders? Plus, you will have to you live with so many men, they are bound to find out you're a girl, and what then? How can I let my sister go to war for me, what would you think of me, what would others say when they found out?' he said hysterically.

'Look, no-one would know as we would swap lives completely, in every way. Think about it Edward, you would be what you always wanted, and I get the chance to do the things I was made for. I want to do this, not just for you, but for me too.'

Edward had clearly started to soften, his view changing from impossible to one where he thought it just might work. The expression on his face eased as her comments finally hit home. Edwina paused again until she could wait no longer.

'So, do we do this?' she said in haste. 'Do we?'

He gently placed his hand over her mouth to stop her talking and shut the door before leading her back towards the two chairs by the fire. He selected the largest log in the basket and tossed it into the eager flames. His stare slowly turned from the blazing fire to Edwina's face.

'We have both read the stories and seen many photographs of the awful conditions in the trenches and how the men live. We have read about the thousands of men who have come home without arms or legs, or both, and the same number who haven't come home at all. What you're suggesting is tantamount to madness at the highest level. How can I agree to this, Ed, you're my sister, there has to be another way?'

'OK, there is another way, of course, you're right. We forget this whole conversation and you simply take your place alongside thousands of other men and go to war yourself. If that is your preference, then fine, but I am more suited to this than you, I have the right mindset, the right attitude to take this on and have never shirked any challenge. I succeed in everything I do and to be blunt, darling brother, I am the son Dad never had.'

Edward jerked back at her bold statement, which took him by surprise. He cringed at the thought of not being worthy and didn't know if she was deliberately trying to be harsh to upset him or confuse him, but as he thought about her last words, he knew deep down that she was right. He fiddled with his hands as he absorbed her words over and over in his head, before looking up at her, nodding gently.

'OK, let's do it,' he said. And they sat holding hands, staring into each other's eyes.

Over the days that followed, they had never been so close. As children, they hardly ever played together, had different interests, and once puberty had been reached, their father had started them on the work trail. Before school each day and again afterwards they would set about their daily chores, often late into the night. Farm life was hard for such young people, but Edwina thrived, accepting challenges way above her age, whereas Edward simply hated it. He would often fail the simplest of tasks, much to the aggravation of their father.

This inseparable behaviour became the key to their preparations, as each evening they sat planning late into the night. Edward realised he had to change perspective entirely, as he would now need to acquire the necessary skills to run the farm alone! Not only that, he would have to do it as Edwina!

This of course hadn't occurred to him at first, but as the thought of being able to dress as a girl settled in his head, he started demonstrating his true commitment to what they were attempting to do. The midnight oil burnt late every evening as they filled a working journal with ideas and solutions to problems. As they discussed bizarre topics and various changes they would have to make, joyous laughter would often grip them as they talked about the changes to come. But when calm, they knew they had to be incredibly thorough to satisfy the closest scrutiny by friends, neighbours and, all importantly, the military. If they failed, the consequences were simply not worth thinking about.

The first week following the arrival of Edward's call-up papers, they continued to run their lives as normal. They planned to start exchanging roles soon, but needed time to satisfy themselves that the lists they had made were full and concise. It was over supper on day six, when Edwina was telling her brother how a girl would wear her clothes, when there was a sudden bang at the side door. It startled them both, as if they had been caught with their hands in the biscuit jar. Edward felt a sudden flash of guilt and peered carefully through the side window of the parlour. He saw Bryan, their vicar, standing on the step. Seeing him there sent a nervous flutter through his stomach and Edward whispered to his sister, 'Its Bryan.'

Ed swung round to pick up the journal and stowed it in the top drawer of the dresser before signalling for him to open the door. Edward swallowed hard, taking a deep breath before welcoming the man who had effectively been their guardian over the years since the Titanic disaster. He was always a welcome face in their home and loved the many cooked meals he'd had there and enjoyed the ale Edward had made so regularly. He stepped in and headed straight over to the fire to warm his hands.

'Tea and cake, Bryan?' Ed asked.

'That would be lovely, thank you,' he replied with a smile.

'To what do we owe this pleasure?' Edwina asked as Bryan sat down. He explained he had been visiting homes in the parish following the vast number of conscription letters that had arrived from the War Office. The twins looked at each other in silence. He went on to suggest some were trying to avoid enlistment due to farming duties, but he had made an enquiry and had been advised by the military themselves that this was highly unlikely.

'I assume you have received your letter, Edward?' he said, without looking up from the fire.

Edward glanced across at his sister. 'Um, yes, I have actually, it arrived last week.'

Bryan turned to look him 'And how do you feel about it?'

Edward didn't answer immediately; instead he walked over to sit down, looking back at Edwina. She gently shook her head sideways, mouthing the word 'no'. He knew he had to be normal as Bryan had known him all his life and could sense a lie at the drop of a hat. He let their trusted friend know of his true fears, but didn't let on what he and Ed were planning. They settled down and drank tea, discussing conscription, the war in general and how it would affect so many people in the village. The conversation was focussed on Edward, with his sibling taking a back seat. She let them talk and made more tea, placing two pieces of carrot cake before them. As they chatted, they slowly devoured the ample slices, sinking the tea without grace. Bryan, in a masterly way, gently probed Edward about his true feelings, but he never once let on about his horror of going to war. Instead, he sold the unlikely tale of having to 'do my bit for King and country', which Bryan took with a pinch of salt, as he knew Edward always lacked the backbone for a fight. To serve his country now was a million miles from where he would want to be. Ed was about to speak when, without warning, Bryan stood up to leave, stating he still had many families to visit. With his hefty gait he waddled out, shouting goodbye and closing the small wooden gate behind him.

As he strode away from the cottage, Edwina blurted out softly, 'Now we have a challenge!'

'A challenge?' said her brother. 'What do you mean?'

Edwina always knew they would have to divulge their secret to Bryan at some stage and hoped he would take it well. He had, after all, become very close over the past few years.

'Look,' she said, 'this is going to be a herculean task and we need help from someone we can trust. Who else is there? It's imperative we get Bryan on side no matter what, as he has to be utterly convinced and support us in every way. He would need to cover for us too if necessary or divert the truth at least, which may be a problem.' Edward looked quite petrified as she spoke.

'Let's invite him over for supper and tell him then,' she suggested. Edward looked at her, his mouth wide open as if the penny had suddenly dropped. He had finally realised this was not a game, but for real!

'Agreed,' he said quietly. 'How about this weekend?'

She paused in thought, staring at him in silence. 'No, let's invite him in two weeks' time and on that day we both swap places for real.'

Edward swung his head round, alarmed. 'Are you serious?' he said. 'I mean, I know it has to happen sometime, but so soon?'

Edwina stood up and went over to collect the journal which they kept in the right-hand drawer of the kitchen dresser. She returned and placed it on the table, opening it carefully, searching for a certain page.

'Yes, here it is,' she said, and began reading to him the issue of changing lives in every single way and practising all aspects of their new lives as soon as possible! She went on to override his negativity about testing themselves and he nodded slowly, sinking back into the old armchair.

'OK, OK, what is your plan?' he asked

'Well, I think it's an opportunity to actually take the first giant step and it gives us time to learn how to be each other. But it will mean from tomorrow we swap lives completely! That means our clothes, our jobs, everything. What do you think?'

Edward didn't speak, frozen as he thought through what she had said. Was it possible to be ready for this immense challenge so quickly? He knew he could not go and fight in the trenches and as if it was a sign, the fire suddenly exploded, sparks flying through the air, reaching their feet, making them both jump.

'Yes, I agree. I have no choice.'

Ed smiled as her mind started to race ahead, almost inhaling the words he spoke. 'OK. We must plan the evening carefully and even set a few traps as we go along, before telling him at the end of supper. His reaction then will be of the utmost importance in how successful we are. If we can't fool our dearest friend, we will surely fail! So, we mustn't flinch for a single second and have to be utterly convincing in every way. We should keep his mind busy and provide plenty of food and beer to distract him. With the room dimly lit by just a few candles, any small indiscretions can be overcome.' She was about to continue when Edward swung round.

'How on earth can you think so quickly, Ed?' he said. 'We have only just agreed and yet you have the night planned, almost in detail.'

'Oh, it's just how I process things. You know me, once I get my head into something, I just get on with it. This is your life we are talking about, Edward. You are in very grave danger if we are caught, as you could go to prison as a coward or deserter or even worse! So, everything must be practised, and we must be convincing, right?'

He glanced across at her, pan faced, and then nodded, slowly in acknowledgement. 'With the enlistment date just ten weeks away, we have a great deal to do!'

Edward swallowed hard and felt his heart rate leap as he realised how little time they had together. 'Sorry, sis, you are right, I am just a little nervous about it all, that's all. No more dilly-dallying I promise.'

The next morning, Ed visited the church to find Bryan, who was busy sweeping behind the altar with his yard brush. He was whistling and seemed quite relaxed, wearing an old pair of trousers with a hole at the knee and a shirt that was not tucked in, with several buttons missing, showing his large, hairy belly protruding through the gap. He stopped what he was doing and leant his brush against the wall. She asked if he was free to come to supper a week on Saturday and before he could answer, his tongue made a sweep of his top lip, as if already tasting every morsel. She didn't stay and turned to leave.

'Six thirty sharp, Bryan, please.' And headed for the village shop.

After supper that day, they began in earnest to transform their lives. They headed upstairs to begin exchanging their possessions, which felt like a party game one might play at Christmas. They went back and forth several times to each other's bedroom, carrying their new clothes, sniggering as they crossed on the landing. It didn't take long, as they had few possessions and Ed finished quickly, while Edward took longer as he tried on each of the three dresses he had been given. Anything they didn't want, was left on the landing for disposal, everything else placed into a small chest of drawers and the wardrobe. When Ed had finished, she glanced into Edward's room, watching him with a smile as he tried on her blue floral dress. She hadn't seen him this cheerful for many years.

'I will head down to start dinner, Edward,' she said, before disappearing into the warmth of the kitchen. As she started preparing the vegetables for their meal in the deep Belfast sink, her mind wandered to what lay ahead. It was important they began to swap roles soon, as Edward had a lot to pick-up. Although he had a sound working knowledge of the general farm duties, he lacked the knowledge to manage the finances, which she would have to teach him, quickly.

She stoked the fire and started boiling the food on the top of the fire tray, placing the cold meat on the table. As she was cutting some bread, Edward appeared in the doorway, wearing the same light blue frock she had seen him in earlier! She pinched her lips tightly together as her sibling paraded in front of her, glorying in his new-found freedom. He had clipped his hair back and applied some lip balm too, and she was struck by how feminine he looked. Edward stared, waiting for her to speak, and with her heart pounding she went over and hugged her brother, a tear coming to her eye. He was the sister she'd never had.

'Well, look at you, brother dear,' she said as their smiles turned to laughter.

Edward broke away and did a spin, almost falling over. 'How do I look?' he asked.

'Incredible, quite incredible,' she said, smiling warmly. Edward then reached into the pocket of the dress, pulling out an object hidden in his hand. Ed could see part of a silver chain in the crease of his knuckle and, before she could speak, he thrust the mystery object into her hand. She gasped as she looked down to see a silver watch and chain, noticing an engraving on the back, which read 'Andrew Mitchell, 4 April 1889'. Their parents' wedding day.

As she looked at her father's watch from his wedding all those years ago, she looked up, happy but confused. Edward explained he had found it when he had sorted through their parents' room after news of their death. He never knew why his father had not taken it with him on the Titanic, as it must have been his greatest possession. But now it was right for it to pass to her as she was doing this monumental thing for him. She stared down at the watch for almost a minute, before reaching for her brother's hand. Words didn't matter, the message was clear that at this moment they were as one.

She opened the watch to see it was holding steady time and put it to her ear to listen to it ticking, before placing it down on the table. 'I will cherish it, Edward, thank you.'

'Right,' he said, 'haircut, come on, sit down.'

She hadn't expected this but sat down by the fire in her trousers and striped shirt, sleeves rolled up to the elbows, as Edward placed a towel over her shoulders and around her neck. He reached for the large scissors and began snipping off her locks to a style that would suit a chap of the day. He explained the way barber shops were run, where men were allowed to be men, and how the stories were more than a little coarse. 'You will need to get used to bad language too, Ed, and laugh, even though things may get very close to the edge.'

Edwina's eyes widened as she listened intently to him. 'Can you tell me a story, you know, like one I would hear at the barber's?'

He shuddered at the thought but commenced to tell her the one he knew about the milk maid and the vicar, but when he delivered the punchline, she didn't laugh, just shrugged her shoulders and said she didn't get it!

Before long, there was a circle of hair scattered on the floor around her feet and Edward pulled the towel from her shoulders. She had never had her hair so short before and felt a slight chill around the back of her neck, making her shiver. She rose up to gaze in the mirror on the far wall, where she saw the new Ed for the first time! Her brother stepped into her view behind her, and that was the first time she realised how similar they actually were. Same nose and high cheek bones, small ears with a round chin. She wasn't sure whether he was like a woman or she was like a man, but either way, they stared at each other, grinning. Supper that night was as relaxed an occasion as Ed could ever remember and she relished the fact that at last her twin was a source of happiness and contentment, for the first time in his entire life. The change had begun!

Over the next few days, they would rise at 5 a.m. and Edward shadowed his sister's every move, until into the second week he was taking the lead. He found a strength and enthusiasm he didn't know he had and slowly but surely got to grips with all she taught him. At four o'clock each afternoon they would finish work and change into their new clothes before prepping food for supper and their evening discussions. Throughout that first week they slowly got used to the new jobs; Edwina learnt to cook basic meals again, and Edward temporarily lost six sheep, finding them again after a hectic search in the wood near the top paddock! He also drafted a letter to the farming union about getting some assistance when Ed had gone to war. It was a long shot, but they would post it the next time they visited the village.

Over the next few nights they focussed on the way men and women differed, and chatted late into the night, discussing topics of daily life and about a range of personal matters, that brought a blush or a snigger. They carefully worked through their long list in the journal, which seemed endless. Ed found she was enjoying being less formal in all that she did, whether it was slurping her drink, sitting with her knees apart and, heavens above, being encouraged she should, when in men's company 'pass wind'. Oh, the joys of being a man, she thought.

Edward too, was becoming very happy with the change and was totally absorbed in his new life in every way. He focussed hard and made a special list of the most difficult things he would undertake, learning about their past, Ed's friends and her closest secrets. It was, however, she who would have the hardest job – becoming a soldier in a man's world, and all that entailed! Edward was truly concerned for his sister, especially regarding military training, and realised that even though she was hugely confident, it would truly test her resolve. She would be at the greatest risk, living amongst soldiers in very confined spaces with little or no privacy, which worried him immensely. But slowly their confidence grew as they completed the list in the journal, and nothing had been missed.

There remained three key issues for Ed to master, which would prove most difficult of all. Firstly, she had to hide her tiny breasts, and decided she could achieve this by wearing a tight-fitting undervest, a size too small, as it would be impractical to wear bandages of any kind. Learning to urinate standing up was unavoidable, and she remembered, as a child, attending the village cricket matches, where as a family they watched their father keep wicket for the village team. While the girls would sit quietly with their mothers in their Sunday best, the boys would play in the trees and stand in line under a tree, urinating freely. Her biggest concern, however, was how she would manage her monthly periods. This was going to need some research and she planned to go to the library in the coming weeks.

But for now, with their big weekend approaching, they felt confident in how their new lives and routines had progressed and could now, not look back.

The next morning, as Edward was eating his porridge, Ed knew the time had come to ask for some special help. If anything was going to make Edward choke, this was it, but to her surprise he took the question totally in his stride and quickly finished his breakfast to head outside.

'Nothing like the present, Ed. Let's go.' and followed him to the outside privy. He opened the door and turned to face her.

'Well, what do you want to know?' he asked.

'Well, how do you stand, how you, err, do it and is there anything I should know, I suppose?' she said nervously. He smiled at her and unbuttoned his fly.

'OK, firstly, men always stand with their feet about a foot or so apart, no more, and in our case, we simply take out our cock and point it in the direction of the toilet or tree or whatever you're aiming at. Now I realise it will be different for you, but you should try to do the same so as not to attract attention. When you have finished, I kind of shake the end a couple of times, or though some chaps squeeze the tip gently back and forth, making sure you don't put it back with any dribbles. Shall I show you?' She nodded, without speaking.

He thought about turning away but instead, stood side on the toilet and followed the action he had just described. She watched, fascinated, as his urine hit the water in the pan below him, like the tap in the parlour sink. It went on for a long time before he stopped and then started again, squirting the last drops, before finishing off by shaking his penis and pushing it back into his trousers. 'There, how was that?'

Ed, slightly embarrassed to have seen her brother have a pee, spoke confidently. 'Well, I see how you did it, but I will now have to practise as I don't quite know how this will work yet. Can women actually pee standing up, do you think?' she said.

'You're asking the wrong person, Ed. Why don't I leave you to it, we can talk later?' And he was gone.

She stood alone, staring into the basin for a moment, but thought better of it and instead shut the door and headed down to the barn, grabbing a bucket of water from the outside tap on the way. She collected the old tin bath and dragged it through the tall doorway, pulling it too behind her. She went over to the back wall and dropped the bath on the ground, nervously peering behind her, even though she knew no-one was there. She quickly removed her work trousers and the new cotton underpants from Edward's wardrobe. Wearing only her work boots, she now stood quite naked from the waist down, with her feet either side of the tin bath. She tried to relax, but it was alien to her not to be sitting down and looked up for inspiration, seeing high on the rafters above, two doves staring down at her. She bent her knees slightly, clutching her shirt above her waist, and tried to relax, her hips quite still, holding her breath. Finally, without looking down, she let it all go.

A stream of hot urine suddenly spurted out, hitting the bottom of the small bath about two feet in front of her. The angle took her by surprise, as it went way forward, towards the front end of the bath. She had thought it would go straight down to her feet and stopped to move back a little to avoid missing the bath altogether. After a little adjustment and widening of her stance, she relaxed again as the gates opened fully for the second time, lasting twenty seconds or so. The last bit of urine pulsed almost involuntarily in short jets, not unlike Edward's earlier. Finally, she allowed herself to breathe.

She stepped away, pretty content at her success, knowing that she must come to the barn every time from now on, no lapses and no avoidance. For the rest of the week, she embarked on her routine several times each day, hidden away in the semi-darkness. As she became more confident, she found she could control the angle of the flow a little by squeezing or pulling up the sides of her genitalia with her fingers, thus easing her concerns about splashback. But trying to pee through the slit in her men's underpants for the first time a few days later proved a wet experience! It was made doubly difficult as during full flow it became hard to stop, and when the cloth slipped from her fingers, a resulting damp patch occurred. Over the days she grew in confidence, but still had not managed to pee without some wetting of her pants and she had yet to try waring trousers!

The vicar's supper was now just one day away. They both felt reasonably confident that they could convince their close friend and pull off a successful evening. They skipped some duties on the farm on the Saturday afternoon, knowing full well they would have time to catch up on Sunday, and set about cleaning the kitchen and preparing dinner. At around five thirty all was complete, and they headed up the stairs to get themselves ready, knowing they had an hour before the vicar arrived. They had discussed their plan at length over the previous days and were happy with what lay ahead.

Bryan was never late for a free meal, and true to form he duly arrived a few minutes before six thirty. Edward, now as Edwina, stood at the kitchen table sorting out the place settings, while Ed was sitting by the fire prodding the logs with the long steel poker. Bryan stepped into the slightly gloomy room, placing a small cask of beer on the end of the table. He headed over to the fire, turning as he got there to warm his rear, before sitting down next to Ed while her brother poured out three mugs of ale. Bryan commented how lovely it was to see Edwina in a dress, something he rarely saw, and they chatted freely as the odours of a busy kitchen spread rapidly throughout the room. The candles at the table had been kept to a minimum deliberately, creating a perfectly cosy atmosphere, with the fire sending ghostly shapes around the walls of the room.

As dinner was served, Bryan was immediately immersed in his oversized portion and tucked in hungrily, gathering pace as he ate. He was a large chap with a waist size that took some keeping up, who always had a soft spot for anything sweet, and he loved his ale too. They knew much of the cask would be drunk that night, and they happily supplied as much as he wanted. As they ate, the twins were conscious of their new-found style and watched each other carefully, ready to confer later. It wasn't long before Bryan brought up the conscription topic and he was pleased to learn that Edward was now coming to terms with the idea of going to war! He wasn't, however, ready for what was coming next.

'Do you think the war will last long, Bryan?' Ed asked.

Through a mouthful of food Bryan said confidently, he was convinced it would all be over in a few months, before reaching for a further helping.

'What about women in war, will we get our chance?' said Edward.

'Why, I don't really know of these things, but I think some women are already working in British field hospitals in England and in France too. I know you would be ready, Edwina, if you ever thought of it, as you are of strong character and hold your own very well, especially since your father died.'

This was music to their ears. 'But I couldn't go to war, who would run the farm?' he said.

'Well, that is a problem, of course, but I was speaking metaphorically, I wasn't really expecting you to give up the farm,' he said. 'Especially as Edward has to go.'

'But you think I would have what it takes to go to war Bryan?' said Edward.

'Yes, I do,' he said, 'And furthermore, it's a shame that you're not your brother, as I know you're as strong as any man, Edwina, you carry yourself well, are courageous and determined and can shoot better than any person I know. No offence intended, Edward, but you are not suited to war, my boy, and I feel sorry you're having to go. Wish there was a way for you to avoid leaving us.'

'There is,' said Edwina, 'with your help!'

Bryan stopped chewing and looked at them in turn, only moving his eyes. He hesitated, then continued to chew his last mouthful, before swallowing hard. He picked up his mug and took a large gulp, before placing his vessel back on the table. He smacked his lips, poked his finger inside his mouth to retrieve a piece of meat stuck between his teeth and leant back in his chair, looking at them again, meeting their eyes in turn.

'I feel as though you are about to feed me to the lions,' he said. 'So, what's going on?'

Ed looked into his eyes and prepared herself.

'Bryan, as a vicar, are you permitted to pass on a secret that you are told in confidence to anyone within the church, or outside of it for that matter, when you have been asked to keep it private? And if we tell you something, um, private like, will you promise not to tell anyone?'

'I am bound by the oath I gave to God that all sins by man are between God and the sinner, so as I represent God, anything you say to me in the form of a confession, whether in church or elsewhere, will stay with me and no-one else. Secrets are not always sins, however, so what is it you are really asking?'

This was it. This was the opening they had sought and soon they would know their fate. 'I appreciate your honestly, Bryan,' said Ed quietly,

'Have you notice anything different about me?' Bryan paused before he answered, looking backwards and forwards to both their anxious faces, unaware of the trap he was falling into.

'Well, Edward, I have always looked out for you, as you know, especially as a young lad when you were picked on by the village children and more recently following your parents' deaths. You are a bright boy but one who has struggled with your life a little and the loss of your parents, your mother especially, I know, had a big impact on you. You are a soft-natured person who has never enjoyed hard labour and you keep yourself closed down a little, away with the clouds you might say. I feel terrible you are leaving us to go to war, as Edwina is more suited to army life than you. It's as if somehow, you exchanged personalities at birth, as life has not always been easy for you. Is that what you wanted to hear?' he asked.

There was a powerful silence in the room, no-one spoke. The twins simultaneously picked up their mugs to take a drink. Edward, dressed in his sister's clothes, was not surprised at Bryan's description and was certainly not offended by it either. But he knew, in that instant, trusting Bryan was the right decision. Edwina smiled at him as she set her mug back on the table, before making her move.

'Bryan, I need you to listen to me without comment of any kind, until I have finished speaking,' she said, thrusting her hands deep into her trouser pockets. 'Is that acceptable to you?'

'Why, yes, of course, dear boy,' he said, as he poured himself another beer from the pitcher.

'You have become a very important man to us, and without you we are not sure we would have survived over the past years, and the farm would probably have gone. So, we are indebted to you for your love and support and for taking the place of our parents in so many ways. We could not have done that without you, Bryan. But today, we now must trust you in the greatest challenge of our lives, which may well become a matter of life and death.'

Ed paused to collect her thoughts and take a sip from her mug. Bryan folded his arms, totally transfixed by the words spoken, casually looking across the table, waiting patiently for Ed to continue. She reached for her brother's hand and gave it a gentle squeeze.

'The war has gone on far longer than anyone ever thought, and this country has lost thousands of good men, some from our own village. It has affected thousands of communities across the country, and families have suffered greatly.' She swallowed hard. 'Bryan, I am not Edward, we have played a trick on you to show you we can swap lives, as I am Edwina and I am going to war in his place!'

Bryan's mouth dropped open and he unfolded his arms as the words hit him. He placed his large hands on the table and leaned forward staring back in utter shock, turning from one face to the other. He sought some sign that this was indeed a huge joke and turned his head briefly up to the ceiling and muttered something under his breath. Ed started to speak again, but Edward cut her off abruptly.

'Bryan, we have been working for several weeks to change our lives completely and what you see tonight is our future. There is a huge risk of course with our plan, Edwina especially, as she will be the one facing the might of the German Army. There is a lot to lose, even perhaps our lives. So we need your absolute support and above all your loyalty to us both and our parents to pull this off. I hope we have not misjudged you?'

A heavy silence fell on the room. Eyes flashed between faces, no-one knowing quite what to say. Bryan bowed his head and breathing deeply clasped his hands together. The twins looked at each other with wide eyes, not knowing what to say. A few moments passed before Bryan stood and walked over to the fire and leant on the mantelpiece, staring into the flames. Suddenly, he turned and placed his hands behind his back, told them to listen carefully.

'I have said nothing while you have been speaking, but you must now allow me the same courtesy. Having briefly spoken to God, I say this: you have embarked on something that is bewildering and terribly dangerous. I do understand the loyalty that exists between you both, but how on earth do you think you can fool the British Army for a single moment?'

Ed started to speak, but Bryan held his hand up and quickly carried on. 'Army training and the front line is something you have absolutely no understanding of and grown men, stronger men than you, are unable to cope, dying by the thousands every month, and yet you seem to think you can fool them and everyone who has ever known you here in the village. I hear what you say and understand, but, think it a foolish undertaking to even consider this plan. I have no doubt it's nothing short of the greatest act of love between siblings I have ever experienced, and I recognise this love is very special between you both, which is why, having spoken to God, I will help you, even though it is a monumental undertaking and is in my view, total madness.'

Edward swung his head around to meet Edwina's gaze. Bryan was clearly flustered and struggled to retrieve his pocket handkerchief from his tight trousers, before blowing his nose loudly. He fussed about his nose for few moments before replacing his handkerchief in his pocket. He looked up for the first time since his outburst.

Ed spoke softly. 'Bryan, do you mean it unreservedly?'

'Yes, I do, Edwina, I do indeed, but you must tell me everything, so I am fully prepared for any eventuality. You undoubtedly have the hardest part to play here, but Edward living in the village under an assumed disguise will be tested also. I have nothing to lose in my life, but you have everything, so, I will come here tomorrow night and every night for as long as it takes to learn of your plans and preparations. You must not hide a single thing from me. Do I have your word?'

They both looked at each other before nodding at Bryan. Edwina spoke for them both. 'Yes, of course,' she said and reached for Edward's hand.

Chapter 4

The meeting called by General Sir Douglas Haig's aide-de-camp (ADC) was to be held at GHQ in London, a long-standing headquarters of the British Army. He had succeeded Sir John French in December 1915 as head of the British Expeditionary Force, later to be relocated to Montreuil-sur-Mer. Today, the agenda included a proposal to create a properly trained team of snipers that would be able to become as effective as those of the German Army. They had deployed their teams along the front line with considerable success, and it was time to give them a taste of their own medicine! With their specialised scoped rifles, they had a huge advantage over the British and allied forces and so it had become high priority to address this imbalance. The prelims of the meeting went ahead with little debate or difficulty, while Major Hesketh-Pritchard sat nervously at one end of the long table. General Haig moved on to item five and invited the major to begin briefing the gathered officers.

'Thank you, sir. Gentlemen, snipers were first used in Admiral Nelson's time on board ships of the line, when marines were sent high into the ship's rigging to shoot officers standing on the quarter decks of opposing ships. It was a successful tactic that has largely been lost over the centuries, but I believe it is time to resurrect this specialist area of operations. I am therefore proposing we form our own specialist sniper school, which would ultimately bring a new dimension, offering commanders in the field additional weaponry and skilled personnel to change the course of the war! Each sniper team would include the shooter and a spotter or observer who would provide support and assist with the range finding, wind speed and direction, fall of shot, etcetera, etcetera. They would work as a pair and do anything that was required to gain a kill.' He looked up; he had gained their full attention.

'This teamwork would initially begin on the sniper course and be developed over time, providing the necessary skills to not only work from the front-line trenches, but also, when required, to be deployed in isolated and hostile locations for long periods in No Man's Land. I believe we can produce a small team of specialists who will encourage, let's say, the Germans to keep their heads down a little more than they do now.'

There was much nodding of heads as the group of senior officers agreed with his summation. He went on with more optimism. 'If you approve my proposals today, gentlemen, we will start to recruit from battalions at the front with a shooting prowess, but also, actively select raw recruits too, as they progress through basic training. A signal would need to be sent to all training establishments to alert commanding officers, and selection and courses would be run from a location I have found in France.'

General Haig had listened intently, even though he had received the written brief from the major over a week before. He sat looking around his staff officers and brushed his large moustache with the back of the knuckle, nodding approvingly. A discussion then followed around the table, before Haig raised a question.

'What's your plan for training these men, Major, where would your location be exactly and how effective do you expect these men to become?'

Major Hesketh-Pritchard was expecting tough questions and was well prepared. 'Subject to your approval, sir, I would set up the training school near an old French Army range, in Linghem in northern France, some fifty miles south east of Calais. It would allow me to standardise the techniques required and develop the individual skills paramount for success. Course length would be eight weeks, and once completed the men could quickly be deployed to front-line battalions in accordance with staff requirements. I have already drawn up plans for your approval, sir, which I have given to your ADC. I hope to start selection and training from May this year, sir. Finally, I have several young officers keen to give this a go and a few experienced senior non-commissioned officers in mind to be part of my training team, all of whom I can personally vouch for. They will be the backbone of the training and uphold the very highest standards.'

As he sat back, placing his pencil on the blotter before him, he scanned the many faces down the long table. He knew his proposal was timely and would be effective, ultimately producing the success Haig wanted. However, convincing this group might be a huge challenge! But what he saw both surprised and encouraged him greatly, as heads around the room started nodding unanimously! As the ADC passed the copies of his report to all the officers present, he waited patiently for the questions to begin.

'Can you cut the training time back a little, Major?' said an elegant looking colonel at the far end of the table, fiddling with his wiry moustache.

'Well, sir, everything is flexible, but this is a new untested course with lots of elements, with modern warfare tactics not done before. They require serious changes to many accepted practices and methods of war, and on top of this we have to produce outstanding shots to carry out these missions in the most difficult terrain any of us can imagine. This is new territory, gentlemen, requiring many changes as we progress, and every day will count. Range days will fill the vast majority of training days, shooting in all conditions and positions. It cannot be emphasised enough that if the training is short or of poor quality, we will not achieve the aims we set ourselves. Furthermore, the German soldiers use a scoped Mauser Gewehr 98 rifle; we have several in our possession and they are particularly good at their trade, having an excellent telescopic sight. This enables accuracy up to four hundred yards, which is why they have been so successful! The Lee Enfield Mk 111 rifle, although a very good weapon for general use, has its limitations in this environment and improvements are being sought as we speak. For example, the .303 ammunition still burnt too hot, although in a sniper's role it had little effect on its accuracy. The British telescopic sights have been developed by the Periscopic Prism Company of London, who have been secretly working on improvements, and a design has now been approved for production. So, gentlemen, I need all the time available, within reason, to get these men up to a level to match that of our enemy.'

He stopped talking and referred to his notes before continuing. 'It is my belief, sir, that eight weeks would be the preferred length, but it is of course your decision.' And then he decided he had said enough, feeling his points had hit home. He stared cautiously at the mighty general, hoping that he would get the resources he wanted.

Haig seemed impressed but said nothing, instead waiting on his senior officers to open the debate further.

'Major, I refer to page six of your document, and notice there is no accommodation present at this range, where do you propose to billet these men?'

'If you look at the back, sir, in the appendixes, I have outlined basic living costs for civilian lodgings for the men and the staff members, as everything else would be provided by the army.' Haig leant sideways to his brigadier on his right to listen to his comment and nodded gently. He wrote something on a piece of paper and held it in front of him. The brigadier adjusted his glasses to the end of his nose, perused the paper for a moment, before nodding slowly. The general caught each officer's eye individually around the room before signing something on his blotter. He then addressed those present.

'Unless gentlemen, anyone has a serious problem with this proposal, I suggest we give it our full support. Major,' he said, looking at him with his head forward. 'We are impressed with your work and expect great things will come from this initiative. The selection of the small range at Linghem is a good choice, but you will need to tighten your training plans, as I will grant you six weeks only for sniper training. I do appreciate you have a lot to get through and this is a new era of operations; however, it is clear you have been very thorough in your planning, and I would be greatly surprised if you do not already have a contingency plan. You will report to Brigadier Norman in two weeks, with your full submission and progress report; get his contact details from him after this meeting. I give you full approval to signal all Brigade HQs as a priority and training Headquarters in Warminster. If we are going to all this trouble, we must capture the very best available men from the ranks and under training. Liaise with the ADC afterwards and he will issue the signal. Finally, I cannot stress how important this matter is, Major. The Hun have had the upper hand, it is now time we showed them what we are made of. You have the power to make a real difference here, I am relying on you! Any questions? No? Good.' He said giving him no time to answer. 'You are dismissed.'

Chapter 5

You could count on one hand the times the Mitchell twins had ever visited the village together, but today was a confidence building occasion, following their successful dinner with Bryan. A golden opportunity, they thought, to test themselves in public after living as each another for nearly two weeks. It was important that they did not draw attention to themselves and simply to act as naturally as possible, so Edwina stepped up to drive the trap as usual, but this time it was of course Edward!

They set off down the hill to the crossroads at the bottom and entered the south end of the village. The early spring sunshine, unusually warming, made the journey rather pleasant and Edward was in his element. Heads turned and people waved, and Bryan peered across at them as he crossed the churchyard. He stopped to smile, arms full of clothes, before heading off down the path to the village hall bazaar. Duchess trotted on down main street, her hooves joining the throng of the busy street. As they came to a stop outside the Bull and Gate pub, Edwina jumped down and gathered the reins, tethering the old mare to the rail, just next to the water trough. They both walked over to the other side of the narrow street, to the small village shop. There was no staring, no reaction at all by anyone, but why should there be? It was of course just a normal day for them, even though Ed's heart was pounding in her chest. They acted as each other would, in perfectly harmony, Ed with her well-practised long stride out in front, while Edward, in his dress and short bonnet, walked more slowly, lagging slightly behind. They looked up the street and saw colourful posters in many shop windows, which were clearly supplied by the Government and were pretty close to the mark.

"*Halt the Hun*" said one, with a British soldier in a pose. Another asked, "*Who's Absent? Is it you?*" with a stout man with a large moustache in a waistcoat made from the Union flag, pointing.

As they reached the path, the village post mistress was shuffling by with her heavy bag, telling them she was late again and heading off without stopping.

They arrived at the shop door, which opened before they had chance to reach for the handle, and two rather stout ladies stepped out, their arms full of packages wrapped in brown paper. They waited until the two ladies had gone before stepping inside, to see Ella, the shop owner's daughter, beaming at them. She walked straight over to greet them, flush with pleasure at seeing them both together and wrung her hands together in delight.

'Hello, you two, it's been ages,' she said. 'Where have you been?'

They both looked at each other sideways on and laughed. If only she knew…

'Oh, you know, busy on the farm, and what with Edward going off to war soon it's all been rather hectic,' said Edward. 'We hope to have a farm worker coming in a couple of weeks to cover for him, so when he settles in, perhaps you might like to come and visit?'

'Yes, I would like that,' said Ella. 'When is he expected?'

'We're not sure yet, as we await confirmation from the Ministry, but it should be soon.'

Edwina, in her disguise, stepped away to collect the items they needed, pulling out a short list from her pocket, leaving Ella and the 'new' Ed chatting, as girls do. With confidence high, she quickly collected the items they needed, before stepping over to the counter, where Ella's father called his daughter over to assist. As she stepped away, Edward coughed, not for the first time since they had arrived, and again a few moments later. Ed thought this odd as he hadn't been coughing earlier and she wondered if she had made a mistake or something and he was trying to alert her. She felt uneasy and so placed the items from the basket next to the till.

'Cash or account?' said Mr Spottiswood.

'Oh, on account please, we will settle up at the end of the month as usual. Could you let me know where we stand please?'

He nodded, making little effort to converse, and listed each item in the large green ledger beside him, before totalling up the month's supplies.

'Your total is three pounds, two shillings and sixpence,' he said. 'Payable at the end of the month, please,' and commenced wrapping everything in brown paper, tied with white string. Ed picked up the goods, thanked him and walked towards to the door, waiting for Edward.

'Time to go' said Ed, and they said their farewells.

As they stepped towards the door, Mr Spottiswood rather sheepishly walked over to Ed with his head down slightly and held out his hand. 'Not sure when I will see you next, Edward, but good luck and keep your head well out of harm's way. You don't want to lose an ear, do you?' He then gave Ed a silver pin in the shape of a clover leaf. It had four leaves. 'That was my mother's, it gave her good luck' and he pushed his hand forward to shake Ed's hand a second time. Ed was moved by this gesture and thanked him, before he turned away into the back of the shop, blowing his nose as he went.

They walked out of the shop, heading back towards the trap, commenting how well it had gone and that Ella, who knew them both very well, didn't notice anything amiss. Ed felt the need to ask her brother why he was coughing so much in the shop.

'Oh, Ella thought I might be ill as she felt my voice sounded a little hoarse, so I coughed a few times to cover myself, didn't know what else to do,' he said.

They both smiled and crossed the road towards the pony and trap. They loaded their supplies into the basket at the rear, and Edwina climbed up. Edward saw the public toilets just ahead and decided he needed to make a visit.

'Won't be a minute,' he said, and walked along the street to the toilets, something he had done a hundred times before. As he entered, the smell of toilet soap greeted him, and then as he stepped behind the dividing wall, it hit him! He had, without thinking, walked into the gentlemen's side, just as an old man was leaving a cubicle at the far end, with his fly gaping open. The old codger suddenly caught sight of what he thought was 'a lady' and yelled loudly swinging his stick at this intrusion, hitting Edward across his arm. He yelled again for her to get out, spittle dripping from his lips! Edward turned and sped out quickly, back into the street, his bladder not seeking relief anymore, his body just intent on freedom.

He ran to the trap and jumped up quickly, taking Edwina quite by surprise. He reached for the reins as he saw the old man appear from the toilet, red-faced, still waving his stick in the air. With haste, he twitched the reins, the horse raising her head as she reacted to this sudden urge to move. They quickly gained speed and trotted past the old man who was still yelling at him. Ed looking sideways at her brother, waiting for an explanation, and then the penny dropped.

'What?' said Edward with an embarrassed grin. Ed bit her lip, peering across at him as they trotted out of the village, but she could not hold back and smiled broadly, before breaking into a fit of laughter.

Chapter 6

In the covering letter attached to Edward's enlistment documents, he was required to have an army medical. It was clearly not something Edwina could possibly undertake, and Edward made it clear, he would go and do his bit. The regimental day was in just a few days' time and was to be held in the town of Lechlade, just twenty miles away. When the letter had arrived the previous week, it stirred all sorts of emotions within him, even though Edward knew all he had to do was quietly attend a brief inspection, and his part would then be over. His weight had remained the same, so borrowed his old suit back from his sister's wardrobe and simply greased his hair back behind his ears. He trusted the past was behind him and any meetings with the boys from the surrounding villages, would pose no problems to him.

When the big day arrived, Edwina made a fuss of him at breakfast and commented that the last time he had worn the suit was at their parents' memorial service in August 1912. Edwina had changed back, too, for the day, in case anyone arrived at the farm without notice, so she donned a woolly hat to cover her short hair before giving Edward a hug as he set off down the hill to catch the bus. He felt nervous as he approached the village square, as two of the boys from the opposite side of the village were standing by the bus stop and sniggered at each other.

'OK, Edward,' said one sarcastically, right into his ear, the other lad sniggering loudly. Not the best start, he thought, so he avoided eye contact and just stepped back against the wall and waited. Then the green bus came down the hill and stopped, the two lads barging their way on first, heading for the back seat. Edward let everyone else on, then sat right at the front to avoid them. The journey took a little over forty minutes and upon arrival it pulled into the car park next to the cricket ground, where a large crowd met his gaze. As he stepped down from the bus, he hurried through the gate into the field, where a vast array of tents and marquees were pitched around the outer edges of the field, with families clearly making a day of it. Many food traders were scattered all over the field and he thought it very strange that people were treating it like a jamboree or a show of some sort, to entertain the masses. Local publicans were taking full advantage by having beer tents and food kitchens to feed the vast throng of people and to entertain the children. There was a great hum of enthusiasm, with handshakes and laughter, drinking games and even a tug-of-war competition going on. A band played in the far corner and men in uniform were scattered around, greeting people with smiling faces. It was not what he was expecting at all.

Two soldiers strolled over in his direction, chatting to anyone who caught their gaze. Children looked up at them as heroes and old soldiers shook their hands and reminisced on their own war stories from past victories, pointing down to the medals on their chests. He walked on and looked through the crowds towards a large tent with several flag poles pointing skywards, the flags hanging limply in the cool air of a February day. On the far side a large huddle had formed by the entrance, and he set off to get the job done quickly, so he could head home. He noticed a kite flying high above being pulled by a man who yanked the cord harshly, and then out of the blue it dipped suddenly almost taking his head off. As he finally approached the tent, he saw a sign above the door which had K6 written in large black letters on it, and he joined a long line of men just like him, all smartly dressed in their Sunday best. The line moved slowly forward until Edward could see a desk just a few feet away. Behind it was a man with three stripes on his upper arms and a nose seemingly battered by too much boxing, or booze! A sergeant he thought. He had a pile of papers before him, all being held down by what looked like an old brass shell head. He was probably in his forties, with greying hair at the temples, wearing full uniform with many coloured medal ribbons above his left breast pocket. The chap in front of Edward was called forward, leaving him frighteningly close to the military for the very first time.

'Next!' said the sergeant.

Edward moved forward and was asked his name. 'Edward, sir,' he replied.

'I'm not your mother, son?' he said sharply. 'Your surname man, your surname,' he said shaking his head.

Edward wanted the ground to open up and stood there nervously as others around him, laughed. He was always at his worst, when people made fun of him and was now unsure of himself. Nervously, he stated his name in full:

'Edward Mitchell, sir.'

'And stop calling me sir, I am a sergeant I work for a living.' He said with a wry smile. An officer behind him gazed across, grimacing and shaking his head, before walking away.

'Yes, Sergeant,' Edward said as the man scanned down the list in front of him, turning several pages before finding Edward's name. He ticked it with his pencil before handing him a piece of green paper and sending him over to another tent next door, where he was told to join another line. He reported once again to another man in uniform, this time with two stripes, and handed over his green paper. He was instructed to go down to bay six, at the far end of the long marquee. The central area was full of people coming and going, with some men doing up their shirt buttons, others looking completely lost. Outside each bay, seats were set out in rows, and he joined two others waiting beneath a large number 6 hanging from the rail. There were at least a dozen cubicles and perhaps fifty men in sight, all waiting to be medically assessed.

'Next,' he heard someone shout and the man nearest to the canvas flap stood and entered, and they all moved up one seat. Five minutes went by and the same man came out, all dishevelled, stuffing his shirt into his trousers, a white piece of paper sticking out of his mouth, as he did up his buttoned fly.

'Next,' came the command again and he moved up one more seat, as the man in front dipped behind the canvas flap. He felt nervous and sat with his arms folded, leaning back, looking around the vast marquee, as people came and went. His mind wandered, his heart pounded, his breathing shallow. He tried hard to think of pleasant things, to avert his nerves and then started to question his moral fibre and whether after all, he should allow Ed to go through with their plan. He knew he was a coward and was ashamed! He started to feel terribly guilty.

'Next,' came a voice from within. Ed stood and stepped coyly through the canvas wall to meet a man wearing a white coat, with a funny loop of tubing around his neck, with a circular pad on one end and two hooks on the other. He had not seen anything like it before and was staring at it, paying little attention to the doctor's questions.

'I say, are you listening to me, lad?' said the doctor, in a broad Scottish accent.

'Yes, sir, err, sorry, sir,' Edward said softly.

'Name?' He wasn't falling for that one again.

'Mitchell, sir.'

He looked down his list. 'Mitchell, Mitchell, ah yes, is that Mitchell, Edward?' he asked.

'Yes, sir,' he replied nervously.

'Sit down, laddie, it's just a routine medical check,' he said writing on a sheet of paper. For the next few minutes Edward was asked various questions about his health, where he was from, about his parents, had he any siblings and so on. He was then told to strip down. He stood up and quickly unbuttoned and removed his jacket and his shirt and then removed his vest, placing them all on a chair. The doctor turned him around and without a word started tapping his back with his fingers rather hard, then repeated this action on his upper chest, before looking into his ears, feeling around his throat and peering up his nose. Finally, he lifted his arms and felt under them in turn, pressing his fingers deep into the tissue, making Edward wince. The doctor then uttered something which Edward didn't understand.

'Pardon, sir?' He said nervously.

'Read the sheet, sonny, read the sheet over there.' Said the doctor, pointing.

Ed looked up and across the tent saw a blackboard several yards away with chalked letters on it.

'G T S U B A X' he said confidently.

'Now touch your toes, laddie' he said. Edward respectfully bent forward until told to stand up again.

'Tongue out and say aaah.' At this point, the doctor peered into his mouth and pushed his tongue down with a flat wooden stick. 'That's all. OK, now drop your trousers!'

This was a shock, but Ed flipped his bracers from his shoulders and the oversized trousers that once belonged to his father fell to the ground, without even unbuttoning the waist. The doctor, who had been writing some details on a sheet of paper, turned back round to see Edward half naked. 'And your underpants, son.' Without question, he did as he was asked and stood back upright in puzzlement, feeling very exposed.

The doctor put his left hand on Edward's shoulder, simultaneously grabbing his balls in his right hand, telling him to look right and cough! Edward, with eyes like a frightened rabbit, froze, not really understanding what was happening to him and turned his head, before looking back nervously and coughing directly into the doctor's face. The doctor stepped back immediately and released his grasp, wiping his face with the hand that had been, until a moment before, clutching Edward's testicles.

With a raised voice, he said, 'What are you doing, man, I said turn your head and cough, not at me.' He shook his head, and watching Edward with cautious eyes, he reached down and again grasped him as before, Edward feeling positively anguished. 'OK, let's try that again, turn your head to the right and cough.'

This time Ed tried to follow his order but quite unexpectedly, just as his testicles were held, he lurched forward, bending at the hip, almost head-butting the doctor in the face. The doctor reacted quicker this time, pulling his head backwards, narrowly avoiding a blooded nose, and released his grip.

'Mitchell, you need to be more careful,' said the doctor shaking his head. 'OK, trousers up and get dressed, you can go,' he said, writing the last of his notes on the sheet.

Edward's first impulse was to charge out half-dressed, but he quickly pulled his trousers back up, quite forgetting about his underpants, which were now crumpled in his crotch. He reached for his vest and shirt and dressed quickly, before pulling his bracers over his shoulders and pulling on his jacket, stuffing his tie into his pocket. He felt terribly embarrassed and wanted the earth to swallow him up!

'Take this paper to the corporal at the exit,' said the doctor without looking up and pointing to the flap in the tent wall.

Edward headed out, his nether regions now caught in the twisted material of his underpants, causing difficulty in walking. He assumed he must be fit for duty and gave the piece of paper to the seated corporal, who he noticed had one leg missing from just below the knee. Edward smiled at him without speaking as the man busied himself writing his name in a ledger and placing the paper into a box on the floor. He then wrote at the top of one of the forms, before handing it to Edward, along with a sheet of paper and a voucher. Just before the exit, he reached down with one hand inside his trousers to adjust his pants, yanking them back into place. From behind, he heard the voice of the doctor, shouting for his next victim.

Ed headed back outside, relieved the ordeal was finally over. He glanced down at his father's old wrist watch with a squint, to see he had over an hour before his bus departed and so he walked over to one of the refreshment tents, away in the corner of the field. When he arrived, it was crammed full of people, many of them clearly the worse for wear, but all in good spirits. Some though were blind drunk, shouting about killing the Hun and doing their bit! He ventured to the end of the bar to get a brew of tea, as he was dry from all the nervous energy and the time spent inside the chilly tent.

He handed over two pence and on finding a quiet spot away from most of the bustle, he took a long swig from the cup, before setting it down and releasing his breath. He wiped his mouth with the back of his hand and glanced down at the papers in his other hand. He noticed he was to report to the barracks in Bristol in just three weeks' time. He was surprised how his body tensed and his heart started pounding, even though it would not be him going to war! The form stated he was to collect his train ticket from the station using the voucher provided on the morning of his departure and not to be late. On the third sheet of paper was a clothing list of items he was to take with him, all typed in neat rows, although he thought it odd that everything was listed backwards:

Vest–Under–2.

Pants–Under–4.

Shirts–dress–1.

And so it went on, down the page.

He placed the papers on the table in front of him, before reaching for his cup to sip the remainder of his tea. As he did so he glanced around the tent, and to his horror saw two of the village lads who were on the bus earlier. He sensed trouble as they were clearly the worse for the drink and laughed at him before heading over in his direction. He started to panic and looked around for an exit, but before he could do anything, they were upon him. He squeezed his lips together firmly, his eyes focussed on their every move, waiting for the verbal tirade that had plagued him since the school playground when he was just six years old. He quickly reached for his papers to place them safely into his pocket, but in his haste, he knocked over the small table and both the cup and the papers fell to the grass. Standing up quickly, as he knew from experience what was coming, he looked for his escape. Alas a few seconds had passed, and they were now standing, swaying arm in arm, about to pounce. He was about to step away when a man much taller than Ed, with mounds of thick black hair, stepped across their path, putting them off their stride and forcing one of them to lose his footing. Almost in slow motion, one dragged the other to the floor, right in front of him. A roar of laughter went up from many people around them, the lads now rolling on the floor.

'Shall we go?' said the man. Ed needed no further hints and collected his papers from the floor and headed away from the throng towards one of the side tent flaps. The sunshine greeted their exit and Ed felt pleased to have escaped the turmoil, turning to thank the stranger.

'I'm Frank' he said. 'Frank Smith. Looks like those lads were out to get you. Do you know them?'

'Hello, Frank, I'm Edward,' and he paused for just a moment, gazing across at the lads as he shook Frank's hand. 'Edward Mitchell, how do you do,' he said warmly. 'Yes, village bullies, that's all, known them all my life and the further I can get away from them the better,' he said, smiling at his new friend.

Two of the army's newest recruits walked away together towards a food tent and joined a short queue. They chatted freely and felt relaxed as they ordered two meat pies before stepping away to find a spot to sit. Ed looked over his shoulder just once, to check the lads weren't following them, but felt happy to have Frank there, just in case. He found him a friendly man who seemed to be ready to do his bit for his country, something Edward most definitely was not! They sat by the fence, near the bus car park.

'Ciggy?' Frank said.

'No, not for me thanks, Frank, never did like the stuff,' but he watched Frank take out some tobacco and a paper and expertly roll a neat cigarette, lighting it with an old petrol lighter that smelt of burnt oil. Frank drew in the strong tobacco and exhaled thick smoke into the air as they sat quietly for a few minutes, talking.

'So, which regiment are you joining, Edward?' said Frank

'Second, fifth Battalion, Royal Gloucesters,' said Edward.

'Oh great, me too, what date have you been given?' Frank asked.

'The twenty sixth of March, just three weeks' time.'

'Ah, we will be together, same regiment, same date,' he said with a smile.

Edward looked at him, thinking 'how wrong you are, old chap', and turned to look around the field, noticing the party atmosphere had remained and many young lads were now very drunk. He and Frank sat watching with interest as hundreds of ordinary people, milled around in small groups, a day many would remember for life. Edward being struck by how pleasant Frank was, felt he had an air about him that he couldn't quite place, and didn't feel it right to ask. After some twenty minutes, Edward peered down at his watch.

'My bus is leaving in ten minutes, Frank, so I had better head over.' They both stood up, brushing the grass from their trousers, returning the plates back at the food tent just across the way. They walked to the exit and down the short lane towards the row of buses now parked up at the end. Edward was confident this would be the last time he would ever see Frank but felt he should remember this moment as his dear sister most probably would. They parted company at the foot of the steps to Edward's number 23 bus, which was preparing to leave. They shook hands warmly and within minutes of taking his seat, the engine came to life and Edward sat looking from the window, wondering what the future would hold. With his job now done, he passed the mantle and all the responsibility of soldiering over to Edwina. Frank waved to his new friend as the bus pulled away.

Chapter 7

From the kitchen window, Edward noticed Bryan scurrying up the track towards the cottage in a fast walk that was clearly causing him anguish. As he approached the gate, he could hardly put one foot in front of the other and he hung on the gate post almost exhausted. His mouth was wide open sucking air into his breathless lungs, then turned his head and spat onto the grass. He blew hard several times, before heading for the door. Edward was puzzled as to why he was in such a hurry and walked to the open door to greet him. Bryan stepped in and almost collapsed, wheezing and quite unable to speak. He quickly sat down, wiping the beads of sweat from his brow with his handkerchief and coughed several times before trying to speak.

'Where is Edwina, we have a problem,' he said, panting. Edward paused for a second and frowned as he looked at the vicar, the smell of his perspiring body filling the air.

'She's in the barn,' he said, 'she won't be long. What's up?'

Leaning forward Bryan looked down at his feet, as his body slowly began to return to normal, moisture dripping from his brow down his overly fat cheeks. 'I'll wait till she gets back. Is there tea?' he said as he turned the chair around noisily on the stone flagged floor.

Edward reached for a spare mug and dribbled in a few drops of milk and three sugars before adding the tea, just as Bryan liked it. As he placed the tea on the table, Edwina came through the door holding a basket of eggs across her middle, discreetly hiding a wet patch in her crotch.

'Ah, there you are,' Bryan said. 'Your farm worker is on his way here, now, right this minute.'

The twins looked at each other with concern. 'But he's not due for another week, we still have things to do,' said Edward.

'Well that may be, but you requested him and, they have sent you someone, so you had better get your skates on. In the meantime, I will take this chap away for a couple of hours back to the church to give you a little time. I can easily find something for him to do. Have you readied his room?' he asked.

'We are giving him the room at the top of the house, but no, we haven't started it yet!' Edward, clutching his mug of tea, turned his head as he spoke to peer through the window and noticed a distant figure coming over the crest of the hill, with a kit bag hanging from one shoulder, taking slow, deliberate steps, and then he noticed he walked with a limp.

'Looks like he's here,' he said. 'He's just coming over the rise.'

'OK, this is what we will do,' said Bryan. 'When he arrives, Ed, you and I will greet him, and I will then ask him to accompany me to the church. I can keep him busy for a couple of hours, have no fears. Will that be enough?' he asked.

'It will have to be,' Edward said, bolting the rest of his tea greedily, before heading through the kitchen door to the hallway. 'I'll make a start,' he shouted, as he disappeared upstairs.

Edwina and Bryan looked at each other in silence, awaiting a new chapter in this complicated affair. A minute later, a young man appeared, looking at the cottage from the gate. As he approached the door, Ed saw his limp. Bryan quickly opened the door just as he stepped down the path making him jump. Ed standing close behind him, peered over his shoulder.

'Hello, I'm David, David Russell. I have been sent to work here.' There was a short pause as their eyes met, before the vicar snapped a look across to Ed.

'Oh, hello David, but you aren't due until next week,' said Ed.

'Yeh, sorry about that, but I was kicked out of my digs so thought I might as well head over, even if it meant sleeping in the barn or something for a few nights. Is that alright?'

'Heavens no, that won't be necessary, David, we can always use your extra help and besides, we have lots of room.'

Bryan then took the lead and turned the conversation, as if by accident: 'An answer to my prayers,' he said, looking keenly at David. 'Look, I need some help in the church this afternoon before the Bishop's visit tomorrow, and just when I had given up hope of finding someone, you turn up. I was just saying to Edward about it, and lo and behold, you appear on the doorstep. God acts in mysterious ways sometimes. Drop your bag, son, and come with me,' he said. 'Oh, this is OK with you, I trust,' he said turning to face Ed.

'By all means, as long as David has no objection,' Before he could even respond, Bryan took his opportunity.

'OK, let's go then. he said, walking down the path.

'I'll take your bag in David, don't worry. By the time you get back, supper will be ready.'

Before David could make any decision of his own, he was trekking back down the hill, the vicar leading the way, calling back to him. Ed waved him off.

'See you later,' she called and turned back into the kitchen. There was a great deal to do.

From the window, Edward had seen Bryan and David leave and came back downstairs. 'Right, we'd better get cracking.'

The twins set about changing the layout of their home, beginning in the kitchen. They firstly turned the large kitchen table to allow for a third armchair by the hearth and slid the dresser over to the right, to give a little more access. Edwina then headed upstairs to the top landing armed with the cleaning box, brushes and mops, coming back for a full bucket of water, while Edward sat to write down the daily jobs sheet they had agreed upon.

She had quite forgotten how dark this upper landing was and all along the top corridor, long cobwebs from years of neglect, hung down, sticking to her face and body. She finally reached the open bedroom door, and what met her gaze was a complete shock. Edward's quick clearance of pieces of furniture and several boxes were now piled up by the door.

She entered the gloomy the room and walked over to open the curtains, where dust flew in all directions, making it difficult to breathe. She coughed repeatedly and reached for the catch, flinging the window wide open, and stuck her head out to suck in some clean air. When she was breathing more easily, she looked back in total disgust. Standing with her hands on her hips, wondering where to start!

Before long, Edward had joined her on the landing and for the next two hours they cleaned the room from top to bottom, removing all sorts of rubbish and furniture that had been stored for many years. While the bed was being made up, Edward dragged the remaining boxes and pieces of furniture down into their parents' room on the floor below and finally, it looked presentable.

Standing in the doorway, they admired their efforts.

'That will do, don't you think?' she said. Edward nodded.

'I am going to change,' he said. 'Better start as we mean to continue.'

Ed grabbed some of her spare work clothes and an old coat from the pile they had discarded only a few weeks before and along with an old woollen hat, hung them on the pegs behind the door, before heading down.

Edwina had been in the kitchen only a few minutes and was just filling the secondary wood basket in the parlour when there was a loud knock at the door. She jumped with a start and stood up, peering through the window instinctively before checking the kitchen one last time.

She opened the door and David, looking quite bedraggled, stood before her, cap in hand. 'Come in, David.'

'Thanks,' he said before stepping inside and wiping his feet. He walked through into the kitchen, looking around to take in his new home. 'Wow, it's big, have you lived here long?' he asked.

'Oh, yes, we were born here and so was my father. It was originally my grandfather's farm and we took it over in 1912. Would you like a brew?' she said.

'That would be great, thanks.'

'So how did it go with the vicar?' she asked as she placed the kettle on the stove..

'OK, I think, but all I have done all afternoon is move the church pews, clean underneath them and put them all back again. Seemed clean to me before we even started, but he did give me some cake and a beer afterwards, so it wasn't all bad. Do you know him well?' he asked.

They chatted freely for several minutes, until steam rose from the kettle. As Ed stood to reach for the pot, footsteps could be heard in the hallway. Edward then stepped into the room to join them, wearing his favourite floral dress, with his hair pinned back.

'Hello, David, I'm Ed. These are for you, your room is all ready, I will show you up if you like. Your bag is over by the dresser.'

David smiled, nodded and walked over to collect it before following Edward from the room. They didn't speak as they climbed the stairs to the top of the house, Edward, carrying a small candle, leading the way, while David struggled behind carrying his large bag. They finally reached the top floor, the door to his room wide open.

'I hope you will be comfortable, David. If there is anything you need, please ask.'

David stepped in just two paces before stopping abruptly, still holding his bag over one shoulder, looking around the room, as if nervous of going any further. He walked forward slowly and placed his bag on the bed before turning towards Edward.

'This is splendid,' he said. 'I have never had a room of my own before.'

Edward smiled and left him to it, telling him supper would be ready soon, closing the door behind him. He stopped after just a few steps, quietly, listening as he was sure he could hear David laughing to himself, laughing loudly.

Inside the room, David was lying on the bed grinning, realising his life had finally changed for the better. He would be happy here, he thought, and jumped up, leaving his unpacking until later and headed downstairs to join his new 'family'. He crept down the two flights of stairs back to the hallway, where he promptly opened the door into a darkened room. Realising he had lost his bearings, he reversed his route and upon hearing voices headed to another wider door and stepped into a kitchen full of life, cautiously leaning in like a man in the wrong house!

'Come in, come in, tea is in the pot, David,' Edward said as he stirred the saucepan with a long wooden spoon.

'Join me by the fire, David,' urged Ed, who was reading the newspaper.

'Thanks,' he said and poured a cup before sitting next to her, taking in his new surroundings. Within a few minutes, Edward announced supper was ready and they both rose and stepped to the table.

As they ate their first meal together, they tried to make David feel at home, talking of the history of the farm and the tragedy that had beset them when their parents had died. He didn't respond, but his face did show much anxiety, his sadness obvious. They talked through supper, discussing David's role, the daily routines and how it was important he learnt quickly, as Edward would be leaving to join the army in a weeks' time. When dinner was finished and the last of the gravy wiped clean from their plates with thickly sliced home-made bread, they moved to sit by the fire. As two fresh logs were placed in the flames, the fire crackled and sparked as they took hold. It was David's turn to speak and he offered his story freely, and with filled mugs of beer, the twins listened intently.

He explained he was a single child from a loveless marriage, his parents having run a small farm on a large estate near Cheltenham. It was owned by Sir Richard Franks who was a Member of Parliament, but was hardly ever present, spending most of his time in London. David said he had found him to be a kind gentleman and through the estate manager made a considerable effort to support his parents. But after years of neglect by his father of the land, the family were finally given notice to leave. Early one morning, his dad left without them, leaving them at their cottage with nowhere to go. His mother presented herself to the estate manager that morning, expecting to be sent packing. The manager took pity on them and found a position for his mum in the great house, offering them a smaller cottage just a short distance from the main house. He was thirteen when all this happened and after school each day he went to work as one of the estate boys under the guidance of old Bill, a chap who took him under his wing. He told them of his fall from a tree when he was ten, which hampered his efforts to work, but he had already learnt quite a lot from his dad before he left. After all their hardships, he thought life was good again, but after several years on the estate his mother died from pneumonia. David stopped talking for a minute, wiping his eyes with the back of his hand, before carrying on. There was clearly a period of pain in David's life.

He went on to explain how he hated school and was not well educated and could hardly read at all. That, he said, was down to him being bullied by the older boys right through school, because he had a limp, and he never concentrated after that. His story was not a happy one, but he did want them to know he was happy to be back where he thought he belonged, on a farm. As David chatted on, yawning more frequently, he rubbed his eyes with fatigue. Edward suggested he went to bed as they all had to be up by 5.30.

'We will do the dishes tonight,' said Ed, and David rose, thanking them before walking to the door, candle in hand.

'Night,' he said as he slipped through the doorway, 'and I am very grateful to you, thanks.' With that, he was gone. On reaching his room, he unpacked his belongings into the old chest of drawers and prepared himself for bed. He set aside a place for his small black and white photo of his mother in a brown wooden frame and held it for a few moments before standing it on the bedside table. He looked around the room before climbing into bed. 'I think I will be happy here mother,' he said talking to the ceiling.

Edward followed soon after and Ed sat for a while by the hearth, running through in her mind what remained to be done. She was very content in all she had achieved and had now even managed to perform her toilet with hardly any wetting, following Edward's suggestion of using her fingers to better effect. Things had indeed improved and she felt more comfortable in front of others, as she had demonstrated when they visited a small local town a few days earlier. The one difficulty that remained was that of her monthly periods, something she had yet to deal with. The hard-physical work on the land had developed a more masculine frame, not that of a woman anymore, but one many men would have been proud of! She now had strong, powerful shoulders and arms, with a big hearty appetite to boot. All this work, for reasons she didn't understand, had reduced her monthly bleed to just a few short days and sometimes not at all. That, however, still meant she had to find a way to hide it from her future comrades sufficiently well to avoid any scrutiny whatsoever. Otherwise all the good work would come to nothing and their lives could be in jeopardy!

She knew full well that in modern Edwardian society woman never talked about menstruation as it was a subject generally passed down from a mother to her daughter at time of need. Her own mother had been very thorough and kind too, during her first months as a young woman, even providing her with an insight into how society ladies would lock themselves away, staying in their beds for the duration. They would use a simply folded cloth or a sewn pad which was placed inside a lady's underwear against the skin or hanging from a belt, being changed at intervals through each day of their cycle. The cloths would then be washed out by their servants, before being reused at another time. It had been this method that her mum had so carefully and lovingly guided her through, when she was just fourteen years old. Ed knew full well that this would not suit her life as a soldier and so had for some weeks been planning to pay a visit to the main library in Gloucester to research how women through the ages had managed this problem, and was leaving the next day, not expecting David to be present.

The following morning, Edward took David out just before 6 a.m. When they had left, Edwina went into Edward's room to pick out a suitable dress from the wardrobe, along with a large blue bonnet to cover her short hair. She packed them into her woven straw bag, along with her black button-up boots, and after her morning chores she grabbed her bag and walked over to the paddock fence where she saw Ed and David. She waved before turning towards the gate and down the track to the village. When she reached the church, Bryan was in the vestry and she stepped in and shut the door, asking him if she could change, as she had to go into town. He was a little confused about what she was up too, but Ed simply said she would explain when she got back, as it was a very private affair. Once changed, she set off for the bus stop near the pub, catching the eight fifty-five bus for the relatively short journey into town. The clothes she wore used to fit well but were now a little uncomfortable, pinching her hips, and they were especially tight across the shoulders. On arriving in town, she walked through the centre towards the railway station, turned right and up George Street to the large Victorian building on the corner. It was probably the tallest building she had ever seen, of Cotswold stone with four floors and a large patriotic Union flag flying in the breeze from the rooftop. She stepped through the swing doors and noticed how dark it was inside, standing in a gloomy reception area. Sunlight filtered through the windows high above, casting beams of light across the floor below. It was an amazing spectacle and something she had never seen before. Shelves upon shelves, floor to ceiling, packed with thousands and thousands of books, surrounded her on all sides. She turned in a full circle, admiring the sight, before a rather stout lady with silver hair, spoke to her from behind a long desk, bringing her back to reality.

'How can I help you, miss?' she said.

Ed stepped over and said softly, 'I would like to read about women from history and how they lived their daily lives.' She said.

The woman stared for a moment, looking blankly at her, then frowned in deep thought. She started to turn but stopped, and glanced back at Edwina and asked, 'What period of history?'

'Greek and Roman I think,' she said.

The librarian started to walk from her desk, calling Ed to follow, her shoes cutting the silence across the stone floor. Ed hurried after her as they headed to the rear of the library, to a small reference section with large volumes covered in dust. The lady looked along the line, bending slightly sideways to observe the section she wanted.

'Ah, here we are, the Roman and Greek sections are on the bottom shelf. Please ensure you take proper care of the books and place them at the end of the table when you have finished. Do not try to place them back on the shelf.' On that, she turned away briskly, leaving Ed to her own devices, the noise of her heeled shoes the only sound that broke the heavy silence.

Ed placed her basket on the chair and bent down to view a long line of reference books. Scanning along slowly, she located a book on the *Roman Empire*, then two books along, she found one titled *Greece and its People*. She lifted the heavy volumes into her arms and stood up, then waddled over to a small table with a tiny light in the corner. Just as she started to lower the books onto the table, the top book slid sideways before dropping noisily onto the table top with a thump! Heads turned sharply, and an old lady dressed in all her finery, who was slightly hidden from view, tutted at her without lifting her eyes from her newspaper.

She sat down before moving the top book to one side, and lifting the heavy cover of the other, she found an index covering several pages. This was going to be a long job, she thought, as the clock chimed ten o'clock. She scanned slowly down the pages in turn until finally locating a small section reflecting the historical facts of Greek Civilisation: 'the living family' two thousand four hundred years ago. She poured over the text and slowly learnt about the primitive life they led, before finding a passage about children and puberty. She turned to the section and read with interest.

'It was widely believed by the Physicians of the day that a girl reaching fourteen or puberty would bleed each month from within. If girls didn't bleed, they were bled by a needle from their arms, by physician, as there was no understanding at this time of the womb lining being shed.'

They clearly didn't understand why this happened, she thought, and assumed they must have seen it as some sort of ailment and as such treated it like any other. The Bible too made mention of 'menstruous rags' which were worn below the crotch on a belt or cloth, as some women of the day didn't wear underwear at all! Edwina tried to imagine this rather primitive state of affairs, content her mother had taught her well. She then stretched her arms up and pulled back on her shoulders, realising she had been sitting for over an hour. As she did so, she peered up to the ceiling high above, the pattern of the roof dome holding her gaze for several moments. It was then, reading with renewed vigour, that she stumbled on a passage that just might be her answer! She read further and on the next page, above a sketch drawing of a young girl being held down on a bench, being bled from her arm, she read:

'Women in Ancient Greece wrapped soft lint, cloth or papyrus around a small stick and penetrated their vagina, acting as a sort of stopper. This would be changed and burnt each day thus avoiding any sign of bleeding and was well hidden.'

This had to be it, she thought, and mumbled under her breath before reading all the material she could find. This would be the way she would hide her monthly ordeal from prying eyes and the men she would share her life with. She read further paragraphs but found very little to challenge her thoughts. Placing the books at the end of the table as instructed, she collected her things and left.

When she got back to the bus station, she checked the timetable and noticed she had a little under an hour to wait, so she went to a small tea room on the opposite corner for some refreshments. On entering, she felt a little nervous as heads turned towards her. She saw many ladies present, talking amongst themselves, their attention only briefly faltering as they looked her up and down! She ventured to a table by the window just as a young girl about her own age, dressed in black with a white apron and a small lace hat, came over, offering her a menu.

'Can I have tea with a bun, please?' she said. The girl bobbed slightly and turned without speaking as Ed peered around the room, admiring how the other half lived, knowing she had not been to a tea room since well before her mother died. The slight rattle of a tea tray approaching brought her back from her memories, the waitress placing a blue patterned tea-set down in front of her. She recognised it as Real Old Willow pattern, her mother having several pieces at home in the sitting room cupboard. She had always loved the blue and it reminded her of China from pictures she had seen as a child. As the waitress turned, she left a folded piece of paper on the table and asked her to pay at the till and left. Ed lifted the lid of the teapot and stirred the lose tea gently as taught by her mother. "Never bruise the tea," she would say bringing a smile to Ed's face. She settled back to let the tea brew, before pouring herself a cup. She glanced at the two ladies chatting in the corner, their faces almost meeting across the table, whispering carefully so no-one else could hear. Secrets, Ed thought, these ladies knew nothing…

She caught the quarter to four bus home and her journey, although uneventful, did provide her with thinking time and before she knew it, the bus had rolled back into the quiet village street. She walked over to the church, entering the vestry by the side door, and finding it quite empty changed quickly and left a note for Bryan before setting off in her man's attire back to the farm. She arrived to find Edward and David already finished for the day, eating bread and cheese by the roaring fire. As she entered, Edward stood and poured her a large mug of tea, mouthing the words, 'All OK?' She reached for the tea nodding gently at him before they sat together for the first time that day. Edward had told David that Ed had to visit the local garrison for 'final orders', which although a lie, was very plausible. He seemed not to be suspicious and chatted freely about his attempts earlier that day to pull a deep thorn from a sheep's leg and how they had between them repaired the hole in the down pipe from the barn roof. She looked at Edward, puzzled, and he stared at her, quietly shaking his head slowly back and forwards behind his huge mug of tea. She would find out the true story later.

The next morning, Ed walked up through the lower paddock to the small wood almost at the extreme edge of their acreage, to the beech tree at the centre of the copse. She found the small twigs of new growth with smooth bark she was seeking, before cutting several and placing them in her jacket pocket, content that she had variety enough to try out the 'Greek method' for herself. Walking back down through the meadows, with fine views all around, she realised how much she would miss the farm and the land she had grown up on, with so many memories! It had been her life and all that she had known since she was very young, and part of her felt great sorrow… But she realised too that it was this land that had given her the hard upbringing that was the sole reason she was now capable of taking her brother's place on the battlefields of France!

On reaching the top stile, she sat for a few moments on the rail, looking at the land that surrounded her, wondering when she might return. She watched as the smoke from the kitchen chimney drifted directly upwards with hardly any movement, before disappearing in a light breeze. She smiled to herself and wondered what her father would think of her now, before jumping down and heading back with a positive heart.

A few minutes later, she stepped into the parlour, silence greeting her arrival, and calling out she found no-one at home. She headed straight up the stairs to her mother's old room to find the sewing box passed down from her grandmother. She looked around the room before locating it behind the old arm chair in the corner, where it had sat undisturbed for many years. She lifted the lid and sifted through until she found what she wanted, placing it back in its hiding place before shutting the door behind her. She headed to her own room, locking the door firmly and went over to sit on her bed. She began cutting the thin twigs into short lengths with her penknife and peeled the bark back to produce several clean and unblemished short, white sticks, with no protrusions of any kind, and placed them on the dresser. She cut several strips of the soft cotton sheet she'd found in the sewing basket and considered carefully how she would wrap the two together. Her first attempt was unsuccessful and so was her second. She pondered her problem further, before trying several more ideas, but nothing worked. This was going to be tricky, she thought, as it had to hold its position firmly and not slip or unfold in any way. It also had to be simple and not need elaborate cutting or fixing as she might find herself in a situation at some point where she only had moments to perform this most delicate practice!

After some time, an idea flashed into her mind and taking her scissors, she cut a rectangular shaped piece of material about six inches by eight, before making a small slit about one inch in from one corner. She then placed the stick on one side of an imaginary line from the opposite corner, rolling towards the slit and folding the spare material in as she did so, until she reached the slit itself. She then poked the end through, making it secure. This then provided a short tail at the opposite end, which by chance might help her extract it when required. She tugged at it a little to test it out and it seemed to hold well, before undoing her work and repeating the process several times more, until she was satisfied she would be able to do it in the dark. She scrutinised her idea carefully but found no fault at all, feeling suitably impressed by her ingenuity! The pad of cloth seemed ideal, and placing it on the dresser, she repeated the process, making five more in quick succession before placing them all in her top drawer. It wouldn't be long before she would be trialling this for real, as her period was due. The Greek women of two thousand years ago had come to her rescue.

Chapter 8

On the west side of Bristol, set back from the river front, a large brick warehouse majestically overlooked the steam boat traffic that had plied its trade for many decades. The old storage building was now in the hands of the War Office as it had been acquired for use as a training depot, due to the huge lack of facilities needed to train sufficient troops for the Western Front! Tens of thousands of new recruits were now being amassed in towns and cities all over Britain, and some from the Commonwealth too, for this hugely testing undertaking. Things were exacerbated when conscription had begun just eight weeks previously, as the general lack of military barracks right across Britain created worrying times for the War Propaganda Bureau. Bristol was now almost overrun by the army, as accommodation and training facilities had been filled to capacity. Detailed plans had been made to locate suitable premises and then to fit them out to make good operational training areas. These would be used as temporary barracks only, although many senior military officers were planning for the long haul! Every available vacant building was considered, and this large warehouse was ideal.

Many fit younger men from general service had already been deployed to France, trained by officers and non-commissioned officers (NCOs) often drawn from retirement, but who offered much experience from previous conflicts. Mostly volunteers, some with long-standing injuries, these old soldiers prepared the next generation of men going into battle.

Men like Captain Alistair Moffat, the officer commanding Bravo Company, 2nd/5th Battalion, Royal Gloucestershire Regiment, who had done his bit for King and country since the last century and now found himself training men for war all over again. His brief was simple. Six weeks basic training to get them to a standard, then shift them over to France for a further week before being deployed to the trenches. He always thought this to be unrealistic; however, his opinion was never sought, and he just did the best he could.

At least he had a good barracks to work from. It comprised five floors, with suitable accommodation, storage and work areas. It was dry, had a good roof, running water, but very little else. The outside area was about half the size of a football pitch. It had been covered in weeds from years of neglect, but they were now flattened by hundreds of boxes full of stores, food provisions and equipment, stacked well above head height, with several large vehicles parked at the far end of the compound. There would be no traditional parade square here, just an uneven piece of scrubland, mainly of mud, with a single track down one side near the building. It would simply have to do and once the new recruits had cleared the area and stored all the equipment, it would be adequate for the task. Captain Moffat was pleased with his lot and set about completing more of the vast amount of administration, until his meeting with the company sergeant major later that morning.

On the ground floor, five of the ten rooms were being allocated for storerooms. A makeshift kitchen would be opposite the food store at the end of the corridor, with the largest room allocated as the armoury. That left two small offices mid-way down the corridor, the small one for the Officer Commanding (OC), the larger one allocated as the company sergeant major's office and billet, a tiny cot being squeezed into the corner of the room. The first floor was completely open and would lend itself to be the cookhouse dining area and double up as the major training facility, where they could assemble all the men together. The top three floors were each big enough to hold up to forty men on double bunks as their sleeping quarters. This space would be shared with the training teams, comprising the sergeant and three corporals for each platoon, sectioned off with curtains and tall lockers. The ablution area near the entrance to each floor was barely large enough for this number but would just have to do. The river was only a stone's throw away and the mobile bath unit was due to visit fortnightly, so he felt sure most would be more comfortable here than their own homes, some having never slept on a proper bed!

It was a little before nine o'clock and the captain was sitting staring out of the window, sucking on his old wooden pipe, gently twisting in his old oak swing chair. He was a veteran from the Boer War where, as a private, he lost an ear during a skirmish and now had a large ugly scar on the side of his head. The surgeons of the time, unused to cosmetic surgery of any kind, had stitched him back together, but one might say it was not their best work! He was promoted through the ranks to staff sergeant when in 1908 he was offered a commission, but he knew he would go no further than captain. Immersed in his daydream, the knock at the door startled him. Swinging round, he saw the sergeant major, a stern-looking man well over six feet tall, standing to attention, his stick neatly tucked under his left arm, holding his salute.

'Morning, Sergeant Major, at ease please. Is everything ready for the weekend arrivals?' he said.

'Not quite sir, we are still awaiting some uniforms that are due later today, but the QM has advised the new Lee Enfield rifles won't arrive until next Friday, but I can work around that and feel confident this won't cause us a problem, sir. We are to be thirteen men down from the personnel list, so I have adjusted each platoon's strength and put thirty-six in 1 and 2 Platoons, and thirty-five in 3 Platoon. I don't know the reasons for these absentees yet and some may still arrive, but let's hope those that do, are of good stock.'

'That won't please the colonel!' he said, stuffing more tobacco into his pipe.

'No, sir, but we can only train what they send us, and with the drop-out rate pretty low, I would expect to get most of them through.'

'Well, let's do the best we can, Sergeant Major. What time do the trains start arriving tomorrow?' he asked.

'First trains arrive at thirteen hundred hours, sir, transport booked for that time with the quartermaster. It will allow us time to locate our chaps from the several trains due. The last report I have received, sir, says over two thousand men will be arriving at Bristol station tomorrow! Last train is due at sixteen hundred hours. All training corporals are all ready to get stuck in at the rail head.'

'Sounds like you have everything in hand, Sergeant Major. Let's meet again at nineteen thirty to cover any last issues. Meet me outside the Officers' Mess at Horfield. You can get to Horfield Barracks?' he asked.

'Yes, sir, of course,' he said, saluting. And then turned about, his left foot stamping the concrete floor with gusto before he stepped off down the corridor, leaving his officer to his pipe.

Chapter 9

The days leading up to Ed's departure were frantic. David had settled in remarkably quickly having grasped his role well in the eight days he had been with them. He was helping in more ways than Ed thought possible, in an effort to be 'part of the family'. There were many loose ends, however, and Edward became irritable in the last days, flying off at anyone who was in his sight, no matter what the issue. Ed had tried to calm him on several occasions, but realised he was clearly stressed about her imminent departure, influencing his ability to separate everyday matters. Managing the farm on his own was not going to be easy for him, and all those years of doing so little were now coming back to haunt him, and he knew it!

One afternoon he entered the parlour in a foul mood, holding his blooded finger and leaving a trail of drips as he walked towards the scullery sink. When he saw David eating a bun from the cake tin, he drew in a deep breath and spat a tirade of abuse at him. Ed stepped out from the parlour, having heard his insulting remarks, but before she could speak, David scooped up his mug, still chewing as he did so, wiped his crumbed mouth with his sleeve, tipped the tea down the sink and stormed out.

'Oh well done, Edward,' said Ed sarcastically. 'He has been out since six this morning, with only a short break at midday for some soup and hasn't stopped all day. You come in with a bloodied finger in another bad mood, and think you have the right to shout and scream at everyone. Well, you don't! We are on the verge of exchanging lives so you can avoid going to war and yet days before I leave you vent your anger on me and David with astonishing regularity. Well, Edward John Mitchell, it stops right now, or I swear I will make your life very difficult.' She started to walk out to follow David, but Edward grabbed her arm and burst into floods of tears. She stopped and pulled him towards her with affection and held him tight. He nuzzled his head into her shoulder, hearing his muffled apology. She knew he was anxious about being on his own, and the thought of losing her was affecting him, greatly, but it was his choice and he had to realise that. She eased herself from him to look into his red, tearful face.

'Edward, this is one of the last times we will have a chance to speak without interruption, so please listen to me.' She held his hand and focussed her gaze on his face as he wiped away the tears with his sleeve.

'David has done well since he arrived, and is trying so hard to make this work, for you, Edward, for you! What has developed since that dark night just ten weeks ago has been somewhat momentous. We are attempting to do something that is almost impossible to pull off but have focussed our minds on many things to the very best of our abilities. The consequences of it going wrong are almost unmentionable as the army won't take lightly to being fooled, and so our mutual strength is paramount for success. I am taking a great risk for you, dear brother, and although I relish the chance to complete in a man's world more than you will ever know, you must step up and dig deep, even deeper than when we lost Mum and Dad. You must stop this childish and irresponsible behaviour, and what's more, you must do it as a woman!' He squeezed her hand affectionately, looking at her with sad apologetic eyes. He knew full well he had done wrong. But Ed didn't let up.

'You have amazed me over the weeks, and Bryan too, with your ability to adapt, to overcome so many things and to learn so quickly. Things I honestly never thought you would grasp. We are on the verge of something quite remarkable, Edward, and it's now we start a new chapter in our lives, before we can be together again.'

He accepted this admonition without complaint. He closed his eyes, trying to calm himself, before looking down at his bloodied finger, which throbbed. Blood was still dripping onto the floor by his feet. He turned to reach for the tap and Ed stepped aside to give him room. With a gush and a splutter, the water ran from the brass tap, cooling his hand and turning bright crimson as it disappeared down the plug hole. Ed reached for a towel and Edward held it tight around his hand, to stop the flow. It was a bad cut and Ed groped in the cupboard for the box of bandages, telling Edward to sit at the table. She wrapped a short bandage around the wound as they sat together.

'I know this probably won't come out right, Ed, but you are a remarkable person and although I have not shown my love over the past years and have not contributed as I should have, I owe you more than I can ever say. I know I will feel lost without you here and understand that I can't have it both ways.

It's good that David has come on so well and I am sorry for my behaviour. That said, and I know you won't want me to say this, but I thank you from the bottom of my heart and beyond, for what you are doing for me, and I will pray for you to come home safely when the war ends. I love you, sis.'

Ed paused as she finished his bandage, looking lovingly into his wide eyes.

'It's not me you should be apologising to, it's David.

She looked at him as his eyes filled with tears once again. Nothing else was said as she returned the box to the cupboard in the scullery. Edward knew he could not let the problems of that day materialise again and stood to head out of the door.

'I'm off to the paddock, have something to put right,' he said, and left Edwina leaning on the door frame, watching him go. She saw the two boys chat and then Edward placed a hand on David's shoulder. It looked to her from a distance that he had put things right and hoped it was the last of his tantrums.

David and Edward worked closely together over the ensuing days, while Ed, as agreed, was content to do the house chores in the mornings before tending to the animals and then preparing all the meals, giving her time to finish her packing in readiness for her big adventure.

Two days before she was due to leave, Ed woke with a tenderness in her lower abdomen and knew her monthly period was upon her. She dressed quickly and went to the outside lav and pulled down her clothing to reveal a smear of blood in her underpants. She reached up above her head, to retrieve a small bag, neatly tucked under the cistern. She removed one of her Greek stick pads from a small bundle to begin her new routine, after years of using the method, taught by her mother. With the limited time she had, it was vital she made this work. She had realised she must moisten the pad with water to help it into place and submerged the cotton bundle into the bucket on the floor. Bending slightly forward and creating an opening with her fingers, she applied gentle pressure and the pad slowly slipped inside her. With a final push with her finger, the cotton strip or tail, was the only part visible. She was delighted, it seemed to work, thanks to the woman in Greece all those years ago! She stood up and dressed quickly, placing the small bag in her pocket to take to her room later.

As the day progressed, she visited the toilet twice, once to check all was well, the other to have a stand-up pee, which she had now become rather good at. She also took the opportunity to change her pad and found that the tail of cloth she had accidently designed allowed her to pull it out easily. This made her feel more confident and she quickly went through her new routine again. When she got back to the cottage, she threw the pad onto the fire before calling the boys in for dinner.

***

The evening of Ed's final night at home, Bryan ventured up to the farm for supper, a date that had been planned for several weeks. He had with him a small gift for his young friend of a small bottle of whisky, along with a small brown journal with a stitched spine, to record her story at the front. Inside the front cover he had written a quotation by someone called Ibsen: *'All life holds a certain risk, the more alive you are, the more the risk!'*

The evening was a rather subdued affair, with practically every conversation about the war. Bryan presented his gifts to Ed, who was unashamedly emotional at his generosity and wanted to hug him, but instead shook his hand firmly, her eyes smiling warmly. Edward, in a pale green dress, with his hair in ribbons at the back, had made a cake, with another, carefully wrapped in brown paper, to go with her. They chatted happily for some time, even finding humour before the light had finally gone and Bryan stood to leave. They parted like a father and son saying a warm goodbye. Bryan tried to hide his emotions, but the tears that welled up were hard to disguise. Ed walked to the gate with him to say a private farewell to a man she owed so much to. He walked slowly away, only looking back once.

As she came back, the room was quiet, and it was David who spoke first to break the awkward silence. He smiled at Ed and saying goodnight left them both sitting by the hearth. They heard him slowly plod up the wooden stairs, then a few seconds later, high above them, the distant sound of his door slamming shut.

'Think I have a cold coming,' said Edward rubbing his nose several times. Then suddenly, he leant forward and reached across grabbing her hand. 'I'm going to miss you Ed, more than you will ever know,' and for the next hour they chatted freely, and talked of their parents and what lay ahead. Suddenly and without warning, he was up on his feet, heading for the door… 'Night,' he said, and was gone.

She wanting to shout after him but stopped herself, as there was time for final words in the morning. She reached down to the basket and placed two large logs on the fire, before standing to blow out the remaining candles. She wondered what her father would think of her now?

At the top of the stairs, she paused outside Edward's room, it was in darkness, and she tiptoed along to her room, quickly getting into bed. She hoped the night would pass quickly, but for much of it she found herself lying awake, creating animal shapes on the walls of her room in the faint light cast by the moon. Her mind was alive with every detail imaginable, and she realised how far they had come in just a few short weeks. Trusting herself to achieve the goal she had set was her driving force, as competing with men at their own game had become the most important thing to her. But she knew it was not only her own life that was at risk, but that of her brother too. If she was to pass judgement by her peers, nothing could be left to chance. Indeed, the immense strength and cunning required to even entertain such a challenge were, in themselves, far beyond the imagination of most people. Her head was too full to sleep, and the night passed slowly.

After several hours, she threw back her covers and reached for a match to light the candle by her bed, before silently opening her side drawer. She reached inside to remove the two most important letters she had ever written. After reading them through for the third time that day, she sat back, feeling content, hoping they would never be needed, before placing them on her bedside table. She knew that the greatest challenge of her short life was about to begin.

By the time dawn provided enough light to see the large picture on the far wall, she had had quite enough, and sat up. She clambered out of bed and pulled back her curtains to see the land she had worked on since childhood stretching out before her. The fields always looked so inviting at this time of day and she had never ceased to enjoy this moment. As the sun slowly crept upwards, casting shadows from the trees across the land, she stepped away from the window and threw her nightshirt to the floor for the last time before pouring water into her floral wash bowl. She knew the razor could actually stay in its holster today, as her smooth face didn't have a single whisker, but decided to soap-up anyway as she could always use the practice. With the blade sitting gently against her firm cheek, she pulled downwards, the soap clinging to the razor, which she then cleaned in the water. After several minutes and no cuts, she wiped her face clean, then brushed her hair before dressing in her brother's old brown suit. Although a fraction tight across her shoulders, it fitted pretty well, certainly well enough to pass inspection. As she adjusted her tie in the mirror, she gazed at the person who returned her stare, pausing just for a moment. She knew she was ready, to face the challenges that lay ahead.

She gathered her suitcase and jacket, before taking one last look at her room, then closed the latch on the door and slipped downstairs, into the warm kitchen. The boys were clearly already up, as she saw the table was laid with a white cloth and their best crockery. A small jug sat in the centre of the table, a few slightly drooping spring flowers adding some colour to the dark room. She placed the old leather-trimmed suitcase by the door and hung her jacket and hat on the chair. She then noticed a simple homemade card at her place, which Edward had written of his undeniable love for his hero sister. She was greatly moved, a tear springing into the corners of her eye. She tucked the note inside her jacket pocket and sat down, lifting the lid of the teapot in front of her and stirring its contents slowly, in deep thought. The door then swung open, the two boys bursting in, laughing loudly. They looked over to see Ed sitting at the table and smiled.

'Nice table, Edward,' she said. 'And thanks for my card, I will treasure it. Now, what's for breakfast, I could eat a horse.'

Edward smiled at her and went straight over to the stove and placed half a dozen thick sausages into the frying pan, before turning back to face her.

'David helped too, Ed, we just wanted to give you a decent send-off, you know, one for you to remember. It's a big day after all.'

Edwina nodded silently, realising Edward had finally accepted his life, and that over the weeks he had grown into someone who cared again, following years of self-pity. She watched him carefully as he chatted confidently, turning the sausages in the pan, the aroma completely filling the air, as fat spat in all directions. Conversation was full-on, and no-one would have known this was indeed a day of both great sadness and joy, as Ed headed off to war. When the large meat plate arrived on the table, Edward placed it next to a plate of eggs, fresh from the hen coop that very morning, cooked to perfection. With fresh bread and copious amounts of tea, they were set for her final meal.

'Last chance to run for it,' David said jokingly, which finally eased the tension of this momentous day. They chatted through breakfast with gay abandonment and before long only smears of egg yolks remained on three empty plates.

'I am absolutely stuffed,' said Edwina, 'thanks for that.' She looked at the clock on the far wall. David looked up too and realised the time had almost come for her to leave. Standing up to vacate the kitchen for their final farewell, he stepped around to Ed's side of the table and pushed his hand out to grip hers warmly. She stood and held it firmly, and then with a few parting words, David left to resume his work outside, leaving the siblings to say their farewells. As the door closed, her brother walked round and sat beside her.

'Don't worry about me, Edward, I will be OK, and you must stay strong and keep the farm running how father would have expected. Always remember what he used to say, "You only reap what you sow", and that has been our motto for life. You have a good man in David, and he seems to know what he is doing. If ever things get too hard, go and talk to Bryan, he will know what to do. I won't be away forever and could be back by Christmas and will write to you as often as I can.'

Edward nodded, but said nothing, and then pulled Ed towards him with his eyes rapidly filling. They squeezed each other tightly for a long time, before Ed released her grip and slapped Edward on the back. 'You'll get me started in a minute,' she said and went to get her jacket.

Nothing more was said as she donned her flat cap, picked up her case and stepped through the cottage door towards the gate. Edward walked over to the door, tears rolling down his cheeks as she walked away to her new life in the army. They had never been apart before.

He had known this day would come, but somehow part of him still felt it was just a game. He willed her to look back, but the last he saw of her was the top of her hat as she disappeared down the hill.

Edwina knew she had plenty of time to catch the bus that would take her to the railway station for her train to Bristol. As she walked down the lane, she peered around, wondering when she would see this wonderful countryside again. She could see from her vantage point that the bus stop was crowded with people, all seemingly in good humour. She recognised many of the young chaps of her own age as they chatted to family members, and she smiled before walking across the road to the church. About to knock on the old oak door, she was surprised when it opened, and Bryan's smiling face greeted her.

'Hello, Ed, all set then, are you?' he said with a forced smile.

'Yes, just about, just wanted to say cheerio and to give you these,' she said, offering two envelopes to him. 'I have written these and want you to promise you will store them for me and only open them if I am ever injured. There are certain things I want done.' she said firmly.

Bryan took the letters and saw his name on one and Edward's on the other. 'Why yes, dear child, of course. I will store them safely and let's hope they never have to be opened.' He offered his hand, which she took readily, and he held hers for several moments. 'Godspeed, Edwina, godspeed.'

She nodded and smiled before wandering back across the road to join the throng. Within minutes, the bus laboured up the rise, stopping with a squeal of brakes. Mums were tearful, girlfriends too, while fathers shook the hands of their brave sons before hugging their wives. Slowly the men climbed aboard, the driver watching the young faces one by one as they stepped up. Ed walked to the back and peered across to the church where Bryan still stood in the doorway. He waved briefly, a gesture she matched, before he turned and closed the door. Ed felt alone, her heart sinking a little with emotion, then the bus pulled away.

Everyone in the crowd waved vigorously, then some mothers sobbed into their handkerchiefs, comforted by loyal husbands fighting to restrain their own emotions. Ed sat quietly thinking, her hands clasped, looking across the fields as the bus gained speed before disappearing over the hill and away.

As they trundled down the valley they passed through several small villages, stopping to pick up two young men who climbed aboard in great humour. In the streets, people waved with smiling faces, which Ed thought a little odd, as they were after all, heading off to war. She soaked up the moment, waving back to people she didn't know, receiving smiles in return. All seemed well, although Ed noticed one chap in the far corner, sitting by himself, his head leaning on the glass window, looking profoundly miserable.

When they pulled up outside Cirencester station hundreds of people were gathered, and Ed, with her new comrades, had to almost fight to get through to the platform. She overheard one chap ranting at an officer in uniform, clearly panicking, as he had forgotten his travel voucher. This didn't seem to stress the man in uniform, who simply furnished him with another and sent him on his way. Ed joined a long line ready to catch the eleven fifty-five train to Bristol and was almost knocked over by an exuberant couple of men who were clearly the worse for wear following their early visit to the pub. A sergeant came over and told them to settle down before heading off to resolve a scuffle across the car park. Suddenly, Ed felt a hand on her shoulder and turned to see a tall chap with black hair, greased back, grinning at her.

'Well, fancy seeing you here,' said the stranger. Ed struggled to place him but allowed a smile to creep across her face as he reached to shake her hand.

'Surely you haven't forgotten me already, we only met a month back.'

Ed suddenly remembered the conversation with Edward about a chap who saved him from the bullies when he went for his army medical, and then smiled broadly as the memory hit home.

'Frank, how great to see you,' she said, with her heart racing. 'I didn't recognise you, that's all, how are you?'

'Oh, I'm very well, thanks, looking forward to getting on with it now, aren't you?'

'Yeh, it seems ages since the medicals. What regiment is it you're joining?'

'The same as you Ed, the 2nd/5th Battalion, Royal Gloucesters.'

Ed realised her mistake. 'Oh, yes, sorry, Frank, my mind is all over the place, what with leaving home and all and saying my goodbyes. Maybe we will be together, in the same platoon.' She said enthusiastically. The two boys then meandered over towards the gate, picking their way through hundreds of family members accompanying their men, to say their own special farewells. It took a full ten minutes to reach the platform, and they walked to the far end, near a small kiosk selling tea. As they finally reached the counter, Frank ordered a mug of tea and a bun each, handing over ninepence. It seemed an almost carnival atmosphere, with laughter from many, some even singing songs, while others stood quietly with their families, emotions clearly high. One chap was standing in the corner with his arms wrapped tightly around his young lady, who, with her bright ginger hair and white dress, stood out in the crowd. She was crying, her shoulders shaking as she buried her head deep into the shoulder of the man she loved. Ed felt a moment of sadness and thanked God she had no-one in her life to complicate her own departure. With a hot tea in one hand and munching on the sweet bun held in the other, they settled back against a wall, away from the mass of people waiting for the train. It was an occasion they would remember for life, as everything seemed to be happening in slow motion: the noise, the faces, the smiles, the sadness, all rolled into massed hysteria on this extraordinary day.

After twenty minutes, they noticed the railway guards coming onto the platform and assumed the train was imminent. The men, smartly dressed in full black attire, quickly ushered people back from the platform edge, and suddenly a loud whistle blew up the line as their steam locomotive announced its presence. It crawled into the station, the large pin wheel spinning wildly just a few feet in front of them. As steam rose from beneath the train, it finally came to a halt way down at the far end of the platform. The whistle pierced the air again, and silence fell over the masses at precisely the same time. The moment had finally come. Many people took their final embrace, with tearful eyes, as the doors were wrenched opened by well-trained porters. Slowly, the hundreds of men began climbing aboard, into the dark, stale carriages. Ed and Frank watched with humility as they placed the mugs back on the counter.

'Well, this is it,' said Frank with a grin, and grabbing their bags, they stepped up through the narrow door into their future. Heads were already poking out from the windows, happy faces, men waving at anyone who was looking in their direction. Ed followed Frank into the very last carriage, just adjacent to the kiosk. Finding a relatively empty compartment, they threw their bags onto the brass luggage racks above their heads before standing by the window to soak up the atmosphere, just like everyone else.

It was difficult to see along the whole length of the train, as the platform curved in a gentle arc, but there must have been fifteen carriages in all, now full to the brim! The sergeant they had seen earlier was trying to get everyone aboard and shouted several times to lacklustre men still holding their sweethearts or wives, grabbing a last kiss. They watched mothers cry unashamedly, with some older men blowing their noses rather hastily to hide their tears. Eventually the mayhem ceased, and the last door was slammed shut, leaving only civilians standing before them. A whistle blew from somewhere nearby, then a few seconds later a sudden jolt shook the whole train beneath their feet. As the wheels found traction, the carriages banged together several times as the couplings took the strain, slowly moving forward. Bodies crushed at the windows as hundreds of men, dressed in their Sunday best, waved enthusiastically, watching their world slip away. The last thing Ed recognised was the young lady in the white dress, her head in her hands, her shoulders hunched. It would be a memory he would savour.

Suddenly, the platform ended as they followed a row of small terraced houses with washing hanging on lines in small back yards, young children looking up, aiming sticks at the train, as if shooting at them. As they slowly gained speed, green fields appeared, and they finally sat down, the exuberance of moments ago now gone. As they left the outskirts of the town, the train's whistle blew several times, almost a sign of farewell as the next batch of young men headed for the battle fields of northern France!

Heading away from town, the gentle rhythm of the steam engine set its tone. Conversation amongst the men died away a little, each man deep in his own thoughts. Ed reached up to her case to retrieve the fruit cake gifted to her by her brother and placed it on the small table by the window. She cut it carefully into small pieces with her penknife and handed them round to the seven lads surrounding her, buying instant popularity for a few important minutes. As they ate, the reality of finally leaving families behind sank in.

Within minutes, several chaps had closed their eyes and were drifting off to sleep, including Frank, who was now leaning his head softly on her shoulder. Their adventure had begun.

Chapter 10

Bristol railway station had never been so busy. As far as the eye could see, military transport vehicles were backed up along the road leading into town. The drivers were clearly bored, aimlessly talking amongst themselves and smoking. Some reclined with their feet up on the dashboards, in a last-ditch attempt to get a few winks of sleep to recharge their tired bodies. Hundreds of men would soon be alighting from the trains that were to arrive this afternoon, and all had to reach their respective barracks by nightfall. The OC, Major Nick Evans, was well into his fifties, and one of many hundreds of retired officers brought back into service to perform the more mundane duties needed in the war effort. He had been tasked with coordinating the troop movement to and from railway stations, in and around Bristol. It was a challenging task as thousands of civilians were expected over the months ahead. He knew full well that trusting the railway timetable was only a hopeful proposition at best, as his temporary office next to the station concourse had already been extremely busy. It would no doubt remain so for the next few days. To his advantage, he did have over a dozen senior NCOs and around thirty corporals running around for him, in a desperate attempt to keep to the schedule. Indeed, from his standpoint, he could see long queues of young men dressed in their best and probably only suits, lining up in-front of the long line of reception tables outside the station. Overseen by his NCOs, they stood patiently with their battered leather suitcases in their clammy hands holding their lifelong possessions, peering anxiously past the man in front to see what was happening.

The first train had arrived at eight thirty that morning and since then almost a thousand new recruits had been processed and moved on. The major felt satisfied the NCOs were properly processing each man in turn before sending them down the line for their onward journeys. But then he heard the phone ring on his desk, just across the way, and stepped back into his squalid office to receive the call. He learnt that several trains were now delayed by up to an hour due to signalling problems and numerous vehicle breakdowns had been reported, which would not help him in his task. As he dropped the handpiece back into its cradle, a knock came at the door. He turned to see a sergeant in full salute, reporting that two trains had just arrived within minutes of each other, on adjacent platforms, creating a huge backlog of many hundreds of men, now milling with no-where to go. Sitting down and reaching for a cigarette, Evans frowned and told the very capable sergeant to sort this one out for himself.

As Ed's train approached Bristol station, all the men in the small compartment peered nervously through the steamed-up windows, eyes wide and mouths open. The first they saw of any military presence was the queue of green army trucks that lined the street across the way, the drivers in khaki uniforms standing idle next to their cabs, gazing up at the new arrivals. As the train slowed, the platform came into view, porters standing at intervals along its length, like black posts in a carpark. Ed watched her companions and smiled to herself; they were arriving as civilians but would depart as army recruits.

As the train finally came to a stop, a sudden jolt rattled and reverberated right through the carriages, forcing two of the chaps to fall into their seats, laughing. With steam rising slowly from beneath the window, screening the platform for a few moments, her new chums grabbed their belongings from the storage racks, ready to join the throng. They all turned towards the narrow door and one by one squeezed into the already busy corridor, crammed full of exuberant bodies heading for the exit. Seeking respite from their confinement and in good humour, they slowly shuffled forward in unison, barging from side to side, bags bruising unprotected shins as they went. Finally, they found their way to the door, where they slowly spilled out onto the crowded platform, into the light of the day. Despite their best efforts to remove themselves from the chaos, Ed and Frank were forced forward by the sheer weight of bodies behind them. Suddenly a shout broke through the cacophony as several blokes tumbled headlong from the carriage onto the concrete below. Although shaken, they brushed themselves down, laughing off the experience before joining the mass once again. With spirits high, Frank grinned at Ed before peering over the hundreds of heads in front of them. Commands from enthusiastic corporals rained down upon them from every direction, in an attempt to gain their attention.

'This way, men, move this way,' said an NCO near them. 'Move to the exit,' said another in the hope of achieving some sort of order. Alas, the sheer mass of bodies stifled any forward motion as more people alighted from the train, creating one giant crowd, going nowhere. As carriages emptied, the station porters began slamming the doors shut in quick succession. Within minutes everything had been secured and a rather rotund station conductor waved his green flag and blew a long blast on his whistle to indicate the train was clear to move, then quickly climbed aboard. With a thunderous rumble, steam in the air, the driver began to reverse the train back out of the station. The noise from the engine slowly increased as it backed up, throwing deep black smoke into the air, until the great locomotive was alongside them, the sooty-faced driver looking down with white eyes, grinning as he went. With steam and smoke all around, the engine noise faded, and relative silence returned, the noxious smell dissipating into the morning air. The peace finally allowed the men in uniform to try and harness the mass of bodies once again, with many voices shouting orders to a thousand ears. As the pigeons, recently disturbed by the train's arrival, flew back to their roosts high above, white droppings splattered down on unsuspecting shoulders and caps, for some, a sign of good omens for the future. In high spirits, the new recruits started to edge forward, shepherded by disgruntled NCOs who probably wished they were somewhere else! It proved to be a highly ineffective method of moving this number of men and the sergeants looking on were not amused.

Suddenly, a high-pitched whistle blasted out repeatedly, cutting through the air and forcing the crowd of five hundred to stop and turn with puzzled curiosity. They saw nothing at first, and then a khaki army cap, under which was a stern soldier's face with a huge black bushy moustache, appeared above the crowd in the centre of the platform. Standing now a good two feet above everyone else, waving a long black stick above his head, he continued blowing his whistle. He looked left and right for several seconds, waiting to get everyone's attention. At last he could see a thousand eyes looking at him and, pulling the whistle from his lips, he wiped his moustache first to the left and then to the right with the side of his index finger. He spoke with a clear, powerful voice.

'Listennnn to me!' he bellowed, pointing his long stick down the platform. 'In a few moments, I am going to ask you to head down the platform to the exit and out onto the large car park to your right. You will do this quickly and quietly, and when outside you are to join one of the many queues and give your name to the corporals seated at the desks. They will then tell you which vehicle you are to go to. These trucks are parked outside in numerical order, from one to twenty-eight, right down the street. When you find your truck, stand by it until you are told what to do next.' He paused before shouting, 'Now go!' he bellowed.

The hundreds of men, slowly started to move as instructed towards the end of the platform, with just a few still skylarking, who then received some stern words from the nearest NCO. The corporals now took the lead, urging them all forward. At the back of the group, Ed and Frank chatted quietly with some of the fellows they had shared a compartment with, shuffling forward as the long queue slowly moved in the right direction. Uniformed voices continued to pipe up now and again to focus their attention, and slowly but surely, people disappeared outside to join the lines, leaving the porters alone in a deserted station to scurry around and ready themselves for the next arrivals.

As they turned the corner, the concourse was totally full. Ed and Frank searched for the shortest queue but struggled to make headway through the mass of bodies. Frank, being well over six feet tall, could see over the heads of most people, and shouted for Ed to follow him, as he pushed his way forward. The chaos steadily grew, but they found a line and slowly but surely, crept forward. Those still chattering behind them, were pulled up by frustrated corporals, encouraged by the sergeants standing behind them, slapping their sticks onto the sides of their legs, in a deliberate attempt to intimidate their new prey. It seemed to do the trick, as order was at last gained and one by one bodies dispersed to join the line of trucks. Finally, they reached the desk. They were in turn asked for their names by a corporal who didn't even look up, and both assigned to vehicle number 17. They picked up their bags, Frank holding his suitcase above his head and moved off swiftly down the line. Ed tucked in behind him, before the space he made closed in again. Large collections of men were gathered to the rear of each vehicle, suitcases resting where they stood. Conversations held by tightly grouped men, helped cause further delays, as people tried to clamber through the mass of luggage and bodies, to trucks further down the line.

Some were boarded quickly by enterprising corporals, the vehicles when full, diving into the afternoon traffic and speeding away, the men in the back jeering and calling out to those still standing at the station. As Ed and Frank jostled through the mass of bodies towards their goal, the army's best continued to try to establish order. As they finally approached vehicle numbers 16, they noticed the next number was 23! They looked left and then right, trying to see if they had missed their truck, but a gathering of men seemed to indicate their transport was not there! One young-looking chap with ginger hair and freckles scuttled off down the street, returning a few minutes later shaking his head, saying their vehicle wasn't around. Most of the one hundred or so men in their group now sat down on their upturned suitcases, sharing cigarettes with their new-found friends, awaiting instruction. After a few minutes, the same sergeant from the platform came into view, pushing his way through the crowd. Upon reaching their group, he leant on the shoulder of the young ginger chap and got up onto a low brick wall. He looked around at them all in turn, waiting for his audience to quieten down, to hear what he had to say. Much to his annoyance, however, two lads at the back were still deep in conversation. The soldier placed one hand on his hip and stared at them with his powerful eyes.

'Good story, lads?' he said sarcastically. Two heads turned quickly towards him, the men stubbing out their cigarettes with grimacing faces.

'Now I have your attention, I am Sergeant Worrall from B Company, 2nd/5th Battalion Royal Gloucester Regiment. Welcome to Bristol, where the beer is plentiful, but the virgins are not!' Laughter broke out amongst the men, but now he knew he had their full attention. 'Now listen, men, transport has let us down and we have no way of knowing whether it's still on its way or has been allocated elsewhere, so we are going to tab to the barracks.' Heads turned quickly, faces frowning, as he continued, 'Tabbing means to march and as it's only two miles or so, it won't take more than forty-five minutes.' He pointed his stick to his left as he spoke, to indicate the direction, before continuing. 'You will, however, have to carry your baggage, so I hope mummy hasn't packed too many heavy things for you.'

A muffled snigger broke through the ranks, one man bursting out loudly with a horse-like laugh that made everyone grin. The sergeant looked down smiling.

'OK, Noddy, it wasn't that funny,' he said as laughter broke out once again. 'Now in a moment I am going to say the words, fall-in. On that command, I want you to line up in three ranks or lines, facing me, one behind the other, stretching from right to left.' He pointed to a tall chap and spoke to him. 'Lofty, come here, lad.' When he stepped forward, the sergeant instructed him to stand still. 'Now gentlemen, form up on this man here and do it quickly and without talking. Now let's give it a try.' There was a short pause before he bellowed 'Fall-in!'

With a sudden eagerness, the men stubbed out their fags and gathered up their belongings, jostling into position. Shuffling to and fro, their heads looking left and right, as they tried to impress the sergeant and do it right first time. Some joined the wrong end of the line, but with gentle encouragement of a size nine boot, the men finally stood in three ranks, facing the hardy sergeant.

'Good, the first bit of military drill in your horrible lives and you have done it well. I am now going to give you the command right turn, and in case anyone doesn't know which direction that is, it's that way,' he said, pointing his black stick to the west. He then paused for a few seconds, and in a crisp order yelled 'Right turn!' He was surprised to find everyone present did indeed turn right, without exception. The sergeant then shouted, 'Quick march' and they all stepped off, leaving the station car park as a single body of men. One corporal ran off ahead, rifle slung over his shoulder, and disappeared, while another shouted rather strange words from the rear:

'Eft, Ight, Eft, Ight, Eft, Ight, Eft…' This went on for a good few minutes before Ed realised what he was actually saying, but it seemed to keep them marching in time.

The process of marching was of course not a complicated one, as an individual, but as a group, many found it difficult to keep in step with the man in front. As the station slipped away, people around her began chatting quietly to one another, watching the new landscape open up all around them. After twenty minutes, they turned left towards a wide bridge over the river. The incline gave some a little trouble, as cumbersome suitcases banged into the legs of those walking too close behind, skinning many shinbones in the process. Despite the corporals' best efforts to maintain a steady rhythm, the inexperienced recruits still found it difficult to stay together. Indeed, several of the men had now dropped back and suddenly, a voice shouted 'Halt' at the top of his voice. As they closed back up, the sergeant piped up once more.

'OK, men, let's try that again,' said Sergeant Worrall. 'But first, line yourselves up one pace behind the man in front and stand still.'

The well-drilled corporals quickly did their work and pushed people back into line. The group set off again, marching over the crest of the bridge as several trucks passed them by, the men inside cheering from the rear in a friendly manner, one man even dropping his trousers to reveal his naked arse. He received a loud cheer for his efforts, as the trucks sped away into the distance, and the sergeant couldn't help smiling to himself beside his men. After reaching the far riverbank, they passed-by a public house called the Boatman before heading west on the south side of the river. Ed was enjoying the march and all the way chatted quietly to Frank, who was regaling her with stories from his past.

It turned out Frank only lived thirty miles from Ed, on a large country estate near Oxford owned by Lord Hardcastle. There, he had been the trainee groundsman and later assistant gillie and was used to long, hard days on the land. He had become an excellent shot and eventually was responsible for culling His Lordship's deer stocks, a position he took very seriously. He mentioned to Ed that he never knew his father, as he had been born out of wedlock, only knowing he had been a weekend house guest on the estate and his mother, then a chambermaid, fell foul of his advances and Frank was the end the result! The matter was never mentioned again, but Lord Hardcastle had always been supportive of him and his mother throughout their lives, and he found much freedom as a child on the two-thousand-acre estate. His Lordship never had children of his own and so gave Frank a great deal of his time, growing close throughout his formative years. When he was older, Frank decided he wanted to leave school early, to work on the estate; however, Lord Hardcastle had other ideas and enrolled him into St Peter's School in Oxford, a private day school. Although his mother had initially protested, she eventually accepted, and he began his new education the following term.

Frank told Ed his life changed that day. But when the war came, Lord Hardcastle tried to push him towards an officer's commission. Frank was determined to leave the Royal Military Academy, Sandhurst to those who were born to it and convinced His Lordship he preferred to be an enlisted man instead.

Enraptured by Frank's amazing life story, Ed hardly noticed the two miles they had marched. And despite telling herself not to get close to anyone, she felt a bond forming with her new friend and hoped they would be billeted together throughout their training.

They finally turned off the road, down a single dirt track, towards a tall, red brick building, their home for the next six weeks. They strode through a large gateway. One dilapidated wooden gate was lying flat on the ground, almost completely covered in weeds, the other was hanging awkwardly at an angle, still attached by a single hinge at the top. As they approached the building, they could see a giant of a man standing in the doorway, watching their arrival, his cane tucked neatly under his arm. Sergeant Worrall shouted out that they were to halt and for every man to listen to his orders. He waited another five or six steps before shouting 'Company, halt.'

As Ed stopped dead in her tracks, a suitcase hit her legs from behind, almost knocking her over. Two chaps just ahead were now scrambling to their feet, having fallen in the dirt, as everyone stood quietly in their new surroundings, panting. The sergeant shouted; 'Stand still!' He then called for them to turn to face the building, the corporals springing into action, pulling them into line once again.

'Stand to attention and be still,' Sergeant Worrall said in a loud, crisp voice. When all was quiet, he marched over and halted in front of the tall man by the door, who stepped forward to meet him. From where Ed was standing, she couldn't make out the muffled conversation that took place for several minutes, but saw the tall man writing in his pocket book. The sergeant then turned to his right and marched off a few paces, before halting and turning around to face them.

'OK, men, I am going to give you the order to stand at ease. Watch me carefully.'

He then moved his left foot sideways bending his knee up slightly and stamping his foot into the ground. He did this several times, before standing back to attention.

'When I give the order, you will move your left foot eighteen inches sideways as I have just demonstrated, then drop your suitcases on the ground beside you.' He paused, looking quickly over the squad before him.

'Stand at ease,' he shouted, and to his utter surprise every man did just that. The tall soldier, with his cane still tucked under his left armpit, stepped forward a few paces, casting his gaze over his new men.

'I am your company sergeant major,' he said sharply. 'You will always address me as sir, and it is my job to ensure you receive your six weeks' regimental training to ready you for war! This is a serious undertaking, men, and it won't be easy. You will have to work harder than you have ever worked before and for long periods, you will be wet, cold and miserable and perhaps a little homesick too. But, you will follow orders at all times and I will personally beat anyone of you who does not do as he is told. This is not a game, it's for real and your lives will depend upon learning how to soldier and survive. It won't be long before you hear the great guns of the German artillery for the first time.' He paused and looked down at the men before him.

'The British Army is your home get used to it and quickly. I am your mother now.' He said before walking along the line of the front rank, looking at every face in turn, before returning to the same position.

'Now, the three sergeants and nine corporals will conduct most of the training, which will test you far more than you have ever been tested before. You will leave here well-trained and ready to meet your enemy, who have already killed tens of thousands of your countrymen, some from your own communities. If you have any gripes, keep them to yourselves, if you have a complaint, keep it to yourself, as I don't wish to hear them. If you do your job, men, we will all get along famously. Do not let yourselves down at a time when your country needs you most.'

Ed felt a cold chill run down her spine, shuddering briefly.

'Finally, well done for marching across town and welcome to B Company, 2nd/5th Royal Gloucestershire Regiment, or as we are better known, The Glorious Glosters.' He turned to look at Sergeant Worrall who marched across to him.

'Carry on, Sergeant,' he said formally and disappeared inside. The sergeant marched across and stood himself at ease. 'OK, you have been split into three platoons,' he said, 'each having a sergeant and three corporals who will be your first point of contact for the foreseeable future and will teach you all the soldering skills you will need. Work hard, men, and enjoy the training.' He then nodded at the corporal to his left and turned, marching off towards the building.

'Senior NCOs on me,' he shouted, leaving the nine corporals to organise what came next. The two other sergeants ran over and disappeared with Worrall into the barracks.

The small wiry corporal, whose trousers seemed far too big for him looked like a boy in a man's clothing. He nodded and spoke in a quiet voice, without looking up from his folder. 'When your name is called, shout "Yes corporal", pick up your belongings and head upstairs to the billet.' He waved with his hand at several corporals standing behind them, who then ran into the building and clattered up the stone steps, their boots being heard all the way to the top.

'OK, the third floor is 1 Platoon, fourth floor 2 Platoon, the top floor 3 Platoon. When your name is called, go to the designated floor, find a bunk and sit down until you are told what to do next.' The corporal then began to read out the long list of names, starting with the letter 'A' and running through to the letter 'K'. Within just a few minutes, thirty-six men had grabbed their kit, and headed into the building to make their way upstairs.

Ed and Frank looked at each other pensively as they waited for their own names to be read out, still hopeful they would be together. The names of 2 Platoon rang aloud, starting with the letter 'L' and Ed knew her name was coming up soon. After a few minutes the corporal read out 'Mitchell, Edward' without looking up. Ed responded as instructed and picked up her case and ran for the door. Just before she entered, she peered back to see Frank grinning at her, before she charged up the four flights of stairs, panting increasingly as she went, until her landing appeared. She was met by a corporal who ushered her through into the main billet area, where a row of double bunk beds on either side stretched out before her. There were two green boxes at the end of each pair of bunks, with three long tables up the middle of the room and chairs scattered around them. She did as instructed and found a bunk, opting for one at the far end next to a window with far reaching views to the river and countryside beyond. She threw her case onto the top bunk and sat down on the lower one, hoping Frank would be joining her soon…

Downstairs, the long list of names continued: 'Pollard, William; Pratchet, Simon', each departing one by one into their new world. 'Rodgers, Peter; Smith, Alan', until he read the last one: 'And finally, Smith, Frank,' said the corporal, turning to speak to another NCO as he folded his page over to the next list.

Frank sighed with relief and set off up the stairs to join his new best friend, running two steps at a time, until he finally ran out of puff. On reaching his goal, panting heavily, he stepped through the door on the fourth floor, the last into the fold. He looked for Ed but could only see men gathered around the centre tables, sharing smokes and chatting to one another. He cursed under his breath, then suddenly at the far end he saw Ed seated on a bunk, grinning at him. As he approached her, she stood to retrieve her case from the upper bunk, placing it on the floor with a thump.

'About time! I had to fight to save this for you,' she said.

Frank beamed with delight at her, dropping his bag by the bed and punching her playfully on the arm, before throwing himself up onto the straw mattress. Laughing, Ed grabbed her striped pillow and hit him over the head with it, before a voice that they would come to recognise shouted into the billet.

'OK, men, settle down,' said the corporal from the doorway. Ed looked round and dropped her pillow on her bed as the NCO walked forward casually, rolling a thin cigarette expertly in his fingers. As he watched them, he waited for silence, before sliding his tongue along the paper and finished the process in one hand, tucking the fag behind his left ear.

'I am Corporal Baker. You should address me as corporal and do not think about shortening it or using any other term. The sergeant will be up to speak with you shortly, so until then stay put – do not move from this room.'

He paused for a brief second, before turning and stepping back past the curtains by the door. As soon as he was out of earshot, the men began milling around, exchanging handshakes in that oh so typically English way. It was true to say, a certain excitement was evident amongst the group, and the light-hearted atmosphere and chatter soon reached fever pitch.

The billet wasn't exactly homely, but it looked comfortable enough and was obviously designed to be practical. The beds were placed in between the many sash windows down each side, not unlike a typical hospital layout. Some of the windows had cracked panes of glass and one pane was missing altogether, where a makeshift repair had been attempted, with a simple piece of wood nailed into the soft timber frame. At the entrance to their floor, the ablutions area had five tin sinks, three cubicle toilets and a long tin urinal to the right. On the opposite side of the entrance was an area sectioned off with tall wooden lockers and heavy curtains from floor to ceiling, marked 'Training Staff Only'. Heaven help anyone who stuck their nose through the gap uninvited, Ed thought to herself!

Frank stood looking out of the high windows and Ed walked over to stand beside him. It was an impressive sight from such a high level, with views over the river, the steam boats loaded to the gunnels, plying their trade. To the far right they could see the outskirts of Bristol and to the left, the hills to the west. They chatted with others in small groups, unpacking their personal belongings into the large green boxes. Everyone seemed to be getting along, although they noticed one chap sitting on his bunk on his own near the entrance, looking down at his feet. Ed realised it was the same bloke who had been on the bus to Cirencester and nudged Frank to look. They decided to go over to say hello, but the sergeant's arrival interrupted their intensions.

'Stand up,' said a voice, as Sergeant Worrall strutted into the billet. He was followed closely by three corporals and everyone stood up as ordered, facing the uniformed men, before being told to sit.

'OK, men, I am your platoon sergeant and these chaps are your training corporals.' The three men came into line and stood at ease, looking sternly at them. 'They are Corporals Bateman, Baker and Bullen.' Each in turn stood to attention, slamming their boots into the wooden floor, before standing back at ease. 'These men are your section commanders for the six weeks' training, and they will travel with you to France on completion.'

Ed thought it an odd view, as the man on the left was a giant of a chap with huge shoulders and what appeared to be swollen ears, a boxing champion perhaps. The man in the middle, whom they had met earlier, was considerably shorter and appeared diminutive compared to the other two men. The man on the right was a handsome chap, well over six feet with a movie star chin. They faced front, not flinching, as the raw recruits looked at them.

'You will grow to loathe and admire these men, but rest assured, they are here to train you, not to be your friends. When the shit hits the fan in the trenches of France, you will be happy to have them by your side, so soak up everything you can, it could well save your life!' The mood suddenly changed, some of the men looked around rather nervously.

'Your billet will be inspected every day, so get used to being clean and tidy in everything you do. There is no excuse for slovenly behaviour or dirty accommodation or equipment. You will be expected to take a brush or mop to keep things spick and span every day you are here. Meals will be eaten in the dining room on the first floor, timings will be promulgated on the company noticeboard on the ground floor, along with daily routine orders or DROs. Tonight, your meal will be at nineteen hundred hours. For the uninitiated, that means seven o'clock.'

The briefing continued for a full thirty minutes, covering a great deal of information including where the company offices were, where not to trespass and when they would be getting their uniforms and equipment. They were told to fall in each day outside on the parade and that the next day would be a very long day, starting at zero six thirty. On that final point, the sergeant stood and gathered his corporals for a brief moment, before telling them to report to him at nineteen thirty hours, before finally leaving the billet.

They were then split into sections, twelve men in each. Ed and Frank were pleased to once again be together in 4 Section, under Corporal Bateman. The remaining chaps were split evenly into 5 and 6 Sections and each NCO took his men off into a corner to brief their new charges about life in the army. Corporal Bateman stood for a moment and surveyed his new charges, before placing his hands on his hips. His height was impressive, with very short, brown wiry hair and a clipped, dark moustache. He began by calmly telling his men to sit on the floor and they gathered round in a small huddle. He began by telling them about himself, in that he came from Devon, and had been in the army for three years. He was a jovial man, who captured their attention quickly, telling jokes and stories and seemed very knowledgeable. He told of his great love of rugby and that he had played for the regiment on four occasions, which was why his ears were swollen and he was so handsome.

Ed felt impressed, however had no idea what rugby actually was… He then impressed upon them all that they had to be honest and deliberate during training, as what they learnt would ultimately save their lives. Everyone focussed on his words, realising this was not, going to be a walk in the park.

Upon completion, they were given fifteen minutes of free time to sort themselves out before falling in again on the parade ground, in their respective platoons. This order was not altogether clear, but as eyes peered around the billet, there was an assumption that someone was bound to shout at them, to sort it all out.

A quarter of an hour later they formed up as instructed, but two chaps were late for their first parade and were told to get on the floor and perform an exercise called press-ups. This went on for a while until they could do no more and collapsed on the floor, grimacing. It became clear to everyone that being late for parade was a risk simply not worth taking. Each new section was then tasked with a variety of jobs, from unloading bundles of clothing to sorting equipment and bedding, which in turn was carried through and placed on the tall wooden shelves in the storeroom on the ground floor. The time passed quickly and before they had opened half of the bundles, it was dark and fine rain had started to fall. They covered the bundles with large tarpaulins and were then dismissed.

At nineteen hundred hours, they joined the back of a long line that stretched down the stairwell from their billets, finally reaching a packed dining room. They collected a platter and some eating irons from the wooden table at the entrance, as they shuffled past. Two cooks, with grubby white shirts, one even smoking, served them a decent portion, before they found some empty seats at the far end. The NCOs were all sitting together on a separate table near the entrance; the sergeants at one end, chatting amongst themselves, the corporals at the other. With mouths full of food, inquisitive eyes stared at people down the rows, men pointing with their knives with curious faces. Within thirty minutes, the meal was finished, and platters were washed under the cold tap above a high steel sink before being stacked neatly on the side. The process was going smoothly until one pile toppled over, falling to the floor with an almighty crash!

'Pick them up,' yelled a voice from the high table, as several men quickly scurried about, grinning to each other like naughty school children. Following a short smoke break, they resumed their tasks, Ed taking advantage of the absence of most of her platoon to nip off to the toilet. It was quite empty, apart from one closed cubicle door nearest the wall. The tin urinal panel fixed to the wall opposite the door reminded her of a large pig trough and she went to stand at one end, turning slightly into the corner. She went through her routine, firstly unbuttoning her flies, then delving inside to spread her underpants with her well-practised fingers. She was just easing herself to relax when she heard footsteps behind her. A chap suddenly burst in and was soon standing just a foot or so to her right, fumbling anxiously at his fly! As he reached down to release his manhood, he sighed loudly.

'Ah, that's better,' he said, as a gush of urine jetted against the tin wall with unexpected force. Ed didn't flinch. She tried instead to relax into her own routine and shut out this extraordinary experience. For anyone watching the scene, it was just two soldiers taking a piss, so nothing unusual, but for Ed, it was a very big moment and she fought against her impulse to turn and run. She stood her ground nervously, staring down at her feet, when the chap started a conversation. She was a little surprised and grunted politely, several times, but found the whole affair rather unnerving. After a few moments, she felt her urine flow and it hit the wall just a few inches in front of her. She breathed out in relief. Then her attention was drawn to the chap as he moved his hips backwards and forwards, shaking himself, before tucking his penis back into his trousers. As he spun round, still doing up his flies, she smiled to herself, just as a small trickle spread into her underpants! Damn, she thought, before doing up her buttons and heading back downstairs to re-join the others.

They worked through to nine thirty that night, when a final brew was provided in the dining hall, before wrapping up for the night. They finally collected their bedding issue, along with some soap, two razors, a long brown towel and a pot of talcum powder, and then they wearily climbed the four flights of stairs to their billet. By the time they had made up their beds, it was lights out, and within minutes the sound of men snoring drifted through the darkened room. After another quick visit to the toilet, Ed placed her belongings inside her green box, leaving both her socks and long-sleeved undershirt on, to sleep in, before clambering into bed. She lay there for a moment, smiling to herself, thinking of Edward back on the farm. She turned on her side to find sleep, knowing her adventure had truly begun, smiling as she heard Frank snoring loudly on the bunk above. Sleep came quickly, for it had been a big day.

Chapter 11

The first week after Ed's departure, passed quickly. Edward was finally coming to terms with her absence, as he and David began to organise their lives without her. He had cried several times since she had gone to war, hoping the noise of his sniffles hadn't reached the floor above! He could do nothing about it now and realised he was missing her more than he ever thought. He vowed to write to her that evening after supper and hoped she was having a decent time of things as she settled into what could only be a very testing time.

Bryan had visited them twice that first week, and they had sat up late the night before, discussing when the war might end. He was very sensitive to the situation and seemed to sense Edward's tension, but couldn't discuss it with him while David was present. Around nine o'clock Bryan stood to leave, his last mouthful of beer still in his mouth, before swallowing hard and placing his empty mug down on the table. As David took the crockery into the scullery, Bryan leant across to reach Edward's ear, and whispered a reminder for him to be sure he kept his guard up. Edward was a little taken aback, feeling he didn't need to be constantly reminded.

The next morning, David was down well before Ed, the kitchen fire already roaring and morning tea in the pot. He was busy preparing eggs for breakfast in the large iron frying pan and smiled at Edward as he came into the room. With nothing to do, he sat at the table, pleased that for once he didn't have to cook, instead watching his new companion serve up eggs on toast. David was making progress each day, gaining Edward's respect and trust, knowing full well how difficult it would be to fill Edwina's shoes. As they ate in silence, David suddenly spoke.

'Ed, I know life has been hard for you, adjusting to Edward going to war, but I am tiring of your constant sniping at me when I am actually working as hard as I can. If you don't think me being here is working, I can always leave you to it.' Ed stopped eating, food still in his mouth, startled at his words! He swallowed to answer, but David continued, 'I say this with some sadness, as even with your constant pressure, I have never felt more content in my life, and ask that you cease bombarding me or simply ask me to go as I can't put up with this much longer!'

Edward put down his fork before wiping the corner of his mouth with his finger. He reached over for the teapot.

'Tea, David?' he asked.

David reached for his mug. 'Uh, yes, thanks,' he said rather startled, before a steaming mug of tea was passed across the table.

'David, I admit to being more than a bit grumpy with everything over the past week and I am sorry if I have picked on you. It's been a huge change for me not having Ed around, and well, I miss him very much.' He paused for a moment, sipping his tea, to select the right words. 'I am glad you feel settled here and I want that to continue, so apologise for being so rude.' David looked across the table at Edward, nodding before wiping his plate with a huge chunk of bread and chewing contentedly. 'Perhaps we should take this opportunity to discuss our workloads, too, to balance things up more equally. I do so want you to be happy here. Shall we run through this tonight after supper?'

'OK, yes, let's do that, thanks,' said David as he rose to his feet, before heading for the door. He turned as he got there. 'I will see you for a morning brew around ten, and thanks, Ed,' he said, before disappearing outside.

Edward didn't ponder over his kitchen jobs that morning as he headed back upstairs to strip both his and David's beds, leaving some clean linen for when he got back. As he was leaving with his arms full of bed sheets, he noticed a diary on David's bedside table with a pencil poking out at one end. He pondered for a moment and looked at the bedroom door nervously before dropping the sheets back on David's bed. His curiosity had got the better of him, and he reached for his diary, even though he knew he shouldn't look. He opened the page to read just a few lines. But quickly shook his head and closed the book, placing it back down on the bedside table. As he collected the sheets from the bed, he saw David looking at him from the doorway!

He froze! His heart started racing twenty to the dozen at this rather awkward situation, before saying nervously, 'Sorry, David, just getting your linen, it's bed change day, hope that's OK?'

David said nothing, just walked past him. 'I had forgotten my hat.' He said coldly and went over to the chair to retrieve it. As he turned back, Edward was still frozen to the spot. The awkwardness was painful, as Edward was sure he must have been seen reading the dairy. He turned quickly and left him in his room.

David didn't come in for his morning break that day, his mug of tea slowly growing cold on the kitchen table. Ed sat waiting anxiously as he watched the clock reach ten fifteen. He knew his actions earlier had caused anxiety and probably a feeling of mistrust between them, so poured a fresh mug, wrapping the cheese butty he had made for David and heading outside. He could see him up in the lower field, fixing a fence, and so slipped his feet into his mucky boots by the door, grabbed his coat off the hook and set off down the path.

As he approached from the valley, David stopped what he was doing and leant on the post, looking at him. Before Ed had chance to say anything, David blurted out, 'Did you find anything interesting?'

Ed stopped dead in his tracks just a few paces away and was about to answer when David stood up straight and spoke again. 'I mean, I don't have much, Ed, but thought my privacy was at least my own. Have I made you feel you must now spy on me, have I not been honest with you, what is it?'

Edward struggled to find the right words, feeling extremely uncomfortable at the situation he now found himself in. His emotions welled up unexpectedly, and within an instant he had burst into floods of tears, the mug of tea partly spilling onto the ground! Before David realised what was happening, Edward placed the mug and bap on the ground, then sobbed into his handkerchief. He who had been offended was now consoling the offender, David thought, as he placed both his hands on Edward's shoulders. He watched his friend get swallowed up in his own guilt. The balance had now changed in Edward's favour, quite by accident, and he looked up at David solemnly.

'I am so sorry, David,' he said between sobs. 'I have offended you, the one person who is helping my family, and I was wrong to take advantage. I was curious what you thought of me, that was all. It won't happen again, I promise. I've brought you some tea and a sandwich,' he said forlornly, picking them up off the grass as a sort of peace offering. David thanked him, as Ed turned to walk away. David, rather shocked at this, stepped quickly forward, spilling more of the tea as he manoeuvred around in front of him. 'Look, I have nothing to hide from you, Ed. I have grown to like you a great deal and just ask that you treat me with respect and honesty, as I will you.' Edward stopped and looked at him, grimacing, and then he nodded gently. 'If you spill any more of the tea, there won't be any left to drink,' he said with a wry smile. And after a brief pause, they both started to laugh!

With the difficulty over, Ed wiped his eyes on his sleeve as David walked back to place his tea on the fence post and then began to devour his butty. With their difficulty over and their friendship back on track, they chatted freely, the incident now forgotten. As David finished his tea, Ed smiled and took the mug from him, before leaving him standing alone. He walked back down the hill towards the cottage, tempted to look back over his shoulder, not knowing that David followed him with his eyes all the way down the hill. Every time he caught a glimpse of Edward through the day, he would stop working and wave enthusiastically, Edward waving back each time. He wasn't sure what was happening, but knew he had feelings for this person, feelings he had never had for anyone before, and knew he wanted to get to know his new friend much better.

At five thirty, David hung his coat on the hook by the back door before rinsing his hands under the cold tap, hunger pains now upon him. He looked round into the kitchen as he dried his hands to see Edward stirring a pot on the stove, music from the gramophone playing a distant melody. He moved his head from side to side to the rhythm before hearing David behind him.

'Oh, hello, David, I didn't hear you come in. Supper won't be a minute,' he said warmly. He knew he had a good man here and opened up more to him that evening, determined to be his new best friend. They sat up late into the night, putting things right, reorganising the farm routines and discussing the war. It was well past ten thirty when fatigue struck them both and they headed up the dark stairway to bed. As David climbed up the final flight onto the top floor of the house, his candle slowly dimming, Edward watched him and thought of happy times ahead.

The next day arrived with heavy rain and an angry sky that created a strange atmosphere, making the animals nervous. By midday it was torrential rain and all outside work ceased for the day. With a positive mood, both Edward and David turned to jobs in the barn, many having been neglected since before Edwina had left for the front. As they toiled to restack a pile of timber, David asked Edward why the tin bath and a bucket of water were lying at the back of the barn. Edward, realising Edwina had forgotten to put them away after her repeated practising, shook his head and changed the subject, just as a rather bedraggled-looking figure appeared in the doorway. They both looked at each other, wondering who it was, before Bryan took off his old canvas hat and bashed it against his thigh.

'Boy, is that raining. I got half way up the hill and the skies just opened. I think you should build an ark with all that timber,' he said, smiling. 'I was rather bored at the church and so have come to help you on what is probably the wettest day of the year,' he said, and flipped off his large, heavy oilskin coat and laid it down on the trap. He gave them four hours' work that day, in all manner of tasks, before Edward slipped away to prepare a meal for them all. While he was gone, Bryan took the opportunity to talk to David.

'So, young man, how has your first week been?' David stopped what he was doing and took a moment before answering. 'Well, we have had our moments, but feel we are now on the same wavelength and becoming friends,' he said. 'In fact, more than friends as I am rather fond of Ed!'

Bryan was suddenly alarmed. He studied David's face, noticing a deep sincerity as he grinned at him, as any man would if he was attracted to someone of the opposite sex. These were dangerous waters, he thought, and struggled for a moment over what to say. 'Let's go in,' he said, and grabbed his coat before dashing across the yard to the parlour as the rain continued to lash down.

Throughout preparations for supper, it was noticeable the two young friends were happy together. There was hardly a glimpse of the old Edward anymore as he had truly transformed himself and had a positivity Bryan had never seen before! His efforts to befriend David were clear and he had become a very passable woman. Bryan, although sitting by the fire, watched them closely as food appeared on the table and he realised then that he had best keep a careful eye on this relationship and was prepared to talk to Edward if needs be. Supper was eaten with great happiness, and a prayer was said for Ed.

As the clock struck eight, Bryan readied himself to leave. It was still raining heavily, and so donned his heavy coat, buttoning it all the way up, for the short journey back to the church. He looked up into the gloom of the night as the rain hit his face, thinking about the comments David had said to him and the signs he had seen between these two chaps. As he shook David's hand, he noticed he smiled coyly, which disturbed him further. He left, pulling his large hat down over his face, as he headed into the darkness. Just as he turned, he saw then standing together and shouted back.

'When are you next in the village, Ed?' he asked.

'Probably Wednesday morning, Bryan. What's up?'

'Oh, nothing, I just wanted to talk to you about your parents. Could you drop in about ten?' Edward nodded, and Bryan shouted a final good night.

As Edward shut the door, David yawned. 'Well, it's been a long day, Ed, I'm going up, I think.' Edward went to place some logs on the fire, knowing he had some book keeping to complete. David said goodnight and disappeared into the hallway. 'Night,' said Edward, and plonked himself into his chair in the dimly lit kitchen. At just after eleven, he placed the books back into the dresser and snuffed out the remaining candles before heading for the door. Within minutes, he was tucked up in the warmth of his bed, the rain still hammering against the window, his curtains moving slightly at the corners as the wind whistled through the gaps in the window frame. Above the noise of the rain, he thought he could hear someone moaning, and sat up to listen. It went quiet and then he heard it again! He threw back the bed covers, grabbed his mother's old gown from the end of the bed and relit the candle. Stepping towards the door, he opened the latch gently and went out, listening in the now silent corridor; 'David, is that you?' he called. There was nothing but the sound of the wind on the roof above his head. He waited for a few moments and shivered, before calling again. 'David!' There was nothing, but as he turned to go back to bed, a voice from the darkness yelled out once again. Startled, he peered along the landing towards the narrow stairway that led up to the top floor. He went back into his room to fetch his slippers before walking along the creaking floor and climbing the narrow stairs at the end. He tapped on David's door, but all was quiet. He started to turn, when it came again. 'No, no, no, aargh!'

He pushed the door open and ventured into the darkened room, the candle providing just enough light to show David sprawled across his bed, muttering to himself. As he went over towards him, he lowered the candle to throw light on his face, and saw sweat beads on his brow, his face contorted by the anguish of his nightmare. He placed the candle on the bedside table, reaching for David's shoulder. He gripped it gently, shaking him several times, calling his name, until he woke with wide eyes in a sudden start. He lifted his head from the pillow, peering upwards to the face above him, screwing up his eyes against the light of the candle.

'What happened, is that you, Ed?' he said, trying to wake.

'Yes, it's me, David, you're having a nightmare, you keep shouting out, are you OK?'

David wiped his face on the sleeve of his nightshirt before exhaling and sitting up fully, now focussed on Edward's face. He was finally back in the land of the living, as calmness returned.

'God, that was awful' he said. 'I was falling away and couldn't stop myself, falling from the roof of the barn, but the roof went on forever. I never seemed to reach the end. God, I'm glad that's over.'

Edward saw him sigh as he rubbed his eyes, and they chatted for a few moments before he lay back onto his pillow, yawning. In an automatic response, Edward yawned too, feeling very tired. He stood and said goodnight, reaching for the candle. As he did so, David stretched out a hand and held Edward's wrist, gently. They looked at each other awkwardly in the semi-darkness, David thanked him for coming up. Their stare connected for a few moments longer than necessary before Ed turned away, heading for the open door. David looked on as the glow faded from his room and his door finally closed. Edward didn't look back, stepping down the narrow stairs, the candle providing just enough light to see by. David lay still, his eyes open, thinking… Sleep didn't come too easily after that, and he could understand why.

Chapter 12

Edwina thought she was dreaming as she could clearly hear a man yelling at the top of his voice and what sounded like a distant drum. She couldn't work out where the noise was coming from. It grew louder and louder until she dragged herself from her deep sleep and opened her eyes to see Corporal Baker, a small cigarette butt sticking out from his mouth, walking up and down the line of bunks, getting immense pleasure from bashing two large mess tins together, with a sadistic smile! Suddenly, people leapt from their beds, as if poked by a cattle prod! Was it five o'clock already, Ed thought looking outside to the dark skies, the moon still visible through the window? She wiped her eyes just as a pair of feet dropped into view, which she flicked with her hand, then Frank jumped down from the bunk above and leant into her space.

'Come on, sleepy head,' he said, grabbing her bodily through the heavy grey military blankets, shaking his new friend playfully.

'Get off, you big mug,' and Frank laughed as he headed towards the light at the end of the billet with his towel and his wash kit. Ed didn't want to be last up so clambered out and slipped on her suit trousers, flinging her bracers over her shoulders before tying her boots. Some of the lads hadn't moved and were still in the land of nod. As she reached the toilets, the enthusiastic corporal was heading back for a second run! Without speaking, he simply grabbed the sides of the mattress of anyone caught still napping, tipping each one unceremoniously onto the hard-wooden floor, with a joyful grin! There were yells behind her and as she joined the short queue, waiting her turn to wash, she enjoyed the spectacle of men being pushed from their beds, some in spectacular fashion. The corporal, having done his duty, disappeared back behind the NCOs' curtain, where laughter could be heard.

The morning routine that day was a little chaotic, to say the least, as the space provided just wasn't big enough for this number of people all at once! Ed and Frank reached for a bucket and then took their turn to use the hand water pump, while others barged in to use the 'pig trough', as Ed called it, to relieve themselves. Men scratched their genitals and picked their noses, quietly waiting for their chance to splash freezing water over their tired bodies that ached for more sleep. Cubicle doors slammed and noises not for the faint-hearted percolated around the tiny room, the smell forever present! Ed suddenly saw a gap and dived to the end as Frank darted for the corner spot of the urinal, his bucket bashing a bloke's leg next to him. Conversations picked up between the newest recruits in the British Army as they went about their morning ritual. She soaped her face to take a shave, knowing it wasn't necessary at all, but the pretence and her well-practised routine were fluent, and she finished in minutes, just as she felt a rumbling call for the loo. She quickly collected her belongings before turning, just as a man stepped out from the end cubicle.

'I wouldn't go in there yet, mate,' he said, but being a farmer's daughter, she was used to smells far worse than anything these men could produce! She left her bucket outside and ducked in below the arm of a taller chap who was caught napping and shut the door quickly, sitting down to relieve herself, paper in hand. There was no time for contemplation and as soon as she was finished, she stood up and had just pulled up her underpants when the door opened, and a head appeared.

'Hurry up, mate,' said a yawning red-head and she quickly buttoned her fly and headed out. She vowed to plan her mornings a little better in future as she went back to her bunk. Those late risers who were still putting their beds back together were now late, and several ran down to the small ablution room, waiting their turn. And so, it went on until finally all that was left was a large pool of water on the floor, slivers of soap around the place, buckets stacked in the corner and a smell that would rot the heavens. As they waited for breakfast, the sergeant suddenly arrived and peered into the ablution room shaking his head! He looked up and called the two men closest to him.

'You two, come here,' he said sternly. 'Mops in the cupboard, now clean this bloody mess up!' he yelled with a red face, before walking on down the room. 'The rest of you, get yourselves moving downstairs and get a brew as we have lots to do today.' And he stood at a window, looking out over Bristol.

'Hope we get more than tea,' Frank said as they walked down the stairs. 'I'm starving.'

The dining area was already filling up with the other platoons, who all seemed a little lost too. They reached for a mug and a metal platter and joined the growing queue, before having a spoonful of grey porridge dolloped on one end of the tray and some brown-looking scrambled eggs on the other, by a fat, balding cook with a spoon in each hand. He was dressed in khaki trousers and a greying undershirt, with a red neckerchief tied below his fat chin. His huge red nose jutted out over the small dog-end hanging from the corner of his mouth, the ash dropping unceremoniously into anything that loitered beneath it!

'Just one bread roll, lads,' said the other cook, as the chaps filled their mugs with hot tea before finding a table. Breakfast, although only just warm, was devoured quickly through muffled conversations around the room, the excitement from the previous day still reverberating amongst them all. As they finished their meal in rapid style, one by one they stacked their trays at the end of the bench and streamed out of the dining hall, disappearing back to their respective billets to grab a few minutes of free time before the busy day commenced. As Frank and Ed got back onto their floor, they noticed some of the chaps writing letters, others headed out for a crafty ciggie, but they sat together, chatting, before a corporal shouted for them to fall in outside. Bodies dived for the stairwell, and the noise of studded boots was almost deafening, as dozens of feet ran two steps at a time down into the open air.

Within minutes, they were fell in on the muddy parade. As purposeful corporals rushed around yelling and pushing people into line, order was finally achieved from the previous chaos. Each platoon now stood as a group, with 1 Platoon to the left, 2 in the centre and 3 to the right. The NCOs all stood to the rear, apart from one sergeant who stood off to one side.

The sergeant major stepped out into the chilly morning air, and everyone stood absolutely still awaiting his orders. They must have looked a bedraggled sight to the uninitiated, as they stood forlorn in their civilian clothes, eyes yet to be fully awake. One of the sergeants shouted for silence and instructed them in the basics of drill, firstly standing properly at ease and then to attention, before repeating the process several times. He marched over to the waiting company sergeant major and reported that the company were present and fallen in, in three ranks. The stern-looking man slowly turned his head, observing his company.

'Now stand perfectly still, eyes to your front, do not look at me,' he barked as a man to his front peered across. The parade fell totally silent, just as an officer stepped out from the building and marched over towards him. The sergeant major turned and marched to meet him, stopping a few feet away, stamping his right foot heavily onto the ground. His right arm then swung upwards smartly to the side of his head. The officer, now standing right in front of him, followed his salute a few seconds later, before both shot their arms back down to their sides.

'Sir, the company is formed up in three ranks in platoon order, ready for your inspection,' The officer thanked him before he turned left and marched away a few paces, where he turned about to face his men. The officer addressed the company for the first time. A man with a history, the men could tell, when they saw a large scar prominent on the side of his head, where his left ear used to be.

'Good morning, men' he said quietly. 'I am Captain Moffat, your company commander, and it is my responsibility to ensure you complete your basic training over the next six weeks, before you head off to France. You have been split into three platoons and will work with your respective NCOs to a strict programme. They will instruct you in basic soldiering skills and provide all the necessary skills you will need to take on the Hun. They will also take the place of your mother, your father and your sweetheart, so if you need anything, ask them. If you have a problem, ask them. But you should understand, they will not be your friends. So, do what is asked of you at all times, and do it to the best of your ability.'

He cast his eyes across the recruits, some looking far too young to be here, others simply looking petrified. There was a general uneasiness amongst the men as heads turned and a mumbled response began to spread through the ranks.

Sergeant Major Woodin stepped quickly forward and yelled loudly, 'What do you think you are doing? Stand still and shut up, the officer is speaking!'

'Thank you, Sergeant Major,' and the officer began again. 'You will be instructed in drill, shooting, rifle management and living in the field. You will be taught to cook basic food and look after yourselves, to dig trenches in battle conditions and survive all that the Germans can throw at you. It won't be easy, men, but tens of thousands have already gone through this training, so we are pretty good at it by now. The CSM will give you orders for the rest of the day and we will have you in uniform by the end of tomorrow, all being well. So, until then you will have to work in your civilian clothes.' He took one last look at his new recruits, before turning to the CSM. 'Carry on, Sergeant Major.'

They both saluted again before he walked off towards his office. Once he was inside the building, the CSM moved over to a standpoint a few yards in front of his company, tapping his stick against the side of his left leg, his face growing red. He then unleashed a tirade of anger.

'If you ever, talk when an officer is speaking again, I will make your lives so uncomfortable you will wish the very ground you stand on would swallow you up whole. Do I make myself clear?'

In one explosive response, the men yelled out 'Yes, sir' and stood facing straight ahead, not daring to move. The CSM nodded without saying another word and stepped away. 'Carry on, sergeants' he said, before disappearing inside the barracks.

With the moment gone, Sergeant Worrall marched to the front, taking a folded piece of paper from his tunic pocket. He split them into their sections and sent them to various areas in the barracks, according to the list in his hand. The tasks were broad and varied, and they hardly stopped all morning, except for a short tea break at nine thirty, then worked on until noon. Frank and Ed got to know their new comrades, and banter began to form part of their daily lives, as they systematically unpacked and distributed boxes of equipment and clothing into the storerooms. Others took the ammunition to the temporary magazine located outside, tinned food to the kitchens and by dusk, the parade area had been largely cleared. The tired recruits finally staggered into the cold building for their final hot meal of the day and some well-earned rest. After spooning down a hot stew with potatoes that tasted burnt, all mopped up with fresh bread, they took the opportunity to visit a small shop that a corporal from 1 Platoon had set up on the ground floor. Ed didn't smoke but did buy a single bar of Rowntree's chocolate and a comb. She finally retired to her bunk to have a square or two of her chocolate and to start writing her very first entry into the fine journal Bryan had so kindly given her. But first, she must write a letter to Edward.

It was not all over yet, as at 7 p.m. Sergeant Worrall told everyone to assemble in the dining hall for a briefing. Some of the chaps had already started to get undressed and quickly re-dressed themselves before charging down the stairwell. Once everyone was seated, the sergeant major arrived and perched himself on one of the tables.

'You have done well today, men,' he said, 'but we have a great deal more to do tomorrow, as all the main equipment will arrive, and you will be issued with your uniforms.' Smiles instantly broke out around the room. 'So, it's another zero five hundred hours start. He then highlighted how important it was to maintain high standards of personal hygiene and didn't want a repeat of that morning's debacle in the ablution areas.

'Section corporals will teach you how to be quick, efficient and clean at all times! Don't let it happen again,' he said firmly. His brief was pretty thorough and spoke of working together in teams, medical advice, doctors' visits and many aspects of the training that lay ahead. He finally told them that if the good work continued, everyone would be permitted to visit the town on Saturday, with each platoon having a three-hour leave pass, staggered throughout the day. As an afterthought, he mentioned it was pay day on Friday afternoon, and a spontaneous cheer went up. He held his hand up with a smile, silently asking for quiet. 'Your platoon sergeants will notify you where to find your platoon notice boards so get in the habit of reading them daily and do not get caught out, as your name will appear for sentry duties and working parties.' He looked back down to his notebook and suddenly stood up, speaking quickly to Sergeant Worrall before leaving the room.

When the CSM had left, one of the corporals brought in a tin bath, placing it in the centre of the room. Bemused faces looked at each other, wondering what was to come next, before one of the sergeants commenced a hygiene lecture covering the billets and ablutions, the kitchen and dining room areas and store rooms. After twenty minutes or so, he nodded to the back of the hall and spoke of 'personal hygiene'. A corporal from 3 platoon then entered the room, wearing just a towel wrapped round his body, and went over to stand in the bath. Two other NCOs brought in several large jugs of water and poured them in over his feet, the steam rising up before them. Ed, who was sitting towards the rear, watched as the corporal ripped his towel away, to the cheers of the men present, and stood quite naked before them. The sergeant explained how important it was to clean the body properly, which the corporal began to demonstrate. He washed himself in front of everyone, lathering himself until he was covered in soap, making a special point of washing his hair, under his arms and around his groin. As he did so, Ed felt a little flushed, but how could she look away? No, she had to laugh along with the rest of them and Frank nudged her in the ribs, grinning. Without flinching, she smiled back not letting on she felt distinctly uncomfortable, until suddenly the corporal turned around and bent forward with his backside now in full view of everyone. He began to wash his arse very thoroughly, creating lots of laughter from the troops, the NCOs enjoying the moment just as much. When all was done, Corporal Bateman arrived with another large jug of water and ceremoniously tipped it over the soaped-up corporal who yelled loudly, standing rigid from shock. It was obviously cold water, which he clearly hadn't expected. He bent down, grabbing his towel, and ran out to loud applause!

As the laughter died down, the sergeant spoke again. 'So, all in a bit of fun, men, but take in the important message here, of how you must look after yourselves and each other too. Wash whenever you can, using your powder to prevent lice and sores. Ticks too will burrow their way under your skin and can cause infections. So, always check yourself and each other when you can. Wash your private areas thoroughly, as no-one else will wash them for you, except perhaps a lady of the night on a weekend pass, but that's another story!' The men laughed and jeered loudly. 'And I repeat, use your powder as often as you can, which will also help with problems you will encounter in the trenches. Any questions?'

People looked at each other but no-one seemed brave enough to open their mouths. Then an arm slowly rose at the back of the room.

'Sergeant, what are the toilets like in the trenches?' said a large chap just a few feet from Edwina.

'Good question, lad. The latrines in the trenches are very basic and mostly consist of pits dug out of the ground, with two logs stuck horizontally over them, your feet go on one and you sit on the other. So, you sit, shit and leave. It's that simple and I promise you, you will want to be quick, as they smell bloody awful. If you stay too long, there is a great risk of falling in, something I don't recommend.' The men turned their faces and groaned aloud. 'OK, if that's it, you are dismissed.'

It was a little after eight thirty, so they had an hour to themselves and they disbursed back to their billets, for some down time. When Frank and Ed entered their room, some of the lads were talking to the quiet chap in the corner, one poking him in the chest, clearly pointing something out to him. They realised it was the chap whom they had seen with his head in his hands the previous day, and as Frank walked over to ask if everything was OK, he was told to mind his own business. He was confused and tried to speak, but was pushed away by the same large bloke who had asked about the toilets. Frank stepped back and wandered back over to where Ed sat, undoing her boots.

'There is something very wrong here,' he said peering across at the small huddle.

'Look, Frank, he is in 4 Section, let his chaps deal with it as we would look after our own too. We can always look out for him a bit, but just be aware of that big bloke.' They glanced at each other, nodding, and set about sorting themselves out for bed.

Five o'clock came far too quickly once again, but Ed was up straight away this time and heading for the toilet before most had even opened their eyes. She went into a cubicle first and then grabbed a bucket to wash, re-entering the barrack room before many had even tied their boots. Frank wasn't far behind her, and after making their beds, they headed down for breakfast, being almost first into the dining hall. They received the promised sausage and beans, which were largely pale and uninviting. They reached for some bread and a mug of hot tea, before sitting on the end table nearest the exit. It was still dark outside, but lights could be seen in the distance, as Bristol awoke for another day.

They fell in at six o'clock in a light drizzle, a single light beaming across the parade from above the door. They were separated into their sections of the previous day and throughout the morning they cleared the remaining stores and bundles of clothing, finishing just before their midday meal. At one o'clock, rainclouds now gone, they were fell in on the parade for their uniform issue! There was excitement in the air as one by one they were called forward into the barracks and down the passage on the ground floor. The sergeant studied each man briefly before shouting large, medium or small. Not quite one size fits all, as some had said, but it was not far off. Items of uniform were then placed on the bench and each soldier was asked for his boot and cap size. The boots were then draped around his neck by the laces, and the cap placed on his head.

Each billet was a hive of activity, with clothes scattered everywhere as uniforms were tried on, casting their civvies aside on their bunks, stepping into a new chapter of their lives, a private in the King's Army. The corporals were moving around their respective sections, giving advice on how to fit the trousers and tunics properly, before demonstrating how to tie leg putties correctly. On each floor, the new recruits finally started to look the part, as they strutted around, proudly, looking at each other. Some of the chaps were sent down to exchange clothing that didn't fit, until finally the whole company was wearing khaki for the first time. There was a real buzz as the men finally became the newest members of the Gloucestershire Regiment!

At four o'clock, they were ordered to fall in on the parade and sped down the stairs to be part of this special moment. Three platoons of uniformed men met the CSM's eyes as he stepped from the building, Sergeant Worrall calling them all to attention. They stood proudly, eyes facing forward as before, heads back and chests out. The CSM eyed his new charges carefully, stepping forward to tell one or two men to do up a button or straighten a cap. He stepped back and chatted to his sergeant, before disappearing back inside. For the rest of the afternoon, they were introduced to drill, which produced much humour and tested many, providing some with very sore feet.

Over the next seven days, training began in earnest, with a short run each morning as a platoon, taking the three-mile route along the river. It was a pleasant regime and often in open spaces, they would stop and do some physical exercises. Breakfast followed the daily run and then battle drills filled most of each day. At the beginning of the second week they were finally issued with their own rifles, a momentous time for most, where they met their new best friend. They were told to cherish them, love them like a woman and never be parted. The corporals taught weapon training, use of bayonets and battle tactics. It was all very new ground and each man seemed to enjoy the freedom of escaping the barracks each day. Some however, struggled to keep up.

With the last of the equipment due any day, the new recruits finally looked and felt like real soldiers. Ed found the almost daily drill on the makeshift parade square somewhat tedious, but it had begun to bring a special bond within the group and it also created much hilarity as arms and legs fought against each other to keep in step.

Ed thrived on anything physical and liked the runs and the exercise they did most mornings, particularly enjoying the field craft exercises, where they would crawl on their bellies in the undergrowth to reach a target unnoticed. Rifle drills had now become a daily occurrence and her own personal routines had settled well. She was almost caught out one afternoon, when some boxing was organised during a gap in the programme and volunteers were sought to fight each other. Several men jumped at the chance to don the padded boxing gloves and batter their comrades, the corporals setting up a makeshift boxing ring in the corner of the parade. She worried she might be included but didn't need to fret as more volunteers came forward than there was time for. Ed was happy just to watch on this occasion, especially as the sergeant made them all strip down to their vests!

On the Friday of the second week, just after dinner, a notice was placed on the company notice board:

The Mobile Bath Unit will be paying a visit on Wednesday. All recruits will take a shower except for 2 Platoon who will be at the rifle range all day.
By Order: Captain Moffat

Ed sighed with great relief.

Chapter 13

The morning of the range day was dismal. The rain lashed down like a winter storm, a low mist hanging over the river as 2 Platoon boarded the trucks. Whilst they waited for their sergeant, the engine fumes drifted up into the back of the vehicle, stinging their eyes and making the men who had fought to get the seats at the tale board, cough loudly. When at last the sergeant finally appeared, the chaps at the back were clearly feeling unwell, and as they set off, the breakfast they had eaten thirty minutes earlier was left in a trail behind them.

Once underway, the wind whistled through the canopy dissipating the fumes, and the fresh morning air settling many upset stomachs. They quickly turned away from the city, heading towards the lower hills to the south. It was only a short journey and within fifteen minutes they were alighting in a crowded parking area, amongst hundreds of other soldiers from various regiments. Ed and Frank formed up on the end of the rear rank, but the platoon was ordered to turn left, and as they marched off, they were leading the way towards the range along the muddy track. The overnight deluge had created huge puddles, and as they marched, some started to step extra heavily into the pools of water, like children, splashing water sideways onto the legs of others. It started off as a joke, but soon turned into, who could splash the most people and laughter quickly ensued. The NCOs grinned at each other, not interfering with this spirited play by the men. They just made sure they weren't in splashing distance. As the rain continued to fall, they were halted and instructed to turn their weapons upside down, before heading across to the short twenty-five-yard practice range at the bottom of the hill. It was a hive of activity as several men were laying out ammunition, while others were placing targets in front of a high bank of sand. They were stood at ease and the range sergeant began briefing them on their first shoot.

'Morning, men, I am Sergeant Brooks and today I will be running your first range day. You will be shooting five rounds of ammunition twice over, firstly to get a zero on your weapons, which means you will aim at the centre of a target and we will then adjust your sights, before you repeat the exercise. This will bring your aim point to the centre of the target and to confirm we have adjusted them correctly. Once done, you will move over to Range D and shoot from one hundred yards. Now, the Lee Enfield has the kick of a horse, so when you are firing, hang on tightly by pulling it firmly into the shoulder for every round you fire. Remember the drills you have been taught. Breath, hold, squeeze. It's pretty simple really. For this practice you will have a spotter sat beside you to help, so listen to their advice and take well aimed shots only. Any questions?'

The men looked along the row at each other, eager to begin and no questions were asked. As they took their places opposite a target, in lines of four, the bull's-eye seemed very small! A corporal handed out pieces of cotton wool for each man, to shove into their ears, and as the first group stepped forward, the remainder sat behind, watching. The front rank moved onto the firing line and the sergeant gave the new orders: 'With a clip of five rounds, load.'

Each man picked up his ammunition and slipped the clip into the top of the rifle, something they had practised routinely with dummy ammunition for over a week. But this was for real.

'In the prone position, down!' yelled the sergeant, each man dropping to lie in the mud. The spotters adjusted their legs and arms, making sure the rifles were aimed down the range at all times.

'Ready' shouted the sergeant and everyone down the line lifted their rear sights and cocked their weapon, the soldiers behind looking through binoculars at the targets.

'Firing five shots in your own time, go on.'

Before anyone could even think, someone clearly had trigger finger, sending a bullet high into the sand, making most people jump. The platoon sergeant went over and kicked the heel of the man on the end several times, before shouting at him. There was a long pause before the shots rang out evenly along the line, each man in turn squeezing his finger gently, until all the magazines were empty. As instructed, each man in turn then raised his arm to indicate he was finished, and once ordered, they were told to stand up and face down the range to prove their weapons. NCOs darted along the line looking inside the chamber, tapping each man on the shoulder and shouting 'clear'. The men then placed their weapons down and walked towards the butts to their respective target, quickly lifting it off the block and replacing it with another. They then headed back to the firing line in quick time to collect their rifles.

As the next batch moved forward, ready for their turn, another sergeant at the rear inspected each man's target, offering advice or a bollocking, with some getting both! He then adjusted the sights in turn, with a small screwdriver, to bring the shots into the centre of their target. The men patched the holes out with paper and glue and placed them back on the pile.

The routine went on for twenty minutes or so as each rank progressed through this first shoot, until it was time for Frank and Ed's rank to step forward. For many years, Ed had been shooting rabbits, pigeons and deer on the farm, but never with a weapon of such power. She had remembered the instructions from her section corporal about the enormous kick the Lee Enfield had, so was determined to grip it tight into her shoulder and use all her experience to show her worth. She listened for the orders in turn, before she was free to engage the bulls-eye to her front. She carefully lined up the small pin at the end of the barrel with her rear iron sight, to the centre of the target. She concentrated deeply, calming her breathing as her father had taught her, before closing her left eye and placing her trigger finger into position. When all was lined up, she held it tight, stopped breathing and squeezed the trigger gently. The round was gone. With rifles singing along the line, she finally released her final shot, then waited for the next command. When all was quiet and safety checks completed, she placed her rifle down and walked with the rest of her small squad to the targets. She was staggered when she saw a small grouping of what looked like three holes to the right of centre of her target. Did I miss, she thought? Frank, to her right, looked at his own target before staring across at hers. 'God, that's brilliant shooting, Ed.'

'Not so bad yourself, Frank,' she said and picked up her target and headed back to the point.

The sergeant was already giving feedback to others when she got there, making stern points and giving some precise instructions, to make some improvements. As Ed offered her target, the NCO stared first at the target, then at her. 'Looks like you missed with two shots, lad,' he said before stopping himself to take another look, poking his pencil through the holes. 'Hang on a minute, you didn't miss at all, you have a one-inch grouping. Bloody good shooting, son,' he said. Smiling for the first time that morning, he took her rifle and adjusted the rear sight slightly, to move the fall of shot to the left. 'That will bring you into line,' he said, and passed the weapon back to Ed. 'Well done!'

As they stepped away, Frank patted her on the back before they sat at the rear with the rest of their squad, awaiting their second chance.

'OK, men, first time nerves for some and some bloody good shooting for others. Now we are going to repeat the routine and remember what you have learnt. Hold the rifle firmly into your shoulder, otherwise you will miss everything you shoot at above one hundred yards. If you are one inch to the side at twenty-five yards, you will be about a foot at one hundred yards. OK, front rank to the point.'

They all repeated the practice once again, and Ed remained way ahead of any of the others, Frank coming in close behind her. When finished, the sergeant stood out in front telling them to head down to Range D, and one of the corporals marched them down.

After ten minutes or so they came to a halt next to the tea wagon and were told to break off for a smoke and a brew. While in the queue some of the chaps spoke to Ed to ask what the secret was. She told them simply to stop breathing and gently squeeze the trigger, never pull it. She didn't want to appear too much of a know-it-all, so tried not to sound cocky! After a short break, they headed on down and commenced the second shoot.

The procedure was much the same, but the targets were much larger and had a figure of a man outlined in black. Firing once again in the prone position, in the same order as before, they went through the same routine, taking longer with all the extra walking to and from the butts. While they waited, the rain started again, and although coming from behind, it still would make it more difficult.

Ed wasn't deterred, her mind drifting back to when she had stalked a large deer the previous Spring.

She rose very early and without breakfast set off into the hills above the farm, creeping into the tree line from the wooded valley, to arrive in position just before daybreak. She had lain very still for many hours on top of one of her father's old, heavy oilskin coats, to protect her from the cool morning. It had all happened quite suddenly. She heard some scuffling to her centre right, and a large pair of antlers appeared out of the bushes, some two hundred and fifty yards away. A proud giant of a beast, he raised his head and sniffed the air before starting to graze. Every mouthful, he lifted his head and peered around, gazing down the valley, before resuming his meal. Every so often, the deer would step forward, a hoof at a time, as he chewed the fine grasses. He was very alert, she remembered, and never once had his head down for more than a few seconds, his two nasal passages sniffing the air as he chewed. It took all of thirty minutes for him to close in enough for

Ed to be comfortable she could take him out with a single shot, as he stood so innocent, so unaware of his ultimate fate. She readied herself for a shot to his torso, aiming behind the front leg mid-way up his chest, aiming for the heart. She slowly dropped her head down behind the rifle sight, so as not to move any grass or for the animal to sense a presence, bringing her eye to the sight. With her finger curling slowly around the trigger she took a slow deliberate breath, which she held for several seconds, and it was over in a flash. As the bullet left the barrel, reaching the target at the exact point she wanted, the beast fell, as if his legs had been cut from under him. He dropped dead in an instant, head forward, grass still between his teeth. It was all over...

Loud shots from the range to their right, brought her back from her daze just as her squad were being called forward, and she took her position to fire. She settled into her steady rhythm: cocking her weapon, *pause*; tightening her body to the rifle, *pause*; closing her left eye, *pause*; then taking her last breath; and only then, squeezing her finger gently around the trigger. The loud crack, when it came rang out, the butt kicking back violently into her shoulder, as her bullet reached its target. The rain had little effect on her and within minutes they were all heading to the butts to check their targets. She was astounded at what she saw! Just to the right of centre, there was a mass of bullet holes, no bigger than a half-crown piece, with just one stray shot just above. She smiled to herself, as someone to her right said, 'Fuckin hell' and she turned to see a corporal looking on. Frank leant across, his target in his hand, peering at her. Ed could see he, too, had shot well, as they doubled back up to the firing line.

When they reached the firing point, the corporal went over to talk to an officer at the rear, pointing to Ed as he spoke. The lieutenant called across, 'Mitchell, come here lad.' Ed ran across with her rifle, holding the target in her left hand.

As she stopped, she almost fell over as her foot slipped in the mud. 'Yes, sir?' she said, standing attention.

'I hear you're a bit of a shot, lad' he said, reaching for the target. He pursed his lips as he inspected her work before grinning at her. 'Once you have had your sights adjusted and have done a reshoot, I want you to move to the two-hundred-yard point and show me what you can do from there,' he said.

'Yes, sir,' and she doubled away to the waiting sergeant, who adjusted the rear sight once more. She quickly patched out her target, before joining the rear line to await her second shoot. Once completed she, along with nine others, including Frank, doubled over to the two-hundred-yard point. When they arrived, they sat down on the wet grass, the fine drizzle now almost gone, as patches of clear blue sky appeared high above. With five minutes to spare, they gave their rifles a quick clean and pulled a piece of cotton gauze up through the barrel with a length of string, before being ushered into line. The briefing this time was given by the young officer Ed had met earlier.

'OK, men, the order has changed so listen up.' He read out the names on his sheet, placing Frank and Ed together on one end of the line. 'This time you will take five shots at the target on the right in the prone position followed by five shots at the target on the left in the standing position, leaning on the post provided. This will be the position you will be firing from most of the time in the trenches and it requires a whole set of different skills. So, listen to the NCOs behind you as you shoot.'

The chaps moved forward and took up their positions, Ed on the far right of the line.

'With a clip of five rounds, load.' The routine repeated itself as before, until they were ready to fire. Ed went through her routine once again, never trying to change it or break her concentration. She fired her five rounds as instructed, with the same pauses as she had before.

'Stand up,' came the order. 'With a clip of five rounds, load,' came the order again and so it went on, but this time it was a whole lot different. Ed had shot birds from a standing position before as they flew over the farm, pigeons mainly, and the odd pheasant too, so standing didn't feel too intimidating. She had always wrapped the rifle sling around her forearm to help support the shot, but on doing so this time, a corporal came across to her position.

'What are you doing, lad?' he said.

She turned to him. 'It gives greater support, corporal, by pulling the stock tight into the hand. I know it may look odd, but it works, and was how I was taught by my father,' she said. The corporal looked at her and shrugged his shoulders, before she leant against the post and got comfortable. The process was repeated as she let each shot go, in the same rhythmical fashion, until all was done.

'Stop,' came the loud voice. 'For inspection, port arms,' came the order. As before, the corporal walked down the line, clearing each man before they laid their rifles down and headed off to the butts and their targets. An NCO went along in turn from left to right, speaking to each man until they got to the end of the line and Ed stood motionless, facing her target, grinning!

'What have we here, Mitchell?' said the sergeant as he peered at her target. Facing him was a sight for sore eyes. Ed had managed to keep all her shots inside a tight circle. The wide-eyed NCO pulled a set of rings from his pocket without taking his eyes from the target. He selected a small ring of two inches and placed it over both of her targets in turn, and grinned. 'Bloody good shooting, lad, bloody good.' He shouted across the line to the lieutenant. 'Sir, do you have a minute?' and he quickly marched over to where they stood. Frank, too, stepped across as the officer got into position to see the two-inch ring.

'By God, who's responsible for this, is it you, Mitchell?' he said.

'Yes, sir,' Ed said, tightening her bottom lip against the top one, trying to hide a smile.

'Patch out and head back up to the firing line. I have something to discuss with you.' And with Frank grinning at her, they both doubled back to the point and commenced cleaning their weapons. A corporal who was with the lieutenant and the sergeant shouted out for Mitchell and Smith. They both jumped up and ran over to hear their fate.

'Ah, Mitchell, Smith. You have impressed us with your shooting, and Mitchell, you are one of the best shots I have ever seen. I will be recommending when your training is over that you receive orders to be sent for sniper selection in France, and special duties. Is that something that would be of interest to you?'

Together, and quite unrehearsed, they both said 'Yes, sir,' grinning like Cheshire cats. 'OK, leave it with me, I will speak to your company commander and pass your names on to HQ. That will be all.'

And they ran back over to re-join the rest of the men who were already sitting eating their snack lunches. They were both jeered by several of the lads as they approached but ignored the jibes and joined the food queue. They only had ten minutes, so devoured their light meal before climbing aboard the trucks to head back to the barracks. As they sped off, they were quizzed about their chat with the lieutenant. Frank joked about them both being invited to the Officers' Mess for dinner, Ed chipping in to support his story, before shocked faces turned to grins as the chaps realised, they were being conned. Ed then explained about the trial to join the sniper squadron.

They had been the first in the company to have a range day so knew they had the moral high ground over the other platoons and were in high spirits as they sped through the open countryside, back to the city. They soon swung back towards the river, and within ten minutes, they rolled into the yard. Some of the chaps were outside taking a smoke, one pointing at them as they came into sight, before parking on the far side of the parade. They all jumped down from the truck in good spirits, collecting their webbing, before heading over to the barracks with an air of superiority. They read DROs that had been posted at the bottom of the stairwell before heading up to their billet. They smiled as they passed several of the lads from other platoons, some stopping to chat about their day on the range. That evening 2 Platoon stood a little taller that the rest...

It had been a good day, Ed thought, and she only had to crack the next three weeks before her sniper training began. As she sat down on the bed to clean her rifle, she felt a slight cramp in her middle. She realised; her monthly period had arrived!

Chapter 14

It had been almost a month since Ed had gone off to war. In that time, four of her letters had reached home, explaining that she had settled into the training well. Edward felt a certain amount of pride in his sister's audacious enterprise on his behalf and always read her letters to David after supper. Ed had been careful when creating her brief letters home never to mention any difficulties she may have endured. In fact, Edward had thought them very positive and full of spirit, as she was seemingly enjoying her time in the army. He had written letters back over the weeks but neglected to mention anything that might make Ed worry, especially the diary reading incident with David. He concentrated instead on news of the farm and how well the crops had taken this year. He also wrote to put her mind at rest about David, who had settled well, and how fond he had become of him.

The post that day brought yet another letter from Ed and once they had cleared up after supper, Edward pulled open the envelope, sitting next to David by the warming fire. He normally read his letters in advance, but this time, trusted his dear sister's judgement.

Dear Sis. I write this after our first successful night out on a patrol exercise with an overnight stay in a basher, which is a small shelter used for sleeping. It was followed by walking through a proper trench system dug by the engineers and running through various battle drills that we all have to get used to and quickly! What an experience, I never realised how difficult it might be, as it was very cold overnight, the sleeping sheets don't give much warmth. Frank has become my closest friend as we do most things together and we have both been selected for a course once we have finished training. Everything else remains well and all my mishaps are now a thing of the past. I hope all is well at home, there is talk of some brief leave before we are deployed to France, but that may be pie in the sky.

Give David my best wishes.

Ed

'Mishaps' said David. 'What does he mean by mishaps?'

'Oh, I don't know, David, it could mean anything,' he said, kicking himself for not reading the letter first. 'Maybe he had a few problems that he hasn't been able to divulge, as I expect they can't write about everything. In fact, he says a course, but doesn't say what.' Edward folded the letter and placed it in his pocket and drank his tea, thinking of what his sister was doing for him. He wondered how he could ever repay her!

The fire cracked and fizzled after David placed a log on top of the flames, and sparks flew across the floor, hitting his feet. He jumped up and brushed his legs quickly, as Edward smiled to himself, before laughing. They had grown closer over the weeks and Edward now trusted David in all but his own private little world, something he could never speak of.

The following morning, before Edward got on with his chores, he placed the letter from Edwina in the top drawer of the dresser, along with the others, and wondered quite how big a pile there would eventually be before she came home. He then placed a new letter written from his bed the previous evening behind the clock, ready for posting. He put on his boots, and grabbing his coat set off to fix the guttering that ran around the small workshop and tack room, as it had been leaking for weeks. David was in the top paddock, fixing the gate, that morning and Edward could see he had already been in the workshop, as yet again the tool box was left open. He rummaged through to find the tools he needed before climbing up, ready to begin.

The damaged sections came away easily, and were dropped to the ground, along with the rotten timbers. Climbing down, he cut the replacements to length and was starting to climb up again when the corner section of the frame holding the platform snapped, the whole structure tipping and sending him spinning in the air to the ground. He landed on top of the old pieces of timber he had discarded earlier, faced down. It took him only a fraction of a second to realise he was now impaled upon several nails that stuck out from them!

With the wind knocked out of him, he felt unable to move and lay still, wondering what to do, wincing at the pain. He tried to sit up but was clearly hooked on several nails in his shoulder and right hip. In great pain, he tried to role sideways, but as he did so, he felt his skin tear along his shoulder. This was going to hurt. Gritting his teeth, he pushed himself through the pain until finally, he was free. He lay on the ground, panting and feeling a little faint! He called out to David as loudly as he could and by chance David was already heading back down the field and was just walking through the paddock gate when he heard Edward's cry. He turned the corner and saw Edward lying on his back amongst a pile of timber. He ran over, in a panic.

'What on earth happened, Ed, are you OK?' he asked anxiously.

Ed was grimacing in pain but managed to answer. 'The corner of the platform slipped and is broken. I fell onto the waste timber I had just cleared from the guttering, landing on some nails.'

'Can you stand?' David asked.

'Not sure, will try,' he groaned, and with David's help he slowly got to his feet. He leant against the wall of the shed to get his breath.

'Let's get you inside to see how bad it is,' David said as he put his arm around Edward's back. As they approached the doorway in the hall, Edward asked David to put some hot water on to boil and get the bandage box from the cupboard and bring it up to his room. David didn't protest but thought he should be helping Edward get upstairs first. Edward had other ideas. Within minutes, he had filled a bowl with hot water, and with the small medical box under his arm, he walked carefully up the stairs to Edward's room. He stepped in to see him sitting on a chair next to the bed and placed the bowl on the table. He helped Edward to take off his jumper.

'Now, is there anything else I can do?' he said.

'No thanks, David, you have been a great help already,' knowing full well that no matter how injured he was, he could never ask David to help him. David walked towards to door, feeling quite uncomfortable, but knew his place and closed the door behind him. She was a woman after all…

Edward struggled to take off his shirt and undershirt, but once off, he stood to look at his injuries in the mirror. On his shoulder, high up, he could see a brown mark about an inch long, with blood oozing gently from it. The one on his hip looked less serious but had a flap of skin about an inch in length ripped back, the blood still seeping out. He could attend to this easily but found the wound on his shoulder more difficult. He picked up his soap and face cloth to wash the areas thoroughly before drying them with his towel. The wounds stopped bleeding and sorted the smaller wound on his hip first. The cut on his shoulder he left open and lay on the bed to relax before dozing off to sleep…

David had gone back downstairs with a view to clearing up the debris Edward had left, but instead thought a brew might be in order. He filled the kettle and placed it on the stove, then noticed the letter behind the clock addressed to Edward. He picked it up and saw the flap was still open. He wondered why Ed hadn't posted it and walked over to the door to see if she was on her way back down. He shouted up but heard nothing, and leaving the door slightly ajar, took the page from the envelope and started to read.

Dear Ed. Thanks for your last letter it was good to read all is well and your coping ok. Great to hear you are past the halfway mark and your experiencing life outdoors. What are they planning for you? We are well and David has settled and is doing good work. We have caught up with a great deal of jobs and I am balancing the budget well.

I am intrigued of your 'mishap' and wonder what you are referring too, have you had any close shaves? Bryan sends his regards to you and promises to write soon. He helped us on a very rainy day a couple of weeks ago and stayed for supper. He is a good friend and we are both lucky to have him with us during this time. I have settled into my new role and hope I can keep David under control although I did make a mistake recently with him, which I regret. I think we are over it now and he is always very helpful. Stay safe and hope nothing comes back to haunt us. Write when you can... Much love. Ed

David realising he had just done exactly as Ed had done when she read his diary. So rather guiltily he returned the envelope to the mantelpiece and poured out two mugs of tea. He sat down, waiting, but after ten minutes the tea grew cold. He crept upstairs to see her asleep on the bed and walked over to her bedside. As he approached, Edward woke with a start. 'What's up, David?'

'Sorry, Ed, are you OK? I've made some tea, are you coming down?'

Edward realised he had nothing on under the covers, so couldn't sit up, so gripped the top of the blanket, holding it tight under his chin. 'It's OK, David, you go down and I will join you in a minute.'

'OK, I'll make something to eat,' he said and left the room, pulling the door closed behind him. Edward quickly covered his shoulder wound before dressing and heading downstairs. David, busy in the kitchen felt he wanted to spoil Ed a bit, so put some soup on the stove before opening the tin of fruit, they had bought the previous day. He brewed another pot of tea, and within minutes they were both sitting together by the now roaring fire.

'So how does it feel, Ed?' David said.

'It's OK, thanks, the wounds are not too bad, and I should be back to normal in a few days.'

As they sat chatting, Edward explained what had happened and how he had fallen, but realised the job was still to be finished. David stood up to leave. 'OK, you sit tight, I'll go and clear up and finish what you started. Should be about an hour,' he said as put on his muddy boots by the door, leaving Edward to ponder his injuries, feeling a bit sorry for himself. He leant his head against the back of the chair to relax, his eyes catching the letter to Ed. He noticed it was not where he had left it...

Chapter 15

Ed sat frozen to her bunk, cautiously glancing around the room to check no-one was watching her. Her heightened fear of being discovered, suddenly started to overwhelm her, but all she saw was normality amongst the men in her billet. Everyone was simply going about their own business. Some were cleaning weapons, others sorting kit or chatting in small groups, no-one was paying her the slightest bit of attention. As casually as possible, she reached into the green box at the foot of her bed for her little green tin and her wash bag before standing and heading for the lavs. She wasn't fazed at the prospect of dealing with her period, as she had been expecting this to happen following several days of tender breasts. She was met at the doorway by Corporal Baker who stopped to talk about her good shooting at the range. This was an untimely interruption, but thankfully, he quickly went on his way. The toilets were largely empty, and she stepped into the cubicle by the wall, which had the best latch, and clicked it shut before dropping her trousers and pants to her ankles. She opened her bag and took out a prepared pad and proceeded to perform her routine as she had practised at home. Within minutes, all was done, and she washed her hands and left without incident…

The evening lecture that night was on first aid in the field, but as soon as they were finished, Ed became the centre of attention as word had clearly got out about her shooting prowess. As men gathered around her bunk, some from the other platoons, she showed off her target with her two-inch grouping from two hundred yards and offered tips to help those yet to shoot. This unexpected popularity cemented her position within the platoon and from that day on she became the person to ask on all shooting matters. She had found her place, which would hold her in good stead for the remainder of their training. As time passed and with lights out imminent, many people were prised back to their own billets by Corporal Baker, who nodded at her with approval. She smiled, before climbing into her bed. It had been a good day.

The next two weeks were largely spent on the ranges and in a battle simulation area, working through various routines and tactics in pre-dug trenches. The rudiments of real soldering came to the fore and made them realise how difficult life would be. During shooting days, each man fired twenty rounds in the prone position, followed by thirty rounds standing, leaning against a post. Ed continuing to show her ability and managed to reduce her grouping even further. At one point the company commander suggested Ed fire at three hundred yards, with the rest of the company looking on. She didn't disappoint and made the same two-inch grouping as before. The whole company gathered round Captain Moffat at the end of the day, as he proudly showed her target to all the assembled men. On the Wednesday, Ed was summoned.

'Mitchell, get over here, lad.' She stood up and doubled over to the OC, and sliding to attention, she saluted in one action.

'Mitchell reporting, sir,' she shouted and stood upright, looking straight to her front.

'Mitchell, this is Major Hesketh-Pritchard, the commanding officer of the sniper squadron, and Lieutenant Cavanagh, who you know. You will be posted to his squadron for your sniper training, along with many other hopefuls. Your orders have come through today.'

Ed didn't quite know what to say but uttered the first words that came into her head: 'Brilliant, sir, Thank you, sir.'

The officer looked at Ed without speaking, as he looked her up and down. He felt a little hesitant, as what stood before him was not a mature soldier, but a boy who was of light build and looked like he should still be at school! 'Mitchell, I hear you're a bit of a shot? A two-inch grouping at three hundred yards is very impressive. Where did you learn to shoot, lad?'

Ed looked at him confidently. 'I grew up on a farm, sir, my father taught me,' she said.

'I'd like to meet your father one day, Mitchell, he has clearly taught you well. You are a very good shot. I hope you are looking forward to the sniper selection course?'

Ed smiled before just saying an enthusiastic yes!

'OK, dismissed, Mitchell,' said Captain Moffat, and Ed saluted and ran back to the others.

'Bit young ain't he, Moffat?' said Hesketh-Pritchard.

'It takes all sorts, sir,' he said. 'It's the shooting that counts and he certainly has great qualities that I have never seen before.' The major nodded and they ambled off towards the tea tent.

In the final week of their short training period, the whole company stayed at the range, sleeping in bashers for three nights using their newly issued canvas sheets, which along with their greatcoats provided reasonable comfort and cover from above. On this occasion, they were within the tree line at the rear of the range, where they used pine needles as a sort of mattress to provide insulation. Compared to what was to come, this was undoubtedly the last time they would experience this luxury. The exercise gave them all ample opportunity to hone their skills for living in the field, albeit they were civilians a little under six weeks ago. At seven o'clock each day they would fall in to be inspected by their section corporals. This would take over an hour checking personal weapons and their equipment and doing a personal welfare check. Many of the chaps were picked up for not shaving or having dirty items within their kit. Punishments were dished out, and men had to run to a large tree and back several times, rifles held high above their heads. A punishment that made the arms and shoulders burn and faces grimace! Ed and Frank, working together, managed to avoid them completely.

On the Thursday morning, they packed up their kit, and following the shooting competition, which Ed won hands down, they headed back into Bristol for one last weekend. They would soon leave the relative peace and quiet of jolly old England, and head to France. Life was about to change dramatically; some would never see the green fields of England ever again. Friday was their last day of training and a night on the town was promised. There was a tremendous buzz around the dining hall at breakfast, the noise incessant as exuberance overtook them. They had been ordered to sit firm on completion, as the OC wanted to brief them inside because the spring rains had made the parade a quagmire.

At seven twenty, the CSM walked in and called for everyone to sit to attention. As he did so, Captain Moffat walked in behind him, the whole room now silent. The sergeant major turned and saluted, reporting to his OC that the company were present and correct. The captain shouted, 'Sit at ease, men,' and took off his cap, perching on the corner of a table before addressing the men for the last time.

'Good morning, men, I hope you have eaten well and you're ready for the next phase of your military life. Now, it's important for you all to remember that you have had a six-week introduction to army life, which will hold you in good stead for the dramatic times ahead, as you experience trench warfare. You must look at and listen to the men you will be alongside in the trenches and never doubt for one moment that if you don't follow the lessons you have learnt here and don't find your feet quickly, you will struggle and die! So, look around you at all times and learn from others more experienced than yourselves. Keep your heads down and look after each other.' He paused to look around the room, reaching for his pipe in his hip pocket as he did so. He took his time lighting it, one eye on his subordinates as smoke drifted upwards.

He stood up and walked over to the CSM, speaking quietly in his ear, before resuming his briefing. 'Orders for where you are being posted have been promulgated on the company notice board downstairs, but Sergeant Worrall will inform you after this briefing too, so listen out for your names. If you have any queries, the sergeant major will fill in the gaps in his office afterwards. It only remains for me to say it has been hard for some of you, so share your experiences and help each other always. Your lives may well depend upon it. Finally, it has been a steady six weeks men, and you should feel proud to wear the King's uniform. So, go to your duties with pride and come back safely. Over to you, sergeant major,' and he replaced his cap, leaving the room. The CSM shouted 'Sit to attention', saluting the officer as he left.

'Sit easy, men. Now I would like to start by reiterating what Captain Moffat has said and to congratulate you all on passing basic training. Your efforts have been noticed by all the instructors and you should feel justly proud of what you have achieved. Your NCOs will be travelling with you all the way to the front as you deploy as a company, except for the OC and I, who start training another batch of one hundred men in a few days. You will stay overnight tonight, but you must be on the ball tomorrow morning, zero five thirty hours start. There remains a great deal to do before you can depart, especially as you all have leave passes tonight.'

A great cheer went up around the room, and every single NCO grinned at this enthusiastic response. The CSM, simply waited for them to settle. The room then fell quiet.

'Your leave starts at nineteen hundred hours, but you must report back here before twenty-two thirty. Do not be late back, gentlemen.' he said sternly.

'Saturday morning you will depart to Bristol station and no, you won't need to march this time, as I have ensured transport will be here, and on time. You will be part of ten thousand men from all over the country being shipped to the front over this weekend. You will need to be patient, as delays may well take place, but if all goes well, you should arrive in a holding barracks in Kent by late tomorrow. The following day you will embark on a ship to get you across the Channel, but one word of warning, watch those sailors, they will try and take advantage of you. I also suggest you don't eat too much before you sail, as although it's a short journey, there is plenty of time to get sea sick. You should arrive in France by late Sunday and your battalion will organise your onward move. There are a few exceptions of course, and Sergeant Worrall has the details. Finally, I would like to say it has been a pleasure, men, and again to reiterate what Captain Moffat said – the more you watch the experienced men around you in your regiment and follow their lead, the more chance you have of surviving longer than five minutes. Good luck, men.'

'Attention,' said a voice, as the CSM replaced his head gear and left the room. 'Sit easy, men' said the sergeant as the NCOs gathered together, with a hum of chatter starting up around the room. The noise steadily grew until Worrall grabbed their attention once more.

'OK, men, listen up.' The conversations around the room petered out. 'I have a list of names for those who are not heading straight into the front line, as some are being sent on courses to support the regiments. So, if your name is not read out, I repeat, not read out, you will follow the instructions posted on the company notice board downstairs.'

The sergeant first read out the names of two men who were going to the Royal Engineers, heading for their training depot in Chatham, followed by six men heading to the artillery battery in Woolwich, London. One chap had been selected for officer training at RMA Sandhurst and three were being sent on a cook's course. 'And finally, Mitchell and Smith are being sent for sniper selection at a place called Linghem, in northern France. Your course, however, doesn't start until the fourteenth so you lucky blighters and are being given a four-day leave pass.' A general moan went up around the room, Ed and Frank receiving slaps on their backs as they grinned at each other!

'OK, chaps, steady down. Now your orders will be issued separately by the CSM, and you are to report to him at zero seven hundred hours tomorrow. Today will be a barrack cleaning day under your platoon NCOs and once completed to the required standard and your surplus kit is handed in, you can go into town. But not, until everything is done. It's up to you men.' Then from no-where, a sudden roar went up around the room, making several of the NCOs jump, as finally these young lads who, until just a few weeks ago, were ungainly, raw recruits exploded with euphoria as their training was over. They were now enthusiastic soldiers, ready to go to war.

'Ok men, settle down, settle down.' And the room came to order. 'Don't be late or I promise you will be charged! Ok, you're dismissed.'

The mass of bright young hopefuls dispersed quickly, back to their billets. It was to be a long day but an even longer night…

Chapter 16

The sun had almost dropped below the horizon as the long arduous day came to an end. Edward and David were sitting at the kitchen table chatting, with large mugs of tea resting on their laps. They were discussing a suitable date to take their lambs to market, following the slow trickle of births through late February and March. At just eight weeks old, they would be sold on, some for fattening up, others straight to the slaughter house. With the enhanced payments from the Government supply chain to feed the army in France, it was going to be a good spring for them. As they chatted, Edward's ears pricked up, catching the familiar sound of the latch on the parlour door as it opened. In full conversation, he stood, thinking the wind had blown it open. However, as he turned, he could see a figure standing in the doorway. Edward's mouth dropped open, stunned, as the broad smile checked his conversation in mid-flow, then, running over to greet his dear sister. He wrapped his arms around her, tightly.

'Oh my God, Edward, look at you. Why didn't you write to tell me you were coming?' he said. Ed dropped her kit bag and hugged him back before answering. 'Well, I thought I would surprise you,' she said as David walked across to greet her.

'Good to see you, Edward, welcome home,' he said, reaching forward to shake the hand that was offered to him.

The welcome was all that Edwina had hoped for, and she took off her cap and headed towards the warm fire she had missed so much. As she turned to face her sibling, she watched as they both looked her up and down.

'So how long does one of the King's soldiers have to wait to get a mug of tea round here?' she said. Edward laughed and placed the kettle back on the range and prepared the pot.

'So how long do you have?' said David.

'I must report to Shorncliffe Barracks on the Kent coast next Wednesday afternoon, ready to catch a boat to France. So, I need to leave here on

Wednesday morning to catch the eleven thirty train from Cirencester. I have three full days to stretch my legs and help you here. You must tell me all you have been up to, sis, and –'

Edward held his hand up, stopping her dead.

'For goodness sake, you've hardly got through the door! There is plenty of time for that. You have to tell us all about your training first. Now sit down and get warm. Have you eaten?' he asked, as Ed removed her tunic, the army bracers showing stark against her greying long-sleeved undershirt. She stood with her back to the fire as Edward touched her arm and smiled.

'No,' she said. 'I'm starving,' as she glanced around the room to see if anything had changed.

'Forget the tea, how about a beer?' suggested David.

'Yes, that's more like it,' said Ed, and David walked into the pantry to retrieve the large jug stored there. He poured three mugs from it and placed Ed's on the table, passing one to the new arrival, before dropping into his armchair inhaling the aroma of the delicious supper to come. They stood chatting for several minutes until Edward announced their meal was ready and spooned the stew into three large white dishes, steam rising gently up to the stained ceiling above. On this occasion Edward asked that they say grace, and thanked God for bringing Ed home safely. They then tucked into a glorious meal of mutton from a sheep that they had killed the previous week.

Edwina was the slowest to eat as she had to answer their constant questions. She talked about the day she left, the journey to Bristol, the meeting with Frank Smith who had become her greatest friend and spoke of living with many people in a small billet. She mentioned all the soldering skills she had learnt and the rifle range, where she had shone. They sat and listened, watching Ed as she finished her stew, finally mopping up the last of the gravy in her bowl.

David had enjoyed the meal and had listened intently to the many stories, wishing at that moment that he also could have gone to war. He felt uncomfortable about being one of those left behind, not an easy pill for him to swallow, but now he was providing a worthwhile service to the men at the front. He yawned suddenly and then stood, telling them both that he was off to bed. Neither of them seemed to object, and David said his goodnights before leaving the two siblings staring at each other across the table.

Ed began smiling again, noticing how her brother had changed, quite taken aback at how he had evolved in such a short space of time. He now looked like a woman in every way, his hair now onto his shoulders, and he looked better in her old dress than she ever did. It would seem they had swopped lives successfully, and more importantly, they were both happy about it. They chatted for over an hour, then Edward yawned and said it was time for bed.

'What time are we up tomorrow, Ed?' said Edwina. 'I would like to get back into things on the farm, assuming you don't mind.'

'Slow down. You are on leave, remember. You should take a walk to the village to see Bryan first, and while you're down there invite him to supper tomorrow night; we have plenty. After all, it is your first morning back, you deserve an extra hour in bed, at least,' he said. 'How about you get the sausages and eggs going for eight o'clock, then take a walk to see Bryan after that? You can always start work later if you wish.'

'Well, how can I refuse, sounds like a plan.' And she yawned widely, too, stretching her arms skywards. 'OK, bed then,' she said.

'Oh, hang on, your bed is not made up,' said Edward.

'Hey, that's no problem, I'll sort that. You go up, I just want to sit a while.'

As Edward rose, he trailed his hand across his sister's shoulders, holding his fingers on her neck for just a moment longer than normal. 'Night, Ed, its lovely to have you back,' he whispered close to her ear, and without looking back he disappeared into the dark hallway, the faint glow from the candle flickering as he went.

Ed sat watching the glowing embers in the hearth for several minutes, the heat still radiating out onto her legs, before placing three large logs on top of the fire to keep it in for the night. She wondered where the last six weeks had gone and was more than thrilled that it had passed without incident. How she had managed it, God only knew, but ahead lay the biggest challenge of her life, the trenches of Flanders and the Hun! On that last thought, she snuffed out all the candles in the room bar one, collected her kit bag and set off up the stairs.

The next morning, she walked down into the village in full uniform. Many people stopped to chat as she headed to the church. Bryan didn't answer the vestry door, so she knocked louder several times, but to no avail. She pulled out her notebook from her top pocket and left a note telling him to come to supper, signing it Ed. Before heading back, she wandered along the main street and went into the village shop. Mr Spottiswood leapt from behind his counter to greet her.

'What a surprise, welcome back, Edward, how long do you have?'

'Oh, just a few days, Mr Spottiswood. How are you?'

'We are all fine, son, all fine. Did you need anything?'

Ed looked around the shop and took some bacon, some pickles and several bars of chocolate and reached for the wage packet that she had placed in her inside pocket. 'Can I settle up the farm's account, please, Mr Spottiswood?' she asked, and cleared the whole month's bill.

As she left, Ed wished them all well, and then she wandered slowly back up the road before crossing the street onto the track up to the farm. She was surprised how fit she felt and took long strides up the hill, all the way back to the small farm gate. On her return, she could see David and Edward in the top field, herding the lambs down towards the barn, but by the time she had changed into her old clothes, they were back, kicking the muck from their boots and calling for tea! Ed joined them at work for the rest of the day until dusk and enjoyed every minute of it. It was like old times, as they retreated into the warm kitchen.

As Edward began preparing supper, Ed disappeared upstairs to change back into her uniform. She thought Bryan would appreciate it. Peering through the window, she saw a familiar shape coming up the hill. She washed quickly and changed, but before she could get back downstairs, she could hear a hearty laugh ringing out below.

'Where is Edward?' Bryan shouted loudly. Ed ran down the single flight of stairs and burst into the room, Bryan's faced gleaming at her as he stepped forward.

He held her by both shoulders, nodding his head several times, and Ed was sure she saw a tear slide down his cheek.

'Edward,' he said with a huge grin. 'It's wonderful to see you. How long do you have?' not releasing his grip for a single second.

'Two more days, I have to leave on Wednesday morning,' she said.

'We must talk. How was the training, was it all you expected? When do you go to France?' he said.

But Ed held her hand up, shaking her head. 'Wow,' she said. 'Let's have some home-made brew, it's been a long time since we have had a beer together.

While Edward and David sped around the kitchen, preparing supper, Ed fed Bryan all the details of her short army career. It was a warming time for this amazing young woman and Bryan recognised an immense change in her. The vicar's dinner, as it was jokingly called, was an evening of laughter and anecdotes for all, and Ed talked about the regiment and the pubs of Bristol! She held her audience in her hands, celebrating her success at the range and her sniper selection course. They all listened, totally engrossed, for several hours, until Bryan decided it was time for him to leave. As he stood, he swayed sideways slightly, catching himself before he fell by hanging onto the doorframe, being very much the worse for wear. They shook hands warmly before he left them and headed out into the darkness.

Over the following two days, Ed found herself back doing what she loved most in life. She relished the opportunity to be working in the fields; mending gates and fences and working with the animals. It was in her blood and she knew that one day she wanted to return and be a farmer once again!

Wednesday morning came far too quickly for Edward, but Ed, was ready for her next challenge. It was certainly more difficult for Edward to say goodbye to her this time, knowing she was now properly off to war. David shook Ed's hand before heading out, leaving them to say their farewells privately. Ed threw her kit bag over her shoulder and walked over to Edward throwing his arm across one shoulder. They didn't speak, they didn't have to. Edwina then pulled away and left the kitchen, walking briskly away down the hill from the farm. She didn't look back.

Chapter 17

It was the middle of May 1916, when twenty hopeful soldiers, many of them just out of training, gathered on the first morning of the sniper selection course in Linghem, France. A sergeant with a full head of white hair and well into his forties ticked names off at the doorway as people arrived, before waving them in to sit and wait for the course officer. Ed and Frank had travelled together from Kent and now sat in the front row of the classroom, housed in the old village schoolhouse. The group were largely silent, except for one chap who had plenty to say and was tipping back on his chair at an almost impossible angle, telling all who might be interested how good a shot he was. Frank looked across at Ed and rolled his eyes. 'There's always one' he said.

Around the room posters were hanging on all four walls, mostly of differing landscapes, with several exploded drawings of rifles and, on the far wall, a picture of a telescopic sight, something that Ed hadn't seen before. In one corner sat a huge pile of old clothes and sacking, with some wooden boxes full of rolls of paper. Pinned in the centre of the blackboard at the front, there was a single rifle target. It sat just below the name of Major Hesketh-Pritchard, which was written in chalk and was the focus of all the eyes in the room. This single target had five neat bullet holes at the very centre, all within a tiny grouping smaller than a shilling!

'Quite some shooting,' Ed said to Frank from the side of her mouth without turning. He nodded slowly, but the bloke at the next table who had overheard, thought little of it.

'It's only an inch grouping.' He said cockily and folded his arms. Frank looked at Ed and shook his head slightly, making her smile.

'I wonder how far he was away from the target,' Frank replied.

'It could be the best shooting I have ever seen,' Ed said.

'Rubbish, I could do better than that.' said the mouthy soldier again.

At the back of the room, the sergeant sat looking at his watch fidgeting. It was just after 8 a.m.

Without notice, the door suddenly sprang open, slamming back against the wall with a crash, making them start. A tall, gangly officer charged into the room, in full khaki uniform, carrying a roll of papers under his arm. He was calling his dog as he entered. The dog, wagging his tale excitedly, was interrupted by the smells of various legs that stuck out down the aisle, and sniffed them all as he came towards his master. The sergeant threw up a salute and shouted 'Attention', but the officer waved his order away.

'Sit down, sit down,' he said in a casual manner and dropped the papers onto the desk; some falling to the floor, the dog immediately jumping on them as if it was a game. 'Max,' shouted the officer, and told him to lie down, which he did, instantly, but on top of the rolls of paper, focussing on his master expectantly.

'Welcome, gentlemen,' said the officer. 'For those who don't know me, I am Lieutenant Cavanagh of the Grenadier Guards and I am your course officer and I apologise for being late.' He paused, looking down at his notebook. 'There is a great deal to get through today so let's get started. Firstly, you all need to complete some paperwork, which Sergeant Johnson will hand out to you.'

The sergeant stood up quickly and rushed forward to gather the paperwork from the desk, before turning to hand out three sheets to each man and a pencil. The officer whose world they were about to step into, was in his mid-twenties, with a moustache that wound side wards across his cheeks, and a tight curl at each end. Ed remembered him from the range, and thought he was a bit of a toff, as he pronounced some of his words in a very unusual way! He was, however, very relaxed as he parked his backside on the corner of the desk and took off his cap, laying it down next to him. He looked round the room, and once the sergeant had delivered all the paperwork, the lieutenant told the men to relax and sit at ease and to remove their head dress. He began by informing them that the training had been designed by Major Hesketh-Pritchard who had been ordered by General Haig himself to form an effective training programme to mastermind a sniper squadron. Soldiers would be selected on ability only, following a range shoot at varying distances. Those who were successful, would immediately attend a six-week training course, starting the following day. He then asked each man to complete the paperwork and stayed quiet. On completion, the sergeant collected everything up, before handing it to the officer.

The next hour and a half was taken up with a detailed description of the course content and what was expected of them all. Lieutenant Cavanagh explained that the bar had been set deliberately high, and that people would indeed fail at every stage, as everyone had to meet the exacting standards necessary. He had a slow but deliberate tone, catching everyone's eyes as he spoke, commanding their full attention.

'The three main components will be camouflage and concealment, observation and scouting, and finally target shooting. Each week, tests will be set and those not attaining a pass will be returned to their regiments. After six weeks, those passing each phase will come with me to the front line where you will be attached to various regiments according to need.' He stressed the importance of high standards, explained the precise structure and design of the course, with certain incentives along the way. He expressed a desire for them not to compete with each other, but to value the man next to them and learn from each other. He highlighted the importance of teamwork and how it would ultimately be the framework for success, and suggested that the best shot wouldn't necessarily pass, if he was not a team player. After some lengthy chats, the group were dismissed for a brew at the canteen tent just across the yard. This was the first time they'd had a chance to chat amongst themselves and whilst some smoked, others grabbed their tea and sat talking. Afterwards, they gathered at the vehicle compound for transport to the range for their shooting assessment. Both Ed and Frank were keen to get started and chatted cheerfully to the other chaps on the short journey, hoping they hadn't come all this way to be sent packing at the first hurdle!

On arriving at the range, Sergeant Johnson split them into two groups of ten. To the rear, a line of twenty shiny new SMLE Lee Enfield Rifles were laid out on two tables, all with the new telescopic sight. Two corporals ran through the drills competently, allowing them all time to set their sights to suit themselves individually before the test fire began. In turn, they all shot the first five rounds into a target, to find their fall of shot. The second five rounds were used as their final practice zero before the test began.

Ed stayed at Range A, while Frank was sent with nine other hopefuls across to Range B, some four hundred yards to the east. As they ran across, Ed focussed on what she must now do, not thinking of anything or anyone else! She had to impress or would be returned to their regiment that very day.

The sergeant paired everyone off, Ed finding herself at the far end acting as observer to the one person she didn't wish to be with – the noisy bloke with the loud mouth from earlier! She lay down beside him, introducing herself and wishing him good luck, but without looking at her he answered with an air of arrogance.

'Don't need your good luck, mate, this will be easy!' he said, not taking his eyes off the target. As everyone settled down on the point, the shoot began.

'With a clip of five rounds, load,' shouted the corporal. 'In your own time, go on.' There was a long pause before bullets started reaching their targets, one hundred yards away. Ed peered through the binoculars to see the fall of the shot for her man and told him where they fell after each round.

'Bollocks,' snarled the chap after the second shot, 'I snatched that one,' before settling back to take aim once again. When all was done, the flag was raised and everyone walked down the range to see the groupings on their respective targets, including the observers. As they trotted down, Ed tried again to converse with the man, but he didn't respond, just sped up, reaching the target several feet ahead of her. As she came up behind him and peered over his shoulder, she could hear him swearing loudly because his shots were scattered all over the target. At that moment, a corporal came up and stood with his hands on his hips, shaking his head.

'Your grouping is rubbish, Becket,' he said, measuring the distance from the centre with his apparatus. 'You're way to the left here and then off to the right and then high. Hold your eye steady on the sight and make love to the trigger, squeeze it gently man, don't let the rifle control you. OK, change targets,' and he moved off down the line to the next man.

Ed was about to offer her advice once again, but as she opened her mouth to speak, he looked at her and said, 'Don't need your help, mate,' and pulled out the target before heading back up to the firing line, leaving Ed standing alone. She shook her head and mumbled to herself before placing a new target into the slot and followed him back up to the point, ten yards or so behind him. When everyone was back, they resumed their positions, the corporal shouting for their attention.

'OK, chaps, don't forget your basic drills and remember to pull the weapon firmly into the shoulder and don't, anticipate it. Hold onto that last breath and only then squeeze the trigger. Listen also to your observer as you will rely on them in the field at all times.' As Ed lay down, she waited for a response, any response, but no, her chap just focussed on his target, awaiting the order to fire. All the riflemen down the line adjusted their sights and lay down for their second attempt, before the order came to load, and shooting began at will. On reaching the butts the second time, Ed's partner was furious with his grouping and was shaking his head, blaming the rifle. 'It's a crap rifle, mate,' he said. And once the corporal had inspected his target, he walked off back towards the firing line, dragging the wooden target in the dirt behind him. Ed changed the target once again just as the shooter was called back by the rather annoyed NCO.

'What's going on, private Becket, I need to see your target, get back here.' The man stopped dead in his tracks and looked skywards. He turned slowly back around and walked the five or six paces to where the corporal stood, looking miserable. Ed had lost interest in him after that and was soon back at the firing point, her partner still some fifty yards down the range, the NCO walking behind him shaking his head. As he approached Ed, he sat down behind her.

'Can I give you some advice?' she said to him kindly.

'What do you know, you're just a boy?' he said and looked away.

'Well, I do know about shooting and just thought I could help,' she said with one last effort.

'Don't need your bloody help,' came his response and he lowered his head once more without further comment. Ed pursed her lips and thought 'do it on your own then' and turned her binoculars over to the other range to see if she could recognise Frank, but they were at the butts, so it was all a bit of a blur. Needless to say, the chap failed both his shoots, gaining at best only a four-inch grouping, not good enough at one hundred yards to pass this first exercise. Later he would find out his fate.

It was now Ed's turn and she was keen to prove it was down to the individual who controlled the rifle, nothing else, and focussed on the job ahead. She took her time on her first shot, never flinching as the rifle butt thumped into her shoulder, controlling her breathing as she had done a thousand times before. Her next four shots were better, and she was confident she had done well. When she arrived at the butts, she saw her grouping was a tight two inches, with a single shot slightly high. As she admired her work, the corporal came up behind her.

'Good shooting, Mitchell, but hold every shot, you can't afford to let one get away.' He adjusted her sight mounting to move her shot over and gave her rifle back to her. 'That should put you right,' he said, and she walked briskly back up to the firing point for her second five rounds.

She wanted to prove her worth and so shut everything else away, other than her rifle, the target and her instructor. The order soon came to load, and then 'Go on'. She pulled the rifle in tight once again, closing off the outside world. With her left eye closed, she slowly took her final breath and gently squeezed the trigger. She cocked her weapon and paused before repeating the whole process, until her magazine was empty. The rest of the men finished a good minute before her and they were cleared, before heading down to the targets. She was nervous as she approached, as what came next would decide her fate.

Her worries were short-lived. Her observer, Becket, looked on in bewilderment. 'How the fucking hell did you do that?' he exclaimed.

'Well, just followed my instincts and remembered my skills from my years on the farm,' she said, smirking to herself as the NCO came and measured her group. He pulled out several rings of copper; her shots fitting inside the two-inch ring comfortably. He reached for the one-inch ring, and all five rounds faced him.

'Great shooting, Mitchell, well done, lad.' She felt her observer's eyes piercing her back, but didn't look up, just smiled and headed back to the point.

After being cleared, they all walked over to the trucks and she could see Frank's team were already gathered. He smiled at her as she approached.

'How did you get on, Frank' she said.

'One-and-a-half-inch grouping and I passed,' he said. 'How about you?' he asked.

'One inch,' she said proudly, and he punched her gently on the shoulder. He offered his hand and they squeezed each other's in competition, Ed giving in to his superior grip! 'Ah, I will beat you yet, Frank,' she said, smiling, enjoying the moment. After a few minutes, following a short conference of the corporals and the sergeant, they were called in to receive the results.

'OK, some good shooting today, men, but sadly some of you have failed to reach the required standard. So, the following five people will be returning to their regiments, transport leaves at fifteen hundred hours.' He then read out the names of the unlucky ones, which included Private Becket. No loss there, Ed thought.

The fifteen men that survived the initial test were being housed on the top floor of an old hotel in the centre of the village that had been acquired by the British military for just this purpose. Ed, Frank and five others were first up to the top floor, as the other truck had stopped outside a small French café at the far end of the village. This allowed a certain amount of room selection to take place before the rest arrived. The seven of them quickly looked the place over, four of the lads from the same regiment wanting to stay together and took a fancy to a large room overlooking the village at the front, leaving the three of them to view the rooms to the rear. Frank saw an opportunity and suggested folding up one of the cots in the other four-bed room to create more space for them. They dashed down to get their kit and set up home for the next month or so, in relative comfort.

As they ran back up to their billet, Frank threw himself onto the bed by the far wall. 'Make the most of it,' it will be last bed you will have for a long while,' said Ed, unpacking her belongings as the other lads were heading up the stairs.

'I'm George, chaps, George Palmer,' said the other man in their room, laughing. They shook his hand, introducing themselves, grinning to each other.

'What regiment are you from, George?'

'5th Battalion, Lincolnshire Regiment. Only finished training last week,' he said proudly. 'And you?'

'We are both from the 2nd/5th Gloucesters,' said Frank. 'We only finished last week, too, trained in Bristol.'

As they chatted, they carried on sorting themselves out, before one of the corporals came up to their floor and called them all down to the dining room at the rear of the building for a briefing. Once they were all sitting down, he stood by the door and looked them over before the staff sergeant spoke.

'OK, chaps, I am Staff Sergeant Phillips, Bob to my friends and lovers, Staff to you lot. I am one of the senior instructors for the course and this will be your home for the next six weeks. I trust you all make the grade and I should say well done at the range, you all did well. The course starts in earnest tomorrow, as you know, so tonight is a free evening. However, you should regard this accommodation as a military barracks, and so you are not permitted to go into town as that requires a leave pass, which haven't arrived. If anyone fails to comply with verbal or written orders, you will be sent back to your regiments with your tail between your legs; there will be no second chances. So, don't, let the call of French ladies of the night beckon you from the street below. They no doubt could use some of your money but keep it in your pockets, chaps, for another night! Any women found in your billet will mean an immediate RTU. Now, the whole building, which was a hotel, has been acquired by the army, and the instructors, me included, are all billeted on the floor below you, so don't make a bloody noise as we will hear every word. Meals will be served in here at zero six thirty and eighteen hundred hours daily, your midday meal will be delivered wherever we happen to be at the time. This is a seven day a week course and each day you will fall in outside at zero eight hundred hours, finishing around seventeen thirty. Sundays will commence at ten hundred, after the morning church service and finish at fifteen thirty to allow for some personal admin and washing your bloody socks. Cleanliness is godliness, chaps, don't let the side down. Any questions?' The room stayed silent as they all absorbed what lay ahead.

'OK, good,' he said, referring to his notes. 'Now, it is a key aim for you all to achieve a level of expertise well above that for the average Tommy. In essence, you will be specialists and you will be put through a variety of key training practices that will provide you with the skills required to kill an enemy in any environment. This role is still developing, so as time goes on, we can expect to adjust our tactics according to what the Germans throw at us. Flexibility within our tasks will be paramount and have no doubts, gentlemen, this will be the most challenging job any of you will have ever done. But that all starts tomorrow,' he said. 'Tonight, is your time, so get sorted out and start getting to know each other, as teamwork will play a key role in the success or failure of the sniper teams. When you are paired off, you will need to know your partner better than you know yourself, so you can communicate in the field with hand signals and gestures, almost knowing what each chap is thinking. Use the time wisely, men, and enjoy your evening,' and he collected his papers, turned and left the room, just as one of the chaps at the back, smirking, said, 'Will you be up to tuck us in later, Staff?' Faces turned to each other, eyes wide, mouths open, before laughter ripped through the room, the sound of the staff sergeant's feet never faltering on the steps as he disappeared, his back masking the smile he had on his face.

On the first morning, following breakfast, they formed up outside the old hotel that, in daylight, was revealed as clearly having seen better days. In spite of a rather drab look and paint peeling off the doors and windows, it was still vastly better than anywhere at the front. As they waited for the NCO, drizzle started to fall, and they moved under the veranda. The duty corporal finally appeared and began reading out various instructions about the day, including their pairings. The training team had coupled men from their own regiments together, and to their great delight Frank and Ed had been paired off. When he had finished, they fell in on the road and marched off, passing many locals along the way. Some doffed their hats politely or waved, and several young girls standing outside the *boulangerie* watched them closely with eager eyes, giggling as one of the chaps blew them a kiss.

On reaching the old school, they saw Staff Sergeant Phillips waiting outside. He instructed them to form a queue. One by one they entered the temporary armoury to sign for their rifles, before clambering aboard the waiting truck. Ten minutes later they arrived at the one-hundred-yard range for a morning of zeroing their weapons. They would shoot ten groups of five rounds alternately, using each other to assess abilities and ways to improve. The instructors monitored and advised them, too, and they slowly got to know their new best friend! Their rifle would now go everywhere with them, at all times, no matter where they went, and anyone not committing to this policy would feel the full weight of the instructors boot. Soon it would feel like they were undressed without it!

The course had been designed in two distinct parts. Mornings would always be range work where the men would be put through various drills and practices, shooting at distances up to four hundred yards. Each afternoon there would be lessons and drills on camouflage and concealment, observation, movement in the field and living under duress for long periods. This was especially pertinent as part of the new role included moving into sniper positions, within No Man's land. On the last day of the first week, they learned how to construct some camouflaged clothing, called a ghillie suit. It was made of sacking, which was enhanced with string, different strands of cloth and stained with oil and paint. This was designed to break up the outline of the body but had the added advantage of providing extra insulation on cold nights.

Over time, the range work became rather repetitious, but shooting in different positions, sometimes over obstacles, at various distances and offering a range of targets, did keep them interested. Each man was expected to hone his personal skills so that eventually he could make a one-inch group at two hundred yards. A very tall order for some, but fully achievable for those expert shots. Ed, who had been shooting rabbits across the fields since she was nine, found these longer distances fairly straightforward and continued to use her own technique of wrapping the sling around her left arm to pull her arm into the stock. This also helped to pull the butt firmly into her shoulder. One of the corporals was less than convinced, until she repeated her result several times over, knocking his doubts away. With coaching to slow the heart rate down with passive breathing, everyone improved throughout the first few weeks. The pairs rotated at each change, so both became efficient in the roles of war. With the empty cylinders piling up beside them each day, they felt part of something really important and longed to be in action.

Firing from the custom-built trench system, set at the back of the ranges provided a realism they hadn't experienced before, especially when battle simulations were used. This created real-life experiences similar to what they could expect, and as the dirt flew with life changing explosives going off all around them, they soon knew what to expect. These initial live battle experiences were a frightening time for many and required a sternness beyond anything Ed had ever endured before. As shells burst overhead, they would crawl a set route, through a simulated No Man's Land battle area, with the incredible noise and smoke grenades dropped for effect, making it all feel very real. They soon became an efficient fighting unit, as each new skill was learnt. And this was only practice!

As the weeks flew by, they were starting to become very accomplished at firing accurately from three hundred yards to the centre of any target, which were made smaller every Friday. Ed and several others hit each one in turn, throughout the range mornings, no matter how small they got. Some, however, were less able, and as the qualifying standards increased, they started to lose more and more men, leaving only twelve to continue into the fourth week.

Entering the middle phase of the course, the standards were stepped up, once again. They would now be instructed in personal disciplines in advance positions, staying out through the night in battle conditions in a firing position, and would be introduced to reconnaissance and information gathering. This differed from their more regular role but would become a vital part of the execution of any task. On the last day of that week, without warning, they were fired upon by a fictitious enemy position, from a controlled area. Ed and Frank found this practice extremely frightening, but soon adapted and kept their heads down. They had earned their supper that night!

Care of their weapons during any operation was absolutely crucial to ensure they would always fire when needed. It was vital they were kept lightly oiled, especially the working parts, but the barrel had to be kept dry, to avoid smoke detection. This was achieved by pulling a narrow piece of cloth attached to a pull-though cord down the barrel length several times. Observer pairings now came into their own and final selections for the front were now considered. It had been clear to the OC that Frank and Ed worked well together, so to their delight they were paired permanently.

Week five focussed on shooting from standing and kneeling at all three distances, with the introduction of dawn approaches to different locations. The observers provided vital information on wind direction and speed, unexpected issues that the sniper might not see, and always protected their rear. Their ability to do this without being seen was an immensely testing period for them, especially within a trench formation, as putting one's head above the parapet was a call to death! Observation skills and the use of binoculars, plus the new telescopic sights, were all vital to beat Jerry at his own game. They had come on well in the few short weeks and were now solid and reliable shots under pressure, good at camouflage and concealment and reliable observers.

On the last week of the course, they had a series of long stalks into positions under the cover of darkness. These combined all they had been taught, demonstrating individual skills to become an army sniper! This was followed by a four-hundred-yard shooting competition which Ed won by a whisker, obtaining best shot on course. At close of play on the final Thursday, the major visited them at the range, to give out the certificates and offer some words of encouragement for what lay ahead. He advised that they would be sent forward to the front at the weekend so had a single day to sort their kit and equipment before heading off. With a grin, he also suggested they make the best of the local café in the village as it might be some time before they got another chance, to have a beer or a woman, in whatever order they wished!

It turned out that Frank and Ed were to be attached to the 2nd/5th Battalion, Royal Gloucester Regiment, and Lieutenant Cavanagh was to be their Sniper Officer. They returned to their accommodation that afternoon in high spirits, before grabbing some food and heading off to the village with the rest of the lads.

It seemed that many British soldiers had the same idea that night, and the cheap wine encouraged many to tell stories before some broke into song. Several ladies of the night were kissed by those prepared to fill their open hands with francs, resulting in several of the chaps disappearing for a while, before scurrying back with red faces and empty pockets. They were some distance from the front line, but tonight they could hear the sound of distant shelling long into the night. They sat outside, drinking merrily for several hours, enjoying each other's company and celebrating their achievements. They had spent little of their hard-earned wages so far and gave generous tips to the serving girls. Ed knew she had drunk too much and when Frank challenged them all to an arm wrestle competition, she was keen to join in.

Unfortunately for Frank, Ed beat him hands down, her strong shoulders from all her heavy work on the farm over many years proving just too much for him, even though he had a bigger frame. He laughed it off, along with all the other chaps, as good friends would, but when she was not expecting it, he dived at her, dragging her to the ground and challenging her instead to a wrestling match! She was not expecting this and suddenly found him sitting on top of her, holding her tightly down on the ground by her wrists, laughing. She tried to lift her arms, but he had them pinned down, so she was pretty helpless! She faked a lift to his left, causing him to lean over, and then she suddenly raised her right side, tossing him down a grassy bank, where he rolled over several times before reaching the bottom. Exhilarated by this, and being egged on by the others, she charged after him to gain an advantage, landing on top of him at the bottom of the slope. She grabbed him round his neck and wrapped her legs around his middle, as he reached up for grip.

'Now who's in charge?' she said, gritting her teeth. But seconds later, he pushed his arm under hers and then twisted round, lifting her bodily over his head into the long grass beyond. She screeched with laughter as she flew over him and he lurched forward to gain his advantage. He reached around her body with his long arms, squeezing her tightly as she laughed and wriggled to loosen his grip. With their bodies entwined, he slipped around Ed's back and pushed his arm down to lift her upwards, by reaching through under her crotch from behind. As he started to pull her upwards from underneath, he suddenly stopped dead, withdrawing his hand. Ed panted for a few seconds before realising what had happened. He sat back up, looking at her, panting heavily, spittle hanging from his mouth.

'What the fuck, Ed?' he said.

She rolled over and squatted up on her haunches, looking casually up to the others sitting on the benches at the top of the slope, before speaking.

'I can explain, Frank, please don't say anything,' she whispered. And they both stood up, Ed trying to laugh, hiding this catastrophic episode. Frank stared at her, bewildered, slapping one hand against the other as if to wipe the grass away as he got to his feet. She realised the other chaps above were paying little attention now and started walking up towards them.

She turned. 'Let's go back up, Frank, but please act naturally. I will explain on our way back to the digs.'

On reaching the top of the bank, he grabbed his glass of beer and drank it down in one hit!

'I think I'll call it a day, lads,' Frank said, not looking at Ed. She nodded her head, too, and said she would go back with him. The others decided to stay in the village for at least one more drink, leaving the two friends to saunter off down the lane back towards the hotel. Frank strode out with his long legs, creating a few yards between them. They didn't speak for several minutes until Ed trotted forward and pulled on Frank's arm. He stopped and turned to face her, pushing his hands deep into his trouser pockets.

'Listen, I never meant for you to find out like this, but I can explain, Frank, you owe me that at least. I have taken a grave risk to be here.'

He looked at her, puzzled, before looking around over his shoulder. 'But you're a bloody girl, Ed,' he said. 'How on earth have you got this far and fooled the army, fooled all of us?'

She stared at him, wondering how to explain it and why she had taken such a grave risk. 'Is that what you think I have done, fooled you? You're my best friend, Frank, the only real friend I have ever had. Have I let you down, have I lied to you?' she said sternly. 'I am protecting my brother, who isn't suited to army life and war, and I have taken a great risk in being here.'

Frank said nothing, just looked at her, frowning, trying to understand. 'Was that him at the medical day in Cirencester?' he asked.

'Yes, yes, that was him, we knew I couldn't attend that day, or our plan would have been scuppered,' she said quietly. 'That was why I didn't know you at the railway station, remember?'

There was a pause as Frank took his mind back to when he saw Ed standing alone in the queue. 'Oh my God, yes, I remember, you looked at me blankly and I couldn't understand why. But you look so alike. I would never have known.' He said. 'So, what happens now?' he said hesitantly, looking up and down the street.

Ed started walking slowly towards the hotel, Frank close beside her, not speaking, awaiting her response. She began to tell him her story about her weak and effeminate brother and his call-up to the army and how they devised a plan to swap lives! How she practised being a man and how she had resolved various women's issues to keep her secret safe. After several minutes, Frank stopped and looked sideways at her. She carried on and spoke of the support she got from her vicar and how he helped with all the preparations they had gone through to get this far! When she had finished, he spoke for the first time.

'Let me get this straight – you have done this to protect your brother, to save him from fighting in a war that all men should stand up for. You have put your life at risk and your brother's, too, if you're caught, and probably this vicar too. And now I know, am I at risk also? What do I do now, Ed, what do you want from me?' he said, shaking his head. 'I will clearly have to protect your secret, too, don't you see? I now see you in a different light, but I will say this, you're bloody amazing, mate, I just never knew, and I have known you for nearly three months.'

Ed looked at him, smiling at the hidden compliment, just for a moment, before she answered. If she got this wrong, she could lose him for good!

'I want nothing more than your friendship, Frank, and hopefully your loyalty. If you can't give me that as your partner, as a soldier and a sniper, you are not the man I thought you were. I will be indebted to you for the rest of my life if you will keep this to yourself. You have become the most important friend I have ever had. We can continue as a team within the squadron or you can shop me, it's your choice.'

Her words stunned him. He looked deep into her eyes and spoke carefully.

'We have a bond, Ed, I grant you that, a special bond at that, but what you're asking is, well, beyond anything I ever imagined. I respect you, Ed, and in fact I respect you more now I know, which in some ways makes it even more difficult. I feel we are a good team, the best.'

Ed looked at him, staring into his dark eyes. 'I have given my all to get here for my brother, who may well be shot as a coward or a deserter if this secret ever gets out. I want to be here in this war and with you by my side I have a confidence I have never felt before. I am good at this, Frank, we are good at this, you and I, and what's more, I trust you with my life!' she said as she stopped to sit on a seat by an old tree. He joined her and leant forward, rolling his hands together, staring at the floor. After a few minutes, he turned slightly and put his hand on her left shoulder, looking directly at her.

'You are right, of course. You are a better man than many we have met so far, and you are as good a soldier as any man I know. You're an excellent shot, Ed, and I am your friend, yes, your best friend I hope, and I will do all I can to keep this secret. But you must tell me everything, Ed, everything I need to know, no matter how small. The whole story from the beginning so if needed I can protect you, no matter how difficult it may be. I need to know it all.'

They stood up and she held her hand out, which he accepted warmly, before they continued walking. He heard her faint reply: 'Thanks. Frank, before they wandered off into the darkness.

Chapter 18

Edward was in his room, sitting at the dressing table, when a tap came on his door. He put down his hair brush and turned around slowly. 'Yes,' he said.

'It's me, Ed, can I ask you something?' Edward, rather surprised, wondered what David was doing outside his door, at this late hour?

'Just a minute, David,' he said, moving towards the door. He hesitated, putting his ear to the door just as another tap came, making him jump. He took a breath and opened it slowly, to see David with his candle in one hand and wearing a pair of striped pyjamas.

'Yes, what is it David, it's quite late you know?' he said, pulling his gown up under his chin.

'Sorry, Ed, it's just that I have a boil on my lower back that's been giving me a lot of jip, and I can't get to it. Could you take a look?' Edward, stared at him for a moment, feeling awkward.

'Oh, yes, I suppose I could, why don't you go down and I will see you in a minute.'

When Edward arrived, David had lit several candles and placed them on the Kitchen table. He was sitting on a chair facing away with his back to the light, his nightshirt off, leaning forward. Edward walked across to him, seeing the red lump from several feet away, right at the crease of his buttocks. It looked very sore, with a yellowy tinge in the middle, and looked like it was about to burst. Edward told him to stay put and went to fetch the old medical book from the bookcase, bringing it back to the table. He sat down and started looking through the index to find the page he needed. He read aloud to David what they were to do.

'OK, treatment for boils.' He read for several minutes, before standing up. 'Sounds easy enough,' said Edward. 'I will get some hot water and some clean cloths, you sit here.' Edward returned a few minutes later with a small bowl and asked David to pull his pyjama trousers down a little, before tucking a clean towel into them. His cold hands made David jump, making Ed laugh, taking the edge off this tricky moment. Edward took a piece of cloth and soaked it in the hot water before applying it over the boil, David flinching as it touched his skin. Edward bathed the boil for several minutes and then pushed a little and yellow pus poured out onto the cloth, causing David to yell. The pus was not a pleasant sight and smelt awful, Edward cringed as he mopped it up, but knew it wasn't all done yet.

'I think I need to push on it again, David, as there is still some more to come out.' Edward positioned himself and said, 'OK, on three.' David tensed his body before Edward suddenly, without warning, shouted, 'Three!' and squeezed firmly, pus oozing out onto the cloth followed by a spurt of blood. David stayed quiet this time, just bent forward slightly, tucking his chin on his chest.

'All done, think it's all out now, David. Are you OK?' she asked with a smile.

David was in so much pain, he lifted his head upwards, releasing his long-held breath, nodding gently, hardly having the strength to answer.

'Good one, Ed,' he said. 'I was waiting for the count and you go straight in on three!' he said, smiling.

'It was something my father always did, helps to get it done,' Edward said, grinning, and beginning to laugh. David swung his head around trying to keep a straight face, alas, Edwards giggling, made him slip into laughter himself.

'What are we, are we laughing at?' Edward said, staggering backwards.

'I don't know,' David said. 'It just seemed better than crying…' And off he went again, until their laughter slowly died away.

Wiping away the tears, David was pleased the boil was now gone. Edward dried the wound with a towel and applied a clean dressing, as instructed on page 264 of the medical hand book. As Edward cleared everything away, David slowly replaced his pyjama top and did up the top buttons. It was all over in a few minutes, but each time he'd touched David's skin he'd felt a strange warmth. A glow he didn't understand. He had never touched anyone, down there, before and now a strange feeling entranced him, that wouldn't go away.

Chapter 19

Their journey to the front line was one of true discovery. As the lorry struck north-east, it slowly penetrated the massed ranks of the rear echelons, the supply chain for the whole war. They realised what hell might look like, as mountains of equipment littered the sides of the road for many miles, piled well over head height, in what looked like total disarray. The faces of hundreds then thousands of men, with distant eyes betrayed the spirit they had expected. Some made an effort to wave as they passed by, others sat idle watching yet another batch of new blood, head to the front and, probably death. Frank and Ed gazed at the sight before them, absorbing the chaos for the first time.

Further up the road, they passed a large area to their left with row upon row of dark green pyramid tents, hundreds of them, all squashed into a small field surrounded by tall trees. To the side, they could see a dozen or more lines of horses tethered on ropes, their feeding sacks hanging loosely from their heads, their hooves swallowed up in thick mud. It was an odd vision, as it gave the impression their legs were cut short, and their skinny bodies indicated, it wasn't just the men having a tough war! They then saw many white tents of the Red Cross, the walls of some splashed with bright crimson stains, stretchers piled high awaiting the next arrivals. They continued for another mile and the great guns of the field artillery appeared, with huge piles of ammunition stacked high just behind the large rear wheels. Small rail tracks stretched backwards away from their positions, with tiny locomotives puffing gently along, dragging the heavy shells forward. Between the artillery positions and the front line, they saw more railway tracks and horses pulling carts with loads, far too heavy for their weary bodies, but being urged on all the same by battle weary soldiers. The vision saddened Ed a great deal, as coming from farming stock she always cared for her animals and this was a pitiful sight. There was no noise on the truck, no speaking, just every man in deep thought as they sped through this horror, until they were once again in clear countryside.

The rest of their journey forward was a little brighter as they came across different regiments and companies of troops scattered across wide areas, with stores and equipment at every turn. Ed was baffled how it was possible to obtain and transport so much equipment from England in such quantities and store it in such a small area. Feeding the tens of thousands of men, would have been a massive responsibility for someone, and she didn't understand how it was ever possible. But there it was for all to see, piled high in the French countryside, as far as the eye could see.

Suddenly, the vehicle stopped, and they were told it was their drop. Frank was the first to move and jumped down, turning quickly to catch his bag that was thrown almost before he had landed. Ed joined him in the mud, and they looked at each other, clutching their precious rifles and kit bags over their shoulders before heading to the HQ tent. They lifted the tent flap and asked a sergeant for directions to the 2nd/5th Gloucesters.

'Ah, new boys, eh, where are your orders, lads?' he said. They reached for their top pockets, both pulling out a single sheet of green paper and handing it over, before being pointed down into the trench system. 'Go right for about eight hundred yards then follow the sign to the left. Look for a small sign saying Gloucester town centre,' he said, laughing, before he turned back to his paperwork. Ed wasn't sure if he was joking, but nodded anyway and slipped away into the trench, Frank right behind her.

'Well, this is it, Ed,' Frank said over her shoulder, as the mud quickly covered their boots. They passed many soldiers along their route and saw for the first time how they lived and, in some cases, how they died. It was not that dissimilar to the training areas in Linghem, but on a massive scale, with so many men crammed into narrow holes in the ground, in the wet, in the cold, and in despair.

For the next thirty minutes, they walked slowly through a series of communication trenches as they headed forward, chatting briefly to the anonymous faces of men cowering over steaming pots of tea, while others asked of home. Water had now penetrated their long-legged putties, the mud so deep in places, their boots were engulfed in the bog! But it was not raining, so the men seemed in good spirits as they went about their day, and at one point an old sergeant stopped them to see if they knew the latest cricket score! At the next turn, they suddenly saw the sign, and smiled. The sergeant wasn't joking after all... Shortly after, they came across the familiar face of Corporal Fletcher from 1 Platoon.

'So, you have finally decided to show up and join us, have you?' he said.

'Hello, Corporal. Yes, we finished our sniper course last week. Do you know where Lieutenant Cavanagh might be?'

'Keep going straight on and then take the next right turn, his shell scrape is down on the left, I think,' and then he turned away to carry on cleaning his rifle.

They set off enthusiastically, realising they were now at the closest point to the enemy. It was a surreal moment, after many months of reading about it, they had now, finally arrived. A familiar voice suddenly piped up.

'All right, mates,' said one of the real characters of the company. Willie Lawrence had kept everyone in good spirits throughout training, his stories on a variety of subjects, holding his audience in the palm of his hands. If he hadn't done something, it wasn't worth doing, if he hadn't drunk it, it wasn't worth drinking and if he hadn't kissed a girl, she wasn't worth kissing! But in spite of his rather loud exterior, he was a splendid fellow and quickly rallied everyone around with an approving roar. With much back-slapping and laughter, cheering from some, and mugs of tea appearing from nowhere, they briefly chatted to the chaps and gloried in their stories. Sergeant Worrall, their platoon sergeant, heard the commotion and looked up, grinning at them from the end of the line, a cigarette stuffed through his large bushy moustache. Ed acknowledged him with a nod as their eyes met, before he came across to greet them. They all enjoyed this brief bit of respite, a gathering of friends.

Finishing their tea, they headed off further along the trench to find Lieutenant Cavanagh's narrow dugout. Frank wasn't sure of the etiquette so crouched down and called out his name. Within just a few seconds, the OC stepped out, half-dressed, smoking a cigar, with his blue bracers showing bright against his grey undershirt. He welcomed them into his little dug-out and they dropped their kit bags before bobbing down to enter the gloomy mud-walled hole in the ground. It was not spacious, about the size of a large cupboard, barely room to stand upright, with a short cot stretched along the wall, a ruffled blanket on top where the lieutenant had obviously been lying just a few moments before. To the side, a used shell case with cigar butts smelling the place out with stale tobacco was illuminated by two short candles, sitting in alcoves just above, in the wall. On the other side, a tiny table stood with an ammo box for a chair, and a piece of a broken mirror was pinned to the wall by a rusty nail. The officer's tunic and his greatcoat hung from a nail near the entrance, alongside his Smith & Wesson handgun and gas mask. A dark green army box, not unlike the ones they had used in training, stood by his cot, completing his possessions. For the next hour, Ed and Frank were briefed on the current situation and their orders for the next day. It turned out two of their number from training had already bought it the week before, sticking their heads up above the parapet, being killed by the same bullet! An example, the lieutenant said, of utter carelessness. He instructed them to use their old dugout, which was just along from his, as their shelter. Without warning, a mug appeared in the doorway, attached to the hand of a private who stuck his head round the tiny entrance.

'Tea, sir' said Jones.

'Thanks. Can you make two more for our new arrivals?' he asked. Jones looked at the two fresh faces and nodded, returning just a few moments later.

Lieutenant Cavanagh carefully explained that squadron orders were changing following new intelligence, and from Friday they had to explore into No Man's Land for the first time. They were ordered to set up an advanced sniper position and he confirmed they would be operating together, Mitchell as sniper, Smith as the observer. The new orders meant moving into position under the cover of darkness to locations yet to be identified, remaining in position for twenty-four to forty-eight hours. They both glanced at each other and grinned enthusiastically at the thought of what lay ahead, realising that all their specialist field training would now be tested to the full. At last the lieutenant finished, the tea dregs were cold, and they were excused.

When they stepped back outside, darkness was almost upon them and moved quickly down the trench system to find the now empty dugout. Frank entered, lighting a single candle that was sitting in an old food tin nailed to the post in the corner. The sudden flame startled a huge rat that immediately scurried away, down a narrow burrow in the corner. Frank peered around his new abode, and finding a lump of wood, hammered it into the hole just vacated by the rat. He stepped back to admire his handy work. 'Not quite the luxury of the digs in Linghem Ed?' he said grinning. But the dug-out was larger than he imagined it would be from the outside and had two narrow sleeping mats made of old duckboards on opposite sides, a few inches above the ground. 'At least we won't drown,' he said smirking. Ed had dropped her bag on the small bunk nearest the doorway, before sitting down for a moment, grinning in the gloom. Frank smiled back, before sorting out his kit.

'Why don't you find the supply sergeant, Ed, for some victuals and I will get a brew on.'

'Roger that,' she said and stood immediately, bumping her head on the earthen roof. When she got back, water was bubbling on the small fire, but Ed was largely empty handed, apart from a box of tea and some sugar. 'We are on central rations,' she said, as Frank poured the steaming water into their two metal mugs.

Before they visited their mates from 2 Platoon, they set about sorting themselves out and cleaning their rifles, before loading them with a clip of ammunition. Then, a familiar voice came from the entrance. Lieutenant Cavanagh crawled in, holding some small boxes of field rations. 'Food, chaps,' he said, dumping them onto the primitive bunk. 'These are only to be used when operating in No Man's land. They are not for general consumption. Dry rations, nothing special, bit like eating cardboard, but they will keep the wolf from the doors. Here is some ammunition, too, fifty rounds each.' As he left, he shouted, 'Briefing at eighteen hundred hours at HQ.' And was gone.

Stand-to was called at dusk and they jumped out of their shelter. Not sure where to stand, they used their common sense and simply joined their friends, leaning against the vast walls of mud on the leading edge of the trenches. It went quiet as darkness fell, men all around them just looking up to the sky with their own thoughts. They all waited, only seeing the man standing either side of them, watching, waiting. Then without warning, a loud whoosh shot upwards from a position behind them. A sky rocket was fired, then another, and light suddenly flooded the area to their front. No Man's Land was lit up and they watched with wide eyes, out into the night. Their war had finally begun.

Over the following days, they quickly got into the swing of things, catching up with the lads and listening carefully to each man telling his own story. It would seem, they had all learnt many valuable lessons, enduring hardship and overcoming some difficult times during their first seven weeks. They were told of the death of Private Cameron, the quiet lad from the train who had sobbed almost every night during the first two weeks of training. He had inadvertently stood with his head over the parapet for a few seconds, replacing sandbags to strengthen their position, when he was decapitated by an enemy sniper! This was just three days after they arrived. The second was a corporal from 1 Platoon, when an artillery shell exploded above them, and he wasn't quick enough to take cover! A rude awakening for them all, but strangely it had benefitted the company and morale seemed high.

Lieutenant Cavanagh decided not to use Frank and Ed straight away, instead letting them adapt to their surroundings and volunteering them to join the regular watch system, before giving them new orders. The days passed quickly to begin with, life soon becoming routine, as they learnt to live in this hell-hole with hundreds of others in close proximity. There was no privacy at all, and bodies were everywhere, some on watch, others repairing the trench walls and laying new duckboards along its length. Every four or five days, the company would rotate back to the rear, with other regiments coming forward, before returning a week or so later. This coupled with many working party's to re-supply ammunition and general supplies, generated lots of movement, and the constant walking to and fro by hundreds of men created paths of deep, thick mud, made worse whenever it rained. They however, stayed put.

Each day, soldiers would search for lice in the clothing and hair of their opposite numbers, and inspect themselves too, especially caring for their feet. Shaving in cold water took some getting used to, although some did the half and half method. This involved making a brew, drinking half and shaving in the remainder! Some luxury…

Life was indeed very primitive, but the Red Cross parcels from home that came from time to time, made all the difference. It was particularly memorable when, along with socks and scarves, a rich fruit cake or a letter from a young woman was discovered. The cakes were eaten by many, the letters read by the lucky finder, who would relish in reading it over and over, before getting the chance to answer his new long-distance love!

The latrine was the biggest shock to the system and was a ghastly sight. Positioned to one side of a trench system, way back down the line, it consisted of two logs fixed across a gap, one for the feet, the other for sitting on, allowing up to four at a time to take their morning shit. It was quite orderly as each man entered from one side, carefully easing himself across, would then perch on the top rail before unloading. Once his daily routine was done, he would slide across to the other side before throwing soil into the pit with a field shovel! It was certainly not a pleasant experience, and the flies were overwhelming. Ed found this whole episode all rather awkward, and would often wait until just after dusk, when most were cooking or getting some shut-eye, allowing a tiny bit of privacy for her, in an otherwise crowded existence. It was however more difficult to keep her balance in the dark, and a fall into the pit at this time, would be a catastrophe!

Apart from the shit trench, life was reasonable, when the sun shone. But, the daily bombardment of mortars would bring them all back to reality. The first week passed quickly and Ed managed to avoid any personal disasters, the small dugout she shared with Frank helping her to perform some of her toiletries, where one night, she explained to Frank about a woman's monthly period. He looked horrified, having no knowledge of this whatsoever, but diligently, whenever required, would sit in the entrance to have a fag, allowing Ed a few private moments.

On their first Sunday, an army padre visited them, wearing his dog collar under his khaki uniform. He looked a picture of health and significantly brightened their day. He told stories and jokes, cheering them all up no end and held brief prayers in small groups along the line, speaking of families torn apart by war. He carried with him a canvas bag, which he filled with letters as he went, to be posted later. At two o'clock that afternoon they were summoned to a rear ops room some eight hundred yards down the trench line for a briefing by Major Hesketh-Pritchard, their commanding officer. He provided information on the new tactic, which he called 48-2 patrols, based on forty-eight-hour sorties by two men, and they were to commence the very next day.

Ed and Frank, the only sniper pair in their sector, were briefed on their particular start position, the code words and the no-move-before timings. They were eager to get started after a week of sitting around. As they headed back to their dugout, an air of excitement bubbled in their minds. At last they would become proper snipers!

It was an overcast and damp evening as they formed up at twenty-three hundred, wearing their new ghillie suits, to the east of their position. They received a final briefing by the OC and carried with them their rifles, ammunition, a knife, a small digging implement, four flasks of water, six packs of dried rations, and some chocolate. Rations had been taken out of their wrappings to avoid noise so close to the enemy and were now contained in small linen bags ensconced in various pockets sewn into their ghillie suits. They were ready to begin their war.

They were to locate a suitable sniper position on an arc of eight to twelve degrees from their start point, a location of particular interest to the brigadier. This was to cover across from the advance trench some half a mile from their own lines. They were to stay put for thirty-six hours, unless compromised or they made a kill, before turning for home.

As they had their last kit inspection, making sure nothing on them made a sound when moving, their hearts pounded as they cocked their weapons and secured the safety catch. It was suddenly very real! Ed shook Frank's hand before they left, nodding, no words spoken. When they went over the top that first time, Ed led the way, Frank following just a foot behind her. As they slipped into the night, a young tommy, not any older than Ed, wished them good luck. Ed moved slowly forward, stopping after five body shuffles, her eyes wide, scanning the horizon and listening for movement. This she repeated over and over, until they were deep into this new strange land that smelled of death. Some twenty minutes later, she dropped down into a large shell hole, Frank sliding in behind her, watching his rear. She grabbed her compass and looked at the dial. She was on course, just nine degrees past north, that would be sufficient to reach her optimal destination. Pulling Frank in close, she made a circle with her finger and thumb, a well-practised signal to ask if he was OK. In return, he squeezed her hand, once, the answer she wanted. After taking a sip of water, they moved forward once again, listening for any movement. She then saw a large knoll on the bearing and crept up towards it, surprised how difficult the going was, as the thick mud from the recent rains acted like a slide at some points and like glue at others. It was terribly wet, and she was sure they must be leaving a trail behind them, like a snail on a frosty morning. Although it could help them on their return journey, she always had a nagging fear it could signpost their position to a German aircraft.

With eyes wide, staring into the dark for signs of wire, shell holes or Germans, they only had each other for company and would have to apply all their skills to stay alive. Ed, lying partly on her side, held her rifle by the stock in her right hand but nestled it on her left thigh, keeping it out of the mud. She retained the ability to pull the weapon forward at any time into a firing position, if she was ever compromised. Before long, they reached the knoll and stopped to listen. This process was repeated several times over. All was going well and as they got closer to the German lines, she was sure she could hear voices. After another hour had passed, sweating from their exertion, Ed stopped, feeling Frank's hand grab her ankle. They hadn't gone far, probably less than three hundred yards, but it was important they tried to calculate which direction the enemy trenches were. Five minutes passed without movement from anywhere then she twitched her foot gently, as practised many times, allowing Frank to know she was moving off. She crawled towards what she thought was a large crater to her front, but, as ever, the darkness played tricks on her brain and it turned out to be a tree lying on its side, blown up many moons ago.

She eased herself in behind it, confident the German lines were the other side, hoping they were well protected. She followed the tree along to the left and noticed a shallow dip beneath it, just wider than her arm, but couldn't see whether it went right underneath. To her right, she established that there was a bank of earth, protecting her flank, and she brought Frank close to whisper in his ear. They were well into the heart of No Man's Land and hopefully close enough to the enemy trenches to find a suitable position. Moving back along to the left again, she carefully started pulling earth back with her hand to make the small channel slightly wider, in the hope she could use it as a rifle chute. She wouldn't know this until first light but felt comfortable with their position and encouraged Frank to get some sleep, as she would do the first watch. He huddled down behind her and she took a sip of water, before listening for anything unusual. Over the next four hours they switched watches every hour, until the dim light from the rising sun alerted them both to the breaking day. Before dawn, they ate some biscuits and drank half a flask of water, the last for many hours. Their arc, she hoped, allowed a good line of sight, but she wouldn't know til morning.

As the sun slowly climbed, the gloom disappeared, Ed could finally see the visibility ahead was limited, but noticed a trench line off to her left and turned her rifle round and settled in for a long wait. As the sun rose fully over the next few hours, life was calm. No rain in sight and no surprises! Ed had been watching all morning and had on occasions seen a periscope and the top of several helmets, but never more than that.

At midday, they switched places, so Ed could rest and take a leak! Throughout the afternoon, nothing stirred until suddenly, far to their left, perhaps four hundred yards away, a single shot rang out and then silence once more. It startled them both, and for a brief second, their minds raced as they studied the arc to their front. Was that one of their own, they wondered, or perhaps a German had bought it. Ed resumed her position just after four o'clock for her last stint at point and was just peering down her sight for the first time when a head appeared. Moving her body over, she looked through the telescopic sight, her finger resting alongside the trigger guard. She kept both eyes open, watching carefully. She twitched her foot to alert Frank, who closed in and lay next to her. Suddenly the head appeared over the rim of the trench once again and she eased her safety catch off in silence, pulling the butt firmly into her shoulder, wrapping her sling tightly round her forearm. Keeping a watchful eye on the helmet ahead, her heart thumped heavily, vibrating up to her ears, as the reality dawned of what was about to happen! She curled her finger gently round the trigger and took the pressure, lining herself to the point where she expected the head to appear. It was a full minute before the head rose again, only a second or maybe two, but long enough for Ed's finger to react. She held her breath and squeezed the trigger all in one go, the crack when it came making Frank jump beside her. The bullet hit its target some two hundred yards to their front, the helmet dipped below the parapet and all was silent. Ed eased her breath from her lungs and slowly cocked her weapon again, Frank catching the spent round. Suddenly, a machine gun opened up, firing across their front. Then again off to their left, wild shooting, but indicating she had her first kill.

She watched as three, four then five periscopes rose up almost together as the German soldiers on the other end peered through the tunnelled glass boxes, but they were looking in the wrong direction to locate them. Ed lay perfectly still, looking along her sights, Frank touching her leg, waiting for her reaction. They lay still for over an hour and the many periscopes held their gaze, turning slowly left and then right to find their foe. Not today she thought, not tomorrow hopefully, and settled down for a long wait.

As the light slowly started to fade, luck came their way, as it started to rain! They remained still until full night had descended and then waited a further hour, before dropping back down below the tree, into a bomb crater. The rain would provide good cover for their withdrawal. As they turned for home, deep pools of water had formed in every dip in the ground. Their progress back was as per the book, only moving quickly when opportunities allowed, crawling back, one beside the other, watching at every turn. For a little over an hour they slid along in the dirt, until suddenly a voice called out '*Halt, who goes there?*'

Frank, now in the lead, stopped his forward motion and called back '*Friend.*'

'Advance, friend, and be recognised,' came the voice. As Frank crawled forward, he was stopped once again, and the voice came again: 'Stop friend, password *London.*'

Frank then answered, '*Amsterdam.*'

The soldier, doing his duty, then called them in one at a time and they slipped back into their own trenches, exhilarated at the outcome of their first successful op. They sat on the ground and shook each other's hand, grinning, before the sentry came over to ask them how long they had been out. They stood up, patted him on the shoulder and said, 'Can't tell you that, mate, or I would have to kill you,' Frank said with a grin, before laughing loudly.

They started to make their way back along the trench system to their own position, but Frank stopped and held out his hand. Ed looked at him.

'What?' she said holding out her hand, and he dropped the cylinder of her first German kill into her hand.

'A memento Ed, the first of many.' She smiled at him before tucking it into her pocket.

It was difficult under foot as they picked their way along the muddy walkways, tripping occasionally over the legs of sleeping soldiers. Some sentries challenged them as they crossed regimental boundaries, but within half an hour they were back in their own lines, this time greeted by a friendly face, that of Sergeant Worrall.

'What are you two up to?' he asked.

'Just returning from an op, sarge,' said Frank

'Oh, right oh, lads, did it go well?' he said quietly.

'It did sarge, it went very well,' said Frank grinning at him.

'OK, I suggest you go back down the line and get de-briefed and grab yourselves some food, see you chaps,' he said before settling back down.

They did exactly as ordered, finding a vast pot of hot tea and plenty of bread and jam at Company HQ where Lieutenant Cavanagh sat reading his book. As they entered the large dugout, he jumped up and greeted them cautiously, as they had only been out twenty-four hours. It was just after two in the morning, and whilst they drank tea, they told him of their exploits. Their first mission was a complete success.

The next morning, they were woken before daylight as the German bombardment began tearing up the silence, the earth shaking violently after each explosion. It was best just to keep their heads down, hoping to avoid a direct hit. Just over an hour later, all went quiet, and Frank dared to put his head out to see a fine morning, with blue sky above, while Ed lit the small a small fire to heat some water from her flask to make a brew. As Frank stepped outside, bodies started coming to life.

'Any luck?' said Corporal Baker, rolling his cigarette. Frank looked up and grinned at him, nodding. 'Yes corporal, our first kill.' He said with a grin. 'Good effort Frank, and stop calling me corporal, Bagsy, will do fine.' And he sat down to light his fag.

'Tea is brewing, Frank, give me your mug.'

'Make that three Ed,' he said, as Bagsy unclipped his mug from his belt order.

And so, the day began again, same routines, same food, same faces. Some of the lads used to say, 'Same shit, different day!'

As they wandered up the trench line a large flock of birds suddenly appeared, high above. They both stopped to admire their freedom, nature hadn't completely deserted them after all.

Arriving at the OC's dugout, they banged their fists on the timber post outside and were called in, their eyes taking a few moments to adjust to the darkness. 'Well done last night, chaps, I have already spoken with the major and he was chuffed that on your first sortie you shot a Jerry. Can you advise on any intelligence of your route and of enemy trenches, something I forgot to ask last night?'

As Frank and Ed relived their 'night out' the lieutenant took notes. They described how they found a good line through various old trenches and shell holes, before locating a fallen tree that provided a good position. Ed explained their line of attack and how patience had played out in their favour, with a clean shot late yesterday, just before dusk. Ed looked at the OC's map and pointed to where she thought they were, considering their departure point, bearing and time and distance. The lieutenant smiled as he wrote down their words, congratulating them once again on their fine work.

'OK, out again tomorrow night, chaps. It's a new moon, though, so there will be some light around, although it is due to rain through the evening.' He took out another map and a black and white aerial photograph and laid them on the table. 'I want you to try a new location,' he said, pointing to a site near a series of zigzagged enemy trenches. 'Here you can see them clearly, here and here,' he said pointing to the many trenches in view. 'You will need to recce it today and through tomorrow morning, through the periscopes at your start point. That is to be at Point Mike-Alpha, here, from the corner heading north-west. You should cross this track,' he said pointing. 'But it has several destroyed vehicles along the route, which potentially could be booby trapped. It's also littered with shell holes following repeated bombardments from both sides over many months in what was once a small wood. The enemy trench line is about six hundred yards, so you'll be on your bellies a lot longer than last night. This target has been selected as we have word that it is where senior officers have been gathering, possibly to recce a future attack. So, getting a high ranker, is, well, top drawer. OK, any questions?' Frank looked at Ed, but she got in first.

'Sir, we found last night that shooting at an angle, and not straight ahead, provided us with greater cover to our flank, plus seemed to confuse the enemy after the kill. They fired way off to our left and not at us at all. So, if it's ok with you, we will try that tactic again?' said Ed.

'That's interesting,' he said. 'It's really your choice Mitchell, but maybe we will talk about this with the squadron. Just make sure you come back safely.

'And, how long are we out for, sir?' said Ed.

'Same as before, short sorties for now, but plan for forty-eight hours. Get your rest and report to me tomorrow at noon for a final update.'

They picked up their gear and crawled out back into the light and unfortunately, they had to drop by the latrine en-route. It was the first time they had both shared the 'log' and the pit was now almost full, the engineers already digging the new one just beyond. As they sat together, Ed realised how well she had adapted and still no-one had the slightest inkling about her secret. Frank finished and carefully slid sideways to remove himself from his perch. As he stepped off, the log shuddered dramatically, Ed just managing to lurch forward to avoid falling back into the abyss! 'Thanks, Frank,' she said with a grin.

The next night was cold with a light breeze coming from the south-west. This had a certain disadvantage as any noise would drift right into the enemy trenches. As they set off light rain was falling, and they slipped into the night from the corner as instructed, Ed leading the way. Within ten minutes she had somehow got caught up in some awful wire, her ghillie suit becoming badly entangled, which required the use of cutters to free it. The noise must have drifted across to the enemy positions, and after waiting an hour they moved down into a small shell hole and stayed deadly still for a long while. They had hardly moved any distance, so decided to slip back the one hundred yards into their own lines. The sentry was more than surprised to see them and they quickly moved up the line to the west for a short distance, until they came across another north-west corner and set off again. They had lost valuable time but the route this time was clear of wire and they were able to move a little quicker. They knew they might well have alerted the German sentries, so paused regularly to listen and watch before moving on. It was some time before they assessed they were within distance and looked around for a suitable position. They had been out now for four hours and knew daylight was fast approaching. As Frank crawled up the eastern side of a large shell hole, he stopped abruptly, waving Ed back down. He stayed still for several minutes before slipping back down the slope next to where Ed lay. She looked at him confused.

He moved his face close to her ear and spoke softly. 'There is a German sniper team about fifty yards to the west of us, just over the rim. I don't think they saw me but there are two of them.'

Ed stared at him as her tactical brain swung into gear, grasping the situation immediately. With the calmness of a veteran, she carefully peered around the rim and saw to the east there was a low point in the edge of the crater, large enough to crawl through without being sky lined. If she could get out and move back south, she would have a clear shot to the nearest soldier, leaving Frank to take out the other. She whispered her intentions to Frank, who nodded approvingly.

'You sit tight for exactly ten minutes then move up to get a decent shot. By then, I will be in position,' she said confidently. 'You must react quickly when I fire, as I will be vulnerable and in the open. Agreed?' He nodded, and she eased her safety catch off before setting off into the darkness.

Within five minutes, Ed had found her way to the small crater and lay as still as possible, watching her foe! She heard them talking quietly together and realised she had not been compromised. She looked at her watch, three minutes to go... She squinted her eyes to try and see Frank, but she was in a dip and he, on the other side of a bank, was out of sight. One minute... Frank started counting, slowly to sixty, knowing his trusted friend would be ready, and slowly eased his safety catch off and lined himself up with the two dark shapes firmly in his sights. Ed some thirty yards away, lifted her head and shoulders, and then aimed at the nearest man. She pulled the rifle butt tight into her shoulder, the barrel now just a few inches above the dirt. She had been drawn in and now had the scent for another kill. She raised the end of the barrel in line with her target and placed her eye behind the sight. Aiming for his chest, she tightened her body, closing her left eye, waiting, counting down in her mind. She held her final breath and gently, squeezed the trigger.

The crack shattered the silence and the bullet tore through the body nearest to her, throwing his torso over against his partner, who was now pinned under him. Ed rapidly cocked her weapon, the empty cylinder flying off into the night, just as Frank let go his round. She didn't look across at him, instead focussing into the targets, and fired again. Ed re-cocked and stayed on aim, but nothing moved. She didn't want to attract any more attention to them than necessary, but equally, didn't want any mistakes either so hit her targets once more, staying on aim. All was quiet. There was no movement.

She suddenly felt vulnerable and pushed herself backwards, dropping into a shell hole and waiting for a few minutes before crawling back round to re-join Frank. As she moved in close to him, she could see his white teeth as he grinned at her. They closed their heads together and he whispered, saying they shouldn't hang about. Before she had answered, he had started to turn, heading directly south, towards their own lines.

She tucked in behind him and they pulled themselves along the soaking mud, sliding through deep troughs, many filled with water, before clambering back up the other side. They were caked in mud as they crawled from shell hole to shell hole, zigzagging when they could, stopping just once to listen for enemy activity. They didn't hear a thing, and knew they were in great danger but, remembered their drills. Both sides would be in their firing positions now, as dawn had arrived, periscopes appearing in their own lines. When they were within one hundred yards of safety, the dawn bombardment started. Ed thought they would be dead meat and so crawled down into a deep shell hole next to Frank. They huddled together as the explosions threw dirt over them, the ground shaking, the noise almost unbearable.

Ed shouted at Frank, 'Do we get blown up here or make a run for it?'

Frank didn't need asking twice. 'RUN!' he shouted and they both got to their feet and charged off towards their own lines.

They ran crouched to begin with, their rifles low in their right hands. Twenty yards, fifty yards, closing in fast through their own wire, the edge of the trenches now visible. They ran zigzagging, across the land, the shells exploding ahead of them, and then Frank tripped, Ed thinking he had been hit. She turned to see him get quickly to his feet grinning at her and set off again. Legs pumping hard to get to safety, one behind the other, until finally they could see the upper sand bags of their lines and several periscopes eyeing their approach. Within seconds, they had jumped over the sandbags, dropping into the bottom of the trench some eight feet below. Startled faces suddenly looked across, as they landed and rolled over exhausted.

And as they looked up from their prone positions, a man eyed them down the length of his rifle. It was Private Barker from 2 Platoon, who slowly lifted his head and grinned at them. Sergeant Worrall had seen their approach too and shouted for Barker to lower his rifle. Frank and Edwina were so covered in mud, their bodies were part of the soil. They caught their breath before scrambling to the forward edge of the trench wall. They took their head covers off, and looked at each other briefly, sweat pouring down their faces. The bombardment continued for twenty minutes, before all went quiet and they leant against the wall of mud, relieved.

'Are you making a habit of this, young fellows?' said Sergeant Worrall.

'That was a close one,' Frank muttered before they headed back down the trench line into familiar territory. They sat down outside their small bunker, and got out of their ghillie suits, Frank immediately reaching for a ciggy. They didn't speak, knowing they had just had a very lucky escape.

The sniper routine spun into weeks and then months as autumn came in wet and thundery. It wasn't the inevitability of falling leaves that gave it away, but the cold nights that slowly crept up on them, making their job all the more difficult. Sleep was harder to find in their forward positions in No Man's Land and concentration was the all-powerful aspect for their personal survival. Mistakes would be made, they knew that, but they just had to ensure it wasn't them who got caught out. During October they secured three further kills, and Frank got two on successive nights in November. Later that month, they were summoned back to the rear echelon for a sniper briefing, along with other teams in neighbouring sectors. Major Hesketh-Pritchard had called the briefing and their OC had told them to stay put for the next two days and take some well-earned rest. The banter around the company was as good as ever.

As November left them, the rain turned white. Winter had arrived...

Chapter 20

Ed and Frank arrived early for the rendezvous, (RV), hoping that someone might have arranged for some soup and bread; however, all that was available inside the brown marquee was a brew of tea. Several of the chaps were already gathered and they chatted freely with another new face to the squadron, a bright faced Londoner, called Ricky Miller. He was keen to hear of their exploits, and eager to get on the ground and do his bit. Ed was drawn to this cheerful young bloke, who brought a different outlook on life, with his charming outgoing style and bright intellect. As a party piece, he suddenly performed a hand stand, holding it for some time, his body bolt upright to the surprise of all present. Frank then shoved him over into the dirt. He simply stood up grinning.

They all huddled together around the pot of tea, reminiscing about their time in Linghem and their latest success, Ricky, focussing closely on everything Ed said. Although they all worked quite separately, there was a certain warmth and understanding between them, as they were an elite group within an army and affections for each other, were very real.

As the last of the chaps arrived, Jerry Swatton, always the course joker, came in wearing a German helmet, sporting a curly moustache greased up and pretended to be shot. He staggered around yelling 'English snipers, English snipers, look out, look out' before dropping to the floor in theatrical style in his death throes! The men laughed and applauded, just as the CO arrived. His dog, who had somehow survived the war so far, ran over and nuzzled him playfully. The chaps settled, and Swatton got to his feet, taking off his helmet and apologising to the officer. But the CO nodded in full approval.

'Nice to see you in such good spirits, Corporal Swatton, nice tash!' The men cheered, with those closest to him slapping him on his back, as he took his seat. With everyone now settled, the major greeted everyone, before placing a large box on the table in front of him. Frank, who was sitting in the front row, was asked to step forward.

'Give one of these to each man, would you, Smith?' said the CO and handed Frank the box. He cautiously opened the lid and smiled to himself before looking up. He turned, grinning at everyone.

'Sticky buns, lads' and quickly nipped round to everyone in turn, as grubby hands reached into the box to take a fruit bun. He returned the box to the table with three remaining. One was quickly devoured by the major, before Frank took one, leaving a lonely bun sitting in the corner of the box. Frank took his seat as the tent fell quiet.

'OK, men, before I begin, I want to read a signal I have received from General Haig:

To: Major Hesketh-Pritchard, CO Sniper Squadron.

Your contribution to date has been somewhat striking and not what I or my senior officers ever expected. The records show that your 13 teams have since Jun, a period of only 4 months, made 42 confirmed kills, with no losses, a credit to the squadron. Please pass on my hearty congratulations to the men.

Haig'

He put the paper down and looked out over his prodigies sitting before him. 'So, a pat on the back all round I think, especially Mitchell and Smith, who have between them made nine kills. Well done, chaps.' The lads cheered loudly and applauded them. Frank and Ed, rather embarrassed, just sat, soaking up this unexpected praise, young Miller, looking on approvingly.

'OK, settle down,' said the CO, and all eyes once again focussed on him as he looked around at the young men before him, many of whom had hardly started shaving. How did he have the right to expect such bravery from this generation while operating in No Man's Land in such terrible conditions? They are a real credit, he thought, and looked back down to his notes.

'I want to begin by applauding each and every one of you for your professional conduct over the past few months. We are only four months in, and have already made a significant impact, stopping many attacks on our own troops due to your diligence and skills in the field. You have taken some key targets, so well done and keep up the good work. The tactics we have employed have largely been successful and your comments passed back to me by your OCs have produced several questions, which have resulted in some changes. The latest one, we must discuss today, is to relay something that happened to Smith and Mitchell, as it occurred to me, we might take advantage of the situation. It was during a sortie into No Man's Land, they rumbled a German two-man sniper team in position, not two hundred yards from our own lines. If it hadn't been for their tactical awareness, we would have been two men short today, but their smart minds and quick action resulted in two kills within minutes. So, we might just use this to our advantage. I want to set up a series of selective opportunities whereby we create some disturbances to lure German teams out to seek kills in areas where we have already planted our own teams. It will mean you may have to be out an extra day or two but, reducing their snipers can only lead to less casualties in our own lines.'

Ed was then asked to run through her story. It took her a full fifteen minutes to explain before answering various questions. She stressed it was the immediate action drills from Frank that stopped them being rumbled themselves and the key, she said, was the element of awareness and surprise, which in this case won the day. Ed finished by saying they didn't hang around after that as their mission had been rumbled and they almost ran back to their own lines during the bombardment.

The major reiterated the tactical necessity of good recces prior to any operation and that the selection of good starting points was crucial and should be varied. OC's take note,' he said. 'Teamwork was absolutely critical and your alertness while operating in No Man's Land saved your lives and the lives of others.' He let that thought hang in the air for a moment as he studied his young team, with grubby faces and eager eyes.

'OK, my second point concerns the irregular opportunities you have to get to the range, so from next week everyone will commence range days, each two-man team will fire fifty rounds at two and three hundred yards to keep yourselves sharp. I have implemented a simple rota on a fortnightly basis, so by splitting the squad into three groups, it will allow enough people to complete any tasks set.' A hand then went up.

'What is it Miller,' said the CO.

'Will that be out and back in a day, sir, or will we need an overnight?' He grinned as he spoke.

'You have been in this war two minutes Miller, and you want a night out with the ladies already, eh. Well, not this time, it will be a one-day affair. Anything else, gentlemen?' he said gazing at these young faces.

'OK, the good news is you will all receive a forty-eight-hour pass, which for a lucky few will begin today!' Shoulders lifted around the tent and faces beamed with delight, followed by a hearty cheer. 'Three lucky pairs, one from each sector, will depart today, transport is already booked for sixteen hundred hours.' He removed his cap carefully and lifted three small bags from within it. 'Everyone's name is here in these bags, so let's see who the lucky ones are!' He then placed his hand into the first one, stirring gently, smiling at his team. The men grinned impatiently before he pulled out one piece of paper, unfolding it carefully before looking up.

'Private Coley and Lance Corporal Jobling from Alpha Squadron,' he said, with both men turning to each other, grinning, as they were jeered by the others. He put his hand into the second bag and repeated the process. 'OK, Bravo Squadron, Private Bell and Private Forrest.' They too jumped up joyously, smiling broadly, gripping each other's arms. The CO laughed before pulling a final piece from the third bag, and read aloud 'Finally, from Charlie Squadron, it will be Privates Smith and Mitchell.' They just looked at each other, smiling, while the others clapped them wholeheartedly. 'OK, I will sort the remaining list and let you all know in due course. Leave your rifles with the QM, chaps, and you can get an advance of pay from Major Brookes the paymaster if you need it, just take your pay book with you. Any questions?'

'Are you coming too, sir?' said Frank.

'No, not this time, Smith, but I will arrange something soon when we can all have that drink together. So, don't be late back and I will see you next week.' The chaps quickly got to their feet, grinning, before heading out of the tent. Just as they were leaving, the CO called Ed back. 'Mitchell, do you have a minute?'

Ed doubled back, while Frank waited outside the tent. 'Yes Sir?'

'I just wanted to congratulate you personally, Mitchell, as you have performed outstandingly well, and much better than I ever expected! When we first met during your sniper training, I saw a man with a small frame and quiet persona, and I honestly thought you didn't have it in you to be a sniper. But you have surprised us all, especially your OC, and your peers too, so well done, lad, you really are an amazing shot.'

Ed felt a little awkward but nodded gratefully before having her right hand squeezed by the big hand of her CO, who nodded, smiled and offered Ed the final iced bun.

She smiled. 'No, sir, you have it,' and walked out to meet Frank outside, the officer smiling before stuffing the bun into his mouth.

'What did the boss want, Ed?' asked Frank.

'Oh, he just wanted to congratulate me on my kills, that's all,' and they walked off together in silence, back into the trench system. Frank hung back a little, slightly miffed his efforts were not praised also. He then realised he shouldn't feel like this, as he was lucky to have her as his sniper partner and quickly swallowed his feelings. She deserved all the praise she got.

'Where shall we go, how about a steak, if we can get one?'

Ed smiled at him, nodding. 'Yeh, that's a great idea, I could eat a horse.'

They got back to their shelter and as they gathered what they needed, Sergeant Worrall stepped over to greet them, a wet cigarette clinging to his lips, which were quite hidden by his ever-growing moustache.

'What's all this, going somewhere, lads?' he asked.

'Hello, sarge,' said Frank. 'Yes, we have a forty-eight-hour pass and are heading to Marle Le Somme for a bath and some rest,' he said with a grin.

'Well, I can't say you two don't deserve it, have a glass for me, won't you?' and he wandered back towards his shell scrape, splitting out the wet ciggy into the mud.

They took just over thirty minutes to reach the paymaster's tent and collected some francs, signing the pay sheet before dropping off their weapons in the armoury. At just after four o'clock, the six snipers headed south towards the village of Marle Le Somme for some rest and recuperation. When they arrived, the other four headed straight to the café' for some wine, while Ed and Frank went straight to their small room at the top of the house. They tossed a coin and frank won the right to bath first. He spent half an hour soaking in the hot water, leaving it tinged with dirt. Ed, didn't care about using his water after him, it just felt bliss…

In clean clothes, they headed down the single flight of stairs to the café, where the rest, were well lubricated and singing songs. They sat talking of home but before long fatigue set in and at 10 p.m. they were lying between clean cotton sheets in soft beds, finding sleep quickly.

The period that followed their forty-eight-hour pass became much less productive for the whole squadron. The heavy snow and freezing conditions meant great hardships for everyone, as it became almost impossible for anyone to do their duty, especially the sniper teams. No Man's Land was a difficult place in the height of summer, but now it was only for the brave, or the stupid. Many soldiers had developed trench foot, a painful and debilitating condition that rotted the flesh of the feet, due to them constantly being immersed in water. The badly fitting military issue boots was the root cause of the problem.

The water was bad enough, but when coupled with the freezing temperatures, life became unbearable and men cried out unashamedly as their feet froze! With limited warm clothing, hyperthermia was a common problem. Life was not a bed of roses…

With a temporary halt called to sniper operations, many of the squadron teams were evacuated from the trenches, to return to the range for several days at a time. This not only kept the men sharp but rested their battered bodies and allowed some basic comforts. But they were not away for long as the changeovers were rostered for several weeks. Christmas came and went with blistering speed, although the sound of carol singing was heard on the breeze from the opposing trenches, just a short distance away. Some men sang quietly to themselves, to tunes they knew so well. Miraculously, not a single bullet, mortar or shell was fired by either side on the 'big day'. It was a whole week before regular bombardments began again, and through January and February, life was most unpleasant in their dire surroundings, where fingers, and toes froze. It was the most barbaric period in many of these young lives, causing great hardships, with grown men crying in the night! The Brigadier, initiated a tot of rum or whisky for their men, and the QM's from each regiment ran a disciplined routine to ensure soldiers didn't drink more than their share. But it became common to find some soldiers drunk on duty, some through greed, others to drown their sorrows. Ed and Frank had been away to the range several times, but were now back, and they enjoyed their tots, usually poured into their hot brew, creating a morale boosting sensation as it slipped down their gullets.

Anyone looking down from on high on these cold, wintery mornings would have seen ghostly figures, white with hoar frost and exhaling hot dragon breath. As the weak sun tried in vain to warm the day for a few short hours, the trenches acted as frost hollows, attracting all the cold air, which sunk to the bottom, where the troops all stood. Men cuddled up together for warmth, under their army blankets that were as effective as a raincoat in the sea. Temperatures in the trenches could be ten degrees and more below those on the surface for days on end, with thousands of bodies all breathing the morning air, it was like looking at the mouth of hell!

On the twenty-first of February, Ed received a long-overdue letter and sat outside her shell scrape, with her brew of tea simmering nicely. She glanced up and from the corner of her eye saw a young soldier just along the trench, who had arrived only days before, pick up his rifle to lick some snow from the barrel, not realising the consequences. Before Ed could react or call out for him to stop, his tongue had frozen to the metal. As he pulled back, the skin of his tongue stayed put, blood quickly pouring from his mouth.

Her mind went back to the letter and news from home, with Edward describing the snow-clad hills across the acreage. He was unusually candid, and she read with interest, before finding a small note at the bottom of the page in Bryan's handwriting. He wished her the very best and to say he prayed for her every day. She felt humbled and vowed to write more often. Edward's finishing paragraph was the most poignant and caught Ed unawares:

I also remind you that it's not long until the fifth anniversary of Mum and Dad's death.

Ed stopped reading, pondering his words as she lifted her metal mug full of steaming tea to her lips. Her memories came flooding back, the pains all too real, just as one of the chaps started playing his harmonica, which although some way off, brought a pleasant calmness to the bitterly cold morning. She realised she had quite forgotten the date was so close and reached into her top pocket, where she kept her father's Bible, with a photo of both her parents tucked neatly inside the front cover. A moment passed before she returned to the letter.

I am hopeful you are still well and it's not too cold for you. Whatever happens Ed, I will always be here for you and although I am lonely at times, David is a great comfort to me, and we have grown close. I hope you approve of all the things we have done here. Keep your head down. Love Ed…

What did he mean, Ed thought, that David is a comfort to him! She read the passage several times over, line by line, realising how the war had even forced her to forget the saddest and most important date in her short life. As she finished her tea, she looked up to the young soldier who was now in deep pain and being jeered by the man opposite. He wouldn't do that again, she thought!

She put more water on for another brew of tea and reached into the dugout for her kit bag and some note paper. While she had time, she wanted to pen a brief letter back to Edward, trying to be upbeat. She wrote freely and honestly, creating the mood of the trenches without compromise, and wished both him and David well. She would write to Bryan separately later. As she finished her note, Frank wandered back from the sniper briefing, wrapped up to the hilt, with a thick brown woollen scarf obtained from a Red Cross parcel several weeks before, wrapped so high around his head it was hard to distinguish it was him. He sat down next to her on an old ammo box before resting his rifle against the timber post and smiled.

'Any tea going, Ed?' he asked.

'Yeh, won't be a minute, anything happening?' she responded.

Frank, not lifting his eyes from the now steaming pot of water, shivered as he spoke. 'Nope, bit of a wasted trip really, oh, except it turns out Jones was shot the other day in the leg. You remember Jones, the small guy who was able to fall asleep standing up! Well, anyway, he is in a field hospital somewhere south of here. Other than that, we are staying put for at least another three days.'

Ed looked back down, spooning some tea leaves into her friend's mug before her own, but it was a case of one lump or two, as they had got rather damp in their tiny, frozen shell scrape! She finished her drink before standing to stamp her feet to help the blood circulate down into the ends of her toes. She left Frank warming his inner soul as she sought the sergeant's permission to leave the sector to make the short journey back down the trench line to the letter box. She collected other mail as she went before dropping them at Company HQ and was back before Frank had finished his tea. They chatted outside their dugout for over an hour about home, about the things they loved, and missed the most. It was bitterly cold again, but a pleasant time, with routine duties only and no bombardment that day. She didn't know how she had endured so much difficulty and how she had become such a key part of the company. No-one had ever suspected she was not quite what she seemed…

Late March brought some better weather and things became a little warmer for everyone. The frozen ground started to cut up, before turning to mush as it melted. Sniper tasks were rumoured once again, much to the pleasure of the men, especially Frank and Ed, who had become stiff in body and stale in their specialist role. Thank goodness they had got to the range through the winter months, keeping their skills sharp. As April approached, heavy overnight bombardments started again, the German lines receiving much the same in return from their British counterparts. Death once again became an everyday thing, the toll of British, French and Commonwealth casualties now reaching desperate numbers. Those lucky soldiers that had remained unscathed in the German onslaught were now so dazed that they simply stared into oblivion for much of the time. Ears ringing like church bells, many unaware of the true carnage that surrounded them. Many buried their heads into the muddy walls of death, their minds in other places, until slowly the realisation hit them that the shelling had actually stopped! Life stirred once more in this little part of England, and then slowly, the death screams started ringing out!

On April Fool's Day, Ed and Frank were at last tasked and were called to their OC's trench for a briefing. They squeezed themselves around the tiny table in the OC's dugout, peering down at a map that was almost in shreds.

'Right, chaps, we have an interesting one that has come directly from General Haig himself! It will take all your skill to both locate and kill a particular German officer who dares to act out a little performance above the trench line to entice a British sniper out of their hide. He has even been given the nickname of The Joker, but we are still trying to locate him. He seems to appear in different locations, but has been seen several times in bravo sector, so you will need to move at short notice and do your recces well. I want you prepared and rationed up, ready to go at short notice, in the hope we can spoil his day. No move before twenty-three hundred hours tomorrow.'

'Any other useful information sir?' Frank asked.

'Not really Smith, but he seems to drift up and down the line at will, with no pattern and has even been seen several miles away from our sector. So, it will make it doubly hard to locate him. That is why it may mean you have to go out for several days and sit tight, waiting for him to appear. He is a performer, that's for sure, but the general wants him dead, and quickly.'

For the next week, Ed and Frank observed through their telescope along a one-mile sector. Reports came from sentries about possible sightings, but even though they moved rapidly, they never actually saw him in action. They moved east and then west for up to a mile each day, watching and studying the land without luck.

That night, they visited their lieutenant to request they go into No Man's Land from 'the pavilion', the nickname given to a small roofed area, over a food pit. Their OC saw two young and daring men, who were still under twenty-one years old, fully prepared to go out to make this kill. How could he dampen this sort of heroic duty and enthusiasm? He studied what intelligence they had received, and agreed a start point, timings, length of task and passwords. They visited the QM for some extra rations and sewed another pocket into their ghillie suits, using a sandbag, allowing another water bottle to be carried, which would now provide six pints for this three-day operation, barely enough to survive.

With the officers and sentries alerted, they waited for the distraction tactics to the east, that would initiate their patrol. While waiting, they did final checks, and then a hand grenade was lobbed over the top and rifles fired to create their diversion. It was precisely 10 p.m. and they cocked their rifles before clambering up and out into the darkness.

As the gunfire and play acting ceased, they made quick progress, travelling several hundred yards in the first hour. Ed signalled to Frank to stop and listen, while she got her bearings. Even at this distance, she was sure she could hear enemy voices. It could have been Welsh for all Ed knew, as either way she couldn't understand the language one bit. They set off again, remaining cautious as always, with Frank crawling forward still in their well-practised zigzag routine, until they literally fell into a large, deep crater. After a few minutes rest, they crawled up to the top edge, listening and peering into the darkness. Nothing moved and the voices of earlier had now stopped. It was just after midnight. They dropped back down, and Ed suggested she would nose forward a short way to see what she could find, on the premise that one person moving across the ground this close to the enemy lines was less of a risk.

Frank lay on the earth just below the rim, rifle at the ready, breathing softly as he waited for his partner to return. He had total faith in Ed as not only had she become his closest friend, but she was a first-class sniper. He checked his safety catch more out of habit than necessity, casting his mind back to more pleasant times, when he first met her brother Edward at the recruitment fair. He never realised it was a different person when they met at the railhead in March of that year, as she looked so much like him. He now trusted her fully with his life, no question! He stared up into the night sky but could see little as there was thick cloud overhead, but at least the rain had stopped. Ed had been gone about twenty minutes when Frank heard a light scuffling sound just ahead. He sat up quickly, rifle at the ready, focussing in that direction as Ed came into view, sliding gently back beside him. She moved close to him and whispered in his ear.

'You're not going to believe this; we are less than one hundred yards from the German lines. No wonder we could hear voices. I have circled round to the rear and found a suitable position to the south west, that lies between two dips in the ground, about thirty yards from the remains of an old vehicle. It's far too obvious a place to set up shop, as it will be a set target for their snipers, but to the right is a good location that should give us cover from both sides and has a good escape route.'

She tapped Frank on his arm and he double tapped back, before she led him away in the darkness. Frank, never more than a few inches behind the soles of her muddy boots, kept checking his arcs, as any tail end Charlie would always do, especially with the enemy trenches so close. It took about ten minutes to circle round behind, to the new position she had chosen, and they scanned each arc for a long time, studying the lines of sight carefully. They seemed to have three fields of fire. The first one was straight ahead but was partially blocked by a bank of earth about twenty yards ahead. The second was off to their left where it was just possible to see a raised platform where two trenches seemed to meet, an obvious sentry position, which had the top of a ladder sticking skywards. The final one was more worrying as it was clearly a gun position but was about forty degrees to their right and the barrel, was currently pointing away on a different arc. Ed was happy with her selection and after eating some cold meat rations and taking another drink, they settled back into a watch system of two hours about, Ed as she always did, taking the first watch. Frank settled down to sleep, not realising that the day would ultimately change their war, in a manner they could never have conceived...

Chapter 21

When they dropped into the void, Frank didn't realise what had happened. He thought they had fallen into a huge shell crater and cursed himself for not staying on his feet. But then suddenly, he was confronted by the sound of a Scottish voice shouting at him over and over for the password. With Ed now laying on top of him, Frank couldn't find the breath to speak, but knew they were in a home trench. Then he heard the soldier cock his weapon. Was he to be shot in his own lines, he thought? No, he had to find the strength to move, and tried desperately to slide her off him, but Ed was unconscious! He just shouted 'English, English' and at last he saw the soldier lower his rifle and peer at him. He eased his body from under Ed and struggled to his feet, narrowly avoiding being pierced by a protruding bayonet. Suddenly a sergeant intervened from just across the trench, the sentry standing back as he approached.

'What regiment are you?' he shouted.

'Snipers, Sergeant, we are with the Glosters, but Ed has been shot!' Frank shouted above the bombardment. He bent down and between them they carried her limp body towards the sentry's dugout a few yards away. Frank realised he could do little until the bombardment was over and lowered his friend, gently to the ground. He reassured her, but she seemed out of it, or was she already dead! Reaching inside his ghillie suit for his note pad and pencil, he lit a single candle in the corner of the dugout, before scribbling a message.

'Sergeant, can you give this note to Lieutenant Cavanagh of the sniper squadron. He will need to know of our success last night.' The sergeant took the note and without reading it, stuffed it into his pocket. 'Sure, no problem, where do I find him?' he shouted above the noise.

'He is with the second-fifth Glosters. Down the line.' The sergeant nodded and went back to his position. Frank then resumed talking to Ed, over and over, and to his great relief, she suddenly answered him.

'I can hear you, Frank. Where are we?' she asked.

'We are in a home trench; I will get you to safety as soon as this barrage stops,' he said as he pulled a flask of water from his suit. He found her mouth and offered it to her, and she took several sips, her breathing still erratic. He looked up and down the trench and opposite saw the burly sergeant who had helped earlier, looking at him. Frank shouted across the trench for more dressings, and without getting out from cover, the sergeant threw one over. Frank unbuttoned Ed's ghillie suit again, placing the new dressing on top of the old one before checking the rear dressing too. All seemed OK and he pulled her clothing back into place, holding her firmly, looking up into the sky. Then suddenly the bombardment stopped!

Frank looked up and down the trench, where several bodies lay, and people started to stir from their holes in the ground. His ears were ringing, and he looked down to check on Ed again, placing his face close to hers. She was unconscious again, but he could feel her breath on his cheek. Though the sounds of the bombardment had ceased, a new sound had begun, that of screaming men. Within minutes a single medic arrived, then another, followed by several stretcher bearers looking for bodies to lift to safety. The trench was alive with people, trying to help all they could; even the sergeant just across the way crawled from his den. For some the war was over as they had been blown to oblivion, with just their boots remaining where a man once stood! The bearers were well drilled, and shouted as they went to clear the way, seeking to save those they could. Bodies were swept up and taken away, but there were never going to be enough stretchers. The deep, wet mud hindered their efforts, and equipment and weapons lay scattered everywhere, creating obstacles for them to overcome. The Hun had a lot to answer for this day.

Frank realised that to get this many to the medical centres at the rear of their lines was an almost impossible task. They would soon be overrun. He called to a chap with a Red Cross armband to come over, but he took one look at Ed and shook his head, running off down the trench to the next casualty. Frank shouted after him as he fled and then realised if he didn't act straightaway, Ed would probably die. He bent down and picked her up and followed a bearer back along the line, passing many dead on the way. She was light in his arms, but he knew he had a long way to go. He called for people to clear the way as he tripped and stumbled along the congested trench line. After twenty minutes, his arms wanted relief, but he recognised the sign for HQ and dug deep, pulling Ed tight into him once more, dragging breath into his burning lungs. He was exhausted, but finally reached a triage point where trucks were parked to ferry the injured back down the line to the field hospitals.

He dropped down on his haunches, giving Ed some water and taking a long swig himself. He didn't have the energy to carry her to the field hospital, and looked up and down the road for help, then when he thought all was lost, a driver pulled up and leant out of his window, peering down at him. Jumping down, he helped Frank put Ed onto a canvas stretcher and place her in the back. Several other wounded were then helped to climb aboard, and one chap with his left leg gone stared at Frank blankly, in obvious shock, bandages hanging loosely where his limb once was. Frank sat opposite Ed as the truck moved off and smiled back at the soldier, but he was in his own world, distant and quiet. Frank hardly took his eyes off his best mate, hoping he had done enough to save her. He stroked her head and talked to her, not knowing if she could hear him. With his bloodied hands, he pulled her collar up and her woollen hat down over her ears. He peered from the rear of the truck as dawn broke. He could see the devastation more clearly following the early morning bombardment, as they sped away.

Ed grunted each time the truck hit a hole in the road, but the driver didn't slow, instead increasing his speed as they headed south. Buildings then came into view, clearly the outskirts of a town, and Frank saw several people on cycles, waving at him with wide smiles. He didn't have the energy to wave back, just looked down at his injured friend, then they turned a sharp corner and with a squeal of brakes, came to an abrupt halt. The door up front slammed shut as the driver got out, shouting to someone ahead. Two stretcher bearers appeared from somewhere and dropped the tailgate, but then stopped to stare at Frank for several seconds, not recognising him as a British soldier. One of the bearers called on him to help and between them they lifted Ed from her temporary bed and slipped her into the hands of his oppo. As the stretcher was pulled slowly backwards, the orderly jumped down and took the front of the stretcher before heading to the entrance of a church.

Frank kept hold of Ed's hand as the young orderly looked once again at Frank, dressed in a bundle of sacking, all in tatters, a style of dress he had not seen before. Walking alongside the stretcher, the medic looked down at Ed's face.

'He's a young 'un,' he said coldly as they approached the church. 'Hardly looks old enough to be out of school.'

'Will he be OK?' Frank asked. The medic, without looking up, said, 'Well, that depends on what happened,' as two men whisked them inside. Ed was taken down a corridor to the right, but Frank was stopped and ushered into an area where some nurses were drinking tea. He turned just as Ed was disappearing around a corner, and he froze for a moment, wondering if he had done enough to save his friend's life. A nurse came across, looking him up and down, but she said nothing. She had learnt never to judge a soldier's disposition and simply asked if he wanted some tea. Frank nodded eagerly, before leaning the two rifles up against a wall next to a church pew.

'Yes, please, nurse, that would be great.' He took a seat, and the nurse bent down, smiling, presenting him with a large mug of tea and a sweet bun. He drank for all he was worth, before peering down to the far end of the church, knowing all hell was about to break loose.

He rested his head against the wall, with his feet up on a chair; he was re-running in his mind the extraordinary escape they had made from No Man's Land, following Ed's miraculous shot and the death of the Joker. She was a bloody hero and surely this time she would receive a medal for her bravery. Getting shot was not part of the plan, of course, but he was pleased he had got her to the hospital, alive.

He could still feel the pain in his arms from carrying her so far but knew she would have died if he had failed her. It was as if someone was helping him, as even though his arms and back ached beyond anything he had ever endured before, somehow, he had managed to keep her tight to his body all the way back along the trench system. He knew his friend's secret was being unveiled while he sat there in the entrance, drinking tea. He couldn't confide in anyone; he had been the only person who knew Edwina's story, until now. Their enemy was no longer the Hun, but possibly some of their own.

He smiled to himself and as he opened his eyes, a nurse was smiling back at him. He sat up and finished the rest of his tea, and suddenly weakness overtook him. Although loyalty to his best friend and sheer fright had driven him to get Edwina back from No Man's Land to the hospital, he was tired and needed to sleep. But his mind continued to race as his despair deepened. How could they have got themselves into this mess? They were silly, stupid youths, all too confident, blinded by this adventure of war. How did they not ever consider Ed might one day be wounded, her innermost secret laid bare?

Whether Edwina survived or not was now out of his hands, but he was sure there would be an inquiry of sorts. They would get to Ed's family, and probably to him too, the Military Police delving into their private lives. He had no idea where it would all end up, but realised she now needed him more than ever before. The full might of the army would undoubtedly fall upon them all, and he now stood alone.

He took a deep breath, remembering his trade, and knew he had had the best training in the world. Above all else, he had been taught to use his brain when in mortal peril. He had done so for the past year, proving himself one of the best. 'So, Frank, think. Think like never before.'

He could claim to have known nothing about Edwina's womanhood. With no proof, it would be his word against theirs, and this would get himself off the hook, scot free. But instantly he shook his head. No, that's the action of a coward, he thought, that is not acceptable. 'Shame on you, Frank. You would be betraying your friend, and her family.'

First of all, he had to warn Edwina's family, but knew all mail from the front was censored, so he couldn't write freely. Plus, letters bearing her name would rapidly be blocked; the army could react surprisingly fast in such situations. He couldn't write to them directly. Too risky. Then an idea dawned on him: *Father Bryan*. He knew the story, Edwina had said. Frank must warn him, but would that work?

Why not, he told himself. He was only a soldier sending bad news to his friend's parish priest back home. The censors would be reading dozens of similar letters every day. The challenge was how to word it so as to give the priest a clear warning without arousing suspicion from the censors.

His mind was slowly working again, his thoughts coming together, and he remembered Ed telling him she had left instructions for her brother and the parish priest if she was ever injured. He stared into space, trying to bring those memories to his mind, and then it came to him.

'Yes,' he said loudly, just as a medic walked past looking at him, rather strangely. Somewhat calmer, with a plan taking shape, Frank stood up, walked to the nurse sat by a small table and asked for some paper and an envelope. He went and sat in the corner, pulled out his pencil and began writing.

Dear Father Bryan,
My name is Frank Smith. I am Ed's mate from the trenches.

Only use Ed, he thought. If the censoring office was looking out for the name Mitchell, the goose was cooked. Chances were that the clerk's job at

HQ was only to check that no sensitive military information got out. He probably wouldn't twig.

Ed has been wounded by a German bullet and is in hospital as I write.

So far, so good, thought Frank. The censor would see it as, 'because my close friend has been shot, I am simply informing him'. Father Bryan was an intelligent man and would understand it for what it meant: 'because Ed has been wounded, they now know she's a woman'.

I am unsure when Ed might get home, as things are pretty serious here.

The censor might wonder why things were pretty serious but would assume it was injury related. Bryan, on the other hand, would understand fully what *'pretty serious'* referred to.

I assume the authorities will inform the family.

The censor would swallow that too. The military authorities always informed families when a relative was killed or seriously wounded. Bryan would get the message: The Military Police are coming.

I thought it might be better if you broke the news to them beforehand.
Although I don't know her brother and sister, Ed has told me all about them.
Sorry to send you such bad news.
Yours truly, Frank.

Now completely calm, Frank re-read his letter and was satisfied he had suitably disguised his message, and it should get past the censors. He just hoped that the priest, now warned, would know what to do. He placed the single page into the brown envelope, addressed it and walked over to the nurse who had provided the tea.

'Could you tell me where the post box is, Nurse?' he asked.

'I'll take it if you like,' she said with a smile. 'I have one to post myself and our mail is collected separately by the post clerk and he is due in about an hour. It should be back in England by tomorrow.' Relieved that he had done all he could, he handed it to her, knowing it was probably the most important letter he had ever written. He then sat back down, wondering how Ed was doing…

Down the corridor, Ed had been taken into a small operating room, with three tables separated only by simple white sheets suspended on wires. The brick floor was stained red, and the blood stuck to the feet of the medical staff as they went about their duties. She was taken to the table at the end nearest the wall and placed down with a bump. Ed stirred slightly as the medics started cutting away the strange sack clothing, then her tunic, shirt and vest from her pale body, leaving her upper torso naked, the dressings soaked in blood. The doctor asked the medics to cut the bandages, before he carefully eased the dressings away. Blood seeped out immediately and he replaced the it quickly. He then turned Ed on her side, to view the wound on her back, but as he did so a nurse at the side stepped across, looking down at Ed's body before her, rather alarmed. The doctor started to inspect the wound at the back, assuming that to be the exit point, but saw only a tiny entry wound.

'This man was shot in the back,' he said, puzzled, and asked for Ed to be turned again. He saw a large exit hole in the upper chest, the bleeding quickly starting again. The nurse looked at him, frowning, and touched his arm to gain his attention.

'Sister, can you go and get Major Leigh-Smith. Hurry now.' She hesitated for a second and was about to object, but he stared at her without speaking, raising a single eyebrow, and she sped off down the corridor. When she returned a few minutes later with the major in tow, the soldier was still lying on his back, his boots and trousers now having been removed, leaving just a pair of cotton underpants over the slim, muscular body of white flesh that had not seen sunlight for many months. As the two doctors chatted about the wounds, the nurse tried to comprehend what she was seeing, and to her horror she realised no-one else in the room had actually noticed.

'Doctor, can I speak to you?' she asked.

But he ignored her. 'So, let's tackle the exit wound at the front first, Simon. It will need careful work to the pectorals major and minor, which are both a bit of a mess. First it will need a thorough alcohol cleanse. Can you do it, old bean?'

Simon nodded and began cleaning the hole in Ed's chest.

'Doctor, I must insist,' said the nurse.

'Sister, what is it?' he answered. 'Can't you see we are rather busy here?'

She went close to him and spoke in a quiet voice directly into his ear.

'Doctor, can you not see, look at the soldier's body.'

The captain stopped what he was doing and looked at her, confused, and then took a step back, scanning the semi-naked body on the table before him. A young soldier, he thought, splattered in his own blood, badly needing an operation. He lifted his arms sideways and shook his head before asking her what she was talking about.

Sister Youngs moved in close once again and whispered something in his ear. The orderlies now hesitated, too, and looked at each other, confused. He jerked his head backwards, peering down once again before leaning over to lift the waistband of the soldier's cotton underpants. He peered inside and gasped!

Chapter 22

Lieutenant General Richard R Davis of General Haig's staff had been described by one of his staff officers as a bad tempered, obstinate hot-headed man and by another as a 'thud and blunder' general, although they had both miraculously managed to remain anonymous. These views, along with his nickname to his friends of the Bull, demonstrated the stern approach he took to his role as a senior officer in the British Army. He was a man who harboured private doubts about Haig's leadership and strategies, following what he called 'repeated blunders', but refused to permit any of his officers to say anything openly critical of him. His intellectual prowess and open mind on battle tactics did allow his officers the freedom to offer ideas about how to end this blessed war, which generated a certain amount of respect from his subordinates.

As a cavalry man he had commanded a division of the British Expeditionary Force, following his promotion to Lieutenant General in 1914, but volunteered to step aside in 1916 to command the Third Army at the Western Front! Today, in the large chateau overlooking the river, some way behind the front line, he was trying to unravel the latest series of orders from Haig, with much frustration. As he contemplated the latest challenge, he rose from his desk and stepped over to the French doors to light a cigar. As he breathed in the strong tobacco, he saw two black Labradors charging across the lawn in front of him. A young captain whom he didn't recognise was whistling to control them from the terrace, but he clearly wasn't having much luck. It was just after four thirty and the sun was already starting to dip, a sign the light would be gone in just a few short hours.

Suddenly, he was distracted by the noise coming from the ante-room outside his office and turned his head towards the door, expecting his afternoon tea and piece of fruit cake, any moment. But as the door opened all he saw was Captain Arding, his staffy, looking at him with a grim face. Irritated that there was no tea tray in sight, he opened his mouth to berate his loyal officer.

'What is it now, Arding?' he snapped, as the captain walked in slowly with a sheet of paper in his hand, pausing only to close the door behind him.

'Oh, please, not more bad news, what does Haig want me to do this time?' he said, heading back to his desk.

'Umm, sir it's not from General Haig, it's a rather delicate matter,' Arding said calmly.

'Well, spit it out, man,' said Davis.

The officer paused before deciding whether he should read the note or offer it to his general, opting for the latter. Davis reached for his glasses from the desk, placed them on the end of his nose and lifted his head back slightly to focus. There was a short pause as he read the five short lines. Arding expected an explosion of some sort, but instead the general pursed his lips, frowned a little, then pulled his glasses from his nose, peering towards the captain with a concerned look.

'Is this some kind of joke, Arding?' he said with a sour tone.

'No, sir, the signal arrived about twenty minutes ago and I immediately signalled the major in the field hospital for confirmation. He has just answered personally. It's genuine, sir. What will you have me do?'

Davis grimaced as if sucking a sour sweet, his eyes focussed on the signal. He turned back to the window, clutching the paper in his hand. Arding stood waiting for an answer, as the officer looked down and read the note again. His head rose slowly, in thought, and seemed to gaze at the dogs still charging around the gardens, before banging on the window with the back of his hand at the young captain, who turned his head towards him. The captain seemed to get the message immediately. The young officer promptly took his leave, calling his dogs and walking away. Without turning to face his ADC, Davis said quietly, 'Get Colonel Wood over here and then call this major fellow. I need to speak to him. Now.'

Captain Arding turned and walked quickly from the office. 'Oh, and Arding, get me Major Clements, of the Military Police on the phone and get my bloody tea!' the general shouted after him. Captain Arding let the door slam shut behind him, fully aware that it irritated his general, but sometimes he felt a yearning to rebel. Davis, dropped into his dark leather chair, closing his eyes, slowly shaking his head.

Captain Arding had been on the general's staff for almost two years, and was an able officer, who had run his offices well during his tenure. Although he disliked the role; the alternative was going back to the trenches and he knew when he was well off! He dialled the exchange and asked the operator to get him Colonel Wood at HQ Hospital, then Major Leigh-Smith of 24th field hospital and then finally, Major Clements from the Military police, before placing the handset back onto the cradle. The colonel had been a regular visitor to the chateau over the past year and had enjoyed many a fine dinner, but today was not a day for socialising. The phone rattled in its cradle, and Arding picked it up eagerly.

'I have Colonel Wood for you, sir,' said the operator and hung up.

'Colonel, it's Captain Arding. Can you come and see the general, sir? It is rather urgent.'

Although the hospital was less than half a mile away, the colonel's voice was faint, almost hidden by the distant crackle that field telephones had. Arding heard a faint response but couldn't hear the colonel clearly, so he repeated his request before hanging up. 'Bloody telephones,' he said as he swung round in his chair, just as a private carrying a tea tray, stepped through the open door from the Mess. Arding stood up and before he opened the general's door for him, he warned him of his current state and nodded, before walking into his office, placing the tray down on the side table.

Private Hill greeted his general in his usual manner, before pouring tea into his large white cup. He received no response. Then he placed it next to the green blotter pad, as he always did, along with a small plate of dark brown army biscuits. He could tell the general's mood in an instant from his demeanour, and today he sensed he should say nothing, simply do his duty and leave. As he headed for the door, the General called after him,

'Where's the fruit cake,' he asked.

'There is none today Sir, just biscuits. Is there anything else General?'

'Can you ask Arding to come back in, Hill, and bring another cup?'

'Yes, sir, will do,' he said, leaving the office quietly. The general swung his chair round, lifting his feet up onto the foot stool beside his desk and placed one foot over the other, staring into space. He reached for his tea and dunked the biscuit to soften it before biting into the dark crust. On this occasion, however, he had left it too long and as he raised his arm, the soft part broke off, dropping back into the cup, splashing tea over his trousers. 'Damn and blast it,' he said loudly, shuffling to his feet. He placed the cup back on the table, the half biscuit sunk without a trace, and he saw a wet patch at the top of his thigh. He quickly pushed the other piece of biscuit into his mouth as he wiped his hand on his handkerchief and shouted for Private Hill, all at the same time. The private scurried in almost immediately, carrying a cup and saucer, as if he had been hovering right outside the door.

'Bring a cloth man, the blessed tea has spilt, and clear up this mess,' Davis ordered. The bewildered private hurried over to see a tiny amount of tea in the general's saucer and a wet stain on his leg. 'And get more tea,' he said abruptly as Hill walked from the room, grimacing. Within minutes, he was back with a fresh pot, and crossing the room he placed the tray back where it had been five minutes before. He announced that the colonel had arrived, before delicately pouring two cups. As the colonel entered, Hill left smartly, glad to be away.

Colonel Wood was an older man with ginger hair greying at the temples and thinning rather badly over the top of his head. He was a little overweight, with a paunch that reflected his love of wine and port, his red nose indicating signs of excess! He was a smoker, too, a little strange for a medical man, the fingers on his right-hand stained nicotine yellow from his twenty-a-day habit.

He had been seconded from the Radcliffe Infirmary in Oxford just after the start of the war, being offered a colonel's commission before his feet had touched the ground. It was fair to say he was, by and large, enjoying the war, especially the long evenings he'd had in the chateau, eating fine food and savouring many French wines. Davis trusted Wood and would now be testing his loyalty.

'Tea, Stanley?' he asked.

'Ah, thank you, sir,' Wood said, and sat down, before enquiring how he could assist him.

'Read this,' said Davis, passing over the signal.

To: Lt General R Davis
From: Major Leigh-Smith. MD 24th field Hospital.
Regret to inform you, Private Mitchell a soldier from 2nd sniper Squadron injured in NML, condition serious. Mitchell is female!
Advise. Major L-S. Med Corps

The Colonel looked up, stunned, pinching the paper in his hand at the corner. He looked down as if to read it again but was simply scanning the page. 'I assume this is genuine, sir?'

'I believe it to be so, Stanley. What do you think, someone would send a prank signal of this nature to me, of all people?'

'No, no, of course not, sir, sorry. Um, can we get to speak to Major Leigh-Smith?' he asked.

'Already onto it. Need to get to the bottom of this and quickly and –' Davis stopped as the telephone rang. He picked it up hastily.

'Major Leigh-Smith for you Sir,' said Arding, before replacing the receiver.

'General, this is Major Leigh-Smith, you asked me to telephone you.'

'Ah, Leigh-Smith, reference your signal. What on earth is going on?'

The major took a deep breath, before explaining how the soldier, a sniper, had turned up at the field hospital that day with serious wounds, having been shot on return from an operation in No Man's Land. He advised they had inspected the wounds in the operating room before stripping the soldier to his underwear, then they had seen it for themselves.

'She's female, sir, I guarantee that, but she is unconscious at present and is very seriously ill, with a bullet wound that has gone right through her body.' He went on to explain his prognosis, but the general was now hardly listening, his mind was racing. 'Hang on, how serious are the injuries?' he said.

'It's going to be touch and go, sir,' said the major, 'as the wounds are serious and infection is likely. She also has internal injuries and we had to open her up to retrieve debris taken in with the bullet.'

'So, I assume, Doctor, she is likely to die,' the general said callously. Colonel Wood sat across the desk, hearing only half of the conversation, but he was acutely aware the line of questioning was out of order. It made him feel extremely uncomfortable and he wanted to interject but, had to wait for an opportunity to do so.

'That's uncertain, sir,' said the major down the phone. 'If God is on her side, she might make it, but she will need comprehensive rest and recuperation before we can move her back down the line.'

'Listen carefully, Major. I assume there are in your charge likely to be other soldiers in greater need of medical support, in other words people who have a better chance of survival than this, umm, Mitchell character. Do I make myself clear, Major?'

Simon paused in his tiny office, trying to understand what the general was implying. Was he trying to get him to waive his duty to bring as many soldiers back from the brink as he could? He gathered his thoughts and spoke deliberately into the mouthpiece.

'Sir, I have many men in my charge, and I will provide the best medical support to all soldiers that come to this hospital, no matter what nationality they are and how serious their injuries. Why, I had a German officer in here last month, and we repatriated him several weeks later, fully recovered. Would you suggest I treat Mitchell with less care than he?' Simon was about to say more but the general cut him off, realising he had not spoken wisely.

'No, no, Major, I am not suggesting anything, but what I am enquiring about is whether you might be stretched a little, and you have a duty to steer your time and efforts to where they are best suited, that is all. If that is the case, you have an obligation to direct that care towards those having the greatest chance to survive, do you not agree, Major?' Not letting the doctor speak and thinking quickly he went on, 'Furthermore, I want you to arrange for the immediate transfer of Mitchell to the hospital here, under the direct control of Colonel Wood, so we can manage things from now on.' He went on briskly, 'I also suggest you keep this matter confidential and brief your team of the consequences if this matter ever gets out. Now, I would like to see you in my office at zero eight hundred hours tomorrow. At that time, I will discuss this matter further.'

Simon, now in total shock, couldn't quite understand why the general would not listen to his medical advice and he knew that to move his patient now would mean almost certain death.

'Sir, you are aware moving Mitchell at this time is not in her best interests as she is very sick after surgery. It is against my medical advice, and what's more –'

Once again Davis cut him off. 'Major, you may be a doctor, but even you must understand that when a general gives you a direct order, it is not up for discussion. So, listen, I will only say this one more time: you are to instruct your QM to send Mitchell back down the line tomorrow and you, sir, will be here in my office bright and early. Do I make myself clear?'

Simon spoke softly into the mouthpiece to acknowledge his order. General Davis looked directly at Colonel Wood as he replaced the phone.

'Don't wish to keep you, Colonel, you must have lots to do. Zero eight hundred hours tomorrow then.'

Colonel Wood was about to argue the point but thought better of it and rose to leave. Davis stepped around his desk, offering his hand to his trusted friend. He squeezed the colonel's hand and grabbed his elbow with his left hand, pulling him in close, talking into his ear. 'This would be best if it went away, Stanley, do you understand me? I will be managing things from now on and I expect your total support.'

Wood turned his head slightly to face the general. Their eyes met for a few seconds, before he was released from Davis's grip. He walked away before turning to salute, the ADC already having the door open.

'Ah, Arding, get me Major Hesketh-Pritchard, CO of the sniper squadron, on the line. I don't know where he might be, but find him,' the general snapped. Arding slipped back to his desk, just as the phone rattled in its cradle again. It was Major Clements, whom he put straight through. He then dug out the battalion telephone listings. Where should he begin…

***

Major Hesketh-Pritchard had been relaxing for the first time for several days when he was summoned to take a call from General Davis. He jumped up as if he was standing before him and rushed to the communication centre deep in the underground bunker, away from the front line of trenches. He walked over to the table, where a corporal offered the phone to him as he approached. He cleared his throat and coughed before speaking confidently into the dirty mouthpiece.

'Major, this is captain Arding, General Davis's ADC, please hold.' He sat down and waited a full five minutes and thought he had been cut off, when suddenly, the general's voice came on the line.

For several minutes, he received a verbal ear bashing, not once getting the chance to speak. He stood silently, as the one-sided conversation finally came to an end, and the line went dead. He stood frozen to the spot, staring into space, as he tried to fathom what the call was all about. One of his men in serious trouble and now being summoned to see General Davis! Must be bloody serious, he thought, but Private Mitchell of all people. Surely there was some mistake, as he was well known to him and probably the best sniper in the squadron. What on earth could he have done that had reached the ears of the general?

He knew he needed to speak with his OC, Lieutenant Cavanagh first and headed down the long, dark passageway to a narrow doorway at the far end. He then turned right up some wooden steps, back to the surface, the cool fresh air hitting him a few steps from the top. The remaining daylight caused him to squint, after being below ground for some time that day. He donned his cap and picked his way back through soldiers working on sandbags along the trench system, heading towards the front line. It took him over twenty minutes to reach his quarters, dug out of the very ground where so many had died. He called for Private Bennett to go and hunt for Lieutenant Cavanagh at once. He returned remarkably quickly and reported that by chance the lieutenant had been in a shell scrape just a hundred yards away, visiting an old Sandhurst friend. Cavanagh followed Bennett through the primitive doorway, took off his cap and sat opposite the major. Bennett disappeared, bringing back a welcome mug of tea just minutes later.

'Corn, we have a serious matter to deal with. What can you tell me about Mitchell?' the major asked.

'Well, sir, I have just started my initial report on his op with Private Smith last night, but info is still a little vague as all I received was a short note and await their patrol report. But you should know, they made another kill, sir, the big one. They got The Joker! The bad news though, is Mitchell was shot during their extraction.'

Hesketh-Pritchard's eyes widened as he absorbed the news, and then he smiled, showing his missing tooth. He jumped up, shaking his fists in the air, simply delighted. He stretched over to shake his lieutenant's hand firmly.

'This is cause for celebration, Corn.' He said joyfully. 'Bennett,' he shouted, 'get in here.' His batman appeared in the doorway. 'Bring some brandy from my supply,' he said, and the batman left.

'So, he does it again, eh? I must get reacquainted with the chaps, you know, too much time gallivanting around HQs and training areas. We must put him up for a medal this time, Corn, bit of a special case, don't you think?'

Corn looked glum. 'Sir, did you not hear me, Mitchell was shot and is probably fighting for his life right now!' he said coldly.

'Ah, yes, sorry, old chap, just got caught up in the joy of The Joker copping it. What's his condition, Corn, and when did you notify General Davis?' As he spoke, Bennett returned, pulling the stopper from a bottle of French Cognac.

'The General? I haven't, sir. All I know is that the sentry reported he was taken to the field hospital in a very bad way yesterday, with Smith at his side. He didn't think he would make it as he was shot in the back during their withdrawal. Smith apparently carried him back from No Man's Land and then took him off to find some transport. I have no more information at this stage apart from what the sergeant gave me. He is a good lad, sir, and has become the envy of many in the squadron. He has also formed a good partnership with Smith, his spotter. Why, is something up?'

'Don't know yet. I have been summoned to see General Davis at HQ tomorrow to discuss this man. Don't have a clue what about, so just trying to fill in some gaps in the info, you see. Can you give me a brief about his life since he joined us, and can I have that unfinished sniper report by zero six hundred hours tomorrow, which I will read en-route?' He paused to think. 'But how does Davis know about The Joker?'

'Well, he can't, the only people who know are Smith, Mitchell and us! It's not public knowledge yet,' Cavanagh said, confused. 'I will head down to the village now to locate Smith and get the full details from him. I will get back to you tonight.'

***

General Davis, sitting in his leather chair, was staring out of the French doors at the rear of his office, rolling a large cigar between his thumb and forefinger. He was plotting. He always plotted better when he smoked a cigar. There was a great deal to do.

Chapter 23

Major Leigh-Smith hung up the phone and sat with his hands over his face, thinking about what the general had just implied. He knew he had to follow orders but felt a deep discomfort at what he was being asked to do. Picking up his cap, he drank the last of his now cold mug of tea before heading out of the operations bunker. He saw his driver across the street in deep conversation with another man in uniform, French he thought, their heads cloaked in cigarette smoke that swirled around in the light breeze. His driver suddenly noticed him and stubbing out his fag under his boot, ran to open the car door. Once his officer was seated, he reached in to set the switch on the dash board and then gave a yank on the starter handle. The engine spluttered into life the first time of asking. He jumped into his seat and revved the engine before driving off.

'Back to the church, sir?' he asked, but there was no response. The major just stared out through the steamed-up window. 'Sir?'

The major slowly turned his head and mumbled, 'Yes, please, and quickly if you don't mind.'

The short journey was done in silence, Major Leigh-Smith lost in something he didn't understand. He watched the world go by as they drove along tree-lined roads that meandered through quite lovely countryside that he probably would never have seen in a normal life. France was a long way from the Gloucestershire village where he grew up, until the war invaded his life. He had been quite happy as a junior doctor in the small local town and he looked forward to the day he could return once more to his community, his family and peace. They were soon pulling up outside the church, a field ambulance was parked outside, two stretcher bearers carrying a stretcher in through the ornate doorway. He had not yet resolved in his mind, what could be done and quite what General Davis was after. But he needed to think carefully and be one step ahead of him.

He stepped from the car and peered into the back of an empty ambulance. Blood stained the floor, lots of it! He steered himself through a small army of porters and medics before calling the orderly at the desk to fetch Sister Youngs and Private Baxter and take them to Mitchell's bedside. He watched him shuffle off down the corridor as he headed to Captain Alan Reece's office. His mind was mulling over his problem and he didn't see the many boxes by the door, tripping as he entered, almost falling flat on the floor. He saved himself by grabbing the corner of the desk, his knee clipping the corner of a wooden crate, and he swore loudly. As he looked up, he saw his friend smiling at him.

'You're not the first to do that today, Simon,' he said, laughing. Major Leigh-Smith rubbed his shin before closing the door and perching himself on a small crate. The QM's curiosity was aroused as no-one ever closed his door. What could be wrong? He folded his arms and looked straight at his friend.

'It must be a favour you are wanting, Simon, a big one perhaps?' he said, knowing he would always do what he could to help this man.

'Alan, I have been told to transfer a very sick patient, a sniper called, Private Mitchell, who we operated on earlier today. This order has come from General Davis of all people and is against my better judgement. The soldier is to go to the divisional hospital under Colonel Wood. I have explained that if we make this transfer, death will almost certainly occur, but I have been overruled. I am powerless.' Simon paused seeing his friends look of concern 'I have my suspicions as to why this order has been made, as something rather serious is amiss. I also have to be in a briefing in his office at zero eight hundred hours tomorrow.' Alan was about to speak, but Simon waved him down and continued. 'I need to sort out a way to somehow delay the transfer or find a way to halt it completely, to give the soldier a chance, and I am going to need your help, old chap!'

He took off his cap and wiped the sweat from his brow. Alan Reece frowned as he contemplated the problem.

'There is one other thing you should know. Private Mitchell is a woman.'

Captain Reece grinned, thinking this was all a ruse and he was being taken for a ride. 'Yes, pull the other one, Simon,' he said laughing. 'Is it April Fool's Day or something?'

Simon leant forward, staring straight into Alan's eyes, waiting for his laughter to subside. 'I am deadly serious, Alan, this is not a joke. Mitchell has managed to disguise herself as a soldier operating as a sniper in the trenches. How she managed to hide her femininity from so many for so long, God only knows, its remarkable. But I can't let this happen.'

Alan Reece, a man who had seen a lot during his service, was suddenly brought back to reality and he found himself embarrassed and said so.

'OK, Simon, sorry about that, how can I help?'

'That's OK, old chap, it is rather extreme, and I am still getting used to this myself. But suffice to say, she is very sick, and believe me her life is in real danger. If we move her tomorrow, I simply don't think she will make it.'

The captain was staring right through Major Leigh-Smith as if in a trance; his mouth had dropped open and his eyes were moving from side to side.

'Are you alright, old man?' said Simon.

Alan Reece stood up to look at the timetable for transfers on the wall opposite his desk. He was clearly plotting something. By nature, he was a compassionate man and a first-class quartermaster. He didn't mind making waves and this was a golden opportunity to do so. 'Well, I can't go directly against General Davis, but we might try some evasion tactics, if you're up for it? It might give you a day or two at best, is that enough?'

Simon shook his head slowly, watching the QM with his deep-set eyes. 'Need to do better than that, old man, much better,' he said.

'What do you mean, Simon?'

'I think the General is considering something quite unlawful and somehow I have to defend and protect this woman from him. So, I wonder if there is any way we might lose her, not for a day or even two, but lose her altogether?' he said with an expressionless face. 'He suggested to me quite clearly that I might turn a blind eye to her recovery and that I probably had more important things to deal with. I was ordered to get you to move her by field ambulance to the divisional hospital tomorrow, even though I advised otherwise. That worries me greatly, Alan. Why would he do that, what is his thinking? Does he want her dead, I ask myself, as that is what could happen if we let this move go ahead!'

Alan frowned, heavy with concern and was struck by the serious expression on his Simon's face. 'That's a mighty big accusation, are you sure? I mean, did anyone else hear this?'

Simon tilted his head back as he thought back carefully, the two men looking at each other for several moments.

'I have no way of knowing for sure but have reason to believe Colonel Wood might have been in his office.'

Reece sat back to think about the situation as he wanted to help and needed to find a way to save a life too. Although an extremely honest and particularly religious man, he felt some skulduggery was needed to overcome this predicament. He thought for a moment and checked his movement roster.

'Well, I do have to move a French soldier by field ambulance to a hospital near Paris tomorrow. He has a serious head injury, you may know of him, but as far as I am aware, he may never regain consciousness.' He reached for a pile of files, selected one from the top and read aloud: 'Serious head injury with full faced bandage, bla, bla, little chance of survival, marked as one over ten. This is signed by Captain Stephens. I think he would be a good candidate for, let's say, a diversion, as if we have sent the wrong patients to the wrong hospitals. That would gain us a day to begin with. But about losing her altogether, I'm not sure even with my network of contacts we could achieve that.'

'Let me see the notes,' said Simon.

Alan passed them across the desk and Simon looked through them with close attention. He couldn't let any patient suffer, as this would be totally unethical and against his own personal views. Plus, the soldier's family may well be expecting him, a family in Paris perhaps. But he may die anyway, even before the morning.

'What time do you normally move patients out on the morning routes?' said Simon.

'Around zero seven thirty, but leave it with me, old man. I will meet you for dinner tonight and we can further put our minds together to solve this.'

Simon thanked the QM, shaking his hand firmly and smiling. He left him in his dark office and headed off to Mitchell's bedside.

When he arrived, the sister was sitting in the room, waiting. Mitchell murmured quietly to herself in the cot in front of them. The major stepped in, thanking the her for coming so quickly and asked where Baxter was. 'He is in theatre, sir,' she said softly.

'OK, never mind, this concerns you more than him anyway, I will brief him later.' The major then explained the problem they all faced, and her eyes widened as he provided his assessment of the situation. He decided not to mention Captain Reece's involvement, thinking the less she knew for now, the better. 'I want someone at her bedside at all times, Sister, and I want you to pack as you may be required to leave here at short notice.'

When he was happy that the sister was sufficiently briefed, he left her sitting by the bed and disappeared down the corridor back to his small office. He sat down to a pile of administrative files that had been on his desk for several days. After an hour's work, there was a sharp tap on his door. He looked up to see Captain Reece's head peering around the door jamb.

'I thought I would find you here.' He said stepping in and shutting the door behind him. 'This can't wait until dinner, Simon,' he said, sitting down opposite the major. 'At zero seven hundred hours tomorrow, you will go to your meeting at the chateau with General Davis in the knowledge that Mitchell will be transferred at ten hundred hours by field ambulance. I have arranged for your car to be here in good time to get you there and that, my dear friend, is all you need to officially know. You will then be in your meeting for most of the morning and so won't know that things have, well, not gone according to plan! With luck, you will be well on your way back here before the problem becomes evident and the shit hits the fan. You're in the clear and Mitchell is safe. Roger so far?'

Simon sat back, his mind racing. 'Yes, that works. So, what have you come up with?' he asked.

'Well, as I see it, we have three options! The first one sounds rather more alarming than it is, but we have a pre-arranged accident, whereby one of our ambulances appears to crash and catch fire en route, and the vehicle and occupants are burnt to a cinder. It is complicated as we would have to obtain several corpses from our morgue, which creates difficulties. But it does kill the matter dead and would stop all follow-ups occurring. Then we hide Mitchell and get her back to England somehow, at a later date.'

Simon was shaking his head, rather shocked at his suggestion, and was about to speak, but Alan continued.

'The second is more complicated in that we care for Mitchell off-site until we find a cadaver of a young woman who we then use as a substitute for Mitchell, as presumably no-one else knows what the girl looks like and therefore wouldn't recognise the body we send anyway. We could simply dress her up and cut her hair as if she was from one of our hospitals. It would mean you performing two small operations to mimic her scars from bullet wounds, in case anyone ever checked. The matter would then once again be closed.' Alan watched his friend for a reaction, but he remained quiet this time, staring at him. 'And the third option?' he asked.

'The third option is we use the French soldier I spoke of earlier, presenting him as her. We then move Mitchell to a safe house, and she recovers in proper time, until she is well enough to move, possibly back to England. However, there is one small problem. The Frenchman, died an hour ago.'

Simon physically sank in his seat. But then realised, this actually helped their cause and he now had no ethical problems to deal with.

'Whatever direction we plan to take, it doesn't quite end there, well, not completely. We then have to find a way of getting her back to England without capture. The troop shipping process is monitored carefully, and it would be tricky, but I do have some thoughts on how we might succeed.' Simon thought carefully, acutely aware they both had a lot to lose!

'OK, I am not happy about vehicle accidents and fires, that could spell trouble if the MPs came sniffing around. Also, finding a suitable female cadaver at short notice especially when we have no access to the French population, might be difficult too, so let's go for option three and dispatch the dead French soldier to HQ. When the mix-up comes to light, he can speedily be repatriated back to his home in Paris, and no-one is any the wiser. Would you be able to take a longer route though, to delay his arrival at HQ?' he asked.

'Yes, that can be arranged, we simply add two other French soldiers in the same vehicle, dropping them off first, the ambulance finally arriving at the divisional hospital late in the day. Telephone calls will be made here, of course, but I will make sure I am unavailable for a while and so must you. In the meantime, we will move Mitchell tonight by ambulance to the small cottage at the end of village we have used before when overrun, so for those taking the slightest bit of interest, they will see yet another transfer without curiosity or question. As far as anyone here knows, Mitchell has then left and will be forgotten about. I suggest you send a trusted nurse to go with her.'

Simon was grinning with admiration at what Reece's mind had come up with in such a short space of time. 'OK, but what if General Davis gets personally involved? Don't lose your head, old man,' he said with concern.

'No, it will be fine, I have to produce a 'move order' each day for every patient transferred. It's a laborious paper exercise and I have boxes of files piled high in the back store from last year's transfers alone. Errors occur more than you think, old man, and even if the Military Police come sniffing, I will be able to show the move order. 'Now for the tricky bit!'

Captain Reece sat forward and looked Simon straight in the eyes. 'How likely is it the general will remember your warning that her wounds would probably kill her if she travelled too soon?'

Simon contemplated his question and thought back to the conversation. 'I would think most likely, as he tried to backtrack on his words. He didn't actually say anything direct, you understand, but his words were selected to direct me to other patients' needs, so I am sure he will remember.'

Simon threw his hands up, as he understood what they were taking on. He started to realise that Alan was a master at this, but it was a great risk!

'General Davis, for his own reason, is taking a particular interest in this, Simon, and so leave it with me. By the time the body arrives at HQ, we will be back here with phase two underway. Let me sort this out, you have more to lose than me! Meet me after supper in the Mess, we can talk more then.'

That evening, Simon and Alan sat together in a quiet corner, throwing further ideas around and committing their final solution to memory. Any slip-ups could cost them long prison sentences, or even their lives. For several hours, they plotted and planned, drinking copious amounts of tea and one or two glasses of brandy. At eleven o'clock, Simon got up to leave.

'Thank you, Alan. I owe you for this.' Reece waved his hand in the air as if it was nothing and said goodnight. He worked on for a further hour before he was satisfied that a workable plan was finally in place.

Later that night, Ed was successfully transferred to a room in the small cottage at the end of the village. Sister Youngs and private Baxter accompanied her, and no-one even noticed another soldier had gone. It would only be a short stay as Alan Reece pondered his next move.

Chapter 24

Frank, now satisfied he had done all he could, went off to find the cook house, and disrobed outside the door, leaving his muddy ghillie suit on the floor opposite. He carried the two rifles with him, and found the cooks sympathetic, finding him some hot beans and mutton and as much bread as he could eat. Fatigue had now caught up with him, and even though he knew he had a report to fill in, he wanted to remain at the hospital to find out how Ed was. He realised any news would be some time coming, so after filling his belly, he collected his things and found a quiet corner down the corridor and sat down. He leaned against the wall, his eyes closed, and was out of it in seconds.

Frank had no idea how long he had slept for but was awoken by someone kicking his boots. He thought at first, he was in the way, so gathered his feet in to let whomever it was to pass. But the kick came again, and he looked up in the dim light to see two men standing above him.

'Are you Private Smith?' said one of the men. 'Private Frank Smith, the sniper?'

Frank sat up awkwardly, before getting to his feet. He could now see the two men had MP armbands and the one who had addressed him, had three stripes. 'Uh, yes, Sergeant,' he said, now standing to attention trying to focus.

In a rather blasé way the sergeant said, 'You are under arrest, sonny,' as the corporal reached for his arm.

'What?' he said alarmed, not quite fully awake. 'But, why sergeant. What have I done?' he asked. The corporal slung both rifles, before grabbing Frank by the arm and guiding him down the corridor to a waiting vehicle. It was dark and he had no idea of time. The weapons were placed into the boot of the car, along with Frank's belt order containing his ammunition. He was then bundled into the back seat, with the corporal now sitting beside him. In the front, the sergeant sat upright in the driver's seat and without haste drove out of the village.

Frank was feeling slightly panicked and wondered what was going to happen. He looked back and forth to each of his escorts, but they didn't talk or return his look. His breathing rate increased, and his heart thumped in his chest. He realised this could only be about Ed and knew he was to be questioned, so started running though in his mind their relationship, when and where they first met, how he had discovered her secret and about their friendship.

Within minutes of leaving the field hospital, the car almost went off the road, throwing him sideways into the MP corporal. He looked at Frank, scowling, before the car settled back into its rhythm and sped off.

Frank looked across at the corporal again.

'It's no good keep looking at me, son, it's not me that's in the shit!' the corporal said before he could say anything.

Frank kept his mouth firmly shut after that, looking dead ahead, feeling extremely nervous. The MPs' intimidation tactics were working! Sometime later, the car swung through a large pair of ornate black gates, an MP standing by the entrance waving them through. He wasn't sure where he was, but could see a large house up ahead, with many lights on. They seemed to be on a long driveway heading up a slight hill and before he knew it, they drove behind the building, the sergeant pulling up in a gravel courtyard. The car swung round in a giant circle, coming to a stop next to some steps. The sergeant jumped out as Frank watched from the car. He disappeared inside the rear door, leaving the corporal with him in the back seat. The sergeant was gone for just a few seconds before he stepped out again and waved for his corporal. The NCO opened the door and jumped out briskly before walking around the rear of the car to Frank's side. He pulled on the handle and the door opened.

'Out,' he said, grabbing Frank's arm. The gravel crunched underfoot as they walked over to the steps, the centres worn down from years of use. Inside was not as Frank expected as it was rather plain with cream-coloured walls, hardly any furniture and a single picture of a landscape hanging at an angle on the far wall. He was told to sit by a door to his right, the corporal standing next to him, while the sergeant disappeared up the stairs. Frank began to get sweaty palms and swallowed nervously, asking for a drink. He then sat in silence, the corporal ignoring his request.

After five minutes, the door next to him opened and another sergeant stepped out, calling for him. Frank stood, took a deep breath and walked through the doorway, the NCO behind him.

'Don't be frightened, it's not a firing squad,' before pausing and then saying, 'Yet!' He giggled to himself, as Frank winced!

'That will be all, Corporal,' said the sergeant and encouraged Frank to come in and sit. As the door closed, he moved into the room and was amazed at how big the office was, for one person. His whole house at home could easily fit inside this single room and all it had in it was a large old desk over in the corner near the window, a few chairs and a single long bookcase full of files against one wall. Above the bookcase he couldn't help noticing a dramatic painting of a cavalry officer at the charge on his brown horse, with his feet back in the stirrups, sword pointing forward, the horse's ears pinned back aggressively, its teeth glowing yellow and foaming at the mouth as it galloped. He had never seen a painting like it before and was so focussed on it, he almost tripped over the carpet, which had rucked up a few feet from the officer's desk.

'Take a seat, Smith,' he was told and as he walked to a chair, he noticed for the first time another man in the room, sitting behind him in the far corner. He sat slowly, looking straight through the man across the desk.

'You can remove your head dress, Private, and sit at ease. Right, I am Major Clements of the Military Police and the officer commanding this sector under the command of General Davis. Now, I assume you know why you are here and so let's not waste time with preliminaries that are not necessary. He shuffled through some papers while Frank sat nervously, peering across at him.

'Firstly, can you confirm that you have been operating in the front line with Private Mitchell within the sniper squadron, under the command of Lieutenant Cavanagh?' Frank nodded before saying yes.

'OK, when did you first meet Mitchell and when did you commence operations within the sniper squadron?'

Frank thought to himself, weighing up his answer. The major watched him carefully, pen poised. He licked his dry lips nervously, wishing he had had that drink, and then began.

'It was in Bristol, sir, in training with the Gloucestershire Regiment, before being selected to join the sniper squadron in May last year. I couldn't be sure of the precise date.' And he stopped, aware he didn't wish to add anything more than he absolutely had to.

As the major wrote Frank's words down, he repeated his comments. 'So, you went through basic training in Bristol and then joined the sniper squadron in May of last year. And when did you find out Mitchell was a woman?'

'Find out, sir?'

Major Clements looked up from his page and paused for a split second before saying, 'You are not going to try and tell me you didn't know Mitchell was female, are you, Smith? There is a lot at stake here so be very mindful of your answers.'

Frank thought for only a moment before stating for the record that he found out she was female at the end of their sniper course in Linghem last Jun. Again, he stopped talking, not wanting to make problems for himself.

'OK, good, now how did you find out and why did you not inform your superiors about this, this matter?'

'Well, sir, Ed, err, Private Mitchell and I had worked together through the course and during week six we were given a 24-hour pass and headed into the local village. It was during some friendly banter Sir, that I found out.'

Major Clements sat back, looking over to the man in the corner, before continuing. 'So how did you find out, and I repeat, why did you not tell anyone?'

Frank was feeling dry and asked for some water, which was declined, before going on. 'Well, sir, we were horsing around, you see, after a few beers in a French café and I kind of noticed during a wrestling game.' He shut up again, hoping no more details were going to be necessary.

'And?' said the major.

'Well, sir, I didn't tell anyone as we had become the greatest of friends and we had both just passed the sniper course. We had been paired up as a team, you see, me as the observer and Mitchell as the shooter. She is a superb shot, sir, and was in fact top of the sniper course.'

The major allowed a smile creep across his face as he realised the loyalty he was showing her, before shaking his head gently from side to side, tapping his page with his pencil as he did so.

'We became very close friends, sir, and did everything together, as we grew close. We had to learn each other's ways and habits, operational actions and abilities. It was full-on, sir, and well, we worked well together.' He stopped talking as the officer rapidly scribbled notes on a pad.

'I would have done anything for Ed, anything, and so we just kept our heads down and did our job.' He folded his arms across his chest, aware he had probably said too much.

'Does anyone else know, anyone at all?' the major asked quickly.

'Not that I am aware of, sir no,' Frank said.

'OK, so who is Private Mitchell, I mean where is the story here and why did he, sorry, she, cheat the army?'

Frank was now slipping into difficult territory and had to refrain from mentioning Ed's brother at all costs, and so thinking quickly, he denied knowing the reasons why and shut up.

'Surely Mitchell told you her reasons. Are you aware of how serious this is, Smith, that you could be culpable in this crime? Because it is a crime, you know, and heads will roll, I assure you of that.'

Frank hesitated for a second but again denied he knew anything more, asking once again for some water. The major stood up and walked to the door, pulling it open and shouting down the hallway for the corporal. He walked back again to sit behind his desk, leaving the door open. Nothing happened for about thirty seconds and Clements was writing on his pad when a voice spoke from the doorway. 'Sir.'

'Yes, bring me a water jug and three glasses and some tea, we are going to be a while yet.'

The man turned about and left quickly, the major continuing to write furiously on the pad in front of him. A full two minutes later, the private returned with a tray holding a large teapot and two cups and saucers along with a jug of water and some glasses. He placed it on the top of the bookcase, poured the tea and served it to the two officers, and then poured a glass of water for each person present, including Frank. He left, and the questions continued.

Frank was thirsty and drank quickly from his glass, water dripping down his tunic. He put his glass down, leaving a wet ring on the officer's desk. But thankfully he didn't seem to notice.

'OK, Smith, let's continue. So, you say you have known about Mitchell's sex since last June. Do you think looking back you should have said something to your OC?'

'Sir, we, that is Mitchell and me, are a first-rate team who have attained more kills in the time than any other sniper pairing since we arrived, in fact it was a daring shot by her that killed The Joker, that put us in the field. She was shot during our retreat.'

'Yes, I am fully aware of that, but that is not relevant!' the major said firmly.

'Yes, sir, sorry, sir, but I just wanted to explain that she is the best in the squadron, sir, and we have become more than good together. Even General Haig sent his congratulations to our team, the signal being read out at our recent briefing by Major Hesketh-Pritchard.'

He paused and noticed Major Clements' face had changed dramatically when he had mentioned Haig's name.

'It is my belief, sir, we have made a big impact in our sector with many kills since we were deployed, mostly officers too, and topping off with the laughing Jerry!' He stopped talking, feeling as if he had won a small battle, the major giving him cursory acknowledgment.

'OK, so tell me about how Mitchell managed to hide herself from others in the trenches. Did you cover for her, did you protect her, what?'

'Sir, you must understand that when we were in the trenches, she was just a soldier like me, like the hundreds of lads around us, and because she was so good as a sniper, she earned great respect from everyone, even General Haig sir, all of us. So, she just blended in and no-one thought otherwise.' She is quite a soldier sir, and a bloody hero too, I hope this is recognised.'

The officer was now staring at him, almost spellbound, not really in the same room for a moment as he puzzled over Frank's comments. He glanced across at the man in the corner, and then back to Frank.

'Your view is interesting, Smith, but army regulations have been broken here and charges will be forthcoming, I assure you. You are culpable, Smith, whether you like it or not, so have a care in how you portray your views now and in the future.'

With that, the major wrote more notes for several minutes before placing his pen back on his desk. He looked Frank squarely in the eyes.

'I think we will stop there for tonight, it's rather late. Smith, as I have to make other enquiries before we can continue, I am sorry to say you will be kept overnight, and as you are under arrest you will be locked up in the cells here under the chateau. I will get the sergeant to take you there in a minute, so go outside and wait there in the seats by the door.'

At that Frank stood up and saluted, before turning about and heading for the door. As he reached it, he turned. 'Sir, Mitchell is a special soldier and deserves a medal for what she has done. She has saved lives and should not be punished.'

The officer said nothing as Frank stepped outside. He sat down and waited for five minutes and then heard a distant clock chime, eleven times.

An escort them took him down the corridor to some stone steps that wound down two flights into a large chilly basement. The cellars were clearly intended for wine, with many racks standing along two walls, some still holding dusty wine bottles. At the far end, he was shown into a temporary holding cell, with a steel-barred door. He was asked to give up his belt and braces and told to take the laces from his boots. He was then locked into his new but hopefully temporary home for the night.

There were no windows, just a straw mattress on the floor that looked stained and lumpy, with two blankets, and a bucket in the far corner. On the table was a drinking vessel full of water and a single mug. As the door closed behind him with a heavy clang, he turned to watch the sergeant walk away, leaving him to his personal thoughts.

Upstairs, Major Clements was still preparing his report for General Davis. He would deliver it at zero seven hundred, sharp the following day. He was not going to like it much.

Chapter 25

Private Oseland, the general's batman, arrived with morning tea, promptly, at six o'clock, but unusually, his officer was already up. He had only been his batman for six weeks, after his predecessor had volunteered to go back to the front line following many difficulties working for this very awkward man. Private Douglas Oseland was a stocky man in his late thirties with considerable personality and experience and was able to deal with his temperament well. He had been promoted several times in his long career, but due to a mister meaner, or two, had been busted three times. No matter, he seemed happier not to have too much responsibility, and after two full years in the trenches, a small room on the top floor of the chateau suited him well. His sound wit and positive outlook seemed to appeal to the general and they got along rather well. Oseland strived to always be one step ahead of his man, often asking him questions to divert his attention. This day was to be no exception.

'Questions, questions, always so many bloody questions, Oseland,' the general said sharply as he sipped his tea, sitting beside his vast canopied bed. He knew he had a good man and was pleased how quickly Oseland had grasped the role and he did actually enjoy his company, but he would of course, never tell him so. He remembered how the previous week he had seen Oseland returning from the chateau gardens with the dog that the headquarters staff had adopted. He was standing with other officers in the rear yard and had called him over to ask him how he had trained the dog so quickly.

'Oh, I have always had dogs, sir,' he said. 'They seem to take to me. Would you like to see a trick, sir?' he had asked him. The general had nodded, thinking nothing of what was to come. Oseland called the dog over to sit and bending down, said; 'What do, Germans do?' and the animal tossed himself onto his back, legs in the air and acted as if dead! The officers chuckled one asking to see it again. Oseland patted the dog on the head but said, he could other things too. At that, Oseland then pointed his index finger at the dog by his feet and made the sound of a gunshot. The dog immediately flopped down on his side and lay deadly still. The officers roared with laughter and Davis smiled at the thought, as he sipped his tea.

'Is there anything else, sir, before I run your bath?' said Oseland, but he got no answer as the general seemed miles away.

Oseland didn't wait, instead walked to the bathroom to turn on the brass taps at the head of the giant roll-top bath. When he returned, the general put his cup down and walked towards him.

'My new boots today, I think, and my second set of number twos, oh, and belt order, no, sword,' he said as he started to push the door shut.

'Yes, sir, would that be with one of your new Savile Row shirts? They arrived yesterday.' The door opened slightly; the general's face just visible. 'Ah, yes, that would be good, thank you, Oseland.'

The private set about his duties and folded back the large white shutters on the tall windows before straightening the bed, noticing a red stain on the sheets. He looked up to see an empty port decanter on the opposite bedside table and knew immediately where it had come from. He would change his bed later he thought, but for now pulled the thick eiderdown up, before emptying the ashtrays and picking up the clothes cast aside the previous evening. He laid out the general's fresh uniform, and then disappeared back downstairs, taking his boots to be polished. Knowing the general was a man of routine, and liked to bathe, shave and then dress himself, he had about twenty minutes, so he grabbed a brew while he chatted to the kitchen porter. When he returned, the general was just stepping from his toilet.

Oseland placed the boots down by the chair as Davis sat on his bed.

'Sir, what can I order for your breakfast this morning?'

The general looked up and smiled, realising how much he liked this chap! 'Fish, I think, Oseland, with eggs and toast,' he said, then stood to pull his trousers up, his bracers hanging by his side.

Oseland went to retrieve his gown and hung it in the wardrobe before going to drain the bath, something his officer never did himself. As he re-entered the room, the general was fully dressed in his brown uniform, his colourful medal ribbons set in three rows above his left breast pocket standing out from the drab colour of the uniform. He knelt by the foot stool to assist the general with his tight new boots, before leaving the room to order the general's breakfast and get on with the rest of his day.

Captain Arding had already eaten when the general came down to the dining room and was busy sorting some papers as he walked in through the far doorway.

'Good morning, sir, I trust you slept well,' he said.

'Bugger off, Arding, you ask me that every day and yet you know full well I don't, Now has the report from Major Clements arrived yet?' he asked.

'Yes sir, I have placed it on your desk.' Captain Arding then paused, for a thank you, but as the seconds ticked by, he realised one was not forthcoming, and left without another word.

He finished preparing the meeting room and finalised the seating plan for the eight o'clock meeting. He surveyed the room from the door. Regimental paintings lined the far wall opposite the windows and ornate silverware was displayed in various cabinets at the end of the room. The table was set with a name card and a large green blotter pad for each attendee, with the agenda set in the centre. He had placed a pencil and a glass with a decanter of water in front, just as the general liked it. Davis, unlike many staff officers, liked to conduct his meetings from the centre of one side of his long table, as many British prime ministers had done for decades. There would be six at the meeting: General Davis, Lieutenant Colonel Wood, Major Hesketh-Pritchard, Major Leigh-Smith, himself and the regional OC from the Military Police, Major Clements. By seven thirty the room was ready. As a final touch he placed a silver statue of a cavalry officer on horseback at the charge as a centre piece, something the general particularly liked, and that had adorned his table on many occasions. He stood back and checked everything before walking back down the corridor to his desk in the general's outer office. A few minutes passed, then he heard the general call for him. He rose and stuck his nose around the door.

'Yes sir, what can I get you?'

'Is everything ready for the meeting, Arding, and has everyone arrived?' the general asked. 'Oh, and what of Mitchell, did the ambulance arrive at the field hospital?' he said, continuing to walk into his office. Just as Arding was about to answer, a voice spoke from behind him. He turned to see Lieutenant Colonel Wood. He stepped to one side to let him pass and he strode in, saluting as he entered.

'Morning, sir, and no, not when I left the hospital, but we do expect him, or rather her, sometime late this morning.'

He started to take off his cap, as the general barked at him, making him jump.

'Can we please stop calling this soldier 'her'. Bloody hell, man, the name is Mitchell!' he bellowed. 'I want to know the moment Mitchell arrives, make sure than happens, Colonel.'

'Yes, sir, we will be notified the moment the ambulance arrives,' said the colonel, wincing.

Captain Arding eased his way out and slipped down to the meeting room. He noticed the MP officer standing on his own by the window and two other officers pouring themselves coffee from the silver jug in the far corner, before returning to the General's office.

'Sir, everyone is present,' he said.

Davis looked up and did a sideways swipe with his head to Colonel Wood, as he collected his blue file and walked towards the door. 'This is going to be interesting,' he muttered to himself with a smile.

Chapter 26

Ed came around from a deep sleep, not knowing quite where she was. She had a faint recollection of being placed in an ambulance, but her memory was full of gaps and she couldn't remember when that was or how long she had been there. She tried to recall when she was shot and getting to the hospital, but it was all a bit of a blur. Her mind was playing tricks on her, but she did remember Frank holding her tightly in the darkness, shells dropping all around them and the next thing was a high vaulted ceiling, of a church, but that could have been days ago.

She blinked several times to clear the feeling of grit in her eyes, before casting her gaze around the room. It was a different room from her last memory, and the light shone brightly through the single window. She turned her head to the other side and could see a figure sleeping in a chair, his arms folded across his chest, snoring quietly. She then realised her right arm was in a sling and as she tried to sit up, a spasm of pain crashing through her chest, and she yelled out as she dropped back down. The man suddenly jumped up from his slumber and rubbed his eyes before leaning over her. She was almost sick; his breath stank of garlic!

'Are you OK, Mitchell, where does it hurt?' he asked.

'Can I have some water please,' Ed said softly. Turning her head away from his violent breath. 'Where am I?' she asked.

'You're in a cottage hospital and very lucky to be alive,' he said, grabbing a tiny cup with a short spout. He poured a little water into the cup before helping her to have a few sips. Putting it down, he then left the room.

Private Baxter, a veteran of hospital duties, rushed down to the sister's room and tapped gently on the door. He spoke to inform her that Mitchell had woken before heading off to fetch the doctor from the church, as ordered. The nurse quickly rose to her feet and walked down the dark corridor to the small room at the end. As she stepped in, she was pleased to see a face with wide eyes and a smile. Ed, happy to see a woman for the first time in months, locked eyes with her as she came close, not expecting the words that came next.

'You are a brave young woman,' said the nurse. 'But before we go into how you have managed to be here at all, I need to know how your pain is and whether your wounds are infected.'

Ed said nothing, just looked up at the grubby ceiling, feeling uncomfortable that her secret was out. As she lay pondering her position, the sister bent forward to smell her shoulder and chest from quite close up.

Ed spoke quietly. 'I don't have much pain as long as I keep still. I tried to turn, but it was very sore.'

'Please don't move too much. You have been through a great deal, but fortunately for you the bullet passed right through your body, although it has left a rather large exit wound in your upper chest. We have packed and dressed it as best we can and are hopeful it will heal well.' As she spoke, she supported Ed's body slightly and placed the spout of the cup to her lips. She drank quickly. 'The doctor is on his way so try and relax.'

Ed didn't answer but wondered how long she had been there, closing her eyes as the cool water settled in her stomach. The sister then turned her slightly to inspect the dressing on her back, sniffing again before nodding her head.

'Well, it looks like your wounds are ok, with no sign of infection, as yet. That's good news Mitchell.' Then suddenly, two men came in panting as if they had been running. One was the man she had seen earlier, the other was wearing a white coat and was striking, as he had a huge moustache with not a blade of hair on his head.

He went to Ed's bedside. 'Welcome back to land of the living,' he said, before introducing himself. 'I am Captain Martin, one of the doctors who helped put you back together. You suffered a gunshot, which I am sure you realise, going through the middle of your back, coming out the top of your chest. It appears to have avoided anything serious, but it did take some material from your uniform into your body, so we had to cut you up a bit to make sure we got it all. It will hurt for a while yet, but we feel confident you will make a full recovery.'

Ed was quite alert now, as the three people in the room stood around her bed.

'Can I sit up, sir? I feel as though lying here is making it hard to breathe,' she said with a slightly husky voice.

'OK, let's see what we can do,' said the captain. 'Baxter, get a couple of pillows, can you, and a blanket.' As Baxter left the room, the sister stepped round to the other side of Ed's narrow cot, ready to help lift her up. When

Baxter returned, they reached under her shoulders. 'OK, when I say lift, I want you, Mitchell, to take a deep breath. Baxter, I want you to place the pillows under her back and head.' Ed winced a little from the pain but stayed quiet so as not to be a sissy! She sagged back into the pillows, her head propped up slightly and breathing more easily.

'Sister, can you give Mitchell a wash down, while Baxter fetches some soup and bread from the cook house. Give Sister Youngs time to finish, Baxter say, twenty minutes?' he nodded and left the room, followed by the sister. Doctor Martin pulled up a chair and sat down beside her.

'When you came in yesterday, Mitchell, it was a huge shock for us all and, well, a day to remember amongst many we would like to forget. I should advise you, at some point in the near future you will have to explain yourself, how you came to be here, how you have hidden your identity, and that we have been ordered to transfer you to a hospital further down the line, near General Davis's HQ. But there is a problem.' He stopped talking, knowing what the major had told him would come as a shock to her, but she should know her fate! 'Major Leigh-Smith, a surgeon and my superior officer, has authorised me to tell you the following. The bottom line is, you have caused quite a stir and some people in authority want answers and for this matter to go away, fast! General Davis, for his own reasons, has arranged for your early withdrawal but we are concerned for your welfare. Because of this, you will stay here as long as we can manage to hold on to you, so your wounds can heal, as the journey could quite easily kill you!'

'What do you mean, they want this to go away, sir? I don't understand, I did my duty, didn't I? Have I not put my life at risk for my Country?' She said quite angrily. 'Am I at risk Sir?'

'I can't answer that, Mitchell, and I am not your enemy here. But, it's not clear why, against all advice, a general takes personal charge of a wounded soldier! That in itself is suspicious and we simply want to give you the best possible chance to survive any journey and so we will apply various tactics to hold you here until we are forced to transfer you and have made plans accordingly.'

Ed put her head back on the pillow and took several deep breaths as she absorbed what he had said. She suddenly thought her plan to take her dear brother's place could now land all of them in deep trouble, and if a general was interested in her, God only knows what might happen next!

Just then the sister came back in, carrying a bowl of steaming water and a towel over her arm. The captain rose and said, 'Rest, young lady, and don't worry, we have your back.' He left the room, closing the door behind him. Sister Youngs placed the bowl down and laid the towel on her legs.

'So, what's your first name, Mitchell?' she asked.

'It's Edwina,' she said quietly. 'But people call me Ed.'

Sister Youngs nodded and smiled at her. 'Well, I am Andrea, and I will be caring for you over the coming days. Firstly, I need to change your dressings, Ed, so why don't you tell me all about yourself and how you came to be here.'

Ed thought carefully before answering, wondering if this was some sort of interrogation process, following what she had just learnt. Instead of speaking, she watched with interest as the dressing on her chest was unwrapped, before Andrea eased it gently from her skin at the corner. She sniffed, then carefully peeled it back slightly, but blood trickled from the wound, so she replaced it sharply.

'That will bleed if I take it off Edwina, the hole made by the bullet is about the size of a small apple, so will leave it for another day or so,' She bound the dressing up again and began washing her down.

'So, how did you find the training with all those men. It must have been very hard for you?' Andrea asked. Ed explained how she just put her head down and got on with it but did enjoy the range work and sniper selection. She decided not to mention anything about Frank, at least for now, until she knew the sister could be trusted. Andrea listened with an enthusiastic ear as she worked her way round Ed's slim body with soap and warm water, something Ed reacted to with much pleasure. She helped her to roll over to clean her back, washing her short hair and checking for lice, still listening intently to her story of life in the trenches.

'But how did you manage your toilet Ed, and your period?' she asked. Ed told her how she had practised her toilet in the barn at home, standing like a man, and how she had become very accomplished. She was even proud to finally tell someone, how she had devised a simple system to manage her monthly periods. The sister stopped and stared at her, shaking her head, having just made the connection.

'Oh, you poor girl, however did you manage?'

Ed smiled. 'Sister, no-one forced me to do this.' She said slightly annoyed. 'I did it because I wanted to compete with men, for the first time in my life, on an equal footing and think I did pretty well. If I hadn't overcome those issues, I would have failed from the outset.' And she sagged back on the pillow, exhausted.

Sister Youngs, was slightly taken aback, as clearly, she could be feisty when she wanted too, even when seriously ill. But recognised what she had achieved was outstanding and no-one would ever take that from her. She dressed her in a clean gown, but Ed was unable to help much and lay as still as possible, saying nothing. She closed her eyes and felt a great deal better, especially as the inquisition had finally stopped.

'There,' said the sister. 'How does that feel?'

'I feel alive again,' Ed said. 'Thank you, before Ed closed her eyes, as a sign she wanted to sleep. She started to wonder where Frank might be and could now remember him placing field dressings on her wounds in the shell hole, ultimately saving her life! She vaguely remembered him carrying her through No Man's Land too, and falling into the trench, but the rest was darkness. With a sudden start, she opened her eyes, wanting to ask someone about him, just as Baxter came through the door with a small tray, a bowl at its centre.

'Enjoy your meal,' said Andrea and with that she was gone.

'Soup and bread for a brave soldier,' he said, placing the tray on the table.

Ed thought this odd, as she didn't think of herself as brave, just doing her bit. 'Do you happen to know where Private Smith might be?' she asked. 'He brought me here.'

Baxter thought for a moment. 'Ah, no, miss, I don't. But I could find out for you. Let's try and get this food inside you first, eh.'

Baxter moved over to her side and placed a cloth over her chest. Sitting next to her, he started stirring the soup around before lifting half a spoonful to Ed's mouth. Her lips parted, and she welcomed the hot, broth, the first food she had eaten for two days. The first few sips seemed to go down well, but then she belched and put her hand up to her mouth, before vomiting onto her chest. Baxter quickly wiped her mouth and took the soup away. She closed her eyes just for a moment to try and settle her stomach and laid back. When she opened them again, she realised she had briefly dropped off to sleep, as Andrea had arrived and Baxter was gone.

'Don't worry Ed, it often happens. We will just stick to water for another day.' Andrea said tucking in her sheets.

'Sister, um, Andrea, sorry. Would you do me a favour, please. Could I dictate a letter as I can't write at the moment?

'Yes, of course, I'll go and get my writing box, be right back,' and she left, returning just a few minutes later. But Ed was fast asleep.

Chapter 27

Major Leigh-Smith was woken by his orderly at just before five o'clock with a firm shake and a hot brew of tea. As he peered at the face behind the candle, the importance of the monumental day ahead suddenly gripped him. He rubbed his sleepy eyes with both knuckles, aware that four hours' sleep was really not enough for any man, especially in this war footing.

'Is the QM up yet?' he asked as he reached for the white enamel mug.

'Not yet, sir, on my way to his quarters next. Is there anything else, sir?' Tomlinson asked.

Simon took his first sip through pursed lips and then shook his head gently, before swallowing. 'No, that will be all, thanks,' he said, as he clambered out of his narrow cot. Standing in his long johns and vest, with his socks still on, he lit his lamp and placed it on the shelf next to his mirror, before pouring cold water from the steel jug into the bowl in front of him. He bent forward and splashed water over his face several times, trying to stimulate life into his tired body, before reaching for his cut-throat razor to shave. He finally rinsed his face, wiped the razor and left the bowl for his orderly to clear away, before dressing quickly and heading out of the door. As he stepped into the corridor a blast of chilled air rolled down the dark passageway, and he pulled the long scarf sent to him by his mother tightly around his neck. He wondered what the day would bring and whether all would go to plan. If not, his career could well be over and his future bleak! He knew they were taking great risks, and as time progressed, more and more people would become involved. He knew what he must do, and he was prepared for whatever lay ahead.

With his mind in neutral, he turned the corner, not noticing Alan Reece in the darkness standing by his office door and almost knocking him over. They grinned at each other.

'Come in, old man,' he said, the QM lighting several candles around his tiny office. Simon sat on the old box as Alan slid behind his desk.

'Right, it took some arranging, but I have managed to get Mitchell to stay at the small cottage hospital in Saint-Denis that we spoke of, but she needs to go today. This will provide us some time to action phase two of getting her back to Blighty.' Simon nodded, comforted in the knowledge that she would soon be far away, and out of the general's grasp. He then confirmed that apart from official ambulance movement logs and the transfers papers, nothing written would exist of their subterfuge. The paper trail ended!

At precisely six o'clock a knock came on the office door, before it was gently pushed open and standing there in the darkness were three uniformed men. The drivers were led by a tall, gangling man with a dark moustache. They were beckoned in, and standing to attention their leader saluted, the others following suit behind him. The QM looked intently at all three of them in turn, trying hard to be as normal as possible, as these chaps had to believe this was just a normal day.

'OK, men, we have three vehicle transfers today. Blake, you have the longest run to the main hospital at Divisional Headquarters with three patients. Two are French soldiers to be dropped off en route at the small French town of Vervins. I think you may have been there before. So, a couple of hours' journey, and then with one of our own for HQ. You will be accompanied by Private Jones, a new man who joined last week. You will collect your patients from the chapel door at the back and report back to me, when your loaded. You will need your overnight kit as you will need to stay at HQ until tomorrow, as there is another run for you in the morning. Liaise with Captain Hargreaves, the QM. Any questions, Blake?' he asked.

'No, sir.' Reece signed the paperwork and handed it to the driver, who left without further word.

'Right, the second run is to a small village called St Bazaire to the south-east, it's about one hundred miles away so it will be a long day for you, Bridges. I suggest you drop by the canteen to obtain rations for the two of you, but I will expect you back by nightfall. The patient is under no immediate danger and can sit upright so there will be no orderly with you. Take vehicle 40 GR 23, which has the internal window allowing you to communicate for drinks and comfort stops. All OK, Bridges?' he asked again.

'Collection point, sir?' he said, looking up from his notebook.

'Front door, patient can walk on his good leg. Report back to me when loaded. Here is your paperwork, now I suggest you get on your way as soon as you can.'

The soldier departed, leaving the tall gangly private standing in the office, towering over Captain Reece's desk.

'OK, that leaves you, Taylor. You are in luck as your run is to take a French soldier who is seriously ill to Saint-Denis on the northern outskirts of Paris. Yes, I did say Paris, Taylor,' he said with a smile. The driver looked down and grinned wildly at him. 'You will be accompanied by Sister Youngs who will also stay overnight before you collect her again tomorrow. The patient has an infection, so I want you to wear your gown and cover your face when transporting him into the cottage hospital. It's most important that you drive steadily making the journey as comfortable as possible. Sister Youngs has the details. All clear, lad?' Taylor nodded, without speaking, and Captain Reece looked up at this giant of a man with a certain affection. 'By the way, Taylor, how long have you been in France now?'

'Just over two years, sir. If you remember I arrived the day after your good self, sir,' he said boldly.

'So you did.' said the QM, a fact he knew very well, but he was reinforcing the bond that existed between them. 'I remember thinking then you must have been brought up standing in a bucket of manure! How tall are you, Taylor?'

'Six feet five inches sir,' he said.

'Well, I think you do a good job here, Taylor, and the men like and respect you too. That is why I have kept the best job today for you.'

Taylor beamed at him, delighted. 'Well, thank you, sir, didn't think anyone had noticed me.'

'Well, I have, and long may your good work continue. Sister Youngs will be at the patient's bedside, so liaise with her. For your troubles, I have authorised you a 24-hour pass.' He said. 'You will meet Sister Youngs at midday tomorrow to return here so don't be late. Your time is your own once your duties are done so enjoy your night out in Paris.'

The private stood grinning, flicking his eyes back and forth across the room from Captain Reece to the major. He rubbed his hands together, joyfully. 'Thanks, sir, thanks very much, you can rely on me, sir' He reached for his transfer papers and his pass.

'Finally, there has been a change. I don't need you to depart until after ten hundred hours and your pick-up-point is the cottage hospital at the end of the village at zero nine thirty. Please liaise with Captain Martin, then report back to me here before you leave.'

'Yes, sir, thank you again, sir.' And he was off and out of the door, realising he had plenty of time, so headed off to the canteen.

All this time, Simon had sat in the corner not uttering a single word, instead just watching a master at work. Alan had a balance of superiority and friendship with his drivers, who clearly respected him. Even giving praise to Taylor, who cherished his overnight pass to Paris, was a stroke of genius, he thought. It had worked too, as he had the men eating out of his hands.

'So, we can do no more for now,' said Simon and Alan grinned at him.

'Breakfast?' he suggested and they both stood to head to the Mess. It was a little after six thirty in the morning and Simon had just enough time to eat before heading off to his big meeting at Divisional HQ! A meeting he wasn't looking forward to one bit!

Chapter 28

Edward woke with a start, the bedclothes strewn across the bed, his right leg hanging over the side. He looked at the old clock on the bedside table, to see it was just after five thirty. He yawned and pulled the covers back across his body, much to the annoyance of David, who lay beside him!

His lover tugged them back before cuddling Edward under the covers. Edward looked into David's eyes and gently touched his cheek, smiling to himself: how much his world had changed and so quickly too! Their urge to love each other was dangerous, they both knew that, but it had happened so gracefully, with David reciprocating from the outset. Edward felt totally relaxed in his company but wondered how long this happiness could last, as he remembered the night, he had told David everything.

He was washing himself down at the back of the kitchen, totally naked in the old tin bath, when the door opened. He looked up to see David staring at him, one hand on the latch, the other carrying the large kettle full of hot water. He was smiling at him and Edward froze to the spot. But, instead of asking him to leave, he stayed quiet and David simply closed the door behind him and walked over. He remembered that he felt calm with no nerves, as he had grown very fond of him. He sat down hugging his legs and David poured the fresh hot water from the fire over his feet, before putting the empty kettle down and kneeling beside the bath. He looked at Edward and said the words that he had never forgotten.

'I think I have fallen in love with you Ed.' He said warmly, not taking his eyes off him. They reached for each other holding hands delicately, smiling. Edward knew he was helplessly in love with this man too and slowly leant back against the end of the bath while David took the soap and started to wash him. Their lives changed dramatically that night, and they cleared Edward's parents' room and moved their belongings in together! The large double bed became their hideaway of love and passion.

It had all seemed quite natural and later, Edward had told David the full story of his life and about Ed. He felt embarrassed that David might think him a coward, but he seemed to understand.

Chapter 29

The meeting was called to order and General Davis took his place in the centre of the long teak table. A fresh coat of polish made the table gleam brightly in the morning sun, the light from the long window creating an almost mirror reflection. The seating plan was clearly designed to be intimidating for some, with Major Leigh-Smith sitting directly opposite him and Major Hesketh-Pritchard to his right. Colonel Wood sat to the general's left and an unknown face from the Military Police on his right. Captain Arding, two seats down, took notes.

'Gentlemen, I thank you for taking the time to attend this meeting so promptly and trust you have answers for me on this immense problem. If you're in any doubt about how serious this matter is, I will tell you now that heads will roll when I find out who is responsible for this almighty embarrassment, that could cause the army and His Majesty's Government great difficulty. It is, gentlemen, a huge affair, make no mistake. Someone has allowed a woman to enter the British Army to fight our country's battles and they have been operating in the front line right under the nose of Major Hesketh-Pritchard for many months without detection. Have no doubts, we will become a laughing stock, across the whole British Army if this gets out and probably the German Army too. So, we have to take some swift and decisive action without delay.' He paused for a moment, feeling rather pleased with his opening salvo, and watched the faces of the men around the table. Good, he thought, I have their attention.

Major Hesketh-Pritchard's heart was pounding, as he tried to make head or tale of what the general had just implied. A woman in the field, under my nose, he thought. How was that possible? He felt the world suddenly close in on him. What had he missed? Davis continued.

'Now, currently only a few people are aware of the situation and most are sat in this very room. I want it to stay that way, and with some careful manoeuvring, we might just keep it quiet. So, a tight lid is to be kept on this and for that reason I am having this private transferred to the field hospital here under Colonel Wood this very day,' he said, before pausing to look at his notes. 'Major Leigh-Smith, I presume my orders of transfer have been carried out?'

'Sir, I left before the transfers began, but assume she is on her way as we speak.'

The general winced as the word 'she' was said aloud! He grunted and carried on. 'I have also invited Major Clements here today as there will be some serious fall-out from this matter, with various consequences. He has already begun his investigation.' The major nodded once, flicking his eyes at the two officers opposite him.

'So, let's start at the beginning. Major Hesketh-Pritchard, how have you allowed a woman to be in your sniper squadron?'

The major was stunned. He was not here to be lambasted, or so he thought, and stuttered, before seeking to clarify the situation.

'Sir, I don't understand the question. I thought I was asked here to discuss private Mitchell, my leading sniper. So, whom are we referring to here?' he said

'Oh, have you not been listening, Major? It would seem you have had a female in your midst for over nine months. Private Mitchell is a woman!' Davis leant back in his chair, hands clenched on the table, looking sternly at him.

The major was stunned and could hardly speak. He sat frowning, looking around the table for support, but everyone's eyes were upon him.

'Well, no, sir. This is the first I have heard of this. Are we talking about the same Mitchell, private Ed Mitchell?' he asked.

The general looked down at his notes. 'Private E Mitchell, attached to the 2nd/5th Gloustershire regiment, under the command of Lieutenant Cavanagh, but ultimately, your responsibility.' He said peering across over his rimmed glasses.

'But I thought we were here to discuss a gallantry medal.' He said seeking support from some of those present.

'And why would we be doing that Major?' the general asked. "You don't know Sir?' Hesketh-Pritchard said with a superior tone. 'Well, two days ago, private Mitchell killed The Joker, the target general Haig had placed on the very top of his hit list.' He's dead sir.

General Davis was clearly stunned at this piece of information and sat back in his chair, totally speechless for several seconds. He frowned and bit his lower lip his eyes glanced down the table at Captain Arding.

'Would you like to offer an explanation as to why I was not informed Arding?' he said sternly.

Captain Arding began to wriggle in his seat. 'Sir, I didn't know about this either, no-one has informed this HQ, I can assure you of that,' he said in his defence. The general was clearly shocked at the statement and seemed unsure about his next move, knowing he couldn't ignore this information.

'That is of course, very good news, major,' he said quietly, 'But we are not here to discuss gallantry medals, we are here to ascertain how a woman has managed to fool you, and others to obtain a foothold in the King's army. Someone who has been under your nose for nine months, a woman, and you had no idea?' The general had in a simple sentence, reversed the pressure off him and thrown his full weight back across the desk to the major.

'Sir, I am shocked to hear what you have just told me.' he said, finding it hard to believe the soldier he first met over a year ago on the ranges at Linghem, was female. He had been tasked to take out the Joker for some time, with the authorisation coming direct from Haig himself, and now Davis was practically ignoring it.

'Sir, with all due respect, this is a monumental achievement and yet you pass over it as if it didn't happen. This has been a top priority for many months and Mitchell deserves a medal, not this, this meeting to cover it up.' But he had said too much.

General Davis suddenly stood up and yelled at him across the table. 'Who do you think you are, Major, telling me how to run my own enquiry, my own division?' he said, his voice rising. 'I will have you arrested if you continue in this vein, and Lieutenant Cavanagh too as he was Mitchell's OC. Now, answer my question, and be damn quick about it.' And he sat back down heavily in his seat.

Major Hesketh-Pritchard gathered his thoughts as his heart pounded in his chest, coming to understand that here was man who had an agenda and if he didn't watch out, he would be part of it.

'Sir, I have recruited many men from the ranks to perform dangerous field work in No Man's Land, selected from regiments throughout Britain. Some were even identified during training, as Mitchell was, and to date we have trained over one hundred successfully, with the loss of only three. These men have killed around fifty German officers and men, some notable targets to boot, including the most recent, The Joker.' He watched the general flinch as he reminded him of their latest success, before continuing. 'Mitchell was found during basic training in Bristol, I think, and we met for the first time during the training course at Linghem last year. Amongst a group of twenty men, Mitchell was the best shot on the course by a country mile and I had no reason to doubt anything at that time as he, um, she had completed basic training without a problem. The course was run by one of my lieutenants and he is now the Officer Commanding for that particular squadron. I only saw Mitchell one other time, at the pass-out, when the best sniper award was presented, to her I might add, until we had a briefing a few months ago.'

'Says a lot for your selection process, eh, Major. You have let a woman into our army and totally disgraced us and I want someone's head for it. Is it yours, maybe, or perhaps this, cavalier lieutenant? What do you say to that, Pritchard?'

The major, feeling as if he was walking headlong into an ambush, steadied himself before answering. 'Well, sir, a one-and-a-half-inch grouping for five rounds at three hundred yards is the pass-out standard we require and is pretty good shooting, I am sure you agree?'

The general nodded, not realising he was heading into a trap.

'Well, Mitchell didn't make that, sir.' He paused. 'She made a one-inch group at that very distance, at every stage of the final week. Fine shooting, sir, don't you agree?'

Davis knew he had been caught out and glanced briefly at the major before swinging his attention across to the doctor without responding. 'Major Leigh-Smith, when did you first see Mitchell?' he asked aggressively.

Simon recognised the general seemed to be trying to set traps for all and sundry and spoke cautiously. 'Two days ago, sir, around thirteen hundred hours. She was brought into the hospital, and I and one of my doctors operated on her.

'And what was Mitchell's condition?'

'Well sir, her condition was very serious and remains so. A gunshot midway up her back coming out below the right clavicle on the front of her chest, taking with it pieces of clothing into her right lung and blowing part of the muscle wall away. But miraculously the bullet did not shatter any bones as it passed through her. We had to open her up and dig for debris, but when I last saw her late last night, she was sleeping. I hope she survives the journey today, sir, which as I said is against my medical advice. I have written my diagnosis and treatment plan down for the record.'

Colonel Wood looked at him with pursed lips from across the table and shook his head slightly, one medical man to another. The major ignored his action and continued.

'As she is still my patient, sir, I plan to visit her before I leave today,' he said, knowing full well she wasn't ever going to arrive.

Davis jumped in quickly. 'Oh, that won't be necessary, the Colonel has control now, you may leave without concern. I am sure you have lots of work back at your field hospital to keep you busy.' Leigh-Smith thought about responding but, knew he had better quit while he was ahead. The colonel was staring at him with wide eyes.

'So, what are the chances of Mitchell surviving with these wounds?' General Davis asked.

'Sir, providing the wounds don't get infected and the journey doesn't kill her, she may have a chance, but as I explained on the telephone, this is a significant risk and against my medical advice, so I would say she only has a small chance of survival.' The general immediately looked down the table at captain Arding and waived a finger at him, shaking his head. Then it dawned on Simon. He was instructing his ADC not to write down what he had said in the minutes!

'Good,' the general continued, not making it clear to anyone in the room whether he meant good that Mitchell might die, or good she might get an infection.

'I have asked Major Clements here to advise on the legal process and whether a court martial should be convened once the matter has been investigated. So, Major, could you please explain your conclusions.'

Major Clements, an old Etonian and experienced soldier, sat forward for the first time and without notes began to recite army law. 'Gentlemen, it is clear that there has been a breach of military law and discipline, as impersonating a member of the British Army is a serious offence. Charges are certain to follow and if the defendant is found guilty of these charges, Mitchell could easily end up in front of a firing squad. Anyone aiding or abetting Mitchell may also be charged with various offences and receive the same punishment, or at best a prison sentence.' He paused for a moment as he looked down at his notes, the officers around the room not moving a muscle, shocked at the seriousness of the statement. Simon looked around for solace, but their expressions gave nothing away. He was about to protest when the general held his hand up, saying, 'Continue, Major Clements.'

'I have sent a signal to Warminster requesting an urgent visit is made to Private Mitchell's home to ascertain whom she is impersonating or whether she is guilty of stealing someone's identity. I should have answers on this within the week. In the meantime, I have already convened an interview with private Smith and will be conducting one with Mitchell, as soon as is practicable. I am also required to interview both of you, gentlemen, and that these take place directly after this meeting.' He stopped talking to look at Hesketh-Pritchard and Leigh-Smith, watching for their reactions, but they both stayed poker faced. 'I stress, that charges will be made for Conduct prejudicial to good order and military discipline, and it may well affect officers present around this table. Her observer, too, whom she had been operating with for many months, and his OC, Lieutenant Cavanagh, may also be implicated, and arrests may take place in England of any family members or friends who knew of this subterfuge.'

The two majors looked at each other pensively, not knowing how to respond.

'Thank you, Major Clements,' said Davis. 'I hope this now makes it clear, gentlemen, how seriously we are taking this and how heads will ultimately roll.' He paused to look at the officers across the table, then looked up at the clock on the wall. 'And on that, we will adjourn for morning tea.'

The ADC closed his minute book and went into the next room, while the steward wheeled in a trolley laden with refreshments. Leigh-Smith and Hesketh-Pritchard helped themselves before walking together towards the window, watched carefully by General Davis from across the room. They looked out at the glorious day outside, as they stirred their tea, wishing there they were anywhere else but in this room. It was Hesketh-Pritchard who broke the silence.

'This is not going to end well.' The doctor took a sip of his tea before answering. 'I think we have to step up,' he said quietly. 'We simply cannot allow this travesty of justice to go forward and must somehow find a way to protect this young woman who has put her country first. I will not allow this to go on without challenge as it is, and as I stand here now, I swear to try and protect her from this, madman, who implied to me only the other evening that this matter would be best gone.'

Hesketh-Pritchard looked at him with deep concern. 'OK, what do you propose?' he said, sipping his tea once again.

'Can I trust you?' Simon asked quietly.

'As an officer and a gentleman, I give you my word.' Simon peered into his eyes, seeking some sign he was a man of his word. He sipped his tea then casually looked across the room, before placing his cup on his saucer silently. 'OK. We can't do this now as eyes are upon us. Let's agree to convene later before we head back.'

He nodded just as General Davis looked across at them. He didn't seem to miss much.

'OK, gentlemen, let's reconvene, I have a lot to do today.' The table swiftly filled, Captain Arding with pencil at the ready.

'Colonel, any news from the hospital?' asked Davis.

'No, sir, I have just chatted to the registration clerk and as yet, the ambulance has not arrived.' The general looked at his wristwatch, then at Leigh-Smith, pursing his lips in obvious annoyance.

'Gentlemen, I would like to remind you all of the seriousness of this matter and your loyalty to King and country comes above all else. I call for a total black-out on you discussing this with anyone outside of this room, unless specifically told to do so. I should also state for the record, that if one of your subordinates slip up, it will not only be their heads that will roll. I hope I make myself clear! Major Leigh-Smith, whom among your team know of the situation?'

Simon paused to think, as he didn't wish to get this wrong. 'Six people, sir. One of my surgeons, a sister, two medics and the QM,' he said confidently.

'OK, you must ensure your team act with the utmost discretion. Give this list to the ADC before you leave and get them together when you return to explain my orders. Is that clear, Major?' Simon nodded. 'Yes, sir, of course.'

'Any questions, gentlemen?' No-one moved, no-one even turned their heads to cast a casual eye around the room, but Major Clements watched them all for any sign of non-compliance, his eyes flicking from side to side.

As everyone was about to close their files, a voice suddenly rang out. 'I have just one thing further to say, General, if I may?' said Major Hesketh-Pritchard, trying to hold his anger in check.

'Yes, go ahead, Major,' said the general calmly as he replaced the top on his Parker fountain pen.

'I just wanted to make this gathering aware that Mitchell is a gallant soldier who in nine months has made ten kills, all of which were German officers. This is more than any other sniper at the front and on the night she was shot, as I have informed you, she killed The Joker. Yes gentlemen, a man we have been after for many months with orders coming down from this very headquarters to make his death a priority.' The head of the British army sniper squadron looked straight into the general's eyes. 'Sir, this person is a hero and due consideration should be given to what happens next.'

Davis was silent, tapping his fingers on the pad in front of him, as he knew those orders had come from him! He stared at the major for a full minute, quite annoyed to be reminded again, of Mitchell's successes. He would drag Arding across the coals later for not finding out sooner.

'Thank you, Major,' he said calmly. 'If that is all, gentlemen, I bid you good day and ask that your interviews with Major Clements take place forthwith.' He stated, looking at both officers across the table. He then stood up quickly, the rest following suit, and walked to his office, calling for Arding as he went. His ADC scurried after him.

Colonel Wood pulled Simon to one side; 'Be very careful of what you do next and consider the consequences of any untoward action, as things could very easily get out of hand. You have to trust the system and not be a loose cannon here. I will look out for Mitchell, have no fears.' Simon looked at him with warmth, as they had been together at the front for over two years.

'If you give me your word, Stanley, I will indeed consider stepping back, but this woman is as brave as anyone I have met at the front. She has put her life at risk for almost a year, entering No Man's Land to take pot shots at German officers, and we cannot stand by and see her hang! What sort of society are we living in?'

The colonel looked at him and nodded, without saying anymore. He knew Simon would not let this rest, but he could only do what Davis told him to, as General Davis had powerful friends. He looked away, the major departed.

***

After Hesketh-Pritchard and Leigh-Smith had finished their interviews with the major, they left a few minutes apart, to rendezvous at a well-known café near the clock tower in the town square. When Simon arrived, two cups of strong French coffee sat on the small table. He sat, without looking round and quietly, two British officers plotted their next move, in a bid to save a British soldier.

Two tables away, a rather inebriated Frenchman had sat down and ordered some wine, before lighting up a cigarette and then dropping his head low, as if sleeping. He was clearly known by the café' owner who tutted at him shaking his head, telling him; 'Juste celui-la' before leaving him to sip his wine. Under his coat was an ID card and his British army issue Webley revolver. He didn't arouse suspicion, but little did the officers know he was a British Military Police officer and had heard every word…

Chapter 30

After Simon had left for HQ, Captain Reece was sat in his office thinking. He had become a master of organisation and had made many phone calls, pulling in favours, to get everything into place. He made sure the paperwork was completed accurately, so as not to draw attention to this special run! Ambulances departed every single day from his location to destinations all over northern France. He knew the roads, the destinations, the personnel and the hospitals too, so relied on his section of drivers and orderlies to perform their duties without question. Today was a big day, but only he and Simon knew the full plan. The rest were only briefed on their own small area of responsibility, to protect them and others from what may ultimately come back to haunt them. It was critical that Taylor's trip to Paris and Blake's run to HQ ran smoothly. Other than that, it was just another day.

From a small door at the back of the hospital, called the chapel entrance, the three patients, all with name tags, were placed in the vehicle without delay. The two French soldiers were placed to the left, one above the other on standard stretcher beds. On the bunk opposite, the label hanging from the soldier's ankle, read; Mitchell.

The two French soldiers were heading to a small town, seventy miles south, where a small hospital had been specialising in amputation recovery. Once the drop was done, the long journey back to the British field hospital at General Davis's headquarters could begin. It was to be an arduous day for the men in the back, but one soldier would know very little, as he died the previous day. A file containing Ed's medical notes accompanied the driver, providing some form of authenticity to avoid suspicion. It was hoped that when they realised it was not Mitchell, it would be seen as a genuine mistake, although Reece was slightly concerned that the general would probably see through his ruse! They left promptly, accompanied by the new man Jones, who had deliberately not been briefed by the captain, to avoid any possible difficulties. If questioned, he would then act perfectly innocently, as any escort would.

As the first vehicle transfer of the day set off, Ed was just waking from a restless sleep in the quiet surroundings of the village clinic. Sister Youngs sat by her bed. 'Good morning, Edwina,' she said. 'How are you feeling?'

Ed looked across at her, in some discomfort, especially across her chest, and a little wary of her disposition. She tried to move but found it all too painful, so rested back where she lay. 'I feel exhausted and the pain is awful today, can you give me anything for it?'

The sister leant over and touched her brow gently with her soft hand, resting it upon her forehead for a moment. 'You are quite hot, I will take a look at your wounds shortly, but remember, you have been through a tremendous ordeal and your body is going through a great deal. Many would have died from the wounds you have suffered.' And she began undoing the bandages to look for infection.

'By the way, your friend was seen by one of the nurses yesterday in the canteen.' Ed's eyes suddenly opened widely. 'Frank is here? Can I see him?' she asked.

'Oh, I haven't seen him Ed, would you like me to find out if he is still at the hospital?'

'Yes, yes please, I would like to see him very much, he saved my life you know!' she said urgently.

Sister Youngs focussed on the job in hand as she gently teased the edge of the dressing, smelling the wound as she did so. There was a distinct odour and she cringed her face slightly. 'I will get the doctor to give you something, we don't want that to get any worse. Look, I have to nip out, would you like to try eating again?' she said.

'I do feel a bit hungry yes, but don't want to be sick again, especially if I am going in the back of an ambulance.' She said

'Well, I will fetch the doctor about your infection and will bring you a little porridge. But that's all, we need to see if you can keep it down. Rest, dear girl, I will be back in a few minutes.'

As she lay there looking at the sky through the high window to her right, Ed fidgeted to get comfortable; however, the pain once again shot through her fatigued body, making her wince. What have I done, she thought? What would become of her and Edward now her secret was out. Frank may now be in trouble too, even Bryan, her carefree pastor back in England. What had she got everyone into, she thought and closed her eyes, her anguish deepening. She lay still and then heard the sister's voice at the door.

'Are you well enough for a visitor?' she asked. And as she walked in, lieutenant Cavanagh wandered in behind her. He grinned at Ed and came to her bedside.

'So, laying down on the job eh?' he said. 'How are you feeling, Mitchell?'

Ed smiled widely and tried to sit up, his arrival cheering her immensely. 'It's really great to see you Sir, and yes, I'm OK, but I don't remember much. What happened?'

Corn shook his head. 'I was hoping you might tell me. I haven't had Smith's report yet so still a little in the dark.' He said sitting down on the end of the cot. Ed was confused. 'But, didn't Frank, I mean Smith go straight back to our HQ?' she asked. The lieutenant frowned before answering.

'Sadly not, Mitchell. He is absent at present and seemingly gone to ground. I am still trying to locate him.' he said. 'He did send me a note and now the news is all over the region, even General Haig is aware, so bloody well-done Ed, I can't tell you how the morale has lifted since news of your success has spread.' Her left hand clung onto the bed sheets not really listening to his congratulations as she stared up to the ceiling, wanting to jump out of bed and find her friend.

'I don't understand Sir. Where could he be?' she asked again. But before he could answer, the sister intervened.

'Sir, I need to attend to my patient. Do you mind coming back tomorrow?' she asked. 'Yes of course. Be back in the morning Mitchell. I will have some news about Smith by then,' And he was gone.

'I don't feel hungry Andrea. Can we leave it for now?' Ed asked solemnly. 'Ok, but I need to clean and change your dressings, Edwina. I am going get some help though as we have to turn you. It's going to hurt but I can give you some morphine if you think you need it.' She collected the bowl and mug and left, returning a few minutes later with Baxter. Between them, they set about taking off the old dressings once again, the smell quite noticeable. They then bathed her chest wound with a salt water solution and placed clean bandages upon the open wounds. The sister went around to the other side of the bed and between them, they eased Ed across to the edge before moving the pillows in behind her to prop her up on one side. This opened up access to the wound on her back, but the movement made Ed yell into her pillow, the pain hitting her hard! Her eyes watered furiously, and she gritted her teeth so as not to shout out for a second time. Slowly the pain subsided, and she felt more relaxed.

'Sorry, Edwina, that's the worst bit over.' Sister Youngs removed the second bandage and aiming at the bucket in the corner, threw it, but it missed, landing on the floor.

'Sister, I need the toilet.'

Andrea nodded. 'OK, I will bring in the commode.'

Ten minutes later and after some difficulty getting her upright, Ed was lying back on the bed, her dignity intact and her dressings changed. Thinking of home and wondering where Frank had got too, she slowly drifted off to sleep, before being awakened by a doctor wearing a stained white coat, what seemed minutes later. He looked at her and smiled, before scribbling some notes in a file on his lap, He spoke quietly to her.

'Hello, Mitchell, I am Captain Martin. How is the pain?' Ed wiped her eyes and nodded gently. 'It's OK, sir, thanks.'

'I will have to perform another procedure I'm afraid. Your chest wound has become infected, so I need to cut away the tissue and then seal the area. It means a trip back to the operating theatre for you. We will get on with it shortly. Do you have any questions?'

Ed was puzzled. She thought Andrea had told her all was well. 'What do you mean seal the area?' she asked.

'It's really nothing to worry about, it's quite a common procedure. All I will do is heat up a small surgical implement and seal the infected skin. It will be all over in jiffy, so we will get you prepped in a few minutes.' And he stood up to leave. Before I go to get scrubbed, I need to talk to you about something else.'

Ed was taken aback at the seriousness of his tone. At that moment Sister Youngs came into the room.

'Shut the door please, Sister, and take a seat.' He stood to address the two ladies and began with a serious message. 'I will try and be brief, but please leave any questions you may have to the end, as there is a great deal to discuss. Firstly, I have had a call from Major Leigh-Smith, and it appears General Davis has instigated a major investigation as to how and why you ended up in the front line. This includes interviews for you, your CO and OC, Private Smith, and your family back in England. To be blunt, miss, I believe you are in danger!' He flashed a look at Andrea. 'Because of this, we, have arranged for you to be hidden away until we can work out what to do. Sister Youngs will be going with you during your transfer, which is to be well away from here. You will be staying in a small village near Paris, with the sister of a French nurse whom I know. As far as anyone is concerned, you will be on a normal transfer route, just do not mention your destination.' Ed sat with her mouth open, staring at the doctor for a moment, before uttering her thoughts.

'What do you mean, I'm in danger?' she asked curiously.

'We have no way of knowing what General Davis is planning but suffice to say he is angry and feels the army is in an embarrassing position and wants heads to roll. Crucially, he wishes for this matter to disappear, and he has dispatched MPs to your family home in England to ascertain whom you are protecting or whether you have stolen an identity. Whatever the outcome, it could be extremely serious. So, a plan has been developed to give us time to collect our thoughts, to allow you to heal and to protect you at all costs.'

Ed was stunned. She just didn't know what to say. For the first time since she was about nine years old, she felt like crying. What had she done? How many people's lives had she inadvertently ruined? She was about to speak, when the captain continued.

'Now I don't know all the details, but it would seem certain steps have been put in place, to provide a cover story to give us all some time by arranging a mix up of patient transfers. By the time the mix up is sorted out, you will be well away from here, in hiding. I hope this all makes sense, but it is, I believe, your best chance of avoiding arrest and charges.'

There was total silence in the room as Ed took it all in. She looked for answers in the major's face but hesitated before speaking.

'Are you saying my life might be in danger, sir?'

'I am afraid so, Mitchell. General Davis seems determined to cover up this matter as he wants no scandal in his division. He truly believes he will be a laughing stock.

'Sir, do I get any say in all this, what of my family, my friends, what happens to them?'

Hang on a moment. Sister, please can you go and get the theatre ready. I will be along in five minutes. Ok, we have no idea what comes after this. We firstly need to get you fully fit and well again before we get you back to England. I can't begin to imagine what is going on in the general's head but, suffice to say we must keep one step ahead of him at all times. We must try to predict his every move, but I must say, so much has happened and so quickly that you will just have to trust us.'

'So, you say he has sent MPs to England, what happens there? And what of Frank, err, Private Smith, is he at risk too?'

'Edwina, I simply don't have all the answers. Major Leigh-Smith will have a better understanding and he will be back this afternoon, so once we have finished your procedure, you can ask him then. Regarding your family, if there is something troubling you at home, I don't wish to know but let's hope whatever it is it stays hidden. Now, if that's all, I need to get you to theatre.'

A few minutes later, Baxter came to transfer her back to the hospital and within the hour, she was back resting, dosed up with morphine. At precisely ten past four in the afternoon, a dark green ambulance driven by Private Arthur Taylor, an overnight pass to Paris tucked neatly inside his tunic pocket, headed south towards Paris with two occupants. Sadly, Taylor would never see the lights of the city and the River Seine…

At the Divisional HQ field hospital, an orderly was running through the corridors desperately seeking his colonel. He found him in the library and informed him an ambulance had just arrived with Private Mitchell on board. The colonel instructed him to place the patient in the isolation wing and he would be along shortly. He finished his report and then walked back to his office to call Captain Arding at the chateau, for him to alert General Davis. But he replaced the receiver before he made the call. Instead, he headed down to the unit, surprising the orderly who was sitting with his feet up on the table, smoking, in his office. He jumped up as the officer entered the room, trying to hide his guilt. The colonel wasn't interested, he just wanted to see the patient.

'Which room is Private Mitchell in?' he asked.

'I have placed him in room seventeen sir,' the orderly said, the colonel leaving almost before he had finished his sentence. He walked quickly down several long corridors towards the isolation wing, feeling somewhat uneasy. The place was always peaceful at this time of night, as the patients had been fed, the orderlies, catching up on their rest. On reaching the door, he walked in to see the slight body of the elusive Private Mitchell, lying quite still under a clean cotton sheet, covered in a single military blanket. He was confused to see the patient had face bandages, something he didn't expect and went to the end of the bed to read her notes. They were both thorough and succinct, completed by Major Leigh-Smith, but there was no mention of any facial injuries…

He looked at her in deep thought, wondering how this lady had managed to survive for so long in such a harsh environment, before replacing the file in the rack. He went to sit next to her on the bed and reached for her left wrist to feel for a pulse, but there wasn't one, the arm was stone cold!

He stood up and looked at the lifeless body and then noticed a slightly raised sheet below his midriff. He suddenly panicked and lifted the sheets to see a man lying before him. He knew instantly what Major Leigh-Smith had done.

Chapter 31

Lieutenant colonel Stanley Wood was sitting in his office, his head in his hands. He had suspected the major would try something to ambush proceedings but hadn't quite counted on this. If he was to protect him, he now had to buy some time. But first, he must speak to Simon, who would clearly know this wasn't going to go away. Alas, for the third time that month the communication lines were down, so made two calls locally, the first to the motor transport office to order a car, the second to Captain Arding to inform him that Mitchell would not arrive until the next day, due to ambulance breakdown. Arding didn't sound concerned and said he would pass the message on to the general. Although he thought his attitude a little unexpected, it bought him at least twelve hours. Grabbing his cap and gas mask, he headed out to rendezvous with his vehicle. It was 7.30 p.m. as he pulled his office door shut, the phone rattled in its cradle. He almost let it ring, but instead walked back in and reached over his desk, lifting the handset to his ear.

'Ah, Colonel, it's Captain Arding. I have informed the general and he has asked that you drop by at zero nine hundred hours tomorrow. Good night, sir.'

He replaced the phone in the cradle, wondering what had changed. Why was the general now so uninterested? Something was amiss, he thought and ran from his office.

It was not the kindest of journeys as the driver wasn't sparing the horses, and in the poor light, seemed to hit every bump and dip in the road throughout the journey. On a good day, the twenty-mile trip would take about forty minutes or so, that night it took well over an hour. They finally arrived a little before quarter to nine and he entered the church to find the place largely battened down for the night. There was an orderly stationed in a small office by the main door, who sprang to attention, asking how he could help the colonel.

'I need to see Major Leigh-Smith and your QM immediately,' he said.

'Yes, sir, I will tell them you're here,' he said.

'No, you won't, just take me to them, now!'

The orderly donned his hat and asked the colonel to follow him as he headed down the dimly lit rear corridor. They first went to the Officers' Mess and the orderly gingerly stepped inside and asked the attendant for the whereabouts of his major. 'He was in theatre, Bill, but that was over an hour ago. Have you tried his room?'

The colonel followed the orderly down the corridor to Leigh-Smith's room, which was empty, so instead they went to the QM's office, and found him working at his desk.

'Sir, there is a colonel from HQ here who wishes to see you and Major Leigh-Smith.'

Alan thought for a moment, before telling the orderly he would get the major instructing him to take the colonel back to the Mess and provide him with refreshment, but the colonel pushed past the orderly, surprising Reece, and said abruptly, 'That won't be necessary, Captain. I need to see you both now!'

Reece knew when he had been outplayed and stood up, asking the colonel to follow him.

'Did you have a good journey, sir?' he said hesitantly. The colonel ignored him completely. Within a few minutes, they arrived at the operating rooms and Reece went in, the colonel close behind him. They put their heads around the doorway to see two officers closing a large chest wound on a soldier, their aprons covered in blood. They both looked up, Simon's heart raced at suddenly seeing the one man he wanted to avoid tonight.

'Can I leave you to close, Stuart?' he said. 'I have to see Colonel Wood.'

He untied his crimson gown and threw it into a large, grey bucket, before rinsing his hands. No words were spoken as they walked from the room, back down to the Mess. Feeling like school children being escorted by the headmaster, they entered a largely empty room and the colonel bellowed to the three doctors present to vacate the room immediately. The officers saw the anger in his face and disappeared. He took off his cap and gloves, placing them on the dresser before turning around to sit at the head of the large dining table. 'Sit,' he said firmly.

'What on earth is going on, what have you done with Mitchell and why is there a dead man in my morgue?'

Simon and Alan looked at each other pensively before leaning forward, elbows on the table, to answer.

'Sir, we have known each other for only a short time and yet I feel I know you well. You are like me in many ways and I know full well you are a dedicated man whose patients mean everything. All I have done is to avoid the probable tragic death of a young soldier who is one of mine. We operated on a war hero two days ago and she deserves better than to be shunted around in the back of an ambulance until her body can take no more. Rest and proper recovery time is vital, as you well know, and we have hopefully, managed to give her a period of stability to recover properly. I wouldn't be doing my job as a doctor if I did anything else. If I had let her go this morning, it would almost certainly have been her in your morgue now! That would have been a travesty of justice on a selfless young woman who has served our country bravely and quite frankly, deserves better. I know this is difficult for you, but I need you on my side here, as all we did was contrive to create a transport error, sending someone to your hospital, who was already dead. So please spare me the bollocking, it has no meaning, no meaning at all, as what I did, I would do again in a heartbeat.' Colonel Wood frowned and looked at him, his anger building.

'Simon, by admitting to me what you have done, you are now liable for a court martial and I am tempted to call the Military Police right now and have you confined. You have probably also implicated Captain Reece and who knows how many other people from your staff in this, this spectacular cock-up. I have a senior General, one of Haig's high command, banging on my door, wanting information, a man who will hang me out to dry over this, so do you honestly think you have acted in everyone's best interests? Is it fair that I don't bring you in to hang with me? Furthermore, do you think this will now go away, do you think all will end happily ever after?'

Simon had slowly sunk back into his chair as he absorbed the colonel's words. He knew what he had done was ethically correct, but understood the grave situation they were all now in. Getting a reprimand was the least of his problems, he thought, but was the colonel really suggesting this was a court martial offence? Had he not many years ago signed the Hippocratic oath, which he stood by now, even under these strange and difficult circumstances. He was not taking this lightly, so decided to fight back. He sat forward once again to address the colonel

'I may be your junior officer, sir, and I may even end up in a military prison, but I would never allow a patient to die, whether he be a German soldier, a French peasant or in this case a British woman! If you are suggesting you would, then my respect for you has gone.' He paused, his words visibly affecting his colonel. 'We owe this girl, this woman, a great deal, after all she has done for her King and her country. So please do not lecture me on a general's impatience or his anger, as we have saved a soldier from certain death by giving her proper care and she now has the chance to live a normal life again! If she were a man, right now she would be a war hero and would be recommended for a gallantry medal. She has even killed The Joker, a man General Haig himself listed as a priority, and was even written about in the *Ypres Times*! So yes, I know all about her heroics, but I am disgusted that you of all people, have suggested you would lower your own medical standards and let a person die just to please a general whose sanity must be questionable!'

He sat back again, feeling Alan Reece's eyes fixed on the side of his head, but didn't look round. Colonel Wood looked at him blankly. A minute passed without any words being spoken, and Reece felt he should speak up himself.

The colonel then held up his hand and had clearly realised he had misplaced his own responsibilities and his loyalty to his staff and patients. His officers deserved better and he had forgotten the fundamental principles of being a doctor. He faced his accuser, deep in thought.

'OK, OK, I won't stand in your way and I will cover for you as much as I can. Just let us try and protect the innocent though. What has been done must not spread to our subordinates, this is our doing and we must take responsibility for it. So where is Mitchell now?'

'She is safe, sir, many miles from here, being cared for by a nurse I can trust. I won't tell you where so you're clear of involvement, but I have it under control. All I need from you is to somehow cover our trail with the body in the morgue,' he said hopefully.

'And how am I to do that, Simon? What if the general wishes to see Mitchell, which he has implied all along? What then? We may also have another problem!'

'What other problem?' said Simon.

'When I found the dead man, I informed the general's ADC that the ambulance had broken down and Mitchell would not arrive until tomorrow. The general had been plaguing me all day to inform him when Mitchell arrived and yet when I called to tell him of the delay, I was told he would see me in his office at zero nine hundred hours tomorrow and not to worry. This is so out of character and I have concerns something has happened. Are you sure Mitchell arrived at her intended location?'

'Well, no,' Simon said hesitantly. 'Alan?'

'Well, Private Taylor, my senior driver, left with Sister Youngs and Mitchell late this afternoon, before I got back from HQ. We, just assumed they arrived safely. We won't know until tomorrow, when Taylor is due to return,' he said, looking at Simon.

'What are you thinking, Stanley?' said Simon.

'I am just concerned that a man who has been vociferously pushing this matter, with several verbal attacks on people and threats of courts martial and with MPs at every door, now seems so calm and uninterested. I am just asking, are you sure they arrived where you have sent them?'

Simon and Alan looked at each other. 'Can we use your driver, now?' said Simon. 'I will go this minute and find out; you have me very worried.'

'Yes, go ahead, how long will you be?'

Alan looked across, calculating in his mind the distance, and spoke for the first time. 'It's about ninety-five miles. Shall I will come with you as I speak better French than you?' he said.

Simon thought for a moment, before nodding rapidly. 'Yes, of course, let's go together.' They stood up to leave.

'Sir, we should be back by about zero one thirty. Use my bunk to get some rest. We will wake you the moment we return.'

The colonel nodded, putting his head in his hands, wondering what he had got himself into.

It was four thirty in the morning when Colonel Wood finally arrived back at HQ and climbed into his small cot. It had been a difficult journey back and his late-night meetings with Major Leigh-Smith and Captain Reece had gone so horribly wrong. The rapid late-night dash by the two officers towards Paris provided answers to his questions. Mitchell never reached her destination and both the ambulance and crew were now missing.

Chapter 32

When Colonel Wood arrived for his nine o'clock meeting with General Davis, he was on edge. He had hardly slept a wink following his excursion throughout the night and upon seeing two Military Police officers sitting in the ante-room, his fears grew. The captain looked at him as he entered and nodded politely but didn't stand. The corporal by his side just faced front. Captain Arding was sitting at his desk opposite, studying a pile of documents in brown folders, avoiding his gaze. As he stood waiting, the phone rang, and Arding listened before setting the handset back in its cradle.

'You can go through, sir; the General will see you now.'

He stepped into the general's office and saw him standing at the window, pulling on his pipe, breathing out thick smoke from the corner of his mouth. The colonel stopped just inside the door, pulled his feet together and saluted. Davis turned his head, his face looking fierce as he chewed on the end of his pipe. He turned back to the window and spoke coldly.

'You think you know better than I, Colonel Wood?'

Stanley swallowed hard. 'Why no, sir, not at all,' he said, not knowing quite what the general meant.

Davis turned and walked back to his desk to sit down. He placed his pipe in a large brass ash tray and waved the colonel forward, stopping him short of his desk. He didn't offer him a chair.

'I gave you clear and precise orders to dispatch Mitchell here and it would seem that you have disobeyed me. I have to ask myself, why you would do that? Are you trying to outwit me, do you think I don't know what is going on?'

Wood then asked to sit, but his request was denied. He drew in a deep breath and recited the story he and Simon had prepared.

'Sir, firstly I can only apologise about the mix-up. I rely on quartermasters all over northern France to get patients delivered to the right place, on the right date and with the correct records. On this occasion things have clearly gone awry, and we hope to be back to normal as soon as possible. When I spoke to Major Leigh-Smith –'

'Balderdash,' said the general.

'I'm sorry, sir?' Wood said, surprised.

'I know full well you visited Major Leigh-Smith last evening, and for what reason, I ask myself? I also know that an unidentified man listed as Private Mitchell is lying in your morgue as we speak. So, cut the lies, Colonel, or I will have you locked up in seconds. Now tell me what has been happening, or you will be charged with conspiracy!'

Lieutenant Colonel Wood, stood before a seasoned veteran of some distinction, feeling totally debagged. He knew he had been caught out and was unsure quite what to say so he simply stared at the man before him.

'Well?' said the general angrily. 'I'm waiting.'

He stared at the colonel, who appeared lifeless although his mind was running amok. Wood decided he would have to come clean but had to try and keep Simon and Alan out of it as much as possible.

'Sir, I wish to resign my commission and –'

'Resign your commission' the general yelled. 'Declined. Now tell me what has been going on!' he said, leaning back confidently in his chair.

'Sir, do you have Private Mitchell?'

'Yes, indeed I do, Colonel, along with a nurse and a dead driver. Do you think I am a fool? Do you think I wasn't aware of your deceit, I have eyes everywhere. Now, I made it very clear what I expected, and you, Colonel, took it upon yourself to go behind my back. If there is one thing I simply won't accept, it's disloyalty!'

The general picked up his pipe from the ashtray, drawing hard several times, just saving the embers, before blowing smoke into the air above his desk. He stared at the now petrified man before him.

'Is she alive?' he asked

'Yes, she is alive, just! And what of it, she is a criminal who falsified documents and impersonated a British soldier. How serious a crime do you think this is, Stanley? Well, I will tell you. It's serious enough to be put in front of a firing squad, that I know for sure. And what's more, Mitchell may well not be standing alone at the post!'

Silence fell over the office as the colonel took in his words.

The general shouted for the captain. In seconds, Arding and the MP officer, entered his office. 'I want you to arrest Colonel Wood and confine him to his quarters under armed guard. We will discuss charges later but get him out of here!'

Colonel Wood was not handcuffed, but the corporal did take him by his arm as he was led away.

*** .

Across the field, just eight hundred yards away, Edwina Mitchell was being moved into a secure room with an armed guard outside. Sister Youngs was by her side, their futures uncertain.

Chapter 33

Bryan, having arranged to meet the church warden, was already in the kitchen when the door knocker sounded. He finished pouring hot water into the tea pot before ambling down the corridor to let him in. He greeted Jonathan, his verger, like a long-lost friend, before closing the large oak door with a thud. They had become close in recent years, and Bryan found him a useful man to have around. As he stepped inside, he gave Bryan a handful of letters.

'Met the postman on the road, Bryan, he gave me these for you. Now, is the kettle on?' he asked, disappearing down the passage. Bryan smiled as he studied the letters in his hand, following him back down the hall. As he sat down at the table, a mug was thrust into his hand, but he was distracted and spilt some of his tea as he realised one of the letters was from France. He put the drink down hastily, wiping his hand on his trousers, before ripping the letter open. He studied it eagerly, then walked over to the window, his mind racing. Jonathan watched perplexed as his friend's mood changed.

'Is something wrong, Bryan?' he asked, concerned. Bryan was miles away in deep thought and didn't answer.

'Bryan?' he said again.

'Sorry, Jonathan, it's young Edward, Edward Mitchell, he has been wounded at the front. I will need to nip up and tell Edwina. But first I have to do something. Give me a minute, will you?' and he disappeared into his office.

He read the note from Frank Smith for the third time, to be sure he had not misread it. Frank, he knew, was Ed's sniper friend and clearly was not only a sharp-shooter, but a sharp-thinker too, as he had managed to warn him despite the censors. Something, however, didn't quite sit comfortably in his mind and he sat staring into space. He quickly opened his desk drawer to retrieve the letters Ed had given him the previous year. It was paramount he read them immediately, now the military knew of Ed's situation. The details inside the letters would be vital.

He reached for his paper knife to open the envelope Ed had given him and found two folded pieces of paper inside. He read a brief note to him personally, then a fact sheet that Ed had mapped out for them both to follow.

Edward and Bryan

I thought long and hard about the possibility that I may get injured at the front, so have made a plan, to try and limit any difficulties. It is very important that we follow it to the letter, otherwise our stories won't match, and we will be in serious trouble. I will when questioned say I stole my brother's enlistment papers, unknown by all of you, and that should avert any wrong doing being placed on your shoulders. I will offer my name as Rebecca Mitchell, our mother, and will take her birth date too, the 1st August, making me one year older. Edward, and you must continue to act as me and I ask that David, assuming he is still with you, agrees to play you, so when the police come it should all fit into place. He will be questioned of course, but his injury, when explained, will eliminate any need for further enquiries, especially with his physical situation. That said, he will have to know all the family history to be convincing, and I realise it's a lot to ask, but without his cooperation, we will not pull this off.

Stay calm and I will hopefully see you all soon.
Good luck
ED

Bryan dropped his hands onto the desk, his mind awash with thoughts. The authorities would soon be aware that two siblings lived on the farm but would not be aware that David was a farm worker, or, how many siblings were in the family. He placed his hand on his chest, feeling his heart pounding as he turned over in his mind how to fix this. He then realised there was no other way, but to falsify the birth register, and create a new birth certificate, as it was bound to be checked. As parish priest, it was his sole responsibility to keep these records accurate and up to date. He himself had written the birth certificates for Edwina and Edward all those years ago and the register was on the shelf above his head. He had to act fast.

He stood up and peered at the row of books dating back to 1625. He took out the relevant register and placed it on his desk, before reaching down into the bottom draw to locate a blank birth certificate. With his ink pen, he started with the entry number, which he copied from the previous certificate, hoping it would not be noticed, before carefully writing Rebecca Mitchell and then completed each box across the page. He then signed and dated it a few days later, before making an exact copy to take to the farm. Opening the register, he detached the binding strings and leafed through the pages until he found the twins' certificates and then flicked backwards one year, before slipping the new certificate into place and re-tying the knots. He slammed the book shut and put it back on the shelf, blowing the dust off all the books along the row, as this register would be checked, and it wouldn't do to have one cleaner than the others.

Had he thought of everything? What would Ed say when she was interviewed? She had simply gone off to war with false papers without anyone knowing. The whole thing sounded simple enough and with a little luck, they *could* get away with it. He closed his drawer, gathered the letters and the new birth certificate into his pocket and returned to the kitchen. Jonathan hadn't moved and was still sipping tea at the table. As he looked past him, through the small window, Bryan's heart sank.

'Oh, crikey,' he muttered as Jonathan looked up.

A military car had just driven past, heading into the village. The Military Police were already here. He now had to think extremely quickly. What if they got to the farm before him? How was he going to stop them when they were in a car? He looked at Jonathan and an idea came to him, but he wasn't sure how much he could tell him.

'Jonathan. Don't ask me to explain now, but I need you to do something of the utmost urgency.' He held up the letter from Ed. 'I have a letter here and Ed Mitchell is in danger, and we must somehow stop that military car going up to the farm until I can get there myself. Can you go outside and flag them down and somehow delay them?'

Jonathan put his cup down, swallowing the last of his tea. 'Well, yes, I suppose so. But what should I tell them?' he asked with a frown.

'I don't know, Jonathan, think of something, this is an emergency.' Bryan said rather loudly. 'I have to run.' He then charged out, leaving the door wide open, before crossing the road and pushing through the hedge into the lane behind the track, running for all he was worth. Jonathan looked around for some inspiration but found little. He had to honour Bryan's wish and ran out, slamming the door behind him without a clue what he was going to say. When he reached the road, the car was turning around at the top of the village. As it made its way back down Main Street, he stepped into the road, waving with both hands. The driver slowed and came to a stop.

'Good day, gentlemen. I am the verger; can I help you with anything?' he said, rather out of breath.

'Good morning,' said the sergeant at the wheel. 'We are looking for the Mitchell farm.'

'It's not young Edward, is it?'

'Sorry, sir, I can't divulge military information to a civilian. Could you point us in the right direction? We are in a bit of a hurry,' the sergeant stated firmly.

'Well, I was just heading that way myself. If you give me a lift, I will show you exactly where it is.' The sergeant nodded his head over his right shoulder for him to get in the back. Jonathan slowly opened the door and climbed into the rear seat, taking his time to shut the door.

'I do hope it's not bad news,' he said as he climbed in. The sergeant looked across at the corporal sitting in the passenger seat but said nothing.

'OK, which way verger?' he asked.

'Oh yes, sorry, you need to take that road,' he said, pointing over his left shoulder. 'Go straight on for about a mile and then you turn right up a track opposite a white cottage. You can't miss it. You can drop me off at the junction if that's OK, as I have to see the family who live there,' he said, feeling rather pleased with his sudden inspiration.

Bryan had stopped halfway up the hill to catch his breath, watching as Jonathan and the army car headed out of the village. He now had a chance to reach the cottage well before them and he started running again. His breathing became laboured very quickly, sweat dripped down his face and his legs began to stiffen. His body objected to this sudden exertion, but he knew he couldn't stop: all their lives could be in jeopardy.

As he reached the crest of the hill, just fifty yards away from the cottage gate, his energy was all but gone and he struggled to put one foot in front of the other. He could feel his heart hammering inside his chest, and he bent forward sucking air into his burning lungs. But then he heard an engine and jerked his head round to see the army car re-enter the village. He now had only minutes and somehow found some energy to run again, praying he was going to make it in time.

'Christ, give me strength.' he yelled, as he covered the last few yards to the back door, just as the car turned into the farm entrance at the bottom of the hill. Bryan stepped through the door and was finally inside.

'Thank God,' he said. 'You're both here.' As a stunned David and Edward stared at him, and then each other. He threw himself into a chair, his mouth wide open as he wheezed loudly, sucking in several deep breaths.

'The Military Police are here,' he whispered hoarsely. 'We have just a few minutes, so listen!' He had their full attention.

'It's Edwina, she has been wounded and is hospital in France. They know she's a woman.' Edward lifted his hands to his mouth and stared at Bryan, gasping.

He turned to David. 'You will now have to be Edward. You have a bad leg and are unfit to serve, make sure they notice and be convincing,' he said, still panting heavily. 'You need to put them off the scent, David, and remember, none of us knew Edwina was going to war and she took your papers. No mistakes now, her life could well depend upon it.' He looked across at Edward.

'I have a letter for you, from Edwina, which she gave me last year when she left.' He passed it to Edward. 'Both of you, read it quickly, now.' He went over to the window, giving them a minute to absorb the short notes.

'As you have seen, Ed will tell the Military Police in France she is Rebecca Mitchell, calling herself after your mother. She will be your older sister by one year and will use your mother's birthday of the first of August.' Then suddenly they heard a car, their time was up. Bryan looked round at them, as two doors slammed outside. They all stared at each other. Bryan ducked away from the window and walked back across the kitchen.

'God help us, they are here. Are you clear?' he asked, and they both nodded. 'Ok, here is a copy of a birth certificate I have just written. It's in the name of Rebecca Mitchell, so tuck it away with the others, they may ask for it.' He said eagerly. Three loud thumps then shook the cottage door.

'Military Police!'

David and Edward stared at the priest, with wide eyes, but David was determined to do his bit and straightened up. 'We can do this, Edward.' He said firmly. Then he waved Bryan away, who quickly stepped into the parlour and closed the door. At the same time, Edward placed the new certificate into the top drawer of the dresser and ran back to sit at the table. David then calmly walked over to open the door.

'Good day, gentlemen. What can we do for you?' he asked.

Doffing their caps, they stepped into the warm kitchen. David knew he must remain calm whatever happened next, as what they were about to do was very risky. They had no idea whether their stories would ever match up completely, but what they could be sure of, anything they said would be passed on, and he knew he was going to have to lie and lie well. He was ready and eager to prove himself.

Bryan had his ear pinned up against the parlour door, while Edward sat by the fire, facing them. The sergeant pulled out his notebook and began reading questions that had been prepared by his officer.

'Firstly, are you Edward Mitchell?'

'Yes, I am Edward. What's all this about, Sergeant?' The corporal turned his head to stare at his sergeant, but their eyes didn't meet.

'Before I answer your question, I will need to see your birth certificate or adoption papers.'

'Oh, yes, of course.' He looked at Edward. 'Sis, do you know where my birth certificate is?' he said, trying to act naturally. 'Am I in trouble?' he asked the MP as he limped over towards the Welsh dresser. At that moment, Edward stood up, nodding to the men, and went straight across to the dresser and opened the top drawer, delving inside.

'Here it is,' he said, handing it to David, before they both walked back across to the kitchen table. He offered the certificate and sat down. As the sergeant inspected it, he spoke, and everything started to become clear.

'Do you have another sister, Mr Mitchell, apart from this lady here?'

'Ah, yes we do,' and he looked over at Edward cautiously. 'You know about our sister Rebecca, do you?' he asked.

'Oh, Rebecca, is it,' the sergeant said, writing her name down on his pad. 'Yes, we do, and that is why we are here. Your sister was shot and injured a few days ago and is recovering in a military hospital in northern France. Let's say her personal circumstances were revealed.' He peered down at the certificate in his hands. 'All seems to be in order here. Is your sister's birth certificate here?' he asked. 'Yes, I think it's in the draw. Sis, do you know where it might be?' Edward got to his feet and walked back to the dresser. He made fuss of finding it, even though he had put it on the top of the pile. After a few moments, he walked back over and gave it to the sergeant.

'Thank you miss,' and he read across the page, taking note of her birth date. 'First of August, same day as my mother,' he said with a smile. But the boys, didn't react.

'Are your parents at home today?'

David was about to answer, when Edward cut in.

'Our parents were killed on the Titanic in 1912,' he said, in a deliberately sad tone. 'We live here alone.'

'Oh, um, I am sorry, miss, I had no idea, but I do have my questions, you see.' And he stuttered a little as he looked at David, before returning his gaze to his notebook.

'I assume you have a death certificate for them,' he said.

'Well, no, actually, none were ever issued, but we have a letter somewhere from the Government as their bodies were never recovered. It was a sort of temporary death certificate, which has never been updated. Will that do?' David asked.

'Yes, I suppose it will, may I see it?'

David was about to stand, when Edward got up and returned within a minute with the letter in his hands. The sergeant held out his hand, but Edward placed the document on the table next to where the sergeant stood and quickly walked back to his seat. The sergeant, used to this sort of behaviour, thought nothing of it and picked up the envelope. He studied it briefly, not having the faintest idea of its originality or accuracy and nodded before placing it back down on the table. No words were spoken; he just pursed his lips.

'Can I ask if you received any papers to join the army?'

'I received papers to go to Cirencester for an army medical, yes, which sadly I failed because of my leg injury. I had an accident falling from a tree as a child, when I broke my leg. I was classified as unfit to serve.' David bent down and pulled his trouser leg up, revealing a huge scar across his knee and upper leg.

'See,' he said with a slight grin. The sergeant took a vague look and nodded.

'Ah yes, OK, thanks, I can see you have a limp too. Does it trouble you much?'

'Not too badly but it is troublesome in the winter and when climbing ladders,' he said, pulling his trouser leg back down.

The sergeant wanted the ground to open up, as he felt awkward. David, on the other hand, felt the questions had played right into their hands.

'I think we are almost done, just one more question. Why did your sister take it upon herself to join the army in your place?'

David took a deep breath for his final encounter with the MP, remembering the tale Edward had told him. He wanted to be convincing.

'You have clearly not met my sister, Sergeant,' he said. 'If you had, you would know Rebecca is the fittest and strongest female any of us have ever known. She has always outdone me in everything in life and it was her I was racing up a tree when I fell twenty feet, breaking my leg. She even carried me home on her back that day, so you see she was always very strong and capable. Following that incident, I was never in favour with my father ever again. I was always second to her, no matter what the situation. So, you see, she was a boy in many ways, Sergeant, in everything she ever did, and after my draft papers arrived unexpectedly, she quietly prepared herself in secret. We never knew until she had gone. She just wanted to prove to the world she could do what any man could do.'

The sergeant looked confused. 'What do you mean, your draft papers arrived? I thought you said you were medically unfit to serve.'

David smiled at him. 'Yes, Sergeant, I was, but out of the blue in December or January last year the papers arrived, and I put them in the drawer and thought nothing more of it. Then in March, Rebecca suddenly disappeared. Once her mind was made up, there's no shifting her, you see.'

The sergeant looked at his corporal before speaking. 'So, you are saying she stole your enlistment papers without your knowledge?' David hesitated before answering, thinking he had made a mistake. He looked at Edward for confidence, who nodded gently.

'Yes, she just took off, leaving us a short note. The next time we heard from her was during her training.' As David spoke, the sergeant looked at his corporal, frowning. The sergeant unbuttoned his tunic pocket and tucked his notebook and pencil away.

'I think that will be all, Mr Mitchell, Miss Mitchell. I don't see we have anything further to ask. On a more positive note, your sister is alive, and we would expect her to spend some time in hospital in France before being moved to England. All we need to do now is to visit the church to check the register of births with the village priest and we will be on our way.' He started to turn when Edward suddenly realised, he had to delay them, as Bryan was in their parlour!

'Would you like some tea and cake, Sergeant?' he said. 'Can't have you coming all this way without having a brew.' David looked at him, wondering what was going on as surely, they both wanted them gone, and quickly. But before he could register any sort of look to Edward, the sergeant smiled. 'That would indeed be most welcome, miss,' he said. 'Thank you.'

'Please take a seat, it won't take a moment,' Edward said, catching David's eye.

'David, could you put the kettle on, I will get the cake from the parlour please?' David suddenly twigged and smiled at her, while Bryan, stepped away from the door to let him in. They didn't speak, but Bryan patted him on the shoulder, before leaving by the rear door.

Twenty minutes later, the men, now refreshed, were driving back down the hill. Bryan sat waiting for them in the vestry, his heart still racing. Jonathan was nowhere to be seen.

Chapter 34

On opening her eyes, Ed's her first vision in the darkened room was of a figure tucked under a blanket in the corner. She wiped her eyes with her left hand and realised it was Sister Youngs curled up in a chair. She looked very peaceful as her tiny chin dropped down and then up again in a rhythm of sleep. The room was only small, with very little furniture to speak of with a single shutter partly covering the window opposite. She couldn't remember where she was after such a long journey the previous day, but did remember arriving in the dark with Andrea and other people fussing over her as she was carried along several corridors to this tiny room. She gently stretched her good arm upwards, then suddenly she remembered the road halt, the voices shouting and a gunshot! She cast her mind back, trying to piece things together, and remembered the military policeman's head peering through the rear doors before slamming them shut again. She could remember the ambulance turning in the road, the gears crunching at every change and then pulling away. She had no idea where they were now, but was pleased Andrea was with her. She then realised she needed the toilet and was forced to wake the sleeping nurse. Gently, she called her name several times before her eyes finally opened to the new day.

'Oh, sorry, Ed, are you OK?' she said, pushing the blanket from her.

'Yes, I feel good actually, but I need the toilet. But before we sort that out, what has happened, where are we?'

Andrea stood and stretched and went across to sit on the bed. 'We were abducted on the road yesterday and brought here to the main hospital at Divisional HQ. I came here some time ago with a patient so recognised the hospital. I will try to find out what's happening, but for now, let me get you comfortable and we can talk later.'

The sister stepped to the door, but it was locked, and she banged on it several times before she heard a key turn in the lock and the door opened. A tall MP stood outside.

'Yes, Sister, what can I get you?' he said.

'I need to attend to my patient, Corporal; can I get to the sluice please?'

'Yes, of course you can,' and he held the door open for her.

Andrea turned. 'I will be just a few minutes, Ed,' and she slipped through the narrowing gap in the doorway. When she returned, she was pushing a hospital trolley, the door being opened wide to allow her in. Ed could see a jug and glasses and various dressings on the top shelf and a bedpan below. She wheeled the trolley to the end of the bed and tied an apron around her waist.

'Right, let's get some normality here, Edwina, and get you comfortable.'

She dealt with her toilet requirements before offering her a drink of water, promising to get some breakfast in a little while. She covered the pan with a cloth and placed it on the lower shelf of the trolley, to dispose of later.

As she started attending to her dressings, the door lock rattled, and a young doctor stepped into the room. He was wearing an army shirt and tie under a white coat and smiled from the doorway, before stepping over to the bed. The door slammed shut behind him.

'Good morning, Mitchell, I am Captain Brown, one of the surgeons here on Colonel Wood's staff. So how do you feel this morning?'

Ed looked at the man who seemed to young to be a doctor, she thought, but then who was she to speak! He stood looking at her, his hands in his coat pockets, smiling.

'Why have I been bought here?' she said firmly.

The young doctor rocked gently on his feet. 'I am not aware of the details of your arrival, Mitchell, just that I have been assigned as your physician. Now, could you tell me how you feel?'

'I feel OK, Doctor, but will you please tell me what happened?'

'All I know is Major Morris placed you on my list and I only have your best interests at heart, so please let us get on. Sister, could you please remove the dressings, so I can take a look?'

Over the next half an hour, Ed's dressings were removed, and her wounds inspected, cleaned and then re-dressed. It was the first time Ed had seen the scars following the quarterisation she received, and it wasn't a pleasant sight. She would clearly have some permanent scarring. The doctor seemed pleased enough though, promising to see her again later in the day, before leaving the room. Andrea bathed Ed from head to foot, and put her in a fresh army gown, before knocking on the door to take away the trolley and dressings. A few minutes later the key rattled in the lock once more, and a young nurse entered and walked up to the bed.

'Hello, I am Nurse Carter, my friends call me Patsy. What should I call you?' she said.

Ed was a little surprised to see her, wondering where Andrea had gone. 'Oh, um, Edwina is fine, as I don't suppose they will allow me to keep my army rank now.' They both laughed, the nurse not knowing why! She started busying herself around the room, tucking the sheets neatly around the end of the bed, drawing back the shutter from the window and ensuring the room looked tidy, before speaking again. 'Can I get you anything, Edwina?' she asked

'I would like to write to my…' she paused briefly, '…my family. Oh, and think I could eat something.'

'Yes, I think we can manage that, I will also bring you a Red Cross parcel and a dressing gown. We will have you comfortable very soon.'

Ed responded quickly. 'Where has Sister Youngs gone?' she asked.

'Oh, were you not told? Sister Youngs has been relieved and is being sent back to her field hospital. I am your nurse now!'

This took Ed totally by surprise and she felt her stomach churn nervously. Andrea had been the face she had woken to for several days and she trusted her more than anyone, and yet she hadn't said cheerio!

'Can you tell me why my door is always locked, Patsy?'

Nurse Carter stopped what she was doing and sat on the bed before looking over her shoulder to the door, speaking quietly. 'Look, I don't know what has been going on, but I was briefed not to talk to you about the security that has been placed on this room. As far as I know, it's because you are the only female patient amongst hundreds of men. It's for your own safety. Now what is your story, Ed, I am dying to know.'

Ed, slightly cautious of saying anything that she might regret, sighed and lay back on her pillow. She concluded nothing would be gained by lying and she might just as well tell Patsy some of the story that had brought her to war. But first, she needed to eat.

'Tell you what, if you can get me some breakfast, I will let you know what bought me here.'

'Right oh, that's a deal.' And she stood up and was gone. Ed looked out through the small window towards the trees on the far side of the field. It was a windy day and the tops were thrashing about in the bright morning. Raindrops clung to the glass. The weather took her home momentarily, as she wondered how Edward was doing, realising she really must write to him, today. She closed her eyes for what seemed like seconds, before she woke to Patsy calling her name, a tray in her hands.

'Breakfast,' she said softly as she placed the tray down on the table. Ed was helped to sit up a little, and with her good arm, managed to feed herself the porridge, which was only just warm and a little lumpy. She hadn't realised how hungry she was and for once, didn't feel sick. A few minutes later, the door was unlocked again and an older man with tight curly hair and a thin moustache appeared.

'Private Mitchell,' he said, 'I am Sergeant Stuttard from the Military Police. I need to inform you that you will be interviewed today by my OC, Major Clements, at ten forty-five. I trust that will not get in the way of any medical issue, nurse?' Ed looked at Patsy and then back to the sergeant.

'Why am I to be interviewed, Sergeant?' she said boldly.

'I am not at liberty to say, miss,' he said, 'I expect they just want to get the facts of your service straight.'

Ed looked at Patsy and shivered, before shrugging her shoulders. 'Well, yes, I think that will be fine, as clearly I am not going anywhere!' she said quietly. And he looked down at his watch and nodded before smiling, rather nicely, and thanking her as he turned to leave. He tapped the door, which opened quickly, and was gone.

'So, come on then, Edwina, I am dying to hear of your story.' The nurse said, as she removed her tray.

Ed sank back into her pillows, acutely aware that she should be careful as she didn't know nurse Carter and she could easily have been asked to gain her trust. Whatever happened now, she must remain disciplined and not drop her guard, as she had so tirelessly done for over a year! After all she had been through, it would be a disaster if it all went wrong now!

'Before I begin, Patsy, tell me about you,' she said firmly.

'OK. Well, I am Patsy Carter and I was brought up in a small village called Tollesbury in Essex. It's a tiny hamlet on the River Blackwater and is famous for its oysters and boat building. I joined the Queen Alexandra's Royal Army Nursing Corps several years ago and have been here just a few months. I have two sisters and a brother. Nothing interesting really. Now, how about you?'

Ed started by telling Patsy about her parents dying on the Titanic and her life afterwards running the small family farm, emphasising that she had a brother and sister. She then discussed her training, briefly, and then how she was selected as a sniper. She made light of living in the trenches and didn't want to glorify her role in any way but, wanted to explain truthfully how life was. She mentioned her first kill, how they lived and how she masked the fact that she was female. She pointed out how life had become quite routine as time had gone on and, in the end, she was just one of boys, living in the same awful conditions, fighting the same war. No-one ever became suspicious, she said, and the only time she fretted was when she had her monthly period, explaining how she overcame this particular problem. Throughout her tale of endeavour and survival, Patsy was wide-eyed and focussed on every word. Finally, Ed told of her getting shot and how her partner and fellow sniper, Frank Smith, saved her life by carrying her back through No Man's Land to safety.

Patsy smiled and told her she had only been briefed at the start of her watch that she would be caring for a female who had been impersonating a soldier. 'I thought they meant a German soldier,' she said with a grimace. 'But you are clearly British, and I am glad about that. They told me you had been shot in the back while operating at the front. That's all I know really. I'm not sure how far we are from the front line, but we do hear the big guns from time to time when the wind is blowing in the right direction.' She looked over her shoulder towards the door before turning back, and almost in a whisper said, 'I was told not to talk to you, just to do my duties and leave. Can't think why.' She continued to ask about Ed's life and probed her a little about her time before the war and asked about her family. Ed a little suspicious, started to feel just a little uncomfortable as many things felt too personal to disclose. She decided to feign tiredness, closing her eyes for a while to avoid more questions, and didn't open them again until she heard gentle footsteps moving away from the bed and the door close.

 Down the corridor, Major Clements was sitting at Colonel Wood's desk when a knock came on the door. Nurse Carter entered and sat opposite him. She had gone straight to the office after leaving Ed's room!

'Now, how did you get on? Did she say anything of interest?' he asked.

'Well sir, I found it difficult to sort of spy on her and to be honest I don't think I can do this again. I feel I will lose her trust, you see, and well, that is a big part of a nurse's job.' The officer frowned as Carter could play a key role in assisting him. 'But to answer your question, she wasn't that talkative really, not about her past anyway but was happy to chat about her time in the army and freely mentioned her training, her role at the front, even her first kill, but she started to drift off when I asked about her family and life before the war. I left her a few moments ago sleeping soundly. I did glean that she had family in Gloucestershire and her parents had died on the Titanic, but that was it really.'

'Do you think there was a reason for her to enlist? Did she mention anything about a friend or talk about taking someone's identity?'

'No, no, she didn't, sir, she didn't allow me into that part of her life and never mentioned why she joined. I think she just wanted to compete with men in the army. She said she ran the family farm after her parents died with her brother and sister and was apparently a very good shot!' The major was scribbling in his notebook, only looking up when she stopped talking.

'What else did she say about her family?' he asked.

'Nothing much at all, sir. I did try but I didn't want to appear, well, pushy, you know. She is a hero Sir, isn't she?'

'Don't get sucked in nurse, she is in serious trouble! Now, is she well enough for questions?' he asked.

'She seems well, sir, considering what she has been through. Her wounds are healing well and there is no infection present, but she is weak and needs lots of rest. You should ask the doctors.'

The major wrote everything down as she spoke. We might know more soon anyway as I am interviewing her myself shortly, as you know. I would like you to be present, too, if that can be arranged?'

'Yes, sir. I would be glad to be there as a sort of female chaperone, if that's what it's called.'

'OK, that's all nurse. I will see you at ten forty-five. You may go. And thank you. Oh, one last thing. It's probably better you don't mention to Mitchell that we have spoken. Don't want to scare the girl, OK?'

Patsy nodded and stood up, heading to the door but turned as she reached it. 'Is she in trouble, sir? It's just that it seems wrong that she is being locked up and –'

'That is not your concern, Nurse Carter and I may need you again, so you are to say nothing. Do you understand?' he said firmly.

Patsy nodded, feeling slightly uncomfortable that she had become his informer. 'Yes Sir.' And stepped from the room.

The major sat, reading his notes, his elbows on the desk, his head resting in his hands. He wondered how hard he should push Mitchell as she was still a sick woman. His instructions from the general were to get the job done and quickly. But how he was to achieve this questioning a woman in this way, he just didn't know. The most serious incidents he had dealt with in the war so far were three desertions, several thefts and various assaults of senior ranks. Quite where this fitted into his life experiences, he had no idea. But question her he must and began scribbling his questions down for later.

Patsy had arrived back at Ed's room within a few minutes and asked the soldier standing guard outside to let her in. He smiled at her and began to flirt a little. 'Doing anything later, nurse, I get my break in an hour,' he said.

'No, but I know one thing, I am not spending it with you,' she said as he pulled the key from his pocket.

'Wow, no need to be hostile, I was only being friendly,' he said.

Patsy tilted her head to one side and folded her arms. 'The door, please,' she said coldly. He paused for a few seconds and then grinned, shaking his head before opening the door. She stepped in quickly without looking back.

The room was stuffy, so she went over to open the small window, before turning to see Ed still sleeping. She felt awful now, almost as if she had betrayed her. She sat down on the chair next to the bed and felt for Ed's pulse on her left wrist, looking at the fob watch hanging from her uniform. She is a strong lady, she thought. God only knows how she had managed to compete with the men at the front, surviving a life of such discomfort and degradation. She studied Ed's features for some time, seeing she was rather pretty, albeit she had a man's haircut. Her breathing was regular, her chest rising and falling in a steady fashion, mesmerising the nurse for several minutes, until suddenly the door opened. The major walked in, with a sergeant behind him, his boots noisily clomping into the room, waking Ed from her slumber. She immediately tried to shuffle up the bed, but pain suddenly wracked her body and she gasped aloud.

Patsy jumped up and spoke. 'It's OK, Ed, stay still, you don't have to move.'

'Yes, stay still, Mitchell,' said the major.

'Could I have some water, please?' Ed looked at Patsy. She reached for the jug and poured some into a glass before helping her to drink. While she was doing this, the major sat down, his briefcase on his knee, the sergeant seated across the room. Patsy stayed beside as instructed.

'OK, Mitchell, I am Major Clements of the Military Police. I have been instructed by General Davis, the Divisional Commander, to question you today as a preliminary enquiry, to decide the way ahead. Sergeant Stuttard will make notes of all questions asked and your replies, but you are not, as yet, under arrest. If you wish, you are eligible to have an officer present here to represent you, a person who can advise you of your rights. But it's not compulsory.'

Ed pushed her head forward a bit and eyed the major with suspicion, before flopping her head back on the pillow. She asked Patsy if she could sit up a bit more and the nurse placed another pillow behind her shoulders, allowing Ed to see the major properly.

Ed coughed before speaking. 'Sir, I don't understand military law and don't know why I am being held in a locked room with a guard outside, if I am not as you say, under arrest! All I have done is serve my country, and to be honest I've been good at it too. I was abducted yesterday by some of your NCOs and brought to this hospital. I am not a threat, sir, to anyone and yet I am being treated like a prisoner. Before we start, can you tell me what I am in trouble over?' and she lay back down to rest.

By the look on his face, the major wasn't expecting this. 'Mitchell, you entered military service illegally by impersonating a male soldier to gain access to secure areas and military operations. So, in effect you are, under military law, an imposter. Now, I must admit there are no direct laws governing a female disguising herself as a soldier, but under regulations, there are various articles that refer to the impersonation of an officer or soldier within the British Army that relate directly to your situation. You may also have implicated others, so any charges brought against you may well be laid against others who may have assisted you. This is a very serious matter, and believe me, you have stirred up a hornet's nest and you should be prepared for charges to be brought against you.'

Ed became dry in the mouth as she listened, and she asked for more water. 'Well, sir, in that case I think I should have an officer present. Am I allowed to choose one myself?' she said cautiously.

'Whom did you have in mind?' asked the major.

'Well, I would like my doctor, Major Leigh-Smith, sir. Would that be permitted?'

'I will need to make a phone call. We will adjourn the interview until I have an answer. If that is not possible, I will take advice and allocate one to you. I trust that is acceptable?'

'Yes, sir, thank you, sir.'

And the major stood to leave, the sergeant followed him out. Patsy felt very guilty as the major peered across at her, as if signalling something, before leaving. Ed sighed, Patsy told her not to worry.

'I don't understand it Patsy, I have done nothing wrong here, except to serve my country dressed as a man! I am no threat.' she said dropping her head back onto the pillow. Patsy started to talk, but Ed lifted her hand up to stop her. 'Can I rely on you, Patsy, because I need someone right now whom I can trust?'

Patsy feeling terribly guilty, looked forlorn and moved forward to grip Ed's hand. 'I am here for you, yes. Please don't worry, I am sure it will all turn out ok I the end.' She said avoiding the question.

Ed smiled at her, just enough to get her confidence.

It was sometime later that the door opened again. Ed had been dozing on and off and wasn't expecting to see three doctors and a sister, with Patsy bringing up the rear. She carried a food tray and placed it on the side. It was too many people for the tiny room, but they spread themselves around her bed while the major took the lead.

'Gentlemen, this is Private Mitchell, or was, until she was shot in No Man's Land several days ago. She was shot high in the back, the bullet exiting from her chest on the right side, through her pectoral major and minor muscles and disrupting her intercostal muscles. Her surgeon did a good job and her wounds are healing well, with currently no infection. She remains in good spirits and is having her dressing changed daily, being cared for by Nurse Carter here. Can you unbutton her gown, please?' Ed was then rolled onto her side, her back uncovered for all to see.

'Now, the bullet entered through her trapezius, missing her shoulder blade and her spine, at a low trajectory, suggesting Mitchell was hunched over somewhat, leaning forward. Would that be right, Mitchell?'

Ed thought for a moment before answering. 'Yes, I think so, sir, we were half crawling and half running so I was leaning forward, yes.'

Major Morris nodded to himself, pleased his summation of events was correct, before addressing the doctors once again. 'OK, good, now the wound, as you can see, gentlemen, is elongated towards her shoulder and the bullet then seemed to dip under the scapular, clipping her lung and then somehow turning fifty degrees or so and popping out through the ribs to the right of her heart, with no major bleeding. Very lucky indeed, as an inch either way and she would not be here today.'

Ed, looking down at the bedsheets, was hearing for the first time how lucky she had been to be shot!

The major continued. 'Her wound has been bathed four-hourly in salt water solution since her operation.' He then took the doctors over to the window to discuss her ongoing treatment, while Patsy replaced the dressing on her back. Major Morris then returned to her bedside and asked her to turn over. She groaned a bit as she did so, but Carter took her weight and laid her down gently. She dropped Ed's gown from her shoulders and removed the old dressing. The doctors closed in around her.

'OK, gentlemen, the exit wound, as you can see, is large and has torn much of the flesh in both pectoral muscles. But these were successfully stitched, along with repairs to her right lung. Her skin was quarterised following some infected tissue and the blackening of the skin are burns and bruising, which will settle in a week or so providing there are no secondary infections. Her condition was very serious, but she is now stable. Captain Brown, she is your patient so keep me abreast of her progress.' The major wrote some notes and handed the file to Brown.

'Good, so plenty of food and water, Mitchell, coupled with some light exercise in a day or so, which should bring you slowly back to full health. You must keep your right arm in a sling for at least two more weeks, and of course you will not be heading back to the front.'

'Sir, can I have a visitor?' she asked with a smile.

'Give the name to Captain Brown, who will have to get approval with the MPs. Is that it?' he asked.

'Well, there is one other thing, sir, what will happen to me now?'

'That is not my decision. Once the general's staff have concluded their deliberations, all will become clear. Rest well, young lady, and we will see you tomorrow.'

They all left apart, from Captain Brown who sat down on the bed.

'What's his name?' he said.

'Private Smith, sir, he is attached to the 2nd/5th Gloucester's and is a sniper.'

Chapter 35

The battered Bakelite phone rattled in its cradle just in front of Captain Arding, causing him to jump in his seat. He picked up the handset, pulling on the twisted flex that had coiled itself in knots from months of use.

'Captain Arding, ADC.' He said

'Argh Nick, Major Clements here, I have an urgent request for the general, is he taking calls?' Captain Arding was a loyal officer who knew when to shut doors on people eager to get to his man and knew he disliked interruptions when in conference, and always preferred to meet face to face.

'No, I'm sorry, Richard, he is in a meeting, but he should be free in about fifteen minutes. Why don't you come over?'

'Roger that' and the phone went dead. What seemed like moments later, the major stepped into Arding's office and sat by the door, taking his cap off and placing it on top of his briefcase. He pulled out the last of his Players cigarette from his silver case, inhaling the strong tobacco, for the twentieth time that day! Before he had smoked half the cigarette, the door opened, and a brigadier stepped out, looking decidedly unhappy. The major stood in respect, replacing his cap, but wasn't acknowledged, the officer just charging from the room. That's all I need, Clements thought, a general in a foul mood.

Arding stepped from his desk and leant into the general's office. Clements faintly picked up the general's voice and then was asked in, Arding holding the door open. 'Good luck,' he said as he pulled the door closed.

The major walked forward and threw up a salute, before being ushered to the desk.

'What can I do for you, Major?' said the general, reaching for his glass of Whisky.

'It's a minor issue, sir. I won't be a minute, just wanted your approval on something. As required under military law, I am obliged to offer any prisoner legal support and although Mitchell has currently not been arrested, officially he, err, sorry, she can have support from an officer at the interview.'

'Yes,' said General Davis, but why are you bothering me with this? Just go ahead and get Mitchell what is required, we must do this by the book!'

'Well, sir, I was going to do that, but she has requested Major Leigh-Smith to be her counsel.'

The general answered immediately. 'Not possible, he may well be facing charges himself, following his interference. Find someone else. Is that it?'

'Yes, sir, that's it. Thank you, I will keep you no more sir.' He reached for his briefcase but realised he had left it outside. He saluted but the general was already looking away at a file on his side table. He walked towards the door and as he turned the door knob, a voice came from behind him.

'I urge you to get this done quickly, Major. Don't drag your feet. I want this woman charged and dealt with, now get on with it!'

He turned to speak but was waved away by the back of the man's left hand, an arrogant gesture to signal his time was up. He didn't speak to Captain Arding on his way out, simply grabbed his case from the chair and headed for the fresh air.

The walk back down the dusty track between HQ and the main hospital gave him a few minutes to think of his next move. He had now to locate a suitable officer to support her, and her OC Lieutenant Cavanagh came to mind. He went straight to Colonel Wood's office, his temporary home, and got on the telephone immediately, placing a call to the 2nd/5th Gloucesters' HQ. All was not done yet, he thought, as the phone rattled deep underground.

'Corporal Higgins, sir.'

'Ah, corporal, this is Major Clements of the Military Police. I need to speak with Lieutenant Cavanagh from the sniper squadron, can you locate him and get him to phone me back at HQ Hospital, Colonel Wood's office. It's extension 28.'

'Roger, wilco, sir,' and the line went dead.

He looked down at his blank writing pad with his Military Law volumes 1 and 2 next to it. He knew he had to prepare his questions, and more importantly the charges he would need to place against Mitchell, but this left him in a quandary as in legal terms she couldn't be charged as a solider. Because of this, he had sent a signal to the UK in Warminster to get some guidance from his brigadier, but as yet had not received any answer. He was aware there was a section in the big red book that permitted him to charge Mitchell as a civilian imposter, but that could result in death by firing squad, making him squirm in his seat. It was half an hour later when the phone clicked rapidly in front of him. He dropped his pen and leant back in his chair, picking up the receiver. 'Major Clements.'

'Sir, this is Lieutenant Cavanagh, I was asked to contact you.'

'Ah yes, Lieutenant, thank you. I am sure you are aware by now that I have Mitchell in custody here at HQ Hospital and also that it turns out that Mitchell is a woman. So, for obvious reasons, I need to interrogate her as a matter of some urgency. She has not been charged, yet, but she needs an officer to be present to act as her military support officer. I thought you might wish to be involved?'

Almost before he had finished speaking, Cavanagh responded loudly down the phone. 'Yes, I am aware of the situation sir, my CO informed me, but I don't understand why she would need to be Interrogated? Are you not aware of her contribution to this war, sir? How can she be under arrest?'

Major Clements was not ready for this and sat back, feeling decidedly uncomfortable. 'Look, Lieutenant, I don't make the rules, I am just following military law, and quite frankly, who are you to question me? I did not say she was under arrest, but that charges will be made, yes. Furthermore, I have a job to do, like you, and as such I must question her about her conduct and how she gained access to a British Army regiment, disguised as a man. For all we know she could be spying for the Germans! So, would you like to represent her or not?'

Cavanagh was stunned! 'Spying for the Germans,' he said. 'That's crazy, sir. Mitchell is the best sniper I have in my squadron and has killed ten Germans, hardly the conduct of a spy. She even bagged The Joker a few days ago, as I am sure you know.' The major was now getting impatient.

'Yes or no, Lieutenant?' he asked again.

'Yes, sir, of course, when and where?' said Cavanagh firmly.

'Good. HQ hospital, tomorrow morning, zero nine hundred.'

'I would walk over hot coals to be there, sir. Mitchell is a bloody war hero and I will put my career on the line to defend her. Perhaps you can also advise me where Private Smith might be tomorrow, as he has not been seen for several days.'

Major Clements did not speak further as that was another tricky situation, simply dropping the telephone in its cradle.

The OC to the sniper squadron waited for an answer, but the line went dead! He stood looking into the mouthpiece and swore. 'Bloody rude man,' he shouted, the corporal's ears across the desk picking up his comment, grinning to himself. Cavanagh sighed as he handed the phone back to him and left without further conversation. He needed to get hold of his CO and fast, before things got out of hand. He would know what to do.

***

The Major got to his feet and set off to the cells at HQ. He needed to interview Private Smith again, to glean as much information as possible, to help secure a list of charges that would be sufficient to gain a conviction and quickly. He was, after all, a co-conspirator at the very least and would probably end up in prison for a very long time!

Chapter 36

Frank had been stuck below ground now for twenty-four hours, only seeing a friendly MP corporal who chatted to him whenever he brought his meals and emptied the bucket. He was very tired having not slept much, and as he pondered his future. He suddenly heard footsteps and stood expectantly at the bars; the army blanket wrapped around his shoulders. Slowly the MP came into view, keys rattling in his hand.

'Hello Smithy,' he said as he reached to unlock the door. 'Time to see daylight. Major Clements wishes to interview you again. Come with me.'

He placed the handcuffs back on Frank's wrists and led him up the narrow stairs to the relative warmth of the landing above. Frank shivered, even though he was now above ground and could see the sun through a large window by the door. He was led back to the area where he'd been interviewed before and told to sit. The NCO tapped on the door and was told to bring Smith in and remove his handcuffs. Frank stood, and the corporal freed his hands. He marched over, saluting as he halted. The seated major didn't acknowledge his action.

'Sit down, Smith,' the major said. The MP corporal turned about and left the room.

'OK, Smith, I have brought you back for further questioning as you admitted to me you knew Mitchell was a woman. I need to know more about her life, her background, and it is in your best interests, I can assure you, to tell me all you know. I need to know how she came to join the army, whether she has ever visited Germany or has any friends or relatives there. So firstly, to recap, you told me previously you discovered her situation in a wrestling match at a café in the village of Linghem, during your sniper course.'

Frank wasn't really listening. All he could focus on was his scandalous suggestion Ed may have a connection with Germany. She is a war hero, she'd saved his life and he hers, and had killed ten enemy soldiers. No, this is not right he thought.

'Sir, I am an educated man, and quite honestly, I fail to understand how you can possible link private Mitchell with Germany. Ed is nothing short of a British war hero.' He paused, hoping his next words wouldn't harm her in any way. 'She does not have any links with our enemy sir, and certainly is not a spy if that's what you are suggesting! I have spent almost every minute of every day for over nine months by her side and she has fought for her country with valour, suffering a great deal in the process.'

The major leant back in his seat, screwing up his eyes. 'A spy, eh, Smith. Why do you mention that, do you know something?'

'What?' Frank said, astonished. 'No, sir, I wasn't saying that, I was just trying to make sure you didn't think she was one, as nothing could be further from the truth.' Frank's mouth had suddenly become very dry and he was trying to stop his tongue sticking to his lips as he formed his words. He swallowed with difficulty but continued. 'She is a first-class soldier, sir, and the best shot in the squadron. Why don't you interview everyone else, get Lieutenant Cavanagh here too, he will vouch for her.'

'That won't be necessary, Smith, as I have you and you know her best of all. So please think carefully, why anyone would impersonate a British soldier to get to the front line, unless they had specific reasons. Furthermore, perhaps she hoodwinked you too, and you don't know her as well as you think. Maybe she has tricked the rest of your squadron and has been passing details to the enemy all this time! Were you ever separated in No Man's Land, for instance, did she ever go off on her own?' he asked, scribbling notes on his pad.

Frank was starting to panic, his heart pounding in his chest, as he sought answers. 'But sir, you can't believe that, she is a soldier and a very good one too. She has been loyal and totally dedicated to the role of sniper, her record speaks for itself by killing many German officers in terribly difficult circumstances.'

'That, my dear man, could easily be a ruse to cover her position and protect herself and others from suspicion. Don't be naïve, Smith, this is real, man, and you are implicated here. If you want to avoid serious charges yourself, you need to come clean and tell me all you know. So, answer the damn question: did she ever go off on her own in No Man's Land?'

Frank thought back and remembered she often did just that, when seeking a shooting position. But how was he to answer?' At that very moment, a noise came from behind him, like a pencil dropping onto the stone floor. He turned to see a sergeant sitting in the corner, bending down to pick up the offending item, and realised they were not alone.

Frank ran through their successful mission and the killing of The Joker and what happened when she was shot. He told her he thought the Germans were just spraying shots wildly and it was just unlucky. He explained how he pulled her back into the dip and managed to get two field dressings into place, before carrying her back to the trenches. But she simply looked puzzled, shaking her head, not remembering much.

'Do you remember us falling into the trench, startling the sentry?' he asked. 'And the sentry screaming, about to stick us with his bayonet?' Ed looked totally blank but laughed aloud, making her wince as a pain shot across her chest. Patsy listened in the whole while, but asked Frank to stop making her laugh. Ed settled back down, but then laughter erupted again, spontaneously, friends caught in a special moment.

'Glad you're OK, mate,' Frank said with a concerned look.

'Frank, you saved my life, I will never forget that,' she said, reaching for his hand.

Nurse carter watched this very sincere moment between two soldiers who had clearly been to hell and back during their time at the front. Indeed, their operations into No Man's Land appeared to her to be the height of bravery and in true historic British spirit. She felt herself welling up with delight as they openly showed the bond that existed between them, almost as though she wasn't in the room. They had obviously become very close during their battle-hardened initiation to war and it seemed a shame that they would now be parted. Frank noticed a bowl of porridge on the table and asked if he could feed his friend. Patsy nodded, but mentioned it was probably cold.

'Army food cold, nothing new there then,' he said smiling. 'Come on,' he said and almost missed her mouth with his first attempt, smearing a spot of porridge on her chin deliberately, creating more laughter until he got the hang of it. They giggled like two school children. Patsy thought, it was a lovely moment.

'So, don't you remember anything, Ed?' Frank asked.

'I remember taking out the German officer,' she said, 'but not much after that. Have you placed a patrol report yet to the OC?'

'No, that's another story. But will tell you about that another time. Do you need anything before I head back?'

'Just a new chest,' she said laughing, which caused further coughing, making her wince once more.

Frank moved closer to her, looking towards the door before speaking quietly. 'You should be very careful Ed, I have been interrogated, twice so far, and they are trying to make a case against you. I don't know all the details, but they are trying to suggest you may have connections to Germany. Be on your guard old friend. I will do all I can from my end to help you.

Ed looked at him, greatly concerned. 'Oh my god! I'm in real trouble, aren't I? I need you to write to my family,' she said nervously. Frank leant forward to speak again.

'Well I already have,' he said smartly. 'I wrote to your priest the day you were shot. He must have it by now. I was careful in my words so nothing would alarm the censors,' he said winking at her. Anything else?' he asked. But just as she was about to speak, the door sprung open and the sergeant walked in.

'I think that's enough for now, Private,' he said. 'We need to get you back.' Ed looked shocked.

Frank then stood up replacing the bowl on the tray and reached for Frank's hand for the final time. They shook, holding on for a few tender seconds. He recognised her concern at the MP standing by the door.

'It's ok, they are just asking me some questions.' Then turned and left the room. As the door closed, Ed realised the letters she left over a year ago with Bryan, would now be read and her plan would commence. Then nurse Carter left the room...

The sergeant led Frank back to the car and handed him over to the corporal at headquarters, who had been waiting patiently outside the back door. He was about to lead him back downstairs, but Frank held back.

'Any chance of having a ciggy?' he said. The corporal looked around the gravel yard, before nodding his head sideways. They went across to the wall behind the kitchen and lit up. His first cigarette for two days. It was a pleasurable moment.

'Hey, Frank, seems like you're getting shafted here. I am no expert on military charges, God, I've only been doing this for eight months, but I overheard most of what was said with Major Clements. The word around the lads is someone is trying to roast you both. I would like to help you, but not sure how. Is there anyone you want to contact, a letter perhaps?'

Frank looked at the man in total shock. Not knowing if he was now being lured into a trap, he didn't speak, and took a last drag before stubbing out his fag. They walked back below ground to the cold cellar. As the corporal unshackled him, he realised he had to try something.

'I just need to write a couple of letters. Can you get me some paper and envelopes?'

'Yes, no problem,' And after locking him back in cell, he nipped back up the stairs and within minutes, he was back. He waited by the cell while Frank scribbled his letters. He completed the addresses and handed them to the corporal.

'Lord Hardcastle. You know a Lord?' said the corporal. Frank didn't answer, just pulled the blanket back over his shoulders, nodding. 'OK, Frank, I promise they will be posted in the headquarters Registry tonight. The mail normally leaves at twenty hundred hours. It will probably be in England by tomorrow afternoon.'

Frank looked at him carefully, his mind racing, and reached out to shake his hand.

'Look, don't trust anyone else, others might not be so supportive. Why, there's already a bet with the chaps on your sentence!'

This shook Frank immensely. He hadn't realised until this moment how serious a position he was in. 'Don't worry, Frank,' and he walked slowly away, back up the stairs, and was gone.

In the office above, Major Clements sat reading his notes, chatting with the sergeant who was now sitting opposite him at the desk.

'I want you to go back to the hospital and speak to the nurse. She may have further information.' As he stood to leave, the sergeant clearly had something on his mind.

'Sir, do you believe Mitchell is a spy? Maybe she does know someone in England who is not sympathetic to the cause.' Perhaps there is more to this relationship with her priest?'

'Thank you, sergeant, but I am already following a specific enquiry, that may indeed provide us with the breakthrough we need.' When the sergeant had left, he reached for his signal pad. He needed to get someone to visit the priest!

***

Later that day, in the Registry, clerks were clattering typewriter keys and shifting paper around the busy office. Unnoticed at the far end of the room, an MP corporal slipped three private letters into the outgoing mail sack: one for his old mum in Berkshire whom he hadn't written to in a while, one to Mr E Mitchell and the final one to Lord Hardcastle! He carefully buried them deep down in the sack and exited quietly by the side door. At 10 p.m. the Divisional Headquarters' mail sack, along with eighty others, were being loaded onto the steamer at Boulogne, ready to sail back to England.

Chapter 37

Ed had drifted in and out of sleep most of the night, her worries constantly on her mind, as she knew the major would be back. Without the knowledge of military procedures, she was always to be at a disadvantage, but was hopeful the officer appointed to her would somehow be on her side. The sun was bright outside the window and she tried to sit up, but the pain shot across her chest making her wince and lay back, holding her breath for a few seconds, until the pain had eased. Just as she was getting comfortable again, she heard the key being turned in the lock, and the door slowly opened. Nurse Carter poked her head around the door, carrying a tray and smiling brightly.

'Morning, Edwina, hope you are hungry, as I have secured you eggs for breakfast with buttered toast and tea, and your support officer is here.

'My support officer, do you know who it is?' she asked looking across to the breakfast tray. 'I did get his name, it's a Lieutenant Cavanagh, I think. Nice looking gentleman.'

Ed's hopes suddenly increased. 'That's good, it will be nice to see him, he's my OC, he'll help me.' She said in a positive tone. Patsy came to her bedside and propped several pillows behind her back, before cutting her food into manageable portions. Ed started feeding herself with a single fork, realising, they were the first eggs she had eaten in a long while. 'Tastes great, Patsy, thank you.'

Nurse Carter, smiled without speaking, wondering what might happen to this brave lady, hoping she was doing the right thing.

After breakfast, Ed was washed thoroughly, her dressings changed, and a few minutes before nine o'clock the key rattled in the lock and a familiar face appeared round the door frame.

'Sleeping on the job, Mitchell,' said a smiling but grubby looking officer, who was still wearing his battle dress uniform. 'Sorry, old bean meant to get here earlier, but had to see someone and we had ops overnight too. But better late than never, eh?' He pulled the only chair to the bedside and took off his gloves, holding his hand out to her. She looked up at him, then shook his hand, firmly. 'Well done Ed, amazing shooting, and you got him.' Ed was a little choked that the first thing he did was to congratulate her.

'Yeh, but look where it's got me.' She said grumbling. He smiled and sat down. 'So, how are you feeling today?'

'Oh, you know, my body will heal, sir, but that is clearly the least of my problems at the moment.

The lieutenant felt for his subordinate and wanted to cheer her spirits, so started their meeting on a positive note and talked first about The Joker!

'Look, before we begin, I wanted to let you that General Haig has sent a signal to congratulate us all on a job well done. I can't tell you what it has done for morale and the lads send their best to you. They are currently not aware of your situation however, as the whole matter has been hushed up. But I imagine it will all come out in due course. You are a good soldier, Mitchell, and I am sorry to be losing you. Now, I have very little information at present, but as you know that under military law you are entitled to have an officer present to act for you. When this Major Clements arrives, I shall try and stall him, so we can have time to prepare.' Before he could continue further, the door suddenly opened, and the two MP's stood before them.

'Ah, you must be Lieutenant Cavanagh,' he said cheerfully.

'I am, indeed, sir. How do you do?' Cornelius Cavanagh threw up a salute in respect, before they shook hands.

'Look, no need for all that, old chap, shall we sit down and get on with it?'

'Well, no, actually, sir, I have only just arrived due to several overnight ops, and will need some time with Mitchell, which I believe is my right. We have much to discuss. Could we delay for perhaps an hour or so?'

Clements was irritated that his hope of moving forward was once again dashed. Cavanagh was right, though, he did indeed have the right to spend time with his charge. The major conceded and agreed to return at ten o'clock. When he had gone, Cavanagh shuffled forward with his writing pad.

'OK, Mitchell, on my way here I stopped at the Gloucesters' HQ to speak to the colonel. He gave me a five-minute introduction to military law and told me what we should ask for, one being time! So, first things first, what, if any, are the charges they have pinned on you?'

'I have as yet not been charged with anything, sir. I have asked repeatedly why I am being locked up as I am no threat and can't even walk, but I am locked up here as a prisoner.'

'OK, that's probably a positive then, as I assume, they are still trying to gather evidence against you. Don't be alarmed, as that gives us some time to dig too. It also means they may be struggling to find a charge that covers this situation. Tell me, what has happened since you have been here?'

Ed looked at him and started to relate what she knew. 'Well, I arrived after a sort of hijacking on the road where MPs stopped the ambulance and brought us here. There was a gunshot too, but I have no idea who was shot! I was initially cared for by Sister Youngs, but she was relieved by Nurse Carter yesterday. My recollections are still vague, however Frank told me yesterday I was shot on our withdrawal through No Man's Land. He carried me all the way back, in his arms.' The officer then interrupted her.

'Hang on, Smith was here, you say? He hasn't reported back. Is he being held here?' he asked.

'I'm not sure sir, but he did say he had been interrogated twice. Is he locked up perhaps?' she suggested. 'Look, don't worry about that for now, I will ask the major later. So, getting back to you. Carry on.'

'Well, my personal situation, I assume became clear while I was on the operating table. Major Leigh-Smith was my surgeon and it was him, I think, who set up my escape to recuperate; however, we were intercepted and brought here. I don't know why he did that but clearly, he must have thought I was in danger or something. I have very little more to tell you, sir. But I would like to know what is ahead for me.'

Corn stopped writing and looked up at her. 'I hope we can sort this out for you Ed and you get what you deserve, a hero's welcome back in Blighty. Even though I would have you back in a heartbeat!'

Ed always did like this man and felt a glow of pride at what she had achieved. 'Thank you, sir, I was only doing my duty and couldn't have done it without Frank.'

'So, to re-cap. No charges have currently been made against you, correct?' he said, looking at his watch.

'No, sir, not yet.'

'Right, the major might well be quite forceful towards you, in an attempt to get certain answers. Don't get sucked in, and if in doubt ask to speak to me privately or lean over and whisper in my ear. I don't have anything like the experience he will have, but I will intervene as necessary. We will be a great team again, Ed, and don't worry.'

Promptly at ten o'clock, the lock gently turned, and the door opened. The sergeant entered, followed by a smiling major, and Nurse Carter bringing up the rear. Lieutenant Cavanagh sat on the side of Ed's bed, so he could be near for any questions she might have for him. The MPs had two extra chairs brought in by the sentry, and sat at the end of the bed, directly facing her, the sergeant's pencil poised over his writing pad.

'Ten zero three, Thursday third of May 1917, at Divisional Headquarters base hospital. Formal Interview of Miss Mitchell conducted by Major R Clements, in the presence of Lieutenant C J Cavanagh, OC of the sniper squadron, and Sergeant P Stuttard.' He selected some papers from the small pile in his briefcase and began again.

'For the purposes of this interview I will call you simply Mitchell, if you have no objection?'

She shook her head twice. She looked at her lieutenant and he smiled, knowing she was totally relying on him.

'Thank you. I ask that you tell the whole truth Mitchell, as it will go against you if in future interviews it is proven that you have lied or obscured the truth.

'So, I would like to start at the very beginning. When did you decide to try and illegally join the army and how did you fool the army medical board?'

Ed knew the questions would come thick and fast and she must be on her toes, carefully reciting the story she had prepared all those months before.

'Well, sir, I had been reading for some time of the war and saw many chaps leave my village to sign up. So, when my brother attended his medical and was dismissed as unfit, I simply prepared myself in secret and took his papers. I just wanted to serve my country you see, and so I had my hair cut short, dressed as a man and went along in the hope I wouldn't be found out. And I wasn't! I was always very strong and powerful, having worked on the farm and even had the appearance of a man. So, it was all very easy really,' she said with an air of confidence.

The major was almost speechless. How could anyone just take someone's identity and enlist in their place? Conscription was supposed to be a legitimate system, with names taken from the national census and the relevant paperwork provided.

'So, is it true you are actually Rebecca Mitchell, your brother's older sister?' he asked without looking at his notes. Ed's heart suddenly raced, as she realised, with some satisfaction, that he must have received notice from England. How else would he know that she was going to use her mother's name? The letter must have got through. She wanted to smile, but controlled herself, before responding.

'Yes sir, I am Rebecca Mitchell.' She said confidently. Corn looked at her a little surprised.

'OK, Rebecca, thank you. Now, during your enlistment, how did you manage to mask the fact you were female from your training team and your platoon?'

'Well, sir, I took the physical demands of training in my stride and had been practising in the barn at home for some time prior to enlisting to be able to pee standing up. I know that sounds pretty awful, but it had to be done, otherwise I would have been rumbled very quickly. I even researched at the library how to manage my other personal issues, which I won't go into, unless you need to know?'

She was right; the major waived his hand and shook his head. 'Please continue,' he said.

'OK, I am already aware Private Smith knew you were female, so please state for the record how he discovered your secret and what happened?' As she began, he opened the page of evidence Smith had told her previously, to see if their stories matched. It did…

'OK, does anyone else know of the situation, anyone at the front, your squadron, your CO perhaps?' he said, looking across at the lieutenant.

'I will answer that for you, Mitchell,' said Lieutenant Cavanagh. 'At no time did I or my CO have any inkling whatsoever. Now a sniper team consists of two snipers working together very closely, so I can assure you sir, the answer would be no,' he said decisively.

'You may well have to give evidence Lieutenant, under oath, but for now, I don't wish to hear your speculation. Now, Mitchell, can you go through what happened in hospital,'

'I don't really know, sir. I was cared for by Sister Youngs and the doctors, including my surgeon who came to visit me every day, twice sometimes, and eventually I was told I was leaving to convalesce. I don't know anything else apart from that. I do remember we were stopped on the roadside and I ended up here.'

Ed's memory suddenly cleared, the incident coming back to her. She leant over to whisper into her lieutenant's ear, masking her mouth with her hand, to ask whether she should ask about it, but he shook his head, pinching his lips. Ed wasn't satisfied with this and spoke up. 'I do have a question though, sir, if I may. What happened to the driver of the ambulance the other day? I thought I heard a gunshot.'

'Oh, he is back in his unit probably, I have no idea. You probably heard a vehicle backfire or something. So, did you correspond with anyone during your time there, letters to England perhaps?'

Ed shook her head rapidly. 'No, sir, I wasn't well enough.'

'How many people visited you in hospital?' said the major without looking up from his note pad. 'Well, lieutenant Cavanagh came for a brief period, the doctors and nurses and Frank, err, Private Smith, came yesterday. There were no others.' She laid her head back and sighed. 'Can I get a drink please?' The officer looked across at nurse carter who was already stepping to her bedside.

'OK, let's continue. Now, Mitchell, I believe you said, your parents died on the Titanic. By my reckoning, you could only have been or sixteen years of age, a very young age to take on such responsibilities. So, who has been your guardian since then?'

'That would be my vicar,' she said with a broad smile. 'Reverend Bryan O'Callaghan. He has advised and supported us, for several years and I could not have survived without him.' She smiled to herself as she thought of him.

'If you were that close, I presume he knew of your enlistment?'

Ed clammed up, not sure how to answer, and reached for her glass of water again to think. 'No, sir. I just left and wrote to him later.'

'Ok, how long has he been your village priest, I assume he is Irish with the name O'Callaghan?' he asked.

'I have known him all my life Sir and yes he had an Irish mother, but is not from Ire, – '. She stopped speaking realising she had almost slipped up.

'Not from Ireland, I think you were going to say. So where was he from, where did he live as a child?' he said leaning forward to encourage her.

Ed froze. How could she answer this one? She would have to lie, nothing else for it. 'I don't know, I never knew his father.' she said firmly. 'All I know is he and his mother arrived in England alone. I don't know anything else about him.'

The major looked at her for several seconds, trying to work out how much she was holding back, and as she avoided his gaze for the first time, he knew immediately. He wanted more.

'Oh,' he said in a curious tone. 'I did not ask about his father,' he said staring straight at her. 'So, where did he arrive from, you must know that at least? Europe perhaps?' Ed's heart was now racing, she had got herself muddled and now was in danger of giving his story away. She started to feel panicked but must continue to deny any knowledge of his upbringing, otherwise, he would be in serious trouble.

'Look Sir, I really don't know anything before I met him as a child.' She said firmly. The major pondered her response, staring at her, knowing she was hiding something. He made a note in the right column to follow this up.

'So, who is running the farm now?'

'My brother, Edward, sir. He still is, and my younger sister of course.' And then she gasped, in apparent pain.

He looked at her and knew instantly she was feigning. He played along, he had things to do.

'Look, you are obviously having some discomfort, let's have a break as I have to make some phone calls and you can have the nurse attend to you,' he said as he stood up. Lieutenant Cavanagh rose too, and the sergeant was already tapping on the door.

'Would you come up to Colonel Wood's office, Lieutenant, at twelve hundred hours. We can then discuss our progress and what remains to be done.' Corn nodded politely.

'Could you give us a minute please nurse?' Corn asked. Patsy carter then stood and followed the MP's out. 'I will be right outside,' she said and smiled before leaving, the door slamming shut behind her.

'You're doing well, Ed, very well, just keep your answers simple and don't say too much. You should not have asked about the roadside incident, that is only drawing attention and we must not antagonise him in any way. But, why is he persisting with questions about your village priest?' he asked pulling his cigarette case from inside his tunic. Ed looked up at him, feeling wretched. She didn't want to tell him, but knew he needed to know. She bit her lip, feeling terribly nervous.

'Because he is German!' she said. Lt Cavanagh stood frozen to the spot, the cigarette in his mouth, drooping downwards.

'Oh my God.' He said shocked. 'this fact must never come out as if they make that connection, it will make things extremely difficult.' He walked over to the door to leave. 'I'm just going to have a smoke. Be back shortly.' He said tapping on the door. As it opened, he saw nurse Carter rushing away up the corridor. She's in a hurry he thought, before exiting through a side doorway to the outside.

Ed was alone, her mind cluttered with too many thoughts. Has she just made a terrible error, she thought and given the major a lead he hadn't had before? Oh my god, what had she done. She clenched her hands to her face and felt like crying. Her mind wandered, her heart raced, how was she going to get out of this? It was over ten minutes before she heard the door open again.

'Are you OK, Ed,' said Patsy. 'What was the matter, where is the pain?'

Ed sat up slightly. 'I don't have any pain, Patsy, I just needed a break, his questions are so difficult, and I am not sure how to answer.'

Patsy sat on the bed and held her hand. 'Well, if you have nothing to hide, just be honest. My mum always says it's the best policy.' Ed smiled at her, knowing she couldn't possibly do that!

A little after twelve thirty, Lieutenant Cavanagh arrived and sat back in the chair by the side of the bed. Nurse carter took the opportunity to take her leave. 'I will be back in a little while. Do you need anything?' she asked. Ed shook her head, now focussed on her OC.

'Give us an hour would you nurse?' asked the lieutenant. She nodded as she closed the door.

He looked at her curiously. 'So, what happened earlier, did I sense some play acting?'

She looked at the man who had supported her since those cold, wet days on the ranges at Linghem during her sniper course and realised, he didn't miss much. She knew she must trust him fully! 'Sir is everything I tell you secret like; you know private?' she asked. He paused looking at this amazing young woman whom he had grown to admire deeply. He smiled. 'I am your councel Mitchell and everything you say is between you and me. No-one, I repeat no-one, will be privy to anything you tell me.' He folded his arms and waited.

Her OC looked at her and opened his arms offering his open hands in friendship. Ed spoke quietly, in case anyone was listening at the door, and began to tell her story. She told him of her parents, how she had a timid and weak brother and how she joined the army to protect him. How they swapped lives completely, and how their vicar, Reverend Bryan O'Callaghan, helped them bring this all together. She spoke of David and how he fitted into the farm, substituting for her when she joined up, and with the details of her basic training, and how she had escaped various problems on a day-to-day basis. She finished up by saying how important Frank had been in her life since they had become snipers. It was a special bond that she felt, which would stay for life! At the end of almost an hour of talking, he looked at her, quite taken aback by the meticulous details of the planning and execution of her life. He stood and walked to the window, before turning to face her.

'You know, you are quite the most extraordinary woman I think I have ever met,' he said. 'I have got fully grown men complaining to me over their conditions and that they can't cope and some even cry at my door with homesickness. But you have a certain determination and courage that is rare, very rare indeed. Quite how I can help for this to go away, I know not, but will seek guidance from Major Hesketh-Pritchard tonight. I am starting to sense a bit of a witch-hunt and we simply cannot let that happen, Mitchell, after what you have done for your Country. I will protect you as much as I can, I promise you that. There will be no more questions to come, difficult questions but for today, I will inform Major Clements you are too unwell to continue. I will come back later to chat further after you have eaten and will brief Nurse Carter on my way out. Well done today, Ed, or should I say Rebecca.'

As he left her small room, she looked lost in a world that now seemed against her. When he had gone, she blubbed into her pillow, something she hadn't done for a very long time.

***

Down the corridor, Major Clements had made one phone call to captain Arding and sent a signal to HQ Warminster, in England. The new information he had just heard from nurse carter, would prove to be most useful...

Chapter 38

The house keeper brought the morning mail up from below stairs on the small silver tray, placing it on the hall table, before getting on with her other duties. The under-butler whose duty it was, waited patiently for the old grandfather clock to strike eleven, knowing His Lordship, a man of routine, would expect the morning mail. When the clock finally chimed, he took them down the corridor to His Lordship's study, where he found him, as usual, sitting in his favourite chair, reading *The Times*

'The morning mail, my Lord,' he said, placing the tray on the small table beside him. 'Can I get you anything, sir?'

'Ah, thank you, Charles, tea I think,' he said without lifting his nose from the financial pages. The man nodded graciously, Lord Hardcastle remaining totally engrossed in the share prices, smiling that his stocks had shown significant improvement over the past months. The tip-off he had received from his friend in the Ministry was proving to be sound, very sound indeed. He always told himself he was doing nothing wrong, just the old boys' network! Thanks to the war, he would do rather well.

He turned back to the front page, to view that day's main story. It ran to a full ten pages and was filled with intrepid actions by British and Commonwealth troops, however the long list of casualties took him back to his own active service, when as a young lieutenant he'd served in the 1863/4 New Zealand Maori wars. He'd been under the command of Lieutenant General Duncan Cameron, later to be knighted, and the skirmishes took over nine months to quell. He'd returned home the following year, after news of his father's death had reached him. Once a soldier, always a soldier, but having no sons of his own, he'd never had the opportunity to encourage his blood kin to enlist and stand up for this great country. As his mind drifted away from his personal experiences, he scanned the pages at random and saw a small article about a German officer called The Joker, who had been shot and killed by a British sniper. It reported that this particular German had been causing considerable anguish to the high command for many months, with antics of hilarity and clowning, to both humiliate British soldiers and humour his own troops. He tittered to himself as morning tea arrived.

'Anything else, Your Lordship?' but he received no answer, just a shake of the head, so he left him to it. A minute or so later, Lord Hardcastle looked up to speak to Charles, but he was alone, so poured his own tea, reaching for his favourite biscuit, a digestive, the kind he had eaten since he was a boy. Out of the corner of his eye, he saw the small pile of letters on the tray and reached across to pick them up. He flipped through, noticing one from the front!

Placing his cup down, he took out a single sheet of paper with just a few lines, but in a style he instantly recognised. Glancing at the signature block at the bottom, he smiled. It was from Frank. His delight was quickly quashed as he read the letter with growing alarm! He quickly reread it before jumping up and going to the door, calling for his butler, who came at the double, noting the tone of his master's voice.

'Ah, Charles, I need to go up to London. Please get the car ready. And get me Lord Symister on the phone in the Foreign Office. The telephone number is in my book on my desk. Put it through upstairs, I need to change.' He walked towards the grand staircase, the letter still in his hand.

'Will you require an overnight, My Lord?' Charles said.

'I hope to be back for dinner, but maybe an overnight bag might be prudent.' and he headed up the grand staircase to dress suitably for a meeting in one of Britain's finest institutions, the War Propaganda Bureau. As he entered his large bedroom that overlooked the rear lawns, his man servant Peter was already in his dressing room, laying out a suit and tie for the occasion. 'I thought the brown tweed, sir?'

'The tweed will be fine, but hurry, I need to leave sharpish!' As he reached for his jacket, the phone rang. Charles had connected him to London.

'Ah yes, thank you, Charles,' he said. And then waited a few moments before speaking again. 'Hugh, hello old chap, sorry to bother you, but something rather urgent has come up and I need to see you, today. Can you find ten minutes this afternoon?' His Lordship listened and then repeated a time: 'One forty-five, that's spiffing, thank you, Hugh.' And hung up.

Within fifteen minutes of opening his letter, they were speeding through the large gates at the bottom of the long drive, narrowly missing several sheep who darted across their path at the last minute. The drive to Buckingham

Gate, London would take a good two hours, so timing would be tight. 'Don't spare the horses, Chapman,' said Lord Hardcastle and he pulled out *The Times* from his briefcase to finish reading the news from the front. After a short time, he rested his head back against the soft leather cushioning of his dark green Rolls Royce, but he was not sleeping; he was plotting, as Frank needed him.

At precisely one twenty-five the car pulled up outside the War Propaganda Bureau, a policeman opening his door before the driver had even got out of the car. He entered the front door and was met by a young man who introduced himself as Mr Brewer, a smart chap with a clipped moustache and wearing a broad pin-striped suit, who had a squeak in his right shoe. He led Lord Hardcastle up the stairs to the first floor where he was shown to a seat in Lord Symister's office and offered tea. He reached inside his jacket for the letter and read it through several times, until the squeaky shoe gave away Brewer's return! It had been some time since he had seen Chuffy, a nickname granted to him by some of the boys in the Lower Fifth at Eton, because of his love for all things steam. Lord Hardcastle sat admiring the array of portraits hanging around the vast room, one of King George taking his fancy, hanging high above Chuffy's ornate desk. As he finished his tea, he heard voices outside and suddenly the door burst open, Hugh rushing in, rather red-faced!

'Hello, Michael,' he said, shaking his hand warmly. 'Sorry I'm late, had to endure the delights of Sir Desmond Allington today. Do you know Allington, works in Defence Procurement? Anyway, big problems now all sorted.'

'That's OK, Chuffy, I am just grateful you have found the time to see me. Is Muriel well, and how are the grandchildren?' he asked politely.

'Oh, they are all fine as usual, don't seem to see them much these days, their mother hardly brings them to see us anymore, since we lost Bertie. Still, what's up, old chap, what's all the rush?'

Lord Hardcastle reached inside his tweed jacket, remembering the day Chuffy had telegraphed him to say his son and heir had been killed at the battle of the Somme. A young Captain of great distinction, who'd played rugger for Cambridge University and whose body had been blown to smithereens! He snapped back from his thoughts and pulled out a folded piece of paper.

'I received this letter today and well, your advice would be deeply appreciated,' he said, handing it over.

Sir
I hope you are well, and your gout is not troubling you too much.

I write from a prison cell below General Davis's Headquarters, and require your urgent assistance.

It's rather a long story, but I am going to be charged by the Military Police for aiding and abetting my sniper partner, Private Ed Mitchell, who they have in custody. There is one problem. Mitchell is a woman and has managed to hide her femininity from the Army for over a year.

I have known Ed since training, and we joined the sniper squadron together. I cannot define our duties, but her skills have taken many German lives and I would put my life down to defend my closest friend. Although she is a war hero, she is about to be imprisoned and probably charged for treason. The man behind this is General Davis.

I have no clue as to why this persecution of an innocent soldier is happening, when if a man, a gallantry medal would be forthcoming. I would appreciate your urgent help Sir, as I am wholly innocent, and things are progressing rather too quickly for my liking.

My warmest regards
Frank

Lord Symister stared at Michael for a full minute without speaking, placing the letter on his desk.

'What can be done, Chuffy?' said Lord Hardcastle.

'I have no idea, old chap, but how on earth has this transpired? A woman at the front, a sniper no less. My God, this is huge, Michael, no wonder the general is hounding your man, err, Smith is it. Can he be trusted?'

Lord Hardcastle leant back in his chair and looked carefully at his old Etonian friend. 'Frank grew up on my estate, Chuffy, when his mother met hard times. You have actually met him several times when you have stayed for weekend shooting parties. He practically became one of my family and without bearing a son of my own, I have kind of mentored him throughout his life and have considered him like a son. He can be totally trusted I assure you and is as honest as the day is long. I would vouch for him above all others,' he said in a clear, precise, but slightly emotional tone.

'OK, this is what I propose. Firstly, can you stay over tonight in London, as sadly I must be at a dinner at Downing Street tonight with various foreign dignitaries, which I can't avoid. And the rest of the afternoon is rather tied up too, I'm afraid. But there is a meeting of the inner cabinet in the morning, which will be over by ten o'clock and if you're available, I think we could speak directly to Spotty Chatterdon. You remember him, don't you, he was two years ahead of us at Eton. Anyway, as you know he runs the War Office with a rod of iron. This face-to-face meeting would allow you time to make further enquiries this afternoon and then discuss your concerns with him directly. You will need evidence, Michael, and you will have to be convincing.'

'Oh, I can be convincing alright. There are innocent lives at stake here and someone must stop this madness. Do you know of General Davis at all?' he asked.

'No, I don't, but I did meet him several years ago before the war. My memories of him are rather vague though. But Spotty will know of him as I am aware that late last year he met with General Haig and several of his senior generals at a two-day meeting here in London. It was all very hush, hush as they didn't want the Hun to know most of the British higher command were not in France at all but drinking port in Whitehall! He will have an opinion, I am sure, but I must dash. Will you stay at the Dorchester?'

'Yes, I think that would suit. Should I come to Downing Street?' he asked.

'No, here I think, old man, then I can bring him across, familiar territory is often an advantage.'

'Thank you, Chuffy, this one is a debt I can never repay!'

'Don't mention it, you would do the same for me, I am sure. See you tomorrow morning, at 11 a.m.'

They shook hands and he disappeared as quickly as he had arrived. Lord Hardcastle's car was outside, with Chapman his driver chatting to another man in a smart grey uniform, both smoking cigarettes. On seeing His Lordship, he quickly stubbed it under his foot and reached to open the door for his master, the other driver stepping away smartly.

'The Dorchester, Chapman, please.' And they sped off across town.

Chapter 39

Bryan O'Callaghan was sitting at his desk, tapping his foot to the music from his old gramophone, as he wrote his Sunday sermon. He wasn't aware of the knocker sounding over and over on the vestry door, as the Mozart concerto drowned out everything around him. He moved with the rhythm, the violins creating a vivid scene in his mind of wild seas and windy days and he was somewhere else at that moment, not really paying much attention to the world outside. Then, as the music subsided, he became aware of someone thumping the door. Standing, pencil still in his hand, he walked over to the gramophone and lifted the arm, the record turning at speed with no sound. He hurried and pulled the door open, revealing two soldiers, both wearing MP armbands, and a policeman.

'Good morning, sir,' said the sergeant. 'Are you Father O'Callaghan?' he asked. 'Yes, I am he, there is nothing wrong, I hope?'

The two men looked each other without indicating anything, before turning back to face him.

'Sir, I am arresting you on a special order from the War Propaganda Bureau. You do not need to say anything, but what you do say may be taken down and given as evidence.'

The smaller corporal suddenly lunged forward and reached to handcuff the priest, almost before he realised what was happening.

'What on earth do you mean, are you deranged, what am I supposed to have done?' he said, twisting his arms away as the soldier tried in vain to clip his right wrist into the heavy iron shackles. 'Now back off, young man, or you will be sorry. I have no wish to hurt you, but I will not be cuffed like some ruffian. Tell me what this is about, and I will oblige you,' he said firmly

'Now, Father, please, I have my orders and that includes arresting you and taking you to Warminster to be interviewed by Colonel Dickson. Now please turn around and let Corporal Slater do his duty,' said the sergeant.

At that, the civilian policeman stepped forward and said, 'Come along, Father, let's be calm and do as the soldiers have asked.'

'No, PC Dodds, I will not stand by and let them cuff me until I know what this is all about.' He looked intently at him as he spoke and said, 'Yes, I know who you are, Constable. Your father used to come to my services here at this very church, holding you by the hand. I know your family. Why are you aiding these soldiers when they have no rights?'

'We have every right, sir, now please would you let the Corporal handcuff you and let us do our duty?'

Bryan stood bewildered. He knew of Ed's plight in a field hospital, but could not work out why they would arrest him? Was it simply because he had helped her, or did they know everything already? One thing was for sure, she would not have betrayed him.

'OK, look Sergeant, I will walk with you to your car and agree to come with you to Warminster, but I will not be cuffed. I am a man of the cloth, so have some decency, would you.' He stepped back into the vestry to get his cloak. As he did so, the large sergeant placed one of his feet inside, so the door could not be closed, and watched his prey go to the coat stand and retrieve his long black cloak, before walking back to the door. Bryan reached round for the big iron key, placing it in the lock on the outside, then slammed the door shut, and with a heavy 'clunk' locked the door. 'Now, shall we go?' he said.

Their vehicle was parked just around the corner and while the sergeant strode ahead, the policeman walked alongside Bryan, the corporal bringing up the rear. The journey to Warminster took over an hour, reaching the small guard house around midday. The sentry didn't speak, just nodded at the corporal at the wheel, and lifted the red and white striped barrier skywards. They drove in, speeding off around the perimeter road, before pulling up outside a small hut on the far side of the barracks. Bryan started to get out but was prevented from doing so by the sergeant sitting next to him. When the engine had been switched off, the corporal got out and headed to the door. Bryan sat still, looking, straight ahead, awaiting his fate. After a few minutes, a head appeared at the doorway, nodding, indicating he should get out.

'Step out of the car please, sir,' said the sergeant. Bryan did as he was asked and was escorted towards the narrow doorway. They walked into the hut and down a dark corridor, Bryan being told to sit outside a door marked Commanding Officer. The sergeant tapped on it gently and stepped inside, his heavy studded boots hammering on the floor as he reported to the officer. Words were spoken and he quickly returned.

'This way, sir.' And Bryan stood up to enter the rather gloomy room that was full of smoke. He saw a heavy-set man right in front of him, sitting behind a tiny desk. He was largely bald and had a long black moustache, that curled at the sides. Bryan thought him to be about his own age and reached forward to shake his hand but, was suddenly pulled back violently by the sergeant and held firmly. He started to sweat, feeling distinctly uneasy at this treatment and was about to say so, when the officer said, 'Sit down, Father O'Callaghan' and he was pushed towards a chair a few feet away from the desk.

'Sir, O'Callaghan refused to wear handcuffs, but to his good grace, he didn't struggle. Will that be all, sir?'

'No, sergeant, stay by the door please, this won't take that long,' Bryan's interrogation was about to begin, and he swallowed nervously.

Chapter 40

General Davis slammed the phone down in anger at being ignored. He had ordered Major Clements to move the Mitchell matter forward quickly as he wanted the court martial completed before the end of the month. He twitched in his seat with impatience. He had already instructed his ADC to be ahead of the game and a warning order had been sent to various staff officers in the division, to support the trial. A venue had been found, but he still sought a suitable Judge Advocate, who would speedily accommodate his wishes.

What he didn't expect was the slow progress by the MPs who had yet to provide details of the charges Mitchell was to face, and information remained vague on any links to her family or indeed, her priest back in England. All Clements had said was that she was apparently too ill to proceed, and further questioning would have to wait until tomorrow. He reached across to the ornate drinks' cabinet presented to him many years before by his officers, to mark his promotion to a three-star general and poured himself a large malt whisky, a Dalwhinnie, his favourite distillery in the Highlands. He tipped his head back, and placing the glass rim to his lips, swallowing the lot in one go, the warmth sinking down into the pit of his stomach.

'Arding,' he bellowed, before belching loudly. His ADC came stumbling through the door with an arm full of files. 'Yes, sir, what can I get you?'

'I need you to draft three signals. The first to General Haig's staff informing them of the impending court martial, as protocol dictates, but don't send it yet. The second to the CO of the Military Police in Warminster, whomever he might be, to question the time being taken to get to the bottom of Mitchell's enlistment saga, and thirdly to Brigadier JJ Norman at the War Propaganda Bureau in Whitehall. Tell him his presence is required urgently here, the day after tomorrow. Tell him there is a dinner or something, that normally does the trick! Oh, and then organise a quiet dinner for the two of us, understand?'

Captain Arding calmly memorised the details of the addressees for the three signals.

'Will that be all, sir?' he said coldly.

'Yes, yes, man. Get on with it and let me know the responses the moment they arrive. Bring the draft signal to Haig and I will sit on it until it's time.'

Across the field in Colonel Wood's office, Major Clements was smiling to himself, following the pointless verbal lashing he had received from the general. He had taken it on the chin, as Davis was yet to learn of his latest piece of information that had arrived from his colonel in Warminster. They had a strong lead, and one that could yet finally link this whole affair to Germany.

At 7 a.m. the following morning, Major Clements sat down in the Mess, as was his custom. He had few friends and when he had tried to get to know fellow officers, they would often give him a wide berth; as they said, 'No MP is ever off duty'! He sat looking across the Mess to see Colonel Wood, the now disgraced Commanding Officer of the Divisional Hospital, who had been detained following his insubordinate actions. He would be called for questioning too and likely charges would follow. But for now, he would leave him alone to simmer!

On the far side of the hospital, Ed had woken feeling much brighter, even though she continued to be a little restless. Nurse Carter had finished changing her dressings and left the room, with the promise of some tea. A few minutes later, the door opened again, and two officers walked in. Ed smiling at them in recognition.

'Private Mitchell, or should I call you Ed?' said Major Leigh-Smith.

'Hello, sir, how good to see you, and you too, Doctor Martin. What brings you here?'

'We are heading to a medical briefing and, well, took the opportunity to drop in on you following the sudden change of plan two days ago. I take it you were unharmed by the diversion?' he said.

'Yes, sir, I am fine and being well looked after. But I am not enjoying it much.

'Sir, do you know why I am being questioned?' she asked suddenly.

'Questioned, by whom?' said the major.

'I have been interviewed by a major Clements from the Military Police. I don't know what I am supposed to have done wrong and he is coming back this morning to continue. I did ask for you to attend me, sir, as I was informed, I could bring an officer in to support me during questioning. Sorry you were too busy.'

'Too busy? I was never asked, Mitchell,' he said furiously, looking across at Captain Martin. 'I will get to the bottom of this, I can promise you that.' The door then suddenly opened, Lieutenant Cavanagh walking through, a little surprised to see the doctors present.

'Oh, you have company, shall I come back?'

'No, come in, Lieutenant' said the major. 'We are here from the field hospital at the front. Major Leigh-Smith and this is Captain Martin,' politely reaching over in turn to shake hands.

'Of course, I thought I had seen you before. I passed you in the corridor when I visited Mitchell the day after she was shot. She is doing well, I think.'

'Yes, indeed, a great deal better than the last time we saw her. What brings you here, Lieutenant, just visiting?'

'No, sir, I am Mitchell's OC in the sniper squadron and now acting as her support officer during her questioning, or should we say interrogation. She is in the hands of the Military Police at present and I am trying to provide suitable advice and support, with my limited experience of military law. Mitchell is doing very well though and holding her own; however, Major Clements the MP is back again this morning to question her further.'

'That doesn't sound good,' said Simon. 'What time is he coming?'

'Well, he's due any time, it's almost eight thirty, I almost expected him to be here by now.'

'Well, we had better be getting along, but be careful what you say, Mitchell. Nothing can be gained by giving too much away. Just say it as it is.'

He nodded once and said his farewell. Alone at last, Lieutenant Cavanagh went up to Ed and sat on her bed.

'I managed to speak with the CO last night, who was aghast at what was happening and promised to make some enquiries today, saying he would go to the very top if necessary.' As he spoke, Nurse Carter entered carrying a dressings tray.

Corn walked away from the bed and out of the room, meeting the major and the MP sergeant in the corridor. 'The nurse has to finish her dressings, Major, she will be about ten minutes.'

The MPs stood motionless together without speaking, just peering out through a small window. It wasn't long before the door opened, and Nurse Carter appeared

'She is ready for you, gentlemen,' as she headed away pushing the trolley towards the sluice.

The major and his sergeant joined the sniper OC and settled back into the same places in the room as on the previous day. Nurse Carter entered a few moments later and sat by the window. The MP Major began.

'Firstly, I trust you are feeling much better, Mitchell. We have a lot to get through.'

She nodded without speaking, but did cast an eye towards her OC, who was now sat to her right, leaning against the wall.

'OK, yesterday we ascertained how you managed to enter the army, how you prepared, who knew about your situation and how you kept this a secret within the regiment. We touched on your local vicar's role, and who was running the farm?'

'OK, moving on, do you know anyone from Germany, and have you ever been there?' said the major

Ed was shocked. How had he made this giant leap to bring Germany into her life? Had Corn spilt the beans? No, he wouldn't do that, but who else knew? She looked at her OC, uncertain, but he offered nothing but a blank look.

'No sir, I have not.' She said trying to avoid mentioning Bryan's German connection.

'What if I was to say your priest was born in Germany? What would you say to that?'

Ed swallowed hard and reached for her glass of water to give herself a moment.

'Bryan has been very supportive to my family, prior to and after my parents died. Without his guidance and physical help at times, we might well have gone under. His love and spiritual guidance meant a great deal to us.' The major, who was now reading from a sheet on his file, looked up.

'And you say he played a very big part in your life following the death of your parents. Did he ever talk to you about Germany, or have Germans stay with him and did you meet any of them perhaps?' he asked, leaning forward.

'Sir, I have never met anyone from Germany. All I have done, is kill them!'

He smiled at her candour and was starting to admire the courage of this young woman. But he wasn't deterred. 'So, did you not ever go to his church, or his house at any time?'

'Well yes, of course I did, he was my friend, is my friend, and he acted out of love for us when our parents died. He became a father figure to us, nothing more.'

'But you admit to fraternising with him for most of your life?' he persisted.

'Well yes, but he has lived in the parish for half of it. I don't remember him ever going away, and believe he thinks himself as much British as you or me.'

The major studied her carefully. 'I am sure you must see how this all looks, Mitchell. You fraternise with a man who may well have arrived from Germany and then lie to join the British Army, in disguise and spend time on the front line and in No Man's Land. Perhaps you made contact with Germans while on your operations. Is that how it was, Mitchell?'

Edwina was stunned how this had all turned around so quickly. She was sweating heavily and once again reached for her glass to try and slow things down. She took a long drink, before placing it back on the table, but as she was about to speak, a friendly voice spoke out.

'I most strongly object, sir, to this line of questioning,' said Lieutenant Cavanagh. 'This is ridiculous, and I ask you to stop.'

'No, I don't think so, Lieutenant. Mitchell has told me she has known a man for all of her life who was born in Germany and has been a father figure to her and her family since the death of her parents. She has further admitted impersonating a British soldier to apparently 'serve her country', but what if she was acting in support of the German nation and was sending information to them, especially as she operated largely alone and on frequent occasions. In other words, acting as a spy!'

Ed snapped her head round to look at her lieutenant in sheer panic! It wasn't true, not a single word of it, and she wanted to shout from the rafters. This was now going extremely badly, and she needed new strength to carry on. She suddenly felt quite sick. Cavanagh interjected again. 'Sir, I need some time to talk with Mitchell.'

'Your request is denied, Lieutenant, that won't be possible. But tell me, what conclusion would you have me draw from this information?'

Lieutenant Cavanagh became quite agitated and stood up, placing his hands on his hips. 'So, she shot ten Germans, putting herself at great risk, even cracking the biggest target of the war, lived in appalling conditions and just for show, she got herself shot in the process. Is that how being a spy works, Major?'

This took the MP a little by surprise and asked the lieutenant to step back!

'I can see you're upset, Lieutenant, but she may well have fooled you too. It's not unusual for spies to be cold and ruthless in this regard, hiding their real allegiances and covering their tracks. Mitchell could quite easily have been doing that, and being fooled would make me angry too, I can see that, but what, –'

The lieutenant suddenly cut him off, giving his own verbal blast.

'Now, just you hang on a minute, sir. What you are saying is quite preposterous, and what's more, Mitchell has shown valour at the front greater than most of her peers all put together. She is the best sniper I have and deserves a medal for gallantry against incredible odds, not victimisation. And she has been applauded by General Haig himself. What more evidence do you want to prove she is innocent of the accusations you are making?'

'Lieutenant, you will not be aware, but certain military information, secret information has reached the German lines over the past year, and with Mitchell's connections and her place in this war, there is every chance that she has had the opportunity to pass these secrets to our enemy! So, with that, I am going to bring formal charges against you, Mitchell, and am arresting you under suspicion of being a German spy. You will be formally charged by one of my lieutenants later, but for now, this interview is over.

The sergeant tapped twice on the door, and they left without another word spoken. When the major got back to his office, he picked up a signal pad. He needed to act fast.

Chapter 41

Anyone who had been watching the two officers from the 24th Field Hospital over the past few days, could well have wondered what they were up to and perhaps been suspicious of their activities. Major Simon Leigh-Smith and Captain Alan Reece were sitting once again in the small stuffy office, as they firmed up their plans to help Mitchell. This had become the single most important thing in their lives, following the disastrous attempt to spirit her away to Paris. They now had to find a way of rescuing her, once and for all.

They knew the layout of the divisional hospital as they had visited it many times and Simon had worked there during his first few months in France. He was also familiar with some of the staff, and, crucially, the routines that ran on a daily basis. With over a million troops all around the north-east, they knew that even if they could get her out of the hospital, onward movement in an already congested transport system would prove difficult. But these vast troop movements in both directions could just offer a small chance of success, although the risks would be compounded by the presence of MPs at every turn!

Captain Stuart Martin, the hospital's 2iC, had been asked to join them at their latest meeting that night, as he would have to cover for them.

'Well, I never had an inkling that she was a woman,' said the newcomer. 'When she came into theatre all covered in dirt, she was just another bedraggled soldier, filthy, dirty, smelling of war, and well, we were programmed to see a man on the table. If it wasn't for Sister Youngs, I would have just carried on!' The men looked at each other and grinned over their tea.

'I don't know, Stuart, you have obviously been here amongst men far too long,' and they all laughed, breaking the tension. 'So, chaps come on, how do we get her away and back to Britain?' said Simon.

'We could dress her up as a civilian, a French girl perhaps. Can she speak French?' asked Alan.

'I doubt that,' said Simon, 'but what had you in mind?' He was rather interested in the idea.

'Well, I remember when I last went back for my leave, the boat had several French families on board, heading to England. They simply mingled with the troops and no-one really took much notice. Maybe we could somehow create a path for her that way?' he said.

'But she would need false papers and I am not sure how we would achieve that. No, we need something else,' said Simon, perplexed.

Stuart stopped talking and sat upright, a grin slowly stretching across his face. 'Of course!' he exclaimed loudly. 'What has she been an expert in for over a year, Simon?' he said. Both men looked at him with a blank expression. 'Come on, think.' Stuart eagerly awaiting a response. He opened his palms upwards as if preaching to a congregation. 'We dress her as a soldier. They won't be looking for a man in uniform and she just mingles in with the thousands of others.' And he sat back triumphantly.

'My God, yes, of course,' said Simon, as the image of Mitchell amongst a throng of fellow soldiers heading for home crept into his mind. 'She is so terribly convincing, and they will be looking for a woman, not a bloke. Brilliant,' he said full of self-gratification. 'All we have to do is get her fit and provide leave papers, which should be easy, and get travel papers from a QM. Do we know a good QM, chaps?' he said with a grin. They sat running over the whole plan, from getting her out of the hospital right up to vehicles and a travel permit.

'All in a day's work, chaps, leave it with me,' said Alan smiling.

Their plan had gathered pace quickly and early the next morning, Simon and Alan set off to make their visit to Divisional HQ Hospital to check out Mitchell's room. They left before sunrise, covering their tracks by telling the assistant quartermaster, they were heading to HQ to see Colonel Wood, who remained confined to his quarters. With Alan driving, the journey along battle-torn lanes took a little over ninety minutes. When they finally arrived, they both put on white doctors' coats and grabbed some files from the back seat, before heading into the building. All was quiet, and they worked their way around the corridors to find what they were looking for. The armed guard sitting on a chair outside a room gave her location away. They wandered over and asked to be admitted. The soldier stood, and without speaking, opened the door and the officers stepped in. They were only there a few minutes and left without bringing attention to themselves, the sentry seemingly not interested in two doctors visiting a patient!

They walked up the corridor and then stopped to chat by a window, before turning and retreating back the same way, taking in all the details they could, to aid their plan. On their second sweep, they were lucky to see a nurse arrive and the sentry duly stood and fraternised with her for a full minute before unlocking the door and letting her in. When they got to the end of the corridor they stood once again and chatted, Simon scribbling notes onto a sheet of paper in the top file. After a few minutes, they heard a door slam shut and the nurse was heading towards them, the door being secured behind her once more. They waited for her and as she got close, Simon stepped up to her and spoke with a deliberate tone.

'Excuse me, are you Private Mitchell's nurse?'

'Yes, sir, I am. Is something wrong, Doctor?' she asked, concerned.

'No, no, but could I have a word?' he said.

'Yes, sir, of course,' she said and stepped to one side of the corridor. Simon looked over at the MP sentry, who was slouching slightly forward. He asked her to follow him and they stepped into the sluice. Alan stood outside, pretending to read from a folder in his hand. Nurse Carter entered the tiny windowless room, Simon followed and closed the door.

'We only have a few minutes, Nurse, so I want you to listen to me very carefully. I am Major Leigh-Smith, the CO of 24th Field Hospital. I operated on Mitchell when she came from the trenches and well, I have a vested interest in her wellbeing. She is, I believe, in grave danger and perhaps even her life is at risk! There are senior officers who are trying to find a way for this matter to disappear and we need to act fast to get her away from here. I have no alternative but to trust you, the one person who can help us, and if I have misjudged you, I am for the firing squad.' He stopped, as her eyes widened. He was pleased his words impacted on her so quickly and looked at the tiny lady before him, dressed in white, with her grey and red trimmed shawl.

'Sir, I am afraid an MP arrested her this morning. She has been charged with espionage. They think she is a spy!'

Simon was utterly speechless. 'Charged as a spy. My God, we need to move fast. Can I rely on you, Nurse, to assist us?'

She swallowed nervously, knowing she had provided key information to the major on two occasions already and she knew he expected more.

'Sir, what do you need?' she said nervously.

'What time do you finish tonight?' he asked.

'I am on until twenty-one hundred, sir,' she said.

'OK, could we meet later, and can you suggest somewhere safe? There is lots to discuss and very little time.'

She thought for a few seconds, looking around the tiny room, biting her lip, and then shook her head slowly. 'There is nowhere safe here, sir. Do you have a vehicle, perhaps we could meet away from the hospital,' she suggested?

'Yes, we do, what do you have in mind?' he asked.

'OK, when I have finished, I will set out to walk to the village café. If you park up along the road, we can drive somewhere quiet, there are lots of spots that I know of. No-one will be bothered seeing me that late as many nurses and medics head down there after their shifts to get some wine and some pastries, it's quite normal. Shall we say about twenty-one fifteen?'

Simon nodded enthusiastically and said he must go. He told her not to leave for two or three minutes and thanked her before he stepped back out into the corridor. Alan, not lifting his head, just followed him, back down the way they had come towards the exit. When they got outside, they went to sit in the car and Simon briefed Alan on the situation, which took him greatly by surprise.

The hours that followed were spent going over their ideas before heading to the Officers' Mess for an early dinner. At eight thirty, they finished their drinks and stood to leave, just as Colonel Wood entered the Mess, catching their eye. He saw them both sitting together and with his guard behind him, walked across the room towards them.

'Oops, that's copped it,' Simon whispered from the side of his mouth. Alan turned his head to see the officer almost upon them and felt as though he had been caught stealing apples from an orchard.

'Good evening, gentlemen, I'm glad you could come down,' said the colonel as he approached. The Military Police sergeant, a couple of steps behind him, looked at them curiously. And then quite unexpectedly, as the colonel began to speak, Simon realised he was providing them with cover, an alibi even, and his heart sped up with anticipation.

'I'm glad you got my message.' He shook both their hands and turned towards the MP behind him. 'Sergeant, I have some medical matters to discuss with these two doctors who are from one of my field hospitals, it will only take ten minutes or so. Why don't you get your meal, I will be sitting here in full view and will join you shortly.'

He had expertly talked down to him and apart from a brief scan of the two new faces, the sergeant nodded and walked over to a table, carefully sitting to face them. As he sat, one of the dining hall attendants came over to take his order. The colonel sat with his back to him and Simon watched the man bury his head in the short menu, before looking back towards his friend.

Stanley Wood, a man from humble beginnings whose parents had run a small shop for many years as he was growing up, always imparted honesty, trust and support to others, especially if the cause was just. He looked at them and smiled.

'I am not surprised to see you both here and assume things have moved on since we last spoke,' he said. 'You are here for Mitchell, correct?'

Simon didn't waste any time as they had to be gone in minutes.

'Stanley, there is about to be a travesty of justice here as Private Mitchell is going to be charged as a German spy and we cannot stand-by and let this happen. I can't tell you how important it is that she leaves here and quickly, even though she really should not travel yet due to her condition. But she is made of strong stuff and with General Davis pushing this forward, we need to move now. Can we trust you, sir, as if not we are dead men,' he said bluntly.

'You have my word, Simon. Can I do anything?' he said quickly.

'OK, thank you, sir, we plan to move her tomorrow afternoon under the pretence of her needing an urgent follow-up operation, with no time for the sentry to alert anyone. We are meeting her nurse in about fifteen minutes, so can't stay long,' he said, looking at his watch. 'She is not aware herself yet, but one of the nurses is going to help us to pull this off. She will simply create a diversion, a sort of act, running from the room to get help. We will then arrive with a trolley and leave as if to head to theatre before the guard can raise the alarm, but will instead, leave by the back door into a waiting ambulance. She will be driven away by Alan to a safe house and then, in slower time, be moved back to Blighty.' As he finished the general outline of their plan, he saw the sergeant gaze across at them. He nodded courteously and smiled before he turned his attention back to the colonel.

'This is hugely risky, chaps, and could easily cost you your own lives, but I am sure I don't need to alert you to this, as once you step out of line with General Davis, you get locked up too. Look at me!' He saw his final words had hit home, but they were pleased that he was finally with them.

'I cannot do much from within my quarters, but I can do one thing to help. Signal Colonel Mathew Briggs at the 2nd Field Hospital in Calais. Don't be worried about him reporting you as he is my brother-in-law. Tell him I have requested he takes a soldier for a few days, don't mention her surname, and mark it as urgent. You can fill him in of the details when you meet. This will give her a few extra days for you to arrange her travel docs back to Blighty. I will of course testify for you, if things go wrong.' He stood and shook both their hands, before saying in a loud voice for people to hear, 'Thank you for coming,' and turned away from them to join his dinner date.

The two officers walked away and out of the Mess to get their staff car. They would never see the colonel again.

It was pitch black when they stepped outside, and their tyres created a small dust storm as they sped towards the main gate. As they approached it, a single sentry lifted the barrier, Alan nodding as he passed through, before swinging the car left and out into the night. After only a few minutes they noticed the figure of a lone nurse, her cloak only partially covering her white uniform, and pulled in just a hundred feet or so past her. Simon opened the rear door as she approached, and she bowed down to peer into the dark interior, before stepping in. She told them to turn right just a little way ahead and they dropped down the hill towards some distant lights of a small farmhouse. At the bottom of the hill, Alan turned into a gateway and pulled to a halt.

'We will be safe here. Now, how can I help?' she said in the gloom.

Simon began by thanking her for her involvement and told her what they were about to undertake. He stressed it involved significant risk to them all; however, they would minimise her role as much as possible and only inform her now of what they needed her to do. So, when all hell broke loose, she wouldn't be implicated.

'What we want you to do is as follows. Tomorrow afternoon at twelve twenty-five, we will position ourselves just around the corner beyond the sluice where we met earlier, with a trolley and blankets. At twelve thirty precisely, you enter Mitchell's room with your usual clean dressings routine and conduct yourself in exactly the same way as you do every day. No difference, it must be a normal visit, and if the guard talks to you, talk back, act completely normally. The only difference will be that you take with you this small bag of blood, which will be used to create a diversion. You will quickly brief Mitchell of what lies ahead and tell her to play along. You then break the bag over Mitchell's chest wound and call the guard into the room. He must see the blood, but then ask him to press down on the wound with a med-pad, so you can get help. Don't ask him, tell him, he will follow orders, they all do. Then leave the room and come quickly down towards us and we will take it from there. Once we arrive, play along and leave with us. I will tell the guard we have to operate, and he should wait as we will only be thirty minutes. When we have her safely onboard the ambulance, you make your way back to the room and sit with him. He will be less suspicious of you if you are in sight and will only get concerned when we don't return. Now do you think you can do this?' he asked.

'Yes, of course, but I won't see Ed again, will I?' she said sadly.

'No, probably not, but I'm sure you will be happier knowing she is safe from persecution and imprisonment?'

'Yes, yes, of course. Can we go back now, please? I am on the early shift tomorrow.'

Alan turned over the engine and swung round in the darkness, before heading up the hill and back to the main road. Just before Patsy got out of the car, Simon gave her the bag of blood, which she stowed inside her cloak, and she smiled at them before walking the last half mile back to the hospital. She headed straight to colonel Wood's office. The light was still on…

Chapter 42

Lord Hardcastle avoided the crowded dining room at the Dorchester, instead relying upon the adequate room service menu, while he made many phone calls and planned his strategy. He had woken to a knock at the door, where a hotel steward gave him a note from Chuffy, which asked him to meet him in his office at 10.30am. He checked his watch. He had plenty of time to enjoy his favourite breakfast of Arbroath smokies, something he always had when he stayed at the Dorchester.

He arrived early for his meeting with Lord Chatterdon, deep within the Foreign Office. He had been supplied with tea and biscuits by the same rather dour civil servant wearing the same squeaky shoes that he had met the previous day. While he waited, he was restless, and walked around the office, admiring the pieces of art that adorned the large room. At the far end, he peered at what he thought was an original Turner, with lashing seas washing over a small boat in the pastel water. As he sipped his tea, he stood back to get a greater perspective, just as the door burst open and Chuffy came in, followed by Lord Chatterdon.

Spotty Chatterdon was a small, unremarkable man, in a tailed suit and with a thick head of hair and wire spectacles. Indeed, when they shook hands, Michael towered over him and he wasn't tall by any means. But he had a firm handshake and commented that it must be thirty years since they had last met. Formalities were over quickly, and more tea was ordered as they took their seats around the mahogany table. Lord Chatterdon looked at his watch pensively and began their discussion.

'Michael, Chuffy told me about the letter you received and the situation in France with your man, and about this woman too, which is clearly rather an awkward situation. But I would like to assist if I can. Could I see the letter?' he asked.

Michael reached into his inside pocket and handed the note across, waiting for him to read it before commenting.

When he'd finished, he lifted his head and looked directly at him. Lord Hardcastle spoke first.

'Spotty, I know this may appear that I am perhaps overreacting, but I fear a travesty of justice is about to happen. I have treated Frank largely as my own son for many years and trust you understand why I need your help. I have grave concerns that he and this Mitchell character could be in huge trouble here and without some intervention things might get rather nasty for them. Can you help me?'

'Firstly, old man, you must appreciate that the senior generals in France take full responsibility for issues in the theatre of war, especially in disciplinary matters and desertion. In this case of possible espionage, it is normal procedure that we are informed, but until we are notified it is rather difficult to intervene. My first call would always be with the commanding officer concerned and if there is something going on, he is bound to protect his interests and produce enough evidence to support his decision anyway. So, at present I have no calls or reasons to get involved. But that said, I would be prepared as a matter of course to signal the Divisionally HQ for clarity on this matter, but that, old man, will no doubt get his back up. I have to be very sure before I charge in, so do you have any other supporting evidence?'

Michael had little to offer other than Frank's letter, but he had come up with one idea to hopefully save the day.

'Firstly, I agree with your summation. However, this whole affair appears to be based upon a rather speculative opinion over a woman who has somehow managed to impersonate a soldier in the British Army while serving at the front, undetected. Yes, all serious stuff I agree, but for all we know, this general may be somewhat personally wounded by a female appearing within his ranks and for some reason wants immediate action. By the sounds of it, though, she is something of a hero, as Frank states, with many kills to her name, so perhaps there might be an angle to approach the Gloucesters' Divisional HQ with an enquiry, just to introduce interest from the War Office. If it is not genuine, then the evidence, or lack of it, would provide sufficient reason for you to intervene and perhaps stall any proceedings, until some sort of investigation could be mounted from here.'

Lord Chatterdon looked at him, thinking carefully. 'I am quite prepared to signal the Divisional HQ with an enquiry, yes, but maybe we attack this from a different direction. I happen to be seeing Field Marshal Haig at a working luncheon tomorrow. I could mention then that I hear there is a bit of a hoot going on regarding a woman soldier, a sniper even, at the front. He would be obliged to intervene I am sure, and there is a very good chap called JJ Norman, his brigadier, who could help too. Now do you know any more about the situation that might help?'

'I am afraid not. Frank has written to me several times but has always remained disciplined on military matters, never giving anything away. But I assume this sniper squadron would have a CO. Could we follow that up as he is bound to know what's going on?'

'Yes, yes, that is a sound idea. I will instigate this immediately. Don't suppose you know his name, do you?' he asked. '

'I am afraid not, Spotty, but surely Haig's staff would know.'

'OK, let's recap. I will send a signal today to the Gloucesters' Divisional HQ, to the commanding officer of the snipers, and see what we get back. If by tomorrow I have some answers, we might be able to push Haig into instigating a temporary halt to proceedings, to ensure fair play. In the meantime, can you stay in London again tonight as your input may well be vital if we must make some key decisions? Also, if you are available, we might meet again tomorrow for a progress report.'

'Yes, I can do that,' said Michael. 'I will be at the Dorchester. I have kept my room from last night in case it was necessary to stay on. Thank you, Spotty, I cannot stress how much this means to me. This man is the closest person I have to a son. I'm sure you understand.'

'Don't mention it, old man, I am glad I am able to assist. Now I have to go so until tomorrow then.' He stood up and Michael shook his hand firmly, then Chuffy escorted him from his office.

Michael sat back down in deep thought, hoping his efforts would be enough to save Frank and his friend Mitchell, who was clearly a person of exceptional qualities, who could so ably compete in a man's world, and was Frank's closest friend. She must be a very special person indeed. Chuffy then re-entered his office and Michael stood up.

'Well, old chap, I think you have your answer. If Spotty can't sort this no-one else can. Shall we meet for dinner tonight; I will come across to you. Eight o'clock OK?' They agreed to dine at the Dorchester and Michael stood to leave, thanking his dear old friend profusely as he left.

He stepped out into the dimming light, rain clouds closing in overhead, and the sudden shower caught him as he walked over to the car. Chapman was sitting inside, but hastily jumped out to open the rear door.

'Back to the hotel, Your Lordship?' he asked.

'No, Chapman, I have to stay over again tonight, so need to visit my tailor's in Savile Row. Did you bring a change with you?' he asked.

'Yes, sir, always do, just in case.' They drove up through Admiralty arch and round Trafalgar square, before heading up to Piccadilly Circus and on to Huntsman's, the family tailor's, first used by his grandfather in 1860.

Chapter 43

Bryan sat nervously a few feet from the desk, the officer scribbling something into a large green book. For several minutes there was silence, and he started to sweat under his heavy gown. He knew he was innocent, but was acutely aware of his involvement with Edwina, so prepared for a roasting by this experienced military man. He had nothing to hide!

While he waited, he casually looked past his captor to the window behind him, which was partly obscured by a dirty net curtain, blocking much of the natural light. He tried to stay focussed and felt pressured by the sergeant now standing by the door behind him. Suddenly, the colonel looked up.

'Father, firstly I need to fill in this interview form. Please can I have your full name?' and he sat poised with his pen over a single sheet of paper on his desk, looking at him.

'My name is father Bryan H O'Callaghan, of Royston parish.'

'And what does the H stand for?' asked the colonel. Bryan suddenly started to sweat, realising his error.

'I never use it colonel. It's just an initial given to me by my parents.' The colonel frowned at this, instantly suspicious of his answer.

'Well, that maybe father, but I need it for the form you see. So, H stands for?' and he waited, pen at the ready.

'Hermann,' he said. The colonel didn't react, just wrote the word down at the appropriate place. He didn't want to spook him, just yet...

'Ok, for your own good father, you should tell the truth during this interview, as lying in any way will only bring trouble for you. I should also explain why we have felt it necessary to bring you here.' He paused for a moment, taking a fresh piece of paper from the pile in front of him. He looked up and spoke deliberately, his accent making the words more defined somehow. 'A young woman known to you was found impersonating a British Army soldier on the front line, in France. She had been shot while in No Man's

Land and I believe you were fully aware of her deceit and possibly encouraged her in this endeavour. But before we talk about that, I want to know why you left Germany and what did you do when you arrived in England?'

This took him totally by surprise and had no clue how he had made the connection of his childhood? He had quite naturally assumed that the questions would be centred around how he had helped Edwina get into the British Army. But Germany! He looked at his questioner, not letting on he was nervous. He knew he must tread carefully here.

'I left Germany in 1895 with my mother, following my parents' separation. They had a difficult marriage and my mother, being of English/Irish ancestry, chose to return to the land of her birth and we settled in Yorkshire. She sadly died of influenza a year later when I was just nineteen. I had little in the way of funds and had to decide what my future was to be and so applied to join the church. I had always been well educated and was offered a place at St Stephen's, London in September 1896. I graduated and was given the Royston Parish in 1900.'

The colonel was writing quickly as he spoke, but in an unusual way managed to keep looking at him as he did so!

'Have you kept in contact with your father over the years and have you visited Germany recently?'

'No, Colonel, I have not visited Germany at all; in fact, I have not been back since I left. My father still lives there but we don't communicate anymore.'

'When did you last hear from your father?' the colonel asked curiously.

'I last saw him at my mother's funeral in January 1896. We have never seen each other since!' he said firmly.

'OK, who else have you contacted in Germany over the last ten years and how frequently?'

'Look, Colonel, what is all this about? I am a British citizen, having lived here for over twenty years, and have served my community for almost seventeen of them. I have absolutely no connection with Germany anymore or its people. I live in a small community in the Cotswolds and apart from visiting my Bishop, I have rarely ventured away from my parish in all these years. So, I would be grateful if you would come to the point!'

The colonel paused for a short moment, before flicking more paper, a veteran of a thousand interviews, over many years. He looked up at Bryan with a stern face.

'It is our belief that Private Mitchell was encouraged by you to impersonate a British soldier to gain access to sensitive military information to support the

German war effort. Furthermore, we believe you have instigated this treachery and driven her to it, thus forging a pact to spy for our enemies!'

Bryan was utterly dumbfounded. The words hung in the air as he tried to work out what to say. He tutted and shook his head, holding his hands open towards his accuser. He suddenly had the urge to abuse this man. Who did he think he was with these blasphemous accusations? But he controlled his answer, as any priest should.

'As God is my witness, I am innocent of your suggestions. I have for many years been close to the Mitchell family, and I am their priest, nothing more, my allegiance is to England not Germany. I haven't been there for a very long time. You are quite wrong, Colonel, to connect me to war-torn Germany, and regarding Ed being a spy, that is quite ridiculous. She is the most loyal, hard-working person I have ever met and clearly a very brave young lady, whom I greatly admire. Can you imagine what she must have gone through to gain a foothold in the army, to fight for her country and be accepted? I urge you, not for myself, but for her, that you think again, before you make a fool of yourself.'

'I expected you to say all of that, Father, but look at it from our point of view. She has grown up with a German priest by her side who has played a big part in her life since the death of her parents. Probably guiding her, teaching her, advising her throughout her young life, and even preparing her. At the outbreak of the war she then dresses to impersonate a man so she can join the army in the front line, knowing her German friend, you, are right behind her, guiding her. And for what? To pass enemy secrets to the German high command, that's what. If you care for Mitchell as you say you do, I urge you to admit your crimes and make this better for all. You are responsible, Father, so I need to ask you to provide the names of your contacts either in France or Belgium. Admit it, you have been caught out and you will later today be charged with high treason!

Bryan began to shake. He shook his head from side to side.

'No, no, no', he said, his voice rising. 'No, this is all wrong. Where do you get these ideas from, man? What proof do you have for any of this? Information, contacts, I have none, I am just a priest, that is all, nothing more, nothing less.' And he sat back with his head in his hands.

The colonel stood and left the room without speaking; the sergeant remained at the door, guarding him. Bryan knew he was in serious trouble, but before he could even think properly, the colonel was back with a lieutenant in tow.

He went behind his desk and stood facing Bryan, asking him to stand. The lieutenant read from a sheet of paper.

'You do not need to say anything, but…'

Bryan was lost in thought and never actually heard all the words spoken to him; instead he said a silent prayer until he heard a raised voice and he opened his eyes and stood facing his accusers.

'I am innocent of the wrongdoings you have laid before me. You should be ashamed, ashamed I say, to accuse me, a man of the cloth who has never had a wicked thought and would defend this England to his last breath. Write that down, why don't you,' he said stoically.

'Take him to the cells, Sergeant,' said the colonel, 'And report back to me afterwards as we have things to do.'

The corporal came in and this time clasped Bryan's wrists firmly, staring at him, as he roughly placed a pair of iron shackles around his wrists. Bryan winced as they bit into his skin, and the two soldiers led him away. The colonel, immediately began preparing an urgent signal to Major Clements, in General Davis's HQ, with some new information.

Chapter 44

Two senior officers sat alone in the main dining room of the chateau, wearing full Mess dress, with several lines of miniature medals over the left breast, as was the military dress code. Neither of them had found time to chat prior to dinner, following the brigadier's transport problems during his journey over from London. They now sat opposite each other at the highly-polished table, with the general's favourite sculpture, a silver cavalry officer at the charge, centre stage. The starter had just been served, the staff then leaving as instructed.

'JJ, you might be wondering why I have asked you here at such short notice. But before I explain, I must have your word that what I am about to tell you stays in this room and you do not utter a word to anyone. Furthermore, I need to know what you told Haig about your urgent trip over here.'

'Sir, my brief from Field Marshall Haig is to follow up any actions deemed necessary to ensure that military discipline remains high so that the men in the field have no doubts that we will come down vary hard on any disruption, desertion and misdemeanours, however they occur. The fact that I have disappeared for a couple of days will not in itself create cause for concern, but I did notify him, yes, simply to follow procedures. I must say, I am intrigued that you have brought me here, so what's all this about, sir?' he said as he picked up the small crystal glass in front of him, filled with a 1903 French Chablis.

The general casually started to eat the fine pâté with small crisp biscuits as he told his story. 'A few days ago, a soldier was brought in from No Man's Land, having been shot through the back returning from a sniper mission. A successful one at that, having shot The Joker, the prominent German officer who had been causing so many problems for us. That was not unusual, but what they found on the operating table the following day was.' He picked up his glass and sipped the delicate wine, before continuing.

'When they opened the tunic of this individual, it turned out that it was a woman in disguise!'

The brigadier almost choked on his pâté and coughed loudly before sipping his wine to clear his palate. The general then moved quickly on.

'I must be honest, JJ, I had hoped this would find its own resolution and quickly, as she was extremely ill and well, it looked likely she would die from her wounds. Alas, that didn't happen, and I now have her in custody in the divisional hospital across the way. Following extensive investigations by the MPs under Major Clements, there is every chance she has been liaising with a German priest back in England, and between them we believe they have been passing military secrets to the Hun!'

JJ Hopkins had heard many things in his life as a soldier, but this certainly stood head and shoulders above them all. He was about to ask a question, when the general continued.

'She will be officially charged tomorrow morning with impersonating a British soldier and espionage, as I believe she is a German spy!'

The brigadier placed his knife down on his now empty plate and sat back. He hesitated, wanting to firstly reassure his general he could be relied upon. 'I assure you, sir, that what you have just told me remain confidential, but firstly I must ask, how on earth has it been possible for this to occur and for how long has she been at the front?'

'It's a long story, JJ, but suffice to say we are currently investigating here in France with the Gloucester Regiment, at the training barracks in Bristol where she did her basic, with the CO of the sniper squadron, a Major Hesketh-Pritchard. Also, we are looking into where the woman enlisted and interviewing Private Mitchell's observer who has worked alongside her for a year and knew of her situation. He by association, is guilty too. Furthermore, we are questioning her village priest, a German, back in Warminster as we believe he is behind this deception and actively recruited her. So, you see, we have been busy, and this is a terribly important issue and one I want closed quickly. In view of this, I have arranged for a court martial to be convened as soon as possible and I want you to be the Judge Advocate.' He finally paused to see the reaction from a man he trusted, who had been a second lieutenant in Davis's regiment during the Second Boer War in 1899. They had known each other for almost two decades and held a certain amount of mutual respect for each other.

Davis expected Norman to be totally supportive of his plan for quick closure and waited for his response as he finished his glass of Chablis. While the batman was in the room to top up their glasses and take their starter plates away, they watched each other, brigadier Norman breathing heavily, unnoticed by Davis just ten feet away. With the glasses charged and the fish course now before them, the general said just one word to his guest:

'Well?'

'Sir, before I left England, I received a memo from Field Marshall Haig's office to attend a meeting with Lords Chatterdon and Symister from the WPB, about a possible travesty of justice about to happen at the front. I made my excuses as I was just leaving to get down to Kent and my boat crossing to France. I can only assume that is somehow connected to this matter you speak of, and whatever you are thinking, I believe this secret is already out!'

The general slammed his cutlery down onto the table, his lips pinched firmly together, an expression like thunder. He almost shouted his retort!

'How on earth could this have possibly got out? I have instructed everyone concerned to keep this highly confidential and only a handful of people are aware. Jesus!'

And he stood up abruptly and started pacing the room. He leaned on the mantlepiece with one hand and drained his glass quickly with the other. He then threw the glass straight into the fireplace, glass shattering onto the floor by his feet. His orderly heard the crash and entered the dining room.

'Get out, get out' the general bellowed as he returned to his seat to fill another glass.

'Tomorrow I want you to head back to London and find out what is known and who is behind this. In the meantime, I will move things forward and attempt to get the court martial running by the end of the week in the hope all the information comes together by then. Can I rely on you, old boy?'

'Sir, I have a duty to fulfil the brief given to me by Haig and as such will always do so. If there is evidence of espionage, then of course I will stand with you, but a word of warning, sir. Make sure your evidence is drum tight as heads could so easily roll the other way if facts are not borne out. Your line of questioning with this woman and your interviews in England must hold water, as many might see her as a hero. The word is out, General, and I am afraid I cannot help you.'

He sat back in his ornate oak chair, looking at a troubled man before him, deep in thought, a light sweat forming on his brow. He picked up his wine glass and sipped it graciously, before pushing his chair back noisily and making his excuses to leave. The general just grunted and walked across to his cigar box. As the brigadier reached the door, he turned.

'Goodnight, General.' He got no response. He decided not to wait for morning, instead raising his driver before heading up the stairs to change and retrieve his overnight bag. The time was a little short of 10 o'clock, when he got into the back seat of his car. It would be the early hours before they reached the coast and a boat back to England.

The general lit a large cigar and walked over to the telephone to call for Captain Arding. A few minutes later the captain appeared in the doorway in his shirt sleeves. 'Sir?' he said in an enquiring tone.

'Arding, I forgot to inform you that I want you to instigate Operation Mayflower at eleven hundred hours tomorrow. That is all for tonight,' he said in a dismissive tone, picking up his fat cigar again.

For once in his life Captain Arding didn't acknowledge him, just left the room annoyed that he had been dragged from his bed by a man whom he had started to doubt. He would go to his desk and do his duty after being notified of the Op order. He prepared the paperwork for the general's signature and stamped it; Confidential. He placed it in the out tray, which he knew would be actioned by zero seven thirty hours the very next day and went off to bed.

Chapter 45

Simon and Alan made an early start, and waited through the morning, to receive the all-important reply from Colonel Briggs. Alas, it never arrived. At just before ten thirty, Alan stuck his head round Simon's door.

'Time to go, Simon. I'll see you in the ambulance, it's parked out front.'

Simon stood wearily from his desk, looking at his watch, before collecting his things and following Alan a minute later. By the time he had reached the vehicle, Alan was already revving up the engine and he jumped in and they slipped away, heading south-west.

By the time they reached the main hospital at Divisional HQ, it was just past mid-day, they had made good time. They parked up behind the rear block as agreed and waited. Time seemed to stand still and for almost twenty minutes, they sat constantly observing their watches. At last it was time to go. They removed the stretcher from the rear of the ambulance and went in the side door, heading to where the trolleys were stored, which they had recced the previous day. They grabbed the nearest one and looked at their watches again, as they didn't want to be seen loitering in the corridor. At twelve twenty-five, they donned their white coats and took a slow walk back down the corridor, Alan pushing the trolley from the rear, halting just around the corner from the sluice. There, they checked the time once again and Simon pulled out a folder from under his white coat and laid it on the trolley. Together they stood as if in conference and waited.

After a few minutes, Simon said nervously, 'She's late.'

'Don't worry, old man, it's probably just taken her longer to get things sorted.'

They both looked pensively at each other as twelve forty came and went, with several hospital staff passing them by. No-one paid any real attention to their presence, just two doctors chatting in a corridor.

'Something's wrong. She should have been here by now,' Simon said, looking at his watch again.

'I'm going to walk down to see what's happening.' Alan nodded while Simon put his hands in his coat pockets and ambled in the direction of Mitchell's room. As he turned the final corner, he noticed there was no guard outside. He was briefly encouraged, assuming Nurse Carter was inside at this precise moment, with the sentry, as planned. A few moments more and it would all happen. He waited on the bend, stepping aside for two nurses, who smiled to one another as they passed him. Nervously he focussed on the door just fifty feet away. Nothing! He became agitated and decided he had to go and see what was happening. His heart pounded as he approached the door. Instinctively, he listened first before gently turning the handle. The door opened slightly, before he stepped into an empty room. Ed Mitchell was gone.

Chapter 46

As Edward finished preparing their lunch, he noticed David making his way back down from the top paddock, after his busy morning in the pouring rain, moving calves up for better grazing. He went to open the parlour door and leant against the frame peering across at him affectionally, rain water dripping heavily from the blocked gutter, just to the side, splashing his feet. When the letter arrived, just a few days before, he knew instantly he must for once, show his strength and find a way of helping Ed. David's world would be disrupted, for sure, but there was simply no-other way. He must help his sister and needed to tell David that he had to go away. What's more, his lie must be totally convincing.

As they sat at the kitchen table, Edward watched David tuck into his sandwich, not seemingly bothered at all, that he was soaked to the skin. Between mouthfuls, he spoke of the work still to be done to the fence line in the paddock, as if it was just another day, but Ed, was about to ruin it for him.

'David, I have received a rather concerning letter from my cousin in Dorset. It would seem that my Aunt Flo, is terribly ill and is not long for this world. So, if you don't mind, I want to go and visit her. You can manage things while I am away can't you?'

David stopped chewing for a moment, before quickly finishing his mouthful, washing it down with tea. He put his mug down on the table and licked his lips.

'I didn't know you had an aunt in Dorset, you never said.'

'Well sorry, it wasn't deliberate. She lives near Dorchester and I will probably need a few days. I will stay with my cousin, Emma, who wrote to me.'

As David listened, he reached across to take Edward's hand, looking straight into his eyes, and smiled.

'These are your family, Ed, so of course you must go. I can cope here there is plenty to keep me busy. When do you need to leave and how long will you be away, do you think?'

'Well, I should go this afternoon really, but how about first thing tomorrow? I am not sure when I will be back, as it all depends how she is. But I will cook us a nice supper tonight and we can have an early night,' he said with a smile.

David grinned at him as he stood up, leaning over for a kiss before heading for the door. He stopped as he pulled on his rain coat, pondering this sudden rush to leave. He stood in the doorway for a few seconds as he placed his cap on his head, before heading out towards the barn.

Edward watched him go, his deceit paining him, but he had no choice. He cleared the dishes before heading upstairs to pack the remaining items he needed to take with him. He sat on the bed, wondering what the days ahead would bring, looking around their room, thinking how life had changed for him since Edwina had left. He had learnt to cope well as a female, finally taking responsibility for his life and making a success of it, albeit under rather strange circumstances.

He knew it was quite wrong to have fallen in love with David, but he was a sincere and thoughtful man, giving him all the support, he had needed over the past year. They had become lovers, and if the truth ever got out, he would be subject to the full power of the law, he knew that. But he had to do what was right and finished his packing, taking everything he needed, before heading back downstairs to make David's favourite meal.

That night, Edward made sure David wanted for nothing. He fussed over him, firstly heating gallons of water on the stove for a hot bath when he returned from work as he wanted to make him happy. In the oven, a stew had been slowly simmering for several hours, full of their own crops and one of their fat chickens. When David came in, Edward jested with him. 'Come along, clothes off, hot bath for you, my lad,' he said with a smile.

'What, is it the end of the month already?' David joked, then proceeded to toss his clothes willy-nilly across the kitchen floor until he stood quite naked. Edward poured the hot water from various pans into the tin bath and then grabbed a tea towel and flicked David's backside playfully, leaving a red welt across his left buttock!

'Ouch,' David yelled, running around the kitchen to avoid further lashings, before stepping into the hot water.

Edward laughed and knelt down beside the bath, a sponge at the ready! The tin bath wasn't big enough for David to stretch out completely, but he slid down and lifted his feet and legs in the air, sticking his head under the water. When he came up for air, Edward had soaped up and started scrubbing him across his chest with vigour, before exploring the rest of his body. David loved it and looked at him, splashing water over his head.

'Hey, you're getting me all wet,' said Edward.

'That's the general idea,' and David grabbed Edward under the arms, pulling him in on top of him. Edward screamed playfully, before submitting. Supper could wait!

That night, they cuddled up as if their lives depended on it. It was special and a night to remember. Before they knew it, the cockerel was crowing, and it was time to rise.

Chapter 47

Frank was glad to be free after six days of captivity and was dropped off at the rear echelon to find transport for himself back to the front line. He found a lift in the back of a three-ton truck, full of rations, that spluttered and rattled on the short journey. He had to resume his duties, but knew he had to locate his lieutenant first, as news of Ed had not been forthcoming from his captors. When he arrived back, there were sad faces in the trenches following a heavy bombardment overnight, killing many, injuring hundreds. He pitied his friends along the line but ignored them all in his need to find Lieutenant Cavanagh.

As Frank approached his shell scrape, one of the guys stood up and crossed over, standing in front of him, his distinctly concerned eyes locked on his. He put an arm on his shoulder. 'Sorry mate, it's not right, you know, but we are all truly sorry to hear about Ed,' he said forlornly.

Frank frowned at the man, rather confused, and tried to speak, but others had now crowded around him, some patting him on the back, others just standing in a tiny huddle in the vast trench system of the British line.

'What? What are you talking about?' he asked.

'Oh Christ, he doesn't know.' Eyes darted around the small group of men. Suddenly, Lieutenant Cavanagh spoke from a short distance away. 'I'll take it from here, chaps. Smith, with me.' And he ushered him away towards his hole in the ground.

'Sit down,' he said, as he took off his helmet and placed in on the makeshift table by the door. Frank sat nervously, his eyes never leaving his lieutenant's face. 'It's not good news, Smith.' He paused and looked down to his feet, shaking his head. 'There is no easy way to say this. Ed was court martialled this morning. She was found guilty of treason and was sentenced to death by firing squad!' he said gravely.

Frank just sat staring at him, saying nothing, not really taking in what had just been said.

'I tried to convince the general and his senior officers that this was all wrong, and with no firm evidence being presented, how could they come to this decision. I explained that Ed was the best we had, but it was not enough. They had convinced themselves she was a spy, along with her village priest, a German chap, who I understand is to receive the same fate, so it's all over. I am terribly sorry, Frank, more than you can ever know.'

Frank sprang to his feet but didn't speak, stood for a moment staring at his officer and then shot out of the shelter and was gone, Lieutenant Cavanagh calling after him.

Oblivious to everyone, he ran down the line as quickly as he could in the thick mud, tears running down his face! He turned right at the HQ crossroads and then after twenty minutes left the trench system about a thousand yards to the rear. All that time his mind was numb, his heart pounding. What he did next would define his very being, and he knew he must try to save her. He walked on back down the rear lines, paying little attention to the many people passing to and fro, until he came to the transport tent. He walked in to speak to the sergeant sitting at the desk inside

'Sergeant, I have to get to the 24th Field Hospital to see Major Leigh-Smith urgently. Do you have any transport heading that way?'

The sergeant, who was sorting paper into a large box to one side, looked up and saw a rather desperate man with a tearful expression before him and stopped what he was doing.

'Lost a pal, eh, son? Yeh, we can sort that. Look, there's a truck leaving from RV-17 in about ten minutes. Speak to the driver, name of Penhaligan, and say Sergeant Simpson said you could travel with him. He will enjoy your company, but take some fags if you have any, he loves a smoke.'

Frank thanked the man, who simply bent down to get on with his mountain of paper. He turned to walk away but was called back to the desk. 'Here you go, chummy, have these,' said the sergeant, throwing Frank a fresh packet of fags and smiling.

He didn't speak much on the journey, just stared out of the window until they came upon the church. He jumped down, shouting thanks, and tossed the cigarettes to Penhaligan, before slamming the door. He made his way into the dimly lit building and asked at the front desk for Major Leigh-Smith. He was directed to his office at the back of the church, the door wide open. He tapped gingerly on the frame before walking straight in. The officer was sitting with his head in his hands as Frank entered, and slowly looked up.

'Smith isn't it?' he said.

'Yes, sir. I have just heard about Ed. Is there anything we can do?' he asked, rather sharply for an enlisted man.

Simon sat back and folded his arms, not taking offence at his manner. 'Look, old chap, there is nothing we can do! What has happened is a complete travesty and I have spoken with all the people I can think of, but to no avail. A legal appeal was placed but was refused by General Davis because of the seriousness of the charges. I just don't know what to say.'

Frank looked at him and asked if he could send a signal to England. Simon was puzzled. 'Why do you need to send a signal, Smith, what good would that do?'

'Sir, my guardian is Lord Hardcastle and I wrote to him when I was imprisoned and, well, I assume he is somehow responsible for my release this morning. I have not been charged with anything and have not heard from him either, but I need to try, sir, I need to somehow get Ed freed!'

Simon reached for an army signal pad. 'OK, what do you want to say?'

Frank thought carefully for a moment and as he spoke, Simon scribbled on the pad.

Sir. I was released today following 6 days held in prison. No charges made. Thank you for helping me. Private Mitchell found guilty and sentenced to death. Your help needed urgently as she is innocent. Reply ASAP, care of Major Leigh-Smith. 24th field hospital.

He gave the address details, and once it was signed, the officer got up and went to present it to the signal office for immediate dispatch, telling Frank to stay put. A few minutes later, he was back.

'Now, you may not be aware, but Ed is due to meet her fate the day after tomorrow. Her execution is to be carried out at Divisional Headquarters, overseen by General Davis. I don't know what Lord Hardcastle can do here, but we should not wait to find out. We must come up with a plan of our own to try and stop this, this farce, in case time and distance halt any measures of help by your guardian.'

Frank was still in shock. How could someone like Ed possibly be found guilty of treason? He wanted to shout and scream aloud for all to hear but knew that was pointless, instead, broke down and cried. The major sat watching, helpless.

After a minute, Frank suddenly sat up and then as though a light had turned on in his head, he looked at the officer across the desk.

'Yes, of course, Ed's brother. An MP at the chateau posted some letters for me. One was to Edward; He might help us!'

The major looked confused. 'Ed has a brother?' he asked.

'Yes, he does, and when I wrote to him, I asked him for help.'

'Well, he probably can't do a lot, but we must consider all angles. You need to get a pass to be free to roam for a couple of days. Where is your OC now?' he enquired.

'I left him in the front line, in his shelter. Shall I go back, sir?'

'No, there is no time. I will telephone the Gloucesters' HQ and get him to call me here. In the meantime, you go down to the canteen and get yourself fed. When your approval comes through, I will come and get you.'

About thirty minutes later, Frank looked up from his dinner to see the major standing in the doorway, with a piece of paper in his hand. He casually walked over and presented a four-day pass to Frank, who quickly placed it in his top pocket. Simon then sat down and began to speak.

'OK. I want you to make your way over to Divisional HQ and seek out this Corporal Forrest. You must be very discreet and contact him only when he is alone. You should seek details of the firing squad, timings, numbers, security, anything you think could help us. In the meantime, I will await the reply to your signal and ask Captain Reece to arrange transport to be available at short notice. He is a good man and can be trusted.'

Frank stood for a second, before pushing his hand forward to shake the officer's hand. A quite unusual gesture, but Major Leigh-Smith smiled at him and took his hand, holding it firmly.

'Thank you, sir,' Frank said, and quietly turned and left the room.

He walked back to the church entrance and stepped out into the light, he felt terribly uneasy and paused, leaning against the large brick entrance to the church to light up a ciggy, a habit he knew Ed always discouraged. He was a million miles away as he pulled on the strong tobacco. He thought of their times together, from when they first met at the railway station, and how their friendship had grown. He was oblivious to anything else, but in the background of his thoughts he heard someone calling his name. He didn't pay much attention, his mind in the clouds. But then it came again.

'Frank,' the voice shouted, and he looked across as a young man in civilian clothes jumped down from the front of a truck. I don't believe it, he thought.

How can this be... He reached for the man's hand and ushered him to the side of the street.

'What on earth? How is this possible?' said a startled Frank.

Chapter 48

At just before 5 a.m. a young man in uniform made his way in the shadows towards the rear of General Davis's Divisional HQ. His uniform was standard issue, as worn by over a million British soldiers, and he looked like any other Tommy, arousing no suspicion. He stood under a tall pine tree in the grounds, some four hundred yards from the building, took out a folded paper from his tunic pocket and studied the map drawn for him. He could see the high wall ahead and made his way over to a small wooden door to the rear, by the stables. He peered around but could see no-one and looked at his watch, waiting for the door to be unlocked. He leant against the wall and dug his hands in his pockets just as the noise of a bolt could be heard from the other side of the door. He was bang on time!

The gate then opened slightly, and a soldier's face appeared through the narrow crack, looking for the man outside the wall. The soldier was quickly ushered in, before the gate was locked with a large bolt.

'Follow me,' he said in a whisper and led the soldier towards a door in the main building and into a corridor, before dropping down some stairs. They entered the lower cellar and the MP told the man to go into a small room full of boxes, mops and buckets, with little room to stand. He told him he would be back shortly and to stay totally silent, closing the door, leaving him in total darkness.

***

Ed had not slept well and was pacing around her tiny cell, waiting for her guards to fetch her and take her to the wall! At five fifteen she was brought breakfast of porridge and eggs with bread and tea. No words were said, she just thanked the corporal as he left but ate nothing, just sipped some tea from the metal mug. A few minutes later, a priest arrived and was shown into her cell for her last confession. From a distance down the corridor, the two sentries listened intently as the priest spoke with sincerity and kindness, before a quiet woman's voice said her confession. They could not make out her words, but it was short, and the priest departed in less than five minutes. They led him up the stairs, back to the ground floor, leaving Ed alone in the cellar.

The difficulties of the previous week were now all a blur, as Ed thought through the traumas of her life in the trenches, getting shot and now the court martial. How it had all come to this, after she had only ever wanted to serve her country, she didn't quite know. All she had put herself through to serve her King in this man's world, was now all for nothing. She never had the chance to prove her innocence. She was now doomed to stand with her back to a wall before her peers, her life taken from her. Her body would be placed in an unmarked grave, that of a traitor.

Her short trial had been a farce, and although Lieutenant Cavanagh had done his very best, her destiny was clear: someone wanted her dead. She wasn't allowed to write home and wondered how Ed would take to the telegram when it arrived. He would blame himself for eternity; she didn't quite know how he would cope! It had been clear from the outset of the proceedings that certain people had created the lies that would ultimately send her to her death, and she would never know why! She was determined to remain calm, as it would serve no purpose to scream and shout. She had after all chosen to be part of this great band of soldiers fighting for freedom. Oh, how she wished Frank had left her to die.

Her greatest regret was involving her dear friend Bryan. God only knew where he might be now, rotting in an English jail somewhere, awaiting his fate! She thought of Edward and David too, and the green fields of their two hundred acres in glorious Gloucestershire. She thought of her parents and their watery grave, and tears welled up in her eyes as the pressures finally exploded within her. She sobbed quietly to herself in her lonely cell beneath the vast French chateau.

***

By a small side door, the MP had been listening carefully and took his chance, stepping into the corridor once the priest had left. He then tiptoed along to the cell door, pulling back the vast bolt slowly to avoid any noise. He peered inside to see Private Ed Mitchell on her knees, with her hands in prayer. She looked up as he entered and saw him holding his finger to his lips. He walked over and whispered for her to remove her tunic and lay it on the bed and then to follow him. Her heart was pounding, and she jumped up, looking at him quizzically as she did as she was told. He then beckoned to her to follow him out of the cell. They moved slowly, stepping quietly on the stone floor, and went through a small door to the left. The corporal then opened another door and told her to step inside.

'Stay very quiet,' he whispered. 'I will be back in a few minutes.'

Puzzled, she tried to speak, but he put his hand over her mouth and shook his head. 'Later. Stay put.'

He shut the door, leaving Ed alone, before walking the short distance down the corridor to the cleaning cupboard. He opened the door and waved to the soldier inside. 'Follow me,' he whispered, and they walked the fifty feet or so to the small wooden door. Pete gently opened it and peered down the passage, seeing all was clear. He nodded his head sideways to beckon the soldier through and they quietly walked into the main cellar to the prison cell, with its open door. When they got inside, Pete spoke calmly to the new resident.

'We don't have much time. Take off your tunic and wear that one on the bed. Give me your cap,' he said, pointing to the one Ed had left on the bed. The soldier quickly undid the many buttons of the army issued tunic, as Pete peered over his shoulder towards the steps. He gave it to the corporal, before picking up the one from the bed, it was still warm to the touch and he lifted it to his face, taking in the smell, before quickly putting it on. When fully dressed, the MP pushed his hand forward to shake a brave man's hand and was about to leave when he noticed the wrist watch.

'Shit give me your watch,' he said and placed into the top pocket of the tunic. 'Look, what you are doing is a superb act of kindness and bravery. You are an amazing man and I salute you.' At that the corporal stood one pace back and saluted him, holding it for a few seconds before locking the cell door.

'Goodbye my friend,' he said sneaking back the way he had come in, closing the small door behind him with great relief, before sliding the bolt into place. He headed the few steps to the small room and opened it to allow Ed out.

'Put this tunic and cap on and follow me and don't make a sound,' Once dressed, he retraced his steps all the way back to the door by the stables, followed closely by a bemused Ed Mitchell. They crossed the gravel courtyard until he reached the side gate. He pulled back the bolt and ushered Ed through it. She stepped outside the wall and to freedom, still not knowing what was happening.

'OK, listen. Head towards the waterfall at the end of the garden and a car will be waiting beyond the wall. Good luck.'

He was about to shut the door, when Ed turned to face him. 'What just happened?' she asked.

'All will be revealed when they get you to safety. Good luck, lady, you deserve it.' And he shut the gate, leaving her to fend for herself, her heart racing like thunder in her chest. She was sweating, breathing rapidly. She was free but, didn't know how or why?

She peered through the early morning mist and headed as instructed towards the large ornate fountain some five hundred yards away. She looked around and no-one was in sight. She didn't want to attract any unwanted attention, so walked in a military fashion along the side of the shrubbery and garden borders, as if on patrol. She suddenly heard a dog barking and stopped and dropped to ground, peering over to her right she saw an officer throwing a stick for his dog. He was some way off and in the opposite direction to her route, so she stood up and continued along the path, reaching the fountain in just a few minutes. On the far side, the wall had regular gaps where the bricks had fallen, and she stepped through the nearest one, to see a dark green army staff car waiting on the other side, the engine idling quietly. The door opened, and she was beckoned into the front seat, the driver looking across at her as she covered the short distance to the car. She bent forward and peered inside to see a familiar face, that of Baxter, the orderly who had looked after her when she was in the field hospital. She got in and closed the door, sitting beside him. Baxter put the car into gear, and slowly pulled away. Ed waited for an explanation of some sort, and kept looking across at him, but none came. Instead, Baxter just smiled at her in sheer delight.

'So, can you please tell me what is happening to me? Am I free, where am I going?' she said.

'All I know is, I was told to pick up a soldier at zero five thirty hours at this location. I think we will both have to wait to find out, Ed, I am as puzzled as you,' he said calmly. 'I am to take you to Boulogne, where we are to be met.'

She felt completely confused, not understanding how she was suddenly free? With a puzzled look, she sat peering out at the green fields that spread all around her. The realisation that she had been released somehow, by people she didn't even know was a little overwhelming. The pressures of the past week finally hit her, and she sank her head backwards onto the leather seat, her eyes filled with tears; which rolled down her cheeks and onto her tunic. She closed her eyes, and within seconds, was sound asleep…

Chapter 49

In the cell below the chateau, Edward Mitchell lay on the bed and closed his eyes, thinking back to his remarkable journey over to France and how fate had played a part, leading him right into Frank's hands. He had said his farewells to his lover in bed on their last morning together and hoped David would forgive him. He probably had clung to him a tiny bit longer than usual, giving David a small sign that perhaps something may be wrong. He had tried to act perfectly normally, however, his letter would explain all! He remembered squeezing David's hand as he dropped him at the bus stop near the church and smiled as David turned the trap around, before a gentle wave as he trotted away back up the hill.

Edward had taken his savings from his bottom drawer, a total of six pounds fifteen shillings, which was now tucked into his wallet. He felt sure it would be ample for his journey. With a change of bus in Oxford and then again in London, he finally found his way to the Kent ferry point of Folkestone. He joined a long queue to buy a ticket for the seven o'clock boat the following morning, and completed the nominal travel forms at the kiosk, which with a small fee, were stamped with the date of travel for entry into France. On the way back to the digs, he bought a fish supper and sat on a wall, looking out over the many ships in the harbour, before returning to his tiny room on the top floor. He slept heavily on the cheap mattress in the dour room, setting off early to board the boat and to post his letter to David on the way. As he held it in the mouth of the pillar box for a few seconds, he felt close to him for the very last time. He released it and it fell inside and was gone.

It was bright and clear, with a stiff breeze from the south-west. The last time he had been at sea, when he was only ten, he was as sick as a dog.

He had not had a lot of time to plan his journey properly and knew he may have trouble with transport details. He had no alternative but to travel as a woman to begin with and then change at some point into the suit he had stowed in the bottom of his bag. He knew, too, he would have to lose his locks of golden hair to complete the transformation.

Within half an hour of departing Folkstone, he saw the French coastline from the top deck, with the English coast now fading away behind him. It was time to make his change so with his bag tucked under his arm, he found a toilet below decks, and avoiding prying eyes, stepped inside, locking the door firmly. The tiny room was only just big enough to undress, with basic facilities and a rather strong smell. He placed his bag on the toilet seat and stripped down completely naked, dropping his female clothes onto the floor to stand on. They were of no use to him anymore.

He rummaged through his bag, quickly slipping into his men's underwear and trousers, and to put on his socks and boots. He hung his jacket, which was rather creased, on the hook behind the door and stood to face himself in the grubby mirror. He reached for the scissors and began cutting his hair, starting at the back. He had no alternative but to grab handfuls of hair and cut through the clumps around his head, until he couldn't grasp anymore. It wasn't the best haircut he had ever had, but he could cover it with his cap until he could get to a barber in France. He dragged all the hair together with his hands, which he dropped into the toilet, before putting on his shirt, flipped his bracers over his shoulders and doing up his tie. He took a final look at himself before donning his jacket and cap. It had all taken a little longer than he thought, so quickly gathered up the clothes on the floor, wrapping them together, placed the scissors in his bag and walked out of the toilet without being noticed.

With his bag over his shoulder, he went to a rubbish bin by the tea shack and threw his past life away, never to return. Feeling nervous, he bought a hot drink and a currant bun before heading up to the top deck to see the coast of France was almost in touching distance. With steam billowing from the funnel high above and the flags at full stretch in the breeze, the ship closed in to the shore and slowed to walking pace as they approached the harbour wall. Boulogne was a busy port, with many ships moored alongside each other. The boat finally docked, and people poured out in their hundreds as stores, vehicles, troops and equipment were disembarked. He picked up his small bag from the floor and set off to find the exit point. Waiting patiently in a long queue he didn't look at anyone in uniform, wanting to avoid any possible conflict. While he waited, he took out the letter from Frank Smith that had arrived a couple of days ago to read – something he had done many times over.

Dear Ed

My name is Frank Smith, we met at the recruitment fare. I am Ed's partner in the sniper team and her closest friend in these troubled times. You may well have had a visit by the Military Police and so I write to inform you that Ed is in serious trouble. The Army have convinced themselves that she is a German spy and has faked her enlistment to pass secrets to Jerry, but it's simply not true and I would stake my life on it. I too am being held in prison at Div HQ and with some help, got this letter out to you, to ask for your help. If it doesn't come, I fear for Ed's life…

It's a long shot, but we are part of the 2nd/5th Gloucester Regiment sniper team and Ed was treated at the 24th Field Hospital, near St Mahon. You are our last hope!

Frank Smith

He folded the note and replaced it in his inside jacket pocket, knowing he was doing the right thing.

After a short time, the passenger ramp was lifted into place and he went ashore. He had landed in France just over a year after his dear sister had done before him, marching, so she hoped, to glory. He left the docks, having cleared immigration, and started the long walk to the centre of town, unsure how he might find his way to the front. He found the bus depot, and nearby a barber's shop and café. He crossed the road and went into the barber's, taking a seat by the window. He spoke no French, so when a man with a huge handlebar moustache and a striped apron spoke, he wasn't sure who he was talking too. He looked around and was waived forward by another chap sat reading and walked over to sit in a fine leather barber's chair. The man wrapped a sheet around his neck, securing it at the back, before taking off his cap. They eyed each other before the Frenchman spoke.

'Ca va?' He pulled the scissors from his pocket and then noticed the mess Edward's hair was in. He looked at him in the mirror and pulled a contorted face.

'Mon Dieu! Qu'est-ce que vous voulez monsieur' and waited this time for an answer.

Ed stayed silent, just looking at him before answering.

'Sorry, I don't speak French,' he said awkwardly and began waving his hands above his head, imitating scissors with his fingers. The barber pulled a face and held his hands sideways before just starting to clip away. Hair of varying lengths fell to the floor for several minutes, then he pulled a cut-throat razor from his pocket and pushing Edward's head forward, used it like a master to trim his hair on his neck and around his ears. He then whipped the cloth from his shoulders and spoke again, holding out his hand. Ed put his hands in his pocket and pulled out some coins, offering them to the man.

'Non. Deux francs s'il vous plait.'

At this point a man in the corner who had put down his paper, took an interest and came over and spoke to Edward.

'Having some trouble, old man?' he said in perfect English. 'Let me help.' And he gave the barber two francs. Ed thanked him profusely and got up to leave.

'Can I pay you back? I have English pounds,' he said.

'Too right, you can buy me a coffee and pastry too,' he said, 'Then we are even.'

Edward wasn't going to question this and nodded keenly, then waited for the chap to have his haircut before leaving together. They walked back across the road to the café. A waiter came over as they sat outside at a table on the pavement. Edward's new friend spoke in fluent French and moments later two tiny cups of coffee in white cups were set down before them, along with two pastries, Edward didn't recognise! The bill was laid on a small saucer to one side. Edward had never had coffee before and certainly not this type of French pastry. The man opposite put two heaped spoons of sugar into his cup and stirred enthusiastically, before dipping the pastry into the cup like an English biscuit and eating it quickly. Edward followed his example and before long, with clean plates and half empty cups, the man spoke.

'I am James Patterson, by the way. What brings you here, old chap?' he said, shaking Edward's hand.

Edward sipped the last of the strong coffee, looking down at the newspaper.

'Edward. Edward Mitchell. How do you do. I am here to write about the Gloucesters,' he said. 'I couldn't join up, you see, as I have a leg injury and failed my medical. I fell from a tree when I was ten.'

'Oh, who are you writing for?' said James.

Edward had not thought of that! He started to offer a bit of a lame answer. 'I have no paper yet, just thought I would write some stuff and try and get it published.'

'Well, good luck, as there are many of us here working behind the official war correspondents and I await daily notes from Henry Robinson, our front-line reporter. We write for *The Times,* so we always hope for a good story. If you have any luck on something meaty, let me know and I will help you. You will have to keep your wits about you though and ensure all your copy passes military censorship. There is a small office on the dockside here in Boulogne, you can't miss it. I live here most of the year in a small room above the barber's shop and send my copy back by boat each day. Where are you heading?'

Edward didn't really have a clue but did have the name of the village supplied by Ed's friend, Frank. 'St Mahon and the 24th Field Hospital,' he said confidently. 'I also need to see the 2nd/5th Gloucester Regiment too at some point,' as if he knew what he was talking about.

'Well, I can't help you, I'm afraid, and you will be lucky to get close to the front line, but you can get lifts sometimes from the army as they have dozens of trains and hundreds of trucks heading across each day. Do you have a pass?'

'Um, no I don't. Didn't know I would need one,' he said, feeling quite stupid.

'That's OK, I have a spare one somewhere, it was a friend's, who returned to England last week.' James reached into his pocket and took out various pieces of paper, finally producing a tatty folded pass with crumpled edges.

'Here it is.' He handed it to Edward. 'Only show it to the Military Police. They don't have a clue most of the time about press passes, so it should hold you in good stead. And on that, I must go, so good luck, Edward, but you need to pay me five shillings.'

Edward looked confused.

'For the haircut and coffee.'

'Ah yes, of course,' he said, and reached into his jacket pocket, taking out a ten-bob note.

'I have no change, Edward,' James said.

'That's OK, James, keep it and thanks for your help.'

They shook hands and James was gone. Edward sat watching the world go by for a few minutes before noticing the many military vehicles heading east, and he stood to take the same road.

As he walked, dozens of trucks came thundering past, loaded to the gunnels, and before he knew it, he was in the countryside. He had walked for over an hour without realising it, reaching green fields and trees, with tracks and roads running in all directions. At last, familiar territory! He knew he couldn't walk all the way, so stopped at a junction and watched as more vehicles passed by. Then, to his great surprise, he saw what looked like buses coming towards him. Thirty, forty even, came up the hill and chugged past him, full of cheerful troops waving at him from the top decks. He tried hitching a lift, but no-one stopped, and why would they, he was a nobody, just a man in civilian clothes. They were soldiers of war!

As the last one went by, he faced forward again, watching them disappear over the horizon, the noise of their engines slowly fading. He was about to set off again when he heard yet another rumble of engines and turned just as a large army truck came up the road, spluttering, with what sounded like a misfire. It chugged a bit further, finally coming to a halt right opposite him. The driver jumped down from the cab.

'Bollocks,' said the driver loudly. 'That's all I need.'

Edward could hear him clearly and called to him across the road. 'Spot of trouble? I can take a look for you if you like.'

'Ah, you're English. You know about engines?' he asked.

'Yeh, sure, do you need help?'

'Thanks,' he said as he lifted the bonnet. Edward took off his jacket and rolled up his sleeves, explaining he lived on a farm and knew about machinery. He stood up on the bumper, leaning into the engine compartment, and immediately noticed a lead hanging off the spark plug. He reached down and clipped it back on.

'That's it,' he said joyously. 'Try it now.'

The driver reset the ignition before winding the starting handle, the engine immediately ripping back into life. Edward dropped the bonnet and jumped down.

'Couldn't ask for a lift, could I?' he said eagerly.

'Yes, sure, jump up,' and Edward climbed into the cab, the hard seat feeling like a pile of bricks. They exchanged names and got settled for the journey, Jock offering him a fag, which he declined. 'So, what are you doing here, mate, and why aren't you in uniform?'

Edward explained his reasons for not being in the war and that he was a journalist, flashing his new press pass in front of Jock's face, just for a second, before sliding it back into his inside pocket. He told him he was writing for a Gloucestershire newspaper and had come to the front to do some stories of local men. He wondered if he could drop him somewhere near to the village of St Mahon, where the 24th Field Hospital was. The driver laughed.

'Ha, I am going to the 24th, I have boxes of field dressings and surgical equipment in the back. What a coincidence.'

The journey took a little over three hours and the two new acquaintances chatted freely all the way. A little after three o'clock they arrived in the village of St Mahon and as they pulled up opposite the church. He said his farewell to Jock and opened the door, looking across the road as he jumped down. The church entrance was busy with people coming and going, but then leaning against the wall to the right of the entrance, he saw a face he recognised. He called out, but the man didn't hear him. He shouted again, but the man blew the last of the smoke skywards from his fag and flicked the butt away with his finger. As he did so their eyes met, the man looking like he had seen a ghost.

Edward walked across, and they greeted each other in the middle of the street. Frank looked stunned and shook his hand enthusiastically.

'The last time I saw you was getting on a bus at the army recruitment day.' said Frank. He shook Edward's hand again and grinned as somehow fate had led them together at this point, in this place, at this time. He started to laugh loudly as they walked to the side of the street.

'How on earth did you find me amongst all this, this madness?' he said. 'Did you get my letter?'

'Yes, I did, Frank, and I have a plan to help Ed. Where can we talk?'

Frank thought quickly. 'The major, we must go and talk to the major, he'll know what to do.' And pulled Edward's jacket as they entered the hospital and disappeared into the dark interior.

Chapter 50

The sound of footsteps stirred Edward back to reality and he sat up to see feet coming down the steps at the far end of the cellar. There were two MPs with armbands and an officer behind them, walking slowly towards him. They had no reason to suspect any foul play and on reaching the door the leading man, a corporal, slid the bolt back and pulled the door open. They stood either side of Edward, leaving the officer in the doorway. He looked down at a piece of paper and began to read.

'Private Mitchell, I am authorised by General AP Davis, Divisional Commander, to take you to a place of execution, where you will stand before a firing squad made up of your peers. Do you have anything to say?'

Edward stood calmly in his uniform, looking at the officer, in readiness for what was ahead. For once in his life he was not taking from others, not shirking his duties, as he so often had done throughout his life. He was at last doing something decent, for his heroic sister. He had no regrets about what was to happen, feeling at peace with himself.

He spoke confidently: 'No, sir.'

The two MPs stepped forward to handcuff him. He wanted to pee and almost let it go where he stood. It had worked, they had believed he was Ed, his twin sister. With the cuffs on, no words were spoken, and they led him away.

He had turned his back on his country's plea when he was needed most, protecting himself selfishly above all others. He had given no thought to anyone else, especially Edwina. He should never have been so frail, so cowardly and let his sister do his duty for him, especially as more than a million men from towns and villages throughout the land had done theirs without hesitation. He would die for his country after all, but in his own disjointed way.

He climbed the stone steps behind his guards and walked along a corridor to a small wooden door, which took them into a courtyard. He saw a line of soldiers to one side, six in total, and a wall over to his left. He stopped in the doorway but, was encouraged on by one of the corporals. He was led forward and positioned on a spot central to the marksmen, his back to the high wall, the corporal briefly standing behind him. As he did so he placed both hands on Edward's shoulders and told him to stand still. He took a white blindfold from his trouser pocket, but Edward refused it. The corporal then pinned a square of white cloth to his tunic, over his heart, before pausing to speak quietly to him.

'You're a bloody hero, mate,' said the soldier who had escorted him to the cellar earlier.

Edward now felt a fraud, as it was his sister Ed, not him, who was the true hero. He had a brief moment of panic but bit into his lip to supress his fears, blood seeping into his mouth. He was calm, he thought of Edwina whom he not seen for almost a year. He looked up to see the top of a tall tree over the high wall, the branches moving in the breeze, the birds flying high above. A voice broke the silence, but he wasn't really listening; instead he looked across as the army priest, dressed in a brown officer's uniform with his dog collar beneath it, with his open Bible in his hand. To his side stood the MP sergeant and several officers, the younger man now taking charge. Edward heard him shout an order of some sort but wasn't focussing on what he said. Instead he thought of Ed running through the top paddock at home, him chasing her during a dreamy summer's day many years before. He heard the officer shout again, but thought only of them as children, rolling down the bank in the long grass, getting scolded by their father for ruining the crop. Life was easy then, freedom meant everything to him, but their lives had changed so dramatically and now his was ending abruptly.

'Ready,' he heard a voice shout, as the men cocked their weapons. But his brain still refused to take it all in and instead, he looked along the line of the soldiers before him, carefully studying each one as they stared at him from just five yards away. They pulled the rifles into their shoulders and he realised most were about his own age. The man on the end of the line looked nervous and shifted his feet several times, his rifle wobbling around uneasily. The officer looked at Edward before sounding off once again.

'Aim,' he shouted.

The men raised their weapons, all arced towards his chest, but Edward still felt at peace and watched with a strange aura, as if looking down from above. He thought of home, he thought of David and of Ed, his eyes never leaving the faces above the line of rifle barrels. He heard a shout and saw only plumes of smoke. His last memory…

His body dropped to the earth, but he was already flying with the birds high above. An officer walked over and reached down to place his hand to his neck. He found no pulse and Edward was pronounced dead. The squad were dismissed.

Postscript

When Ed woke, her face was pressed against the side window of the car, her skin feeling sticky, the glass misty and damp. As she moved her head, her neck was stiff and she slowly sat upright, rubbing her neck with her hand, before easing her head back and forward to ease the cramp that had set in. But then she realised she was looking straight out to sea!

She sat bolt upright, eyes wide, before wiping the window with her sleeve and peering out, struggling to remember what had happened to her. She could see ships away to her left, docked in rows, and looked blankly out over the water, trying to think. To her front, she saw a ship sailing past, black smoke pouring from its funnel as it fought against the waves. She realised the driver's seat was empty, placing her hand on the soft leather to feel it was still warm. The driver had clearly not been gone long and she turned her head left and right, searching for some sign of life.

With her heart pounding, she slowly opened the door and stepped out onto the jetty, the wind almost flinging the door out of her hand, before she slammed it shut. She blinked several times, still waking, and walked over to the edge, peering down at the sea lapping against the sea wall. She put her hand over her eyes to shield the bright sunshine and could see ships unloading their holds onto wagons and trucks alike, and then saw two men approaching her. One of the men was wearing a fine suit, his homburg putting his face in shadow, his long cane in his left hand tapping the concrete jetty at each step. She then recognised the man in uniform beside him as Baxter, the face at the wheel when she had got in the car in the grounds of the chateau. They came up to her, the stranger removing his hat before speaking.

'Edwina, welcome to Boulogne.' She straightened up and looked at him pensively. 'I am Lord Hardcastle, Frank's guardian. He probably spoke of me. I am here to take you home!'

Ed was dumbstruck! Home, she thought, how was that possible? Until early that day she had been a prisoner, about to be shot by a firing squad. She couldn't quite fathom what had taken place.

'I know this will all seem rather strange, but we will board a boat to England within the hour. Your war is over! There is great deal to tell you and all will be revealed shortly. But if you follow me, I have reserved a cabin for us on board. There you can change and make yourself more comfortable. There is also someone who wants to see you.' He took out his watch that hung on a gold chain from his waistcoat. 'It's now eight thirty, we have lots to do. Shall we go?' He gestured with his right hand and they started walking away.

'Good luck, Ed, you deserve it,' said Baxter as he climbed back into the car.

Ed looked at Frank's guardian whom she had been told a great deal about and walked beside him as they headed towards the dock. She was unsure what lay ahead, but with a real sense of freedom walked easily for the first time in weeks, with a gentleman she didn't know. She longed to get home and see her brother and Bryan too, and wondered who the person was on board that Lord Hardcastle had referred to. As they approached the gangway, people were milling around, and tickets were being checked. The purser saw Lord Hardcastle from a distance and they were escorted by a crew member up the gangplank and then up two flights of stairs, onto 02 deck. The door to their cabin was opened from the inside by a steward, and she went in to see a man with his back to her, wearing a grey suit. He turned, and Frank Smith grinned at her, looking a proper gentleman.

'Well, you finally made it, Ed, it's good to see you.' They shook hands and he gave her a hug, which he held for more than a few seconds. As she pulled away, she felt a bulge in her tunic pocket and reached in to find a watch that she didn't have yesterday. She recognised it but couldn't quite put her finger on where she had seen it before. She frowned and then realised it was Edward's, but how did it get there? She kept calm and tried to take in her surroundings as the door closed behind her, Lord Hardcastle leaving them to talk. Frank led Ed to a seat by the window and refreshments that sat on the low table. He began to explain. It wasn't going to be easy!

***

At a military barracks near Warminster, England, after fifteen days of confinement and interrogation, Reverend Bryan O'Callaghan was charged and then quickly tried for espionage against the State. His case was brought before a military court but was not clear-cut, as the only evidence the prosecution had was circumstantial! Although he was found guilty, no connection was ever made to persons or organisations within Germany, nor any proof offered of a connection to Private Ed Mitchell at the front line. He was about to be sentenced, then at the twelfth hour the charges were suddenly dropped due to the personal involvement of the Earl of Derby, the Secretary of State for War. He was discharged and sent to convalesce at Hardcastle Hall in Oxfordshire. He died of pneumonia within six months of being released.

***

Following interventions from the War Propaganda Office in Whitehall, London, General Davis was relieved of his duties with immediate effect before he could instigate a witch-hunt for officers and other ranks who tried to get Private Mitchell released! He was ordered to resign from the army and retreated north to his Yorkshire estate, but died within a month of his dismissal in a shooting accident, or so it was reported.

***

The three officers who were so instrumental in Mitchell's release – Colonel Wood, Major Leigh-Smith and Captain Reece – all saw out the war and returned home to their families. Colonel Wood retired and set up practice in Harley Street, London. Major Leigh-Smith left the army and moved to Scotland to become a top surgeon in an Edinburgh hospital, while Captain Reece stayed in the army and eventually served in World War Two as a brigadier. He was killed on the beaches of Normandy three days after D-Day, stepping on a mine. His son, a lieutenant with the Royal Engineers bomb disposal, was also killed while disarming a German bomb in a London Street. He was awarded a posthumous Military Cross.

***

David Russell never got over the loss of Edward but stayed on the farm, receiving regular visits from Edwina over the years between the wars. He never paid her any rent, but the farm was eventually sold when David passed away within months of the start of World War Two.

***

Edwina returned to England with Frank and they moved into the Hardcastle estate, destined to be together. Within a week, late into the night, she slipped away, leaving a letter for Frank, which simply, asked for his forgiveness, telling him she had to go away, as there was some unfinished business... She finished the short note by telling him; she loved him.

Within a month of returning, Frank was officially adopted by His Lordship and in the Spring of 1927, the twelfth Lord Hardcastle inherited the estate, his future certain.

A short distance from the main house, under a large oak tree, a small gravestone stood alone. The citation reads:

A coward is incapable of exhibiting love;
it is the prerogative of the brave.
Rest in peace, dear brother.

Lightning Source UK Ltd.
Milton Keynes UK
UKHW011845221120
373874UK00001B/58